Melanie [illegible]
seventeen, [illegible]
co[illegible]ting a Master's Degree in Education she decided to [illegible] novel in between settling down to do a PhD. She [illegible]so hooked on writing romance the PhD was shelved [illegible]areer as a romance writer was born. Melanie is an [illegible]or for the Australian Childhood Foundation, is a [illegible]-lover and trainer and enjoys long walks in the [illegible]n bush.

[illegible]**nmi** can't remember a moment when she wasn't lost [illegible]k—especially a romance, which was much more [illegible]han a mathematics textbook. Years later, Tara's wild [illegible]on and love for the written word revealed what she [illegible]nted to do. Now she pairs Alpha males who think [illegible]v everything with strong women who knock that [illegible]*d* them off their feet!

[illegible]**lliams** can remember reading Mills & Boon books [illegible]ger, and now that she is writing them she remains an [illegible] For her, there is nothing like creating romantic [illegible] engaging plots, and each and every book is a new [illegible] Cathy lives in London, and her three daughters— [illegible]Olivia and Emma—have always been, and continue [illegible]reatest inspirations in her life.

Scandalous Sins

MELANIE MILBURNE
TARA PAMMI
CATHY WILLIAMS

MILLS & BOON

All rights reserved including the right of reproduction in whole or in part in any form. This edition is published by arrangement with Harlequin Books S.A.

This is a work of fiction. Names, characters, places, locations and incidents are purely fictional and bear no relationship to any real life individuals, living or dead, or to any actual places, business establishments, locations, events or incidents. Any resemblance is entirely coincidental.

This book is sold subject to the condition that it shall not, by way of trade or otherwise, be lent, resold, hired out or otherwise circulated without the prior consent of the publisher in any form of binding or cover other than that in which it is published and without a similar condition including this condition being imposed on the subsequent purchaser.

® and ™ are trademarks owned and used by the trademark owner and/or its licensee. Trademarks marked with ® are registered with the United Kingdom Patent Office and/or the Office for Harmonisation in the Internal Market and in other countries.

First Published in Great Britain 2018
by Mills & Boon, an imprint of HarperCollins*Publishers*
1 London Bridge Street, London, SE1 9GF

SCANDALOUS SINS © 2018 Harlequin Books S. A.

Unwrapping His Convenient Fiancée © 2016 Melanie Milburne
The Sheikh's Pregnant Prisoner © 2016 Tara Pammi
Snowbound with His Innocent Temptation © 2016 Cathy Williams

ISBN: 978-0-263-27469-1

1218

MIX
Paper from responsible sources
FSC™ C007454

This book is produced from independently certified FSC™ paper to ensure responsible forest management.

For more information visit: www.harpercollins.co.uk/green

Printed and bound in Spain
by CPI, Barcelona

UNWRAPPING HIS CONVENIENT FIANCÉE

MELANIE MILBURNE

To my dear friend Jo Shearing.
You are such a gorgeous person
and I value our friendship so much.
This one is for you. xxxx

CHAPTER ONE

IT WAS THE invitation Violet had been dreading for months. Ten years in a row she had gone to the office Christmas party *sans* partner. *Ten years!* Every year she told herself next year would be different, and yet here she was staring at the red and silver invitation with her stomach in a sinkhole of despair *again*. It was bad enough fielding the *What, no date?* looks and comments from her female colleagues. But it was the thought of being in a crowded room that was the real torture. With all those jostling bodies pressing up so close she wouldn't be able to breathe.

Male bodies.

Bodies that were much bigger and stronger and more powerful than hers—especially when they were drunk…

Violet blinked away the memory. She hardly ever thought about *that* party these days. Well, only now and again. She had come to a fragile sort of peace over it. The self-blame had eased even if the lingering shame had not.

But she was nearly thirty and it was time to move on. More than time. Which meant going to the Christmas party to prove to herself she was back in control of her life.

However, there was the agony of deciding what to wear. Her accountancy firm's Christmas party was considered one of the premier events in the financial sector's calendar. It wasn't just a drinks and nibbles affair. It was an annual gala with champagne flowing like a fountain and Michelin star quality food and dancing to a live band. Every year there was a theme and everyone was expected to be part of the action to demonstrate their commitment to office harmony. This year's theme was *A Star-Struck Christmas.* Which would mean Violet would have to find something Hollywoodish to wear. She wasn't good at glamour. She didn't like drawing attention to herself. She wasn't good at partying full stop.

Violet slipped the invitation between the pages of her book and sighed. Even the London lunchtime café crowd was rubbing in her singleton status. Everyone was a couple. She was the only person sitting on her own. Even a couple pushing ninety were at the table in the window *and* they were holding hands. That would be her parents in thirty years. Still with the magic buzzing between them as it had from the first moment they'd met. Just like her three siblings with their perfect partners. Building their lives together, having children and doing all the things she dreamed of doing.

Violet had watched each of her siblings fall in love. Fast-living Fraser first, racy Rose next and then laid-back Lily. Been to each of their weddings. Been a bridesmaid three times. *Three times. Groan.* She was always in the audience watching romance develop and blossom, but she longed to be on the stage.

Why couldn't she find someone perfect for her?

Was there something wrong with her? Guys occasionally asked her out but it never went past a date or two. Her natural shyness didn't make for scintillating conversation and she had no idea how to flirt… Well, she did if she had a few drinks but that was a mistake she was *not* going to repeat. The problem was that men were so impatient these days, or maybe they always had been that way. But she was not going to sleep with someone just because it was expected of her…or because she was too drunk to say no. She wanted to feel attracted to a man and to feel his attraction to her. To feel frissons of red-hot desire scoot all over her flesh at his touch. To melt when his gaze met hers. To shiver with delight when he pressed his lips to hers.

Not that too many male lips had been pressed to hers lately. She couldn't remember the last time she had been really kissed by a man. Pecks on the cheek from her father and brother or grandfather didn't count.

Violet was rubbish at the dating game. Rubbish. Rubbish. Rubbish. She was going to end up an old and wrinkled spinster living with a hundred and fifty-two cats. With a chest of drawers full of exquisitely embroidered baby clothes for the babies she had longed for since she was a little girl.

'Is this seat taken?'

Violet glanced up at the familiar deep baritone voice, a faint shiver coursing down her spine when her gaze connected with her older brother's best friend from university.

'Cam?' Her voice came out like the sound of a squeaky toy, an annoying habit she hadn't been able to correct since first meeting Cameron McKinnon. She had been eighteen when her brother brought Cam home for the summer—or at least the Scottish version of it—to their family's estate, Drummond Brae, in the Highlands. 'What are you doing here? How are you? Fraser told me you've been living in Greece designing a yacht for someone super-rich. How's it all going? When did you get back?'

Shut up! Funny, but she was never lost for words around Cam. She talked *too* much. She couldn't seem to help it nor could she explain it. He wasn't intimidating or threatening in any way. He was polite, if a little aloof, but he had been a part of her family for long enough for her to get over herself.

But clearly she *hadn't* got over herself.

Cam pulled out the chair opposite and sat down, his knees gently bumping against Violet's underneath the table. The touch was like an electric current moving through her body, heating her in places that had no business being heated. Not by her brother's best friend. Cam was out of her league. Way out.

'I was in the area for a meeting. It finished early and I remembered you mentioning this café once so thought I'd check it out,' he said. 'I've only been back a couple of days. My father is getting remarried just before Christmas.'

Violet's eyes widened to the size of the saucer under her skinny latte. 'Again? How many times is that now? Three? Four?'

His mouth twisted. 'Five. And there's another baby on the way, which brings the total of halfsiblings to six, plus the seven step-siblings, so eleven all together.'

Violet thought her three nephews, two nieces and the baby in the making were a handful—she couldn't imagine eleven. 'How on earth do you keep track of all of their birthdays?'

His half smile looked a little weary around the edges. 'I've set up automatic transfers via online banking. Takes the guesswork out.'

'Maybe I should do that.' Violet stirred her coffee for something to do with her hands. Being in Cam's company—not that it happened much these days—always made her feel like a gauche schoolgirl in front of a college professor. He was an unusual counterpoint to her older brother who was a laugh a minute, life of the party type. Cam was more serious in nature with a tendency to frown rather than smile.

Her gaze drifted towards his mouth—another habit she couldn't quite control when she was around him. His lips were fairly evenly sculpted, although the lower one had a slightly more sensual fullness to it that made her think of long, blood-heating, pulse-racing kisses.

Not that Violet had ever kissed him. Men like Cameron McKinnon didn't kiss girls like her. She was too girl-next-door. He dated women who looked as if they had just stepped out of a photo shoot. Glamorous, sophisticated types who could hold their own in any company without breaking out in hives in case someone spoke to them.

Cam's gaze briefly went to her bare left hand where she was cradling her coffee before coming back to hers in a keenly focused look that made something deep in her belly unfurl like a flower opening its petals to the sun.

'So, how are things with you, Violet?'

'Erm…okay.' At least she wasn't breaking out into hives, but the blush she could feel crawling over her cheeks was almost as bad. Was he thinking—like the rest of her family—*Three times a bridesmaid, never a bride*?

'Only okay?' His look had a serious note to it, a combination of concern and concentration, as if she were the only person he wanted to talk to right then. It was one of the things Violet liked about him—one of the many things. He wasn't so full of himself that he couldn't spare the time to listen. She often wondered if he'd been around to talk to after that wretched party, during her first and only year at university, her life might not have turned out the way it had.

Violet stretched her mouth into her standard everything-is-cool-with-me smile. 'I'm fine. Just busy with work and Christmas shopping and stuff. Like you, I have a lot of people to buy for now with all my nephews and nieces. Did you know Lily and Cooper are expecting? Mum and Dad are planning the usual big Christmas at Drummond Brae. Has Mum invited you? She said she was going to. The doctors think it will be Grandad's last Christmas so we're all making an effort to be there for him.'

Cam's mouth took on a rueful slant. 'My father's decided to upstage Christmas with his wedding on Christmas Eve.'

'Where's it being held?'

'Here in London.'

'Maybe you could fly up afterwards,' Violet said. 'Or have you got other commitments?' Other commitments such as a girlfriend. Surely he would have one. Men like Cam wouldn't go long between lovers. He was too handsome, too rich, too intelligent, too sexy. Too everything. Cam had never broadcast his relationships with women the way her brother Fraser had before he'd fallen madly in love with Zoe. Cam was intensely private about his private life. So private it made Violet wonder if he had a secret lover stashed away somewhere, someone he kept out of the glaring spotlight that his work as an internationally acclaimed naval architect attracted.

'I'll see,' he said. 'Mum will expect a visit, especially now that her third husband Hugh's left her.'

Violet frowned. 'Oh, no. I'm sorry to hear that. Is she terribly upset?'

Cam gave her a speaking look. 'Not particularly. He drank. A lot.'

'Oh...'

Cam's family history was nothing short of a saga. Not that he'd ever said much about it to her, but Fraser had filled in the gaps. His parents went through a bitter divorce when he was six and promptly remarried and set up new families, collecting other biological children and stepchildren along the way. Cam was jostled between the various households until he was sent to boarding school when he was eight. Violet could picture him as a little boy—studious, quietly observing on the sidelines, not making a fuss and avoiding one where it was made. He was still like that. When he came to visit her family for weddings, christenings or other gatherings he was always on the fringe, standing back with a drink in his hand he rarely touched, quietly measuring the scene with his navy-blue gaze.

The waitress came over to take Cam's order with a smile that went beyond *I'm your server, can I help you?* to *Do you want my number?*

Violet tried to ignore the little dart of jealousy that spiked her in the gut. It was none of her business who he flirted with. Why should she care if he picked up a date from her favourite café? Even if she had been coming here for years and no one had asked for *her* number.

Cam looked across the table at her. 'Would you like another coffee?'

Violet put her hand over the top of her latte glass. 'No, I'm good.'

'Just a long black, thanks,' Cam said to the waitress with a brief but polite smile.

Violet waited until the girl had left before she spoke. 'Cra—ack.'

His brow furrowed. 'Pardon?'

She gave him a teasing smile. 'Didn't you hear that girl's heart breaking?'

He looked puzzled for a moment, and then faintly annoyed. 'She's not my type.'

'Describe your type.' *Why had she asked that?*

The bridge between Cam's ink-black eyebrows was still pleated in three tight vertical lines. 'I've been too busy for any type just lately.' His phone, which was sitting on the table, beeped with a message and he glanced at it before turning off the screen, his lips pressing so firmly his mouth turned bone-white.

'What's wrong?'

He forcibly relaxed his features. 'Nothing.'

The phone beeped again and his mouth flattened once more. He clicked the mute button and slipped the phone into his jacket pocket as the waitress set his coffee down on the table between them. 'So, how's work?'

Violet glanced at the invitation peeping out of the pages of her book. Was it her imagination or was it flashing like a beacon? She surreptitiously pushed it back out of sight. 'Fine…'

Cam followed the line of her gaze. 'What's that?'

'Nothing… Just an invitation.'

'To?'

Violet was sure her cheeks were as the red as the baubles on the invitation. 'The office Christmas party.'

'You going?'

She couldn't meet his gaze and looked at the sugar bowl instead. Who knew there were so many different artificial sweeteners these days? Amazing. 'I kind of have to… It's expected in the interests of office harmony.'

'You don't sound too keen.'

Violet lifted one of her shoulders in a shrug. 'Yeah, well, I'm not really a party girl.' Not any more. Her first and only attempt at partying had ended in a blurry haze of regret and self-recrimination. An event she was still, all these years on, trying to put behind her with varying degrees of success.

But secret shame cast a long shadow.

'It's a pretty big affair, isn't it?' Cam said. 'No expense spared and so on, I take it?'

Violet rolled her eyes. 'Ironic when you consider it's a firm of bean counters.'

'Pretty successful bean counters,' Cam said. 'Well done you for nailing a job there.'

Violet didn't like to admit how far from her dream job it actually was. After quitting her university studies, a clerical job in a large accounting firm had seemed a good place to blend into the background. But what had suited her at nineteen was feeling less satisfying as she approached thirty. She couldn't shake off the nagging feeling she should be doing more with her life. Extending herself. Reaching her potential instead of placing limitations on herself. But since that party… Well, everything had been put on pause. It was like her life had jammed and she couldn't move forward.

The vibration of Cam's phone drew Violet's gaze to his top pocket. Not just to his top pocket but his chest in general. He was built like an endurance athlete, tall and lean with muscles where a man needed them to be and where a woman most liked to see them. And she was no exception. His skin was tanned and his dark brown hair had some surface highlights where the strong sunlight of Greece had caught and lightened it. He had cleanly shaven skin, but there was enough dark stubble to suggest he hadn't been holding the door for everyone else when the testosterone was dished out.

'Aren't you going to answer that?' Violet asked.

'It'll keep.'

'Work or family?'

'Neither.'

Violet's eyebrows lifted along with her intrigue. 'A woman?'

He took out the phone and held his finger on the off switch with a determined set to his features. 'Yeah. One that won't take no for an answer.'

'How long have you been dating her?'

'I haven't been dating her.' Cam's expression was grim. 'She's a client's wife. A valuable client.'

'Oh… Tricky.'

'Very. To the tune of about forty million pounds tricky.'

Forty million? Violet came from a wealthy background but even she had trouble getting her head around a figure like that. Cam designed yachts for the super-wealthy. He'd won a heap of awards for his designs and become extremely wealthy in the process. Some of the yachts he designed were massive, complete with marble en suite bathrooms with hot tubs, and dining and sitting rooms that were plush and palatial. One yacht even had its own library and lap swimming pool. But, even so, it amazed her how much a rich person would pay for a yacht they only used now and again. 'Seriously? You're being paid forty million to design a yacht?'

'No, that's the cost of the yacht once it's complete,' he said. 'But I get paid a pretty decent amount to design it.'

How much was *pretty decent*? Violet longed to ask but decided against it out of politeness. 'So…what will you do? Keep ignoring this woman's calls and messages?'

He let out a short, gusty breath. 'I'll have to get the message across one way or the other. I'm not the sort of guy who gets mixed up with married women.' His mouth twisted again. 'That would be my father.'

'Maybe if she sees you've got someone else it will drive home the message.' Violet picked up her almost empty latte and looked at him over the rim of the glass. '*Is* there someone else?' *Arrgh! Why did you ask that?*

Cam's gaze met hers and that warm sensation bloomed deep and low in her belly again. His dark blue eyes were fringed with thick ink-black lashes she would have killed for. There was something about his intelligent eyes that always made her feel he saw more than he let on. 'No,' he said. 'You?'

Violet coughed out a self-effacing laugh. 'Don't *you*

start. I get enough of that from my family, not to mention my friends and flatmates.'

Cam gave her a wry smile. 'I don't know what's wrong with the young men of London. You should've been snapped up long ago.'

A pin drop silence fell between them.

Violet looked at her coffee glass as if it were the most fascinating thing she had ever seen. The way her cheeks were going, the café's chef would be coming out to cook the toast on her face to save on electricity. How had she got into this conversation? Awkward. Awkward. Awkward. How long was the canyon of silence going to last? Should she say something?

But what?

Her mind was blank.

She was hopeless at small talk. It was another reason she was terrible at parties. The idle conversation gene had skipped her. Her sisters and brother were the ones who could talk their way out of or into any situation. She was the wallflower of the family. All those years of being overshadowed by verbose older siblings and super articulate parents had made her conversationally challenged. She was used to standing back and letting others do the talking. Even her tendency to gabble like a fool around Cam had suddenly deserted her.

'When's your office party?'

Violet blinked and refocused her gaze on Cam's. 'Erm…tomorrow.'

'Would you like me to come with you?'

Violet had trouble keeping her jaw off the table and

her heart from skipping right out of her chest and landing in his lap. *Best not think about his lap.* 'But why would you want to do that?'

He gave a casual shrug of one broad shoulder. 'I'm free tomorrow night. Thought it might help you mingle if you had a wingman, so to speak.'

Violet gave him a measured look. 'Is this a pity date?'

'It's not a date, period.' Something about his adamant tone rankled. 'Just a friend helping out a friend.'

Violet had enough friends. It was a date she wanted. A proper date. Not with a man on a mercy mission. Did he think she was completely useless? A romance tragic who couldn't find a prince to take her to the ball? She didn't even *want* to go to the ball, thank you very much. The ball wasn't that special. All those people drinking and eating too much and dancing till the wee hours to music so loud you couldn't hear yourself shout, let alone think. 'Thanks for the offer but I'll be fine.'

Violet pushed her coffee glass to one side and picked up her book. But, before she could leave the table, Cam's hand came down on her forearm. 'I didn't mean to upset you.'

'I'm not upset.' Violet knew her crisp tone belied her statement. Of course she was upset. Who wouldn't be? He was rescuing her. What could be more insulting than a man asking you out because he felt sorry for you? Had Fraser said something to him? Had one of her sisters? Her parents? Her grandfather? Why couldn't everyone mind their own business? All she got these days was pressure. *Why aren't you dating anyone? You're too fussy. You're almost thirty.* It never ended.

The warmth of Cam's broad hand seeped through the layers of her winter clothing, awakening her flesh like a heat pack on a frostbitten limb. 'Hey.'

Violet hadn't pouted since she was about five but she pouted now. She could find a date. Sure she could. She could sign up to one of any number of dating websites or apps and have a hundred dates. If she put her mind to it she could be engaged by Christmas. Well, maybe that was pushing it a bit. 'I'm perfectly able to find my own date, okay?'

He gave her arm the tiniest squeeze before releasing it. 'Of course.' He sat back in his chair, his forehead creased in a slight frown. 'I'm sorry. It was a bad idea. Seriously bad.'

Why was it? And why *seriously* bad? Violet cradled her book close to her chest where her heart was beating a little too fast. Not fast enough to call for a defibrillator but not far off. His touch had done something to her, like he had turned a setting on in her body she hadn't known she'd had. Her senses were sitting up and alert instead of slumped and listless. Had he ever touched her before? She tried to think… Sometimes in the past he would kiss her on the cheek, a chaste brotherly sort of kiss. But lately…since Easter, in fact…there had been no physical contact from him. None at all. It was as if he had deliberately kept his distance. That last holiday weekend at home, she remembered him coming into one of the sitting rooms at Drummond Brae and going straight back out again with a muttered apology when he'd found her curled up on one of the sofas with her embroidery. Why had he done that? What was wrong with her that he couldn't bear to be left alone with her?

Violet picked up her scarf and wound it around her neck. 'I have to get back to work. I hope your father's wedding goes well.'

'It should do, he's had enough practice.' He drained his coffee and stood, snatching his jacket from the back of the chair and slinging it over his shoulder. 'I'll walk you back to your office. I'm heading that way.'

Violet knew the tussle over who paid for the coffee was inevitable so when he offered she let him take care of it for once. 'Thanks,' she said once he'd settled the bill.

'No problem.'

He put a gentle hand in the small of her back to guide her out of the way of a young mother coming in with a pram and a squirming, red-faced toddler. The sizzling heat of his touch moved along the entire length of Violet's spine, making her aware of her femininity as if he had stroked her intimately.

Get a grip already.

This was the problem with being desperate and dateless. The slightest brush of a male hand turned her into a wanton fool. Stirring up needs that she hadn't even registered as needs until now.

But it wasn't just any male hand.

It was Cam's hand...connected to a body that made her think of smoking-hot sex. Not that she knew what smoking-hot sex actually felt like. The only sex she'd had was a surrealist blur with an occasional flashback of two or three male faces looming over her, talking about her, not to her. Definitely not the sort of romantic scene she had envisaged when she'd hit puberty. It was another thing she'd miserably failed at doing. Each of her siblings had successfully navigated their way through the dating minefield, all of them now partnered with their soul mate. *Was* she too fussy? Had that night at that party permanently damaged her self-esteem and sexual confidence? Why should it when she could barely remember it in any detail?

She had been surrounded by love and acceptance all her life. There should be no reason for her to feel inadequate or not quite up to the mark. But somehow love—even a vague liking for someone of the opposite sex—had so far escaped her.

Violet walked out to the footpath with Cam, where the rain had started to fall in icy droplets. She popped open her umbrella but Cam had to bend almost double to gain any benefit from it. He took the handle from her and held the umbrella over both of their heads. Her fingers tingled where his brushed hers, the sensation travelling all through her body as if running along an electric network.

Trying to keep dry, as well as out of the way of the bustling Christmas shopping crowd, put Violet so close to the tall frame of his body she could smell the clean sharp fragrance of his aftershave, the woodsy base notes reminding her of a cool, shaded pine forest.

To anyone looking in from the outside they would look like a romantically involved couple, huddled under the same umbrella, Cam's stride considerately slowing to match hers.

They came to the large Victorian building where the accounting firm Violet worked as an accounts clerk was situated. But just as she was about to turn and say her goodbyes to Cam, one of the women who worked with her came click-clacking down the steps. Lorna ran her gaze over Cam's tall figure standing next to Violet. 'Well, well, well. Things finally looking up for you, are they, Violet?'

Violet ground her teeth so hard she could have moonlighted as a nutcracker. Lorna wasn't her favourite workmate, far from it. She had a tendency to gossip to stir up trouble. Violet knew for a fact their boss only kept Lorna on because she was brilliant at her job—and because she was having a full-on affair with him. 'Off to lunch?' she asked, refusing to respond to Lorna's taunt.

Lorna gave an orthodontist's website smile and aimed her lash-fluttering gaze at Cam. 'Will we be seeing you at the office Christmas party?'

Cam's arm snaked around Violet's waist, a protective band of steel that made every nerve in her body jump up and down and squeal with delight. 'We'll be there.'

We will? Violet waited until Lorna had gone before looking up at Cam's unreadable expression. 'Why on earth did you say that? I told you I didn't want a—'

He stepped out from under the umbrella and placed

the handle back in her hand. Violet had to extend her arm upwards to its fullest range to keep the umbrella high enough to maintain eye contact. 'I'll strike a deal with you,' he said. 'I'll come to your Christmas party if you'll come to a dinner with my client tonight.'

Violet screwed up her face. 'The one with the persistent wife?'

'I've been thinking about what you said back at the café. What better way to send her the message I'm not interested than to show her I'm seeing someone?'

'But we're not…' she disguised a little gulp '…*seeing* each other.'

'No, but no one else needs to know that.'

You don't have to be so darned emphatic about it. Violet chewed at one side of her mouth. 'How are we going to keep this…quiet?'

'You mean from your family?'

'You know what my mother's like.' Violet gave a little eye roll. 'One whiff of us going on a date together, and she'll be posting wedding invitations quicker than you can say *I do*.'

There was another yawning silence.

I do?

Are you nuts? You said the words 'I do' to the man who views weddings like people view the plague!

Something shifted in Cam's expression—a blink of his eyes, a flicker of a muscle in his lean cheek, a stretching of his mouth into a smile that didn't involve his eyes. 'We'll cross that bridge if we come to it.'

If we come to it? There was no *if* about it. That bridge

was going to blow up in their faces like a Stage Five firecracker on Guy Fawkes Night. Violet knew her family too well. They were constantly on the lookout for any signs of her dating. MI5 could learn a thing or two from her mother and sisters. How was she going to explain a night out with Cam McKinnon? 'Are you sure we should be doing this?'

There was a slight easing of the tension around his mouth. 'We're not robbing a bank, Violet.'

'I know, but—'

'If you'd rather not, then I can always find someone—'

'No,' Violet said, not even wanting to think about the 'someone' he would take. 'I'll go. It'll be fun—I haven't been out to dinner for ages.'

He smiled a lopsided smile that made the back of Violet's knees feel like someone was tickling them with a feather. 'There's one other thing...'

You want it to be a real date? You want us to see each other as in 'see each other'? You've secretly been in love with me for years and years and years? Violet kept her face blank while the thoughts pushed against the door of her reasoning like people trying to get into a closing down sale.

'We'll have to act like a normal dating couple,' he said. 'Hold hands and...stuff.'

And stuff?

What other stuff?

Violet nodded like her head was supported by an elastic band instead of neck muscles. 'Fine. Of course.

Good idea. Fab. Brilliant idea. We have to look authentic. Wouldn't want anyone to get the wrong idea… I mean, well, you know what I mean.'

Cam leaned down and brushed her cheek with his lips, the slight graze of his rougher skin making something in her stomach turn over. 'I'll pick you up at seven.'

Violet took a step backwards to enter the building but stumbled over the first step and would have fallen if it wasn't for Cam's hand shooting out to steady her. 'You okay?' he asked with a concerned frown.

Violet looked at his stubble-surrounded mouth that just moments ago had been against the smooth skin of her cheek. Had he felt that same sensation ricochet through his body? Had he wondered in that infinitesimal moment what it would feel like to press his lips to hers? Not in a brotherly kiss, but a proper man-wants-woman kiss? She sent the point of her tongue over the surface of her lips, her breath hitching when he tracked every millimetre of the movement. *Keep it light.* 'For a moment there I thought you were going to kiss me,' Violet said with a little laugh.

The navy-blue of his gaze turned three shades darker before glancing at her mouth and back again. But then his hand dropped from her arm as if her skin had scorched him. 'Let's not go there.'

But I want *to go there. I want to. I want to. I want to.* Violet kept her smile in place even though it felt like it was stitched to her mouth. 'Yes, that would be taking things too far. I mean, not that I don't find you attractive or anything, but us kissing? Not such a great idea.'

There was the sound of heels click-clacking behind her and Violet turned to see Lorna coming back. 'Silly me. I forgot my phone,' Lorna said and with a sly smile at Cam added, 'Aren't you going to kiss her and let her get back to work?'

Violet sneaked a glance at Cam but instead of looking annoyed at Lorna's comment he smiled an easy smile and reached for Violet's hand and drew her against his side. 'I was just getting to that,' he said.

Violet assumed he would wait till Lorna had gone back into the building before releasing her but Lorna didn't go back into the building. She stood three steps up from them with that annoying smirk on her mouth as if daring Cam to follow through. Cam turned his back to Lorna and slipped a hand under Violet's hair, cupping the nape of her neck, making every nerve beneath her skin pirouette.

'You don't have to do this…' Violet whispered.

Cam brought his mouth down to within a whisker of hers. 'Yes, I do.'

And then he did.

CHAPTER TWO

CAM PRESSED HIS lips to Violet's mouth and a bomb went off in his head, scattering his common sense like flying shrapnel. *What are you doing?* But he didn't want to listen to his conscience. He had wanted to kiss her from the moment he'd walked into that café earlier and now her annoying workmate had given him the perfect excuse to do so. Violet's mouth tasted like a combination of milk and honey, her lips soft and pliable beneath his. He drew her ballerina-like body even closer, his body responding with a fierce rush of blood to his groin. Her small breasts were pressed against his chest, her slim hips against his, her hands gripping the front of his jacket as if she couldn't stand upright without his support. Hell, he was having trouble keeping upright himself, apart from one part of his anatomy.

It's time to stop. You should stop. You need to stop. The chanting of his brain was attempting to drown out the frantic panting of his body. *Yes. Yes. Yes.* Clearly it had been too long between drinks. His self-control was usually spot on. But he didn't want the kiss to end.

He felt as though he might *die* if it did. Lust pounded through his body, rampaging, roaring lust that made every cell in his system shudder with need. Intense need. Need that made him think of sweating, straining bodies and tangled sheets and blissful, euphoric release.

She gave a little mewling sound when he shifted position, her mouth flowering open to the hungry glide of his tongue. He explored her sweet interior, his pulse rate going off the scale when her tongue came into play with his. Her tongue was hesitant at first, but then she made another whimpering sound and grew more and more confident, flirting with his tongue, darting away and coming back for the sensual heat of his strokes. He put his hands on her hips, holding her to the throbbing ache of his body.

She felt so damn good, like she was made for his exact proportions. Had he ever felt so aroused so quickly? It was like he was a hormone-driven teenager all over again. He seriously had to get his work/life balance sorted out. How long had it been since he'd slept with a woman? Too long if his trigger was being tripped by just a kiss.

A car tooting on its way past was the only thing that got through to him. Cam put Violet from him, holding her by the hands so as to help her keep her balanced. He did a quick glance over his shoulder but Violet's workmate had disappeared. Not surprising given he'd lost track of time during that kiss.

Violet blinked as if trying to reorient herself. Her

small pink tongue did a quick circuit of her lips and his groin groaned and growled with need. He could almost imagine how it would feel to have that shy little tongue move over his body. He couldn't remember a kiss being so…consuming. He had forgotten where they were. He had darned near forgotten who he was. He might be seriously hot for Violet but he wasn't going to act on it. She was his best mate's kid sister, the baby of the family he adored.

It was a boundary he was determined not to cross. Or at least not to cross any further than he just had.

Cam released her hands and gave a relaxed smile he hoped disguised the bedlam of base needs in his body baying for more. 'That was quite a kiss.'

Violet gave him a distracted little smile that seemed to set off a rippling tide of worry in her toffee-brown eyes. 'Y-you caught me by surprise…'

Right back at you, sweetheart. 'Yes, well, I figured your workmate wasn't going to go away until we got it over with. Is she usually that persistent?'

'You caught her on a good day.'

Cam wondered how much bullying went on in that office. Violet was a gentle soul who would find it hard to stand up for herself in a dog-eat-dog environment. Even within the loving and loud bosom of her family, she had the tendency to shrink away to a quiet corner rather than engage in the lively banter. Before he could stop himself, he brushed a fingertip down the pinked slope of her cheek. 'You're completely safe with me, Violet. You do know that, don't you? Kissing is all we'll do if the need should arise.' *I hope fate isn't listening, otherwise you are toast.*

Her small white teeth sank into the pillow of her lower lip and she lowered her gaze to a point at the base of his neck. 'Of course.' Her voice was not much more than a scratchy whisper.

He stepped back from her. 'I'd better let you get back to work.'

She turned without another word and climbed the steps, not even glancing back before disappearing into the building when she got to the top.

Cam let out a long breath and walked on. It was all well and good to kiss her but that was as far as it could go. He wasn't what Violet was looking for. He wasn't the settling down type. Maybe one day he would think about setting up a home with someone, but right now he had too much going on in his career. That was his focus, his priority. Not relationships.

Marriage might work for some people, but it didn't work for others—his parents and their collection of exes being a case in point. Too many people got hurt when relationships broke down. It was like a boulder dropped into a pond; the ripples of hurt went on for years. He was still sidestepping the pain his parents' divorce had caused. It wasn't that he'd wanted them to stay together. Far from it. They hadn't been happy from the get-go because his mother had been in love and his father hadn't and then his father had dumped his mother for someone younger and more attractive and had been outrageously difficult about the divorce.

His mother had responded by being equally difficult and, inevitably, Cam had got caught up in the middle until eventually he'd been dumped at boarding school and left to fend for himself. In the years since, his parents had changed partners so often Cam had trouble keeping track of names and addresses and birthdays. He'd had to set up a database on his phone to keep on top of them all.

But he needed to get Sophia Nicolaides off his case and taking Violet was the way to do it. Sophia was too crafty to spot a fake. He couldn't bring someone he'd only just met to the dinner. It had to be someone he already felt comfortable with and her with him. Violet was shy around him, but then, she was shy around most people. It was part of her charm, the fact that she didn't flaunt her assets or draw attention to herself. He'd been upfront about the fact it wasn't a date and he was sure she too wouldn't want to compromise the friendship that had built up over the years.

At least they'd got the first kiss out of the way.

And what a kiss. Who knew that sweet little mouth could wreak such havoc on his self-control? He would have to watch himself. Violet wasn't street smart like the women he normally dated. She wasn't the sleep-around type. He wondered if she was still a virgin. Not likely since she was close to thirty, but who knew for sure? It wasn't exactly a question he'd feel comfortable asking her. It was none of his business.

Cam ran his tongue over his lips and tasted her. Even

if he never kissed her again, it was going to take a long time to forget that kiss.

If he ever did.

Violet tried on seven different outfits until she finally settled on a navy-blue velvet dress that fell just above the knee. It reminded her of the colour of Cam's unusual eyes. *Maybe that was why you bought it?* No. Of course not. She'd bought it because she liked it. It suited her. She loved the feel of the fabric against her skin. She slipped her feet into heels and turned to view her reflection in the cheval mirror.

Her flatmate, Amy, popped her head around the door. 'Gosh, you look scrumptious. I love that colour on you. Are you going out?'

Violet smoothed the front of her dress over her stomach and thighs, turning this way and that to check if she had visible panty line. No. All good. 'You don't think it's too…plain?'

'It's simple but elegant,' Amy said, perching on the end of Violet's bed. 'So who's the guy? Have I met him? No, of course I haven't because you've never brought anyone here, that I know of.'

Violet slipped on some pearl drop earrings her parents had given her for her twenty-first birthday. 'He's a friend of my brother's. I've known him for ages.' *And he kisses like a sex god and my body is still humming with desire hours later.*

Amy's eyes danced. 'Ooh! A friends-to-lovers thing. How exciting.'

Violet sent her a quelling look. 'Don't get your hopes up. I'm not his type.' Cam couldn't have been more succinct. *'Kissing is all we'll do.'* She hadn't turned him on… Well, she had, but clearly not enough that he wanted to take things further.

The doorbell sounded and Amy jumped off the bed. 'I'll get it. I want to check out your date to see if he passes muster. Flat twenty-three B has certain standards, you know.'

Violet came out a few seconds later to see Amy giving an impression of a star-struck teen in front of a Hollywood idol. Violet had to admit Cam looked heart-stoppingly fabulous in a suit. He wasn't the designer-wear type, but the sharp tailoring of his charcoal-grey suit fitted his tall frame to perfection and the white dress shirt and blue and grey striped tie highlighted the tanned and healthy tone of his skin and the intense blue of his eyes.

Cam's gaze met Violet's and a tiny invisible fist punched her in the stomach.

'You look stunning.' The deep huskiness of his voice was like a caressing stroke down the entire length of her spine. The way his eyes dipped to her lipgloss-coated mouth made her relive every pulse-racing second of that kiss. Was he remembering it too? How it had felt to have their tongues intimately entwined? How it had felt to taste each other, to feel each other's response? How it had felt to end it without the satiation both their bodies craved?

Violet brushed an imaginary strand of hair off her

face. 'This is one of my flatmates, Amy Kennedy. Amy, this is Cameron McKinnon, a friend from way back.'

When Cam took Amy's hand, Violet thought her flatmate was going to fall into a swoon. 'Pleased to meet you,' he said.

Amy's cheeks were bright pink and her mouth seemed to be having trouble closing. 'Same.'

Violet picked up her coat and Cam stood behind her and helped her into it. His body was so close she could feel its warmth and smell that intriguing blend of his aftershave. He briefly rested his hands on the tops of her shoulders before stepping away. While he was facing the other way, Amy gave her the thumbs-up sign, eyes bright with excitement. Violet picked up her purse and followed Cam to the door.

'Have a good time!' Amy's voice had a sing-song quality to it that made Violet feel like a teen going out on her first date.

Cam led her to his car, parked a few metres down the rain-slicked street. 'How many flatmates do you have?'

'Two. Amy and Stefanie.'

Violet slipped into the plush leather seat of his showroom-perfect convertible. There was no way she could ever imagine a couple of kids' seats in the back. His car was like his lifestyle—free and fast. Not that he was a hardened playboy or anything. But he was hardly a monk. He was a healthy man of thirty-four, in the prime of his life. Why wouldn't he make the most of his freedom? How many women had experienced that divine mouth? That gorgeous body and all the sensual delights it promised?

Probably more than she wanted to think about.

'I'm sorry about Amy back there,' Violet said after they were on the move. 'She can be a bit over the top.'

Cam glanced her way. 'Did I pass the test?'

Violet could feel an annoying blush creeping over her cheeks. 'The girls have a checklist for potential dates. No smokers, no heavy drinkers, no drugs, no tattoos. Must be gainfully employed, must respect women, must wear a condom… I mean during…you know… not at the time of meeting… That would be ridiculous.'

Cam's deep laugh made the base of her spine quiver. 'Good to know I tick all the boxes.'

Violet swivelled in her seat to look at him. 'So what's on your checklist?'

He appeared to think about it for a moment or maybe it was because he was concentrating on the traffic snarl ahead. 'Nothing specific. Intelligence is always good, a sense of humour.'

'Looks?'

He gave a lip shrug. 'Not as important as other qualities.'

'But you've only ever dated incredibly beautiful women. I've seen photos of them. Fraser showed me.'

'Mere coincidence.'

Violet snorted. 'Well-to-do men are selective when choosing a lover. Women, in general, are much more accepting over looks. It's a well-known fact.'

'What are you looking for in a partner?'

Violet looked at her hands where they were clutching her purse. 'I guess I want what my parents have—a partner who loves me despite my faults and is there for me no matter what.'

'Your parents are a tough act to follow.'

She let out a long sigh. 'Tell me about it.'

The dinner was at a restaurant in Soho. Cam's client had booked a private room and he and his wife were already seated at the table when they arrived. The man rose and greeted Cam warmly. 'So good you could join us. Sophia has been excited about it all day, haven't you, *agapi mou*?'

Sophia was excited all right. Violet could see the sultry gleam in those dark eyes as they roved Cam's body like she was mentally undressing him.

Cam's arm was around Violet's waist. 'Nick and Sophia Nicolaides, this is my partner Violet. Darling, this is Nick and Sophia.'

Partner? What was wrong with girlfriend? Partner sounded a little more…permanent. But then he wanted to make sure Sophia got the message loud and clear. 'Darling' was a nice touch, however. Violet quite liked that. No one had ever called her that before. She got 'poppet' and 'wee one' from her parents and her grandad called her Vivi like her siblings did. 'I'm very pleased to meet you both,' she said. 'Cam's told me all about you. Are you in London long?'

'Until New Year,' Nick said. 'Sophia's never had an English Christmas before.'

Sophia looked like all her Christmases and New Year's Eves had come at once when she slid her hand through Cam's arm. 'You're a dark horse, aren't you?' she said. 'You never told us you had a partner. Are you engaged?'

Cam's smile looked a little tight around the edges as he disentangled himself from Sophia's tentacle-like arm. 'Not yet.'

Not yet? Didn't that imply he was actually considering it? Violet had trouble keeping her expression composed. Even though she knew he was only saying it for the sake of appearances, her heart still gave an excited little leap. Not that she was in love with him or anything. She was just imagining what it would be like if she was. How it would feel to have him look at her with that tender look he was sending her way and actually mean it. For real.

Sophia smiled but it didn't crease her eyes at the corners, although that could have been because of Botox. *Meow.* Violet wasn't normally the critical type but something about the predatory nature of Nick Nicolaides' wife irritated her beyond measure. Sophia looked like the type of woman for whom the word 'no' was a challenge rather than an obstacle. What Sophia wanted, Sophia got. No matter what. And Sophia wanted Cam. It was a wonder Nick couldn't see it. Or was Nick so enamoured with his young, stunningly beautiful wife he couldn't see what was right before his eyes?

Violet decided it was time to draw the line, not in

sand but in concrete. She gazed up at Cam with what she hoped passed for besotted devotion. 'I didn't know you were thinking along those lines this early in our relationship.'

He leaned down and dropped a kiss to her upturned mouth. 'It's never too early to say I love you.'

Violet smiled a blissfully happy smile. Who said she couldn't act? Or maybe she wasn't acting. Hearing him say those words, even though deep down she knew he didn't mean them, had a potent effect on her. No one, apart from her family, had told her they loved her. 'I love you, too, baby.' She turned her smile up a notch.

Nick slapped Cam on the shoulder. 'Let's have a drink to celebrate in advance of the announcement.'

Champagne was ordered and served and the glasses held up in a toast to an engagement that wasn't going to happen. It felt weird to be part of such a deception but Violet had no choice but to run with it. Sophia kept looking at her, sizing her up as if wondering what on earth Cam saw in her. Violet didn't let it intimidate her, which was surprising as, under normal circumstances, she would have retreated to the trenches by now.

Dinner was a long, drawn-out affair because Nick wanted to discuss business with Cam, which left Violet to make conversation with Sophia. Never good at small talk, Violet had exhausted her twenty question checklist before the entrées were cleared away.

Cam came to her rescue after what was left of their mains was removed. He excused them both from the table and escorted her out to the restroom. 'You're doing great, Violet. Hang in there.'

'If looks could kill, I'd be lying in a morgue with a tag on my big toe right about now,' Violet said through clenched teeth. 'She is *such* a cow. She's not even trying to hide how she's lusting after you. Why can't Nick see it? She's so brazen it's nauseating.'

Cam's mouth was set in a grim line. 'I think he does see it but he's in denial. I don't want to be the one to take the bullet for pointing it out to him. This project is too important to me. It's the biggest contract I've done and more could follow. Nick has a lot of contacts. Word of mouth is everything in my business.'

Violet studied his tense features for a moment. 'If she weren't married would she be the type of woman you'd be involved with?'

'God, no.' His tone was adamant. 'What sort of man do you think I am?'

'She's incredibly beautiful.'

'So are you.'

Violet moistened her lips. 'You're terrifyingly good at lying.'

His brows came together. 'You think I'm lying? Don't you have mirrors at your flat? You turned every head when you walked through the main restaurant just now.'

Keep it light. Violet smiled a teasing smile to cover her self-consciousness. Compliments had never been her strong point. She knew it was polite to accept them with thanks but she could never quite pull it off with sophisticated aplomb. And if people noticed her when she came into a room, she never saw it. She was always too busy keeping her head down trying *not* to be noticed. 'You *were* lying about the intended proposal.'

His dark blue eyes held hers in a lock that made the base of her spine tingle like sherbet. 'I can be ruthless when it comes to nailing a business deal, but not that ruthless.'

'Good to know.'

His phone pinged with an incoming message. His expression turned sour when he checked the screen.

'Sophia?' Violet's tone was incredulous. 'She texted you while her husband is sitting right next to her?'

Cam expelled a breath and pocketed his phone. 'Go and powder your nose, I'll wait for you here.'

Cam led Violet back to the private dining room. She had reapplied her lipgloss and it made her lips all the more tempting to kiss. *Get a grip.* This was an act, not the real deal. He wasn't interested in the real deal. Not with anyone just now and particularly not with a girl he had viewed as a surrogate sister for the last twelve years.

But then last Easter something had changed.

He had changed.

He had suddenly noticed her. As in *noticed* her. The way she smiled that shy smile that made the corners of her mouth tilt upwards and then quiver, as if uncertain whether to stay there or not. The way she bit her lower lip when she was nervous. The way she moved her body like a graceful dancer. Her beautiful brown eyes that reminded him of caramel. Her creamy skin with that tiny dusting of freckles over the bridge of her nose that he found adorable.

Adorable?

Okay, time to rein it in. He had no right to be thinking about her that way. If he crossed the boundary any further it had the potential to ruin his relationship with her whole family. Three generations of it. He had so many wonderful memories of spending time at Drummond Brae, the big old house set on a Highland estate just out of Inverness. He had met Fraser Drummond in his fourth year at university in London when they were both twenty-two. It felt like a lifetime ago now.

But he still remembered the first time he had visited the Drummond family. It was nothing like any of the families he had been a part of, his nuclear family in particular. He had been struck by their warmth, the way they loved and accepted each other; the easygoing bonhomie between them was something he had never witnessed outside of a television show. Sure, they argued, but no one shouted or swore obscenities or threw things or stormed out in a huff. No one went through an insanely bitter divorce and then refused to have the other person's name mentioned in their presence ever again. Violet's parents were as in love with each other as the first day they'd met. Their solid relationship was the backbone of the family, the scaffolding providing the safety net of stability that allowed each sibling to grow to their full potential. Even the way

Margie Drummond was taking care of her ill ninety-year-old father-in-law Archie was indicative of the unconditional love that flowed in the family.

Cam had become an ancillary part of that family in a way he wouldn't dream of compromising, even if it meant ignoring the persistent drumbeat of lust he had going on for Violet—the baby of the clan. Who was doing an excellent job of pretending to be in love with him at the moment.

But it was far more than the fear of compromising his relationship with her family that held him back. How could he even think about settling down when he was all over the place with work commitments? He was driven to succeed and the only way to succeed was to put everything else on hold. Work was his focus. His first priority. His only priority. If he got distracted now, he could jeopardise everything he'd worked so hard for since the day he'd been left at boarding school. He was used to being an island. Self-sufficient.

Violet resumed her seat next to Cam at the table and looped her slim arm through his, gazing up at him with those big brown eyes as if she thought the world began and ended and only made sense with him. This close he could smell her perfume, a bewitching combination of spring flowers that tantalised his senses until he felt slightly drunk. Or mad. Definitely mad. Mad with lust. He could feel it pounding in his pelvis when she leaned closer, her slim pale hand sliding down to his.

Her touch should not be having this effect on him. He was not a lust-crazed teenager. Normally he could control himself. But if she looked at his lap right now, he'd have some explaining to do. He still had some explaining to do after that kiss. He had been hard for her with one kiss. One kiss, for God's sake! What sort of tragic did that make him? Yes, he hadn't had sex in a while but he'd been busy since Easter… And no, it had nothing to do with seeing Violet that weekend. Nothing to do with noticing her in a way he had never done before.

Or had it?

Had he not pursued the many opportunities he'd had for a casual fling because something had gnawed at him since Easter? The sense that there had to be something more…something more than a few drinks or dinners, a few mostly satisfactory tumbles and a 'goodbye, thanks for the memories'?

For years he had been perfectly content with his lifestyle. He enjoyed the freedom to take on extra work without the pressure of being responsible for someone's emotional upkeep. He had seen both of his parents struggle and fail to meet the needs of each other and their subsequent partners whilst juggling the demands of a career and family. It had always looked like too much hard work.

But there was something to be said for feeling something more than basic lust for a sexual partner. Kissing Violet had felt…different somehow. The connection they had as long-term friends had brought a completely different dynamic to the kiss. He couldn't quite explain it. Maybe he would have to kiss her again… *There's a thought.*

'Smile for the camera,' Sophia said from the other side of the table, holding up her phone.

Cam smiled and leaned his head against Violet's fragrant one, her hair tickling his cheek, her closeness doing something dangerous to his hormones. The photo was taken and Sophia sat back with a Cheshire cat smile. He didn't trust that smile. He didn't trust that woman. He didn't trust his deal with Nick would be secure until the contract was signed, sealed and delivered. But Nick was dragging things out a bit. This trip to London was obviously part of the stalling campaign. Cam couldn't help feeling he was being subjected to some sort of test. Maybe Nick knew exactly what his flirty young wife was up to but wanted to see how Cam would deal with it.

He was dealing with it just fine. With Violet's help. But how long would he have to play pretend? This weekend was fine. But after that? There was only one more week before Christmas. If word got out… His gut seized at the thought. Why had he got himself into this? Seeing Violet in that café earlier had been purely coincidence.

Or had it?

He had felt drawn to that café as if a navigational device inside his body had taken him there. When he'd seen her sitting there all alone something had shifted inside him. Like a gear going up a notch. He had gone from *noticing her* to wanting her…as in *wanting* her. He had offered to take her to the party not because he felt sorry for her but because he couldn't bear the thought of some sleazy colleague trying it on with her.

Green-eyed monster?

You bet.

CHAPTER THREE

VIOLET WASN'T SURE she liked the idea of Sophia having photos of her and Cam but what could she do? She had to play along and pretend everything was fine. Thing was, it *felt* fine. Leaning against him, smiling up at him, looking into those amazingly blue eyes of his that crinkled up at the corners when he smiled—all of it felt so fine she had trouble remembering this was all an act. That it wasn't going to last beyond the weekend.

'Nick and I are going to dance at the nightclub down the road,' Sophia said. 'Come and join us.'

It wasn't an invitation—it was a command. One Violet would have ignored but for the forty million pounds that were hanging in the balance.

And because she didn't want Sophia to think she was one bit intimidated by her. It was how mean girls worked. They manipulated and caused trouble, striking mischief-making matches and standing back to watch the explosion like Lorna had done outside the office.

But there was another reason Violet walked into that nightclub on Cam's arm. She had never danced with anyone. Not since that party. She hated the crush of bodies. The threat of strangers touching her, even by accident as they jostled on the dance floor, had always been too threatening.

But if she danced with Cam it would prove she was moving on. Taking back the control she had lost. She had never danced with him, not even at one of her family's famous *ceilidhs*. He had always refrained from joining into the fun, citing the fact that he had no co-ordination or wasn't a true Scot and there was no way he was ever wearing a skirt. But this would be the perfect opportunity to get him on the dance floor. A legitimate excuse to be in his arms. Where she felt safe.

But Violet hadn't factored in the music. It wasn't the swaying-in-your-partner's arms sort. It was loud, an auditory assault that made conversation other than sign language virtually impossible. The nightclub dance floor was cramped with sweaty, gyrating bodies. It was exactly the sort of place she normally avoided. There wasn't room to swing a cat, let alone a dance partner.

But Sophia and Nick seemed to be enjoying every eardrum-splitting moment. They were jigging about, weaving their way through the knot of dancers as if they did it every day of the week. They waved to Cam and Violet on their way past, shouting over the music, 'Come and join us!'

Violet looked up at Cam, who looked like he was suffering from indigestion. She stepped up on tiptoe and cupped her hand around his ear. 'Are you going to ask me to dance? Because, if so, let me spare you the embarrassment of being rejected.'

'You call that dancing?'

A smile tugged at her mouth and she stepped up to his ear again. 'You ever get the feeling you were born into the wrong century? Give me a traditional Gay Gordon dance any day.'

He drew her closer in a quick squeeze hug that made her breath hitch. 'I feel about a hundred and fifty in here.'

'Age or temperature?'

He gave a crooked smile and took out his handkerchief—*why did classy men always have one?*—and gently blotted the beads of perspiration that had gathered on her forehead. Violet couldn't tear her eyes away from the deep steady focus of his. What was he thinking behind the screen of his gaze? His eyes dipped to her mouth, his lashes going to half-mast, giving him a sexily hooded look that made her belly quiver like someone bumping into an unset bowl of jelly. She moistened her mouth…not because it was dry but because she liked seeing him watch her do so. He moved closer, his thighs strong and muscular, so very male against her trembling legs. She felt the ridge of his arousal. It should have shocked her, would've shocked her, if it had been anyone else.

But it was Cam.

Who desired her even though he didn't want to. It was a force they were both fighting…for different reasons. Violet didn't want to waste time in a relationship going nowhere even if it was with the most desirable man she had ever met. Cam wasn't interested in finding a life partner. He didn't want to be tied down to family life. Understandable, given the atrocious example his parents had set. But Violet couldn't help wondering if deep down he was less concerned about his loss of freedom and more concerned about not being the sort of husband and father he most aspired to be. He was a perfectionist. Doing a good job wasn't enough for someone like Cam. If he put his mind and energy to something he did it brilliantly. That was why he was one of the most celebrated naval architects in the world.

'Let's go someplace else,' Cam said against her ear.

Had he suggested leaving because he knew she was uncomfortable in that environment? Violet couldn't help but be touched by his concern. 'But what about Nick and—?'

'They'll survive without us.' He took her hand and led her out of the nightclub. 'I'll send Nick a text to say we had to leave. He'll think I want to whip you away somewhere private.'

Please do! Violet followed him out of the nightclub to the wet and cold street outside. Within a few minutes they were in the warm cocoon of his car. But instead of driving her back to her flat he turned in the direction of his house in Belgravia. She hadn't been there before...although she'd walked past. Purely to satisfy her feminine interest, of course. During the drive he'd suggested a nightcap, which could have been code for something else but she took it at face value. Besides, going back to her flat, which would be empty now because both Amy and Stef had steady boyfriends and spent most weekends at their homes, was not the most exciting prospect.

Violet had to pretend to be surprised by the outside of the house when he pulled up in front of it. 'Is this your place? Wow! It's gorgeous. How long have you had it? It looks massive.'

'I bought it a year or so ago.' He led her up the black and white tiled pathway to the front door. 'I've done most of the renovations myself.'

Violet knew he was good with his hands; she had the humming body to prove it. But she hadn't realised he was a handyman of this sort of standard. The house was amazing. A showcase similar to those you would see in a home and lifestyle magazine. It was a three storey high Georgian mansion with beautiful features throughout. Crystal chandeliers tinkled above when Cam closed the door against the wintry breeze. The plush Persian carpet runner that led the way down the wide hallway threatened to swallow Violet's feet whole. The antique furniture made her mouth water. Some girls loved fashion and jewellery but anything old and precious did it for her. There were priceless works of art on the walls in gilt-edged frames. Sculptures on marble stands, a white orchid in full bloom on another softening the overall effect.

Cam led her through to a sitting room with a fireplace with a stunning black marble surround with brass trim. Twin cream sofas, deep as a cloud, sat opposite each other with a mahogany coffee table in between. A Louis XV chair was featured in one corner next to a small cedar writing desk next to a full bookcase. It looked like the perfect room for curling up with a book…or cuddling up with the one you loved.

Stop it. You're letting it go to your head.

Violet realised then with a little jolt that this was the first time they had been completely alone. At Drummond Brae there had always been members of her family about the place, if not in the same room. She had never truly been alone with Cam without the threat of interruption.

Violet turned from taking in all of the room to find him looking at her with an unreadable expression. The air seemed to tighten and then to crackle as if an invisible current was being transmitted through their gazes. She could feel her body responding to the magnetic presence of his. She was half a room away but it felt like a force was drawing her to him, a force she could not control even if she wanted to. 'Why are you looking at me like that?' she asked, barely recognising the breathy voice as coming from her.

'How am I looking at you?'

'As if you don't want me to know what you're thinking.'

His mouth lifted in a wry smile that tugged on something deep inside her. 'Believe me, you don't want to know what I'm thinking.'

'Try me.' *Did you just say that? Isn't that flirting? That thing you never do?*

He closed the distance in a couple of strides, standing close enough for her to feel the potent energy of his body calling out to hers. 'This is all sorts of crazy.' He didn't touch her. He just stood there looking down at her with that inscrutable expression on his face.

Violet disguised a tiny swallow. 'What is?'

She heard him draw in a breath, it sounded as if it caught on something on the way through. He lifted his hand, brushing the backs of his bent fingers down the slope of her cheek. 'Being alone with you. It's… ill-advised.'

Ill-advised? Violet wondered what other word he'd considered using. Dangerous? Tempting? Inevitable? All three seemed to apply. She looked at his mouth, knowing it was a signal for him to kiss her. Knowing it and doing it anyway. It was what she wanted. It was what he wanted. She might not be very experienced but she could tell when a man wanted to kiss a woman.

She lowered her lashes over her eyes, swaying towards him. *Kiss me. Kiss me. Kiss me.* She placed her hands on the wall of his chest. The feel of his firm male form beneath her palms sent a thrill through her body. It was like being plugged into a power source. She felt the sensual voltage from her palms to the balls of her feet…and other places. Places she mostly ignored, but not now. Her feminine core responded to his closeness with a tight, clenching ache. His head came down, his mouth hovering within a breath of hers as if some fraying thread of self-control was only just keeping him in check.

Violet took matters into her own hands…or mouth, so to speak. She closed the minuscule distance by placing her lips to his, her heart kicking in excitement when he made a low, deep groaning sound before he took charge of the kiss. His lips were firmer than the last time, not rough but with an undercurrent of desperation as if the self-control he had always relied on had finally let him down. She felt it in the way his tongue came in ruthless search of hers, tangling with it in an erotic dance that made her skin pop all over with goose bumps. The spread of his fingers through her hair made every nerve on her scalp tingle at the roots, his mouth continuing its sensual teasing until she was mindless with longing. His stubble grazed her cheek and then her chin but she didn't care. This was what she'd been hungering for all evening…or maybe for most of her adult life.

The insistent sound of her phone vibrating and chirruping from within her evening bag would have been easy to ignore under normal circumstances, but it was late at night. Late night phone calls usually meant something was wrong. And with her frail grandfather it was hard not to worry something terrible had happened. Violet eased back from Cam's embrace and gave him a wincing look. 'Sorry, better answer that. It might be urgent.'

'Sure.' He rubbed a hand over the back of his neck and stood back while she fished her phone out of her purse.

By the time Violet got her phone out it had stopped, but she frowned when she saw she'd missed six calls from her mother. There were three each from all of her siblings. Her stomach dropped like an elevator with sabotaged cables. She pressed speed dial and looked at Cam with a grimace as she braced herself for bad news.

'Mum? What's wrong? You called me—'

'Poppet, why didn't you tell me?' Her mother's clear voice carried as if Violet had put her on speaker. 'It's all over social media. I've had everyone calling to confirm it. We're so delighted for you and Cam. When did he ask you? Tell me everything. It's just so exciting! Grandad's taken on a new lease of life. He got out of bed and had a wee dram to celebrate. He says he's going to make it to your wedding and no one's going to stop him. Your father's beside himself with joy. Here, speak to him.'

Violet looked wide-eyed at Cam for help, mouthing, *What will I say?*

Cam gestured for her to hand him the phone. He took it and held it to his ear, his eyes on Violet's, his expression was calm on the surface, but she could see a tiny muscle in his jaw going on and off like a miniature hammer. 'Gavin? Yes, well, we were hoping to keep it quiet a little longer but—'

'Congratulations,' her father said. 'Couldn't have asked for a better son-in-law. You have my every blessing, Cam. You're already a big part of the family—this has just made it formal. You and our little Vivi. I'm so thrilled I can barely tell you. I know you'll look after our baby girl.'

After a few more effusive congratulations from both her parents, Cam handed back the phone to Violet and she was subjected to the same. This was the trouble with having parents who were enthusiastic and encouraging in anything and everything their children did. There was barely a space for her to put a word in. Finally her parents ended the call and Violet switched her phone off. Her siblings would be next. There would be another barrage of verbiage she wouldn't be able to contradict for fear of disappointing everyone.

But her brother and sisters would have to wait until she figured out what Cam was up to. Why hadn't he denied it? Why let it continue when so many people would be hurt when the truth came out?

'Okay, so apparently we're now engaged,' she said, shooting him a *please explain* look. 'Any idea how that happened?'

His mouth was set in a rigid line. 'Sophia Nicolaides must have made an announcement on social media with that photo she took of us at dinner. Do you know how many followers she has?' He turned away and let out a stiff curse. 'I should've known something like this would happen.'

'But we could've just denied it.'

He swung his gaze back to hers. 'You heard what your mother said. Your grandfather practically came out of a coma at the news. No, we'll have to run with it—at least until after Christmas.'

Violet's heart was doing a rather good impression

of having some sort of medical event. 'Why till after Christmas?'

'Because I don't want your family's Christmas to be spoilt,' he said. 'It's the time when everyone comes together. Your mother puts such a lot of effort into making it special for everyone. Can you imagine how awkward it would be if we were to tell them it's all a lie?'

Violet chewed her lip. He was right. Of course he was. Christmas was a big thing in her family and it would be ruined if she and Cam put them straight about the charade they were playing. And surely poor old Grandad deserved to have his last Christmas as happy as they could make it? It wasn't like Cam was going to keep this going for ever. He didn't want to settle down. The last thing he would want to do was tie himself down with a woman he wasn't in love with. He liked her, loved her even in a platonic sort of way, but he wasn't in love with her. She wasn't his type. She wasn't anyone's type.

'But we're going to have to tell them some time…'

Cam dragged a hand down his face, momentarily distorting his handsome features. 'I know, but there's too much at stake. And no, I'm not just referring to this deal with Nicolaides.'

'Apart from my family, what else is at stake?'

He let out a ragged-sounding breath. 'There's my family for one thing. I'm not sure I want to show up to my father's fifth wedding on Christmas Eve with a broken engagement under my belt. He'll never let me hear the end of it. I can hear everyone saying it now. *Like father, like son.*'

Violet could understand his point of view. From what she knew of his father, Ross McKinnon would make the most of any opportunity to rub in Cam's mistakes as a way to take the focus off his own behaviour. His mother, Candice, would also not let a chance like that go by, given Cam had been so critical of how both his parents had behaved over the years.

'Right, well, it looks like we run with it then.'

At least her office Christmas party would be less of an ordeal with him there as her fiancé. For once she would be spared the sleazy flirting from male colleagues, and at least there would be no more pitying looks from some of the women who thought it fine sport to make a mockery out of her being single. It was a win-win…she hoped.

Cam picked up his keys from the writing desk where he'd left them earlier. 'I'd better take you home. It's late.'

Violet's spirits slumped in disappointment. Didn't he want to finish the kiss they'd started? 'I don't have to be back by any set time,' she said. 'The girls are sleeping over at their boyfriends' so…'

His sober expression halted her speech. 'Violet.' The way he said her name with that deep note of gravity was a little disquieting to say the least. 'We're not going there, okay?'

There? Where was 'there'? All she wanted was a

little more kissing and…a little fooling around. Okay, *lots* of fooling around. Violet forced a smile.

He looked at her for a long moment, his eyes moving back and forth between each of hers in a searching manner that made her feel like someone was trickling sand down the column of her spine. 'I said we'd kiss and that's all.'

'Fine. No problem. Best to be sensible about this.' The words kept tumbling out. 'Way, way too awkward if we go there. I'm not your type in any case. Not enough experience for one thing.'

His brows formed a bridge over his dark-as-midnight blue eyes. 'How much experience have you had?'

Violet gave a self-deprecating grimace. 'Well…let's put it this way. I haven't been around the block, I got to the corner and then got kind of lost.'

His frown deepened. 'What do you mean?'

What are you doing? You haven't ever told anyone about...that.

Violet pressed her lips together, wondering if she should go any further. Would it make him see her differently? Make him judge her for being a naïve little fool to get into such a situation? But something about his concerned expression made her realise he would be the last person to pass judgement on her. 'I'd rather not talk about it…'

'You can tell me, Violet.' Cam's voice was so steady, so strong, so calm. But then he had always been a good listener. Violet remembered an occasion during her teens when she'd found herself telling him about the mean girls at school who had taunted her for not wearing the right label of clothes to a party. *What was it with her and parties?* Cam had listened to her frustrated rant and then assured her the girls were probably jealous because she didn't need designer wear to look gorgeous. Violet remembered blushing to the roots of her hair but feeling a strange sense of warmth every time she recalled that conversation since.

Telling him about what happened at that university party was not on the same level of having a moan about a bunch of vacuous schoolgirls at a teenage birthday bash. Telling him about the trauma of her first sexual experience would be laying herself bare. Opening old wounds that had never properly healed. But there was something about Cam that gave her new strength. Maybe it was time to get it off her chest so she could breathe without that lingering pinching feeling of shame.

'During my first year at university, I went to a party…' She took a short breath before continuing. 'I was trying to fit in instead of being on the outer all the time. I had a couple of drinks—too many drinks, really…'

Violet glanced up to see him frowning so intensely his eyebrows met over his eyes. But it wasn't a frown of disapproval or judgement, it was one of raw concern. It gave her the courage to continue. 'Things got a little hazy and I…well, I woke up and there were three…' She took a painful swallow. 'At first I wasn't sure if it was a dream—a nightmare or something. I was on a bed and there was a man, not someone I knew…'

'Did he…rape you?' Cam's voice came out sounding rusty as if he had trouble getting the words through his throat.

This time Violet couldn't quite meet his gaze but aimed it at a point just below his chin. 'I'm not sure… I don't remember that part. Can you call it rape if you don't remember anything? There wasn't just one man… I'm not sure if they were just…watching or…'

He took her by the hands and drew her close but not quite touching his body as if he was worried about making her feel uncomfortable after her confession. 'Did you report it?'

Violet shook her head. 'I couldn't bear anyone knowing about it. I didn't tell anyone, not even Mum or Rose or Lily. I felt so ashamed I'd got myself into that situation. I just locked it away and…and, well, I quit my studies. I couldn't help feeling people were looking at me differently around the campus…you know? I just thought it best to move on and pretend it never happened.'

He drew her against him in a gentle hug, resting his head on top of hers. 'I wish I'd been at that party because there's no way those lowlife creeps would have got away with that.' The deep resonance of his voice from his chest where it was pressed against hers was a strange sort of comfort. She felt safe in a way she hadn't felt in years. If only he had been there. If only she had been able to run to him and have him hold her, protect her. He was that type of man. Honourable. Chivalrous. There was no way he would spike anyone's drink and take advantage of a woman when she was too out of it to give proper consent. The world needed more men like Cam. Men who weren't afraid to stand up to bullies. Men who were brave and steadfast in their values. Men who treated women as equals and not as objects to service their needs.

Violet looked up at him. 'Thank you.'

He gently stroked her hair back from her face. 'It wasn't your fault, Violet. What those men did was wrong. You're not the one who should be feeling ashamed. They committed a crime and so did anyone else at that party who witnessed it and didn't report it.'

'I was so worried there might be…photos…'

He winced as if someone had stabbed him in the gut. 'Do you remember anyone taking any?'

Violet shook her head. 'No, but there was so much I didn't remember so I could never be sure one way or the other. It's made the humiliation of that night go on and on. For ten years I've worried someone out there has photos of me…like that, and I can't do anything about it.'

Cam's expression was tight with rage on her behalf. There were white tips around his mouth and his jaw was locked. 'Think of it this way. If photos were to surface they could be used as evidence in court. You could identify the perpetrators and lay charges.'

Violet hadn't thought of it that way and it was like a weight coming off her, like taking off a heavy backpack after a long, exhausting walk. She leaned her head against his chest, breathing in the clean male scent of him. He continued to stroke her head, gentle soothing strokes that made her feel as if she was the most precious person in the world instead of someone dirty, tainted, someone to be used for sport and cast aside.

Violet didn't know how long they stood there like that. It could have been seconds, minutes or even half an hour. All she knew was it felt as if she had come to a safe anchorage after years of tossing about in an unpredictable sea.

But finally he eased back from her, still holding her, his thumbs rhythmically stroking the backs of her hands. 'I want you to know something, Violet. You will always be safe with me. Always.'

Violet wasn't sure she wanted to be safe. The feelings she had for him were dangerous. Dangerous and exciting. 'Thanks…' *I think.* 'But please, I'd rather you didn't mention this to my family. I want to put it behind me. For good.'

'Am I the only person you've told?'

Violet nodded. 'Weird, huh? You of all people.'

His frown was still pleating his forehead. 'Why me of all people?'

She shifted her gaze. 'I don't know… I never thought I'd tell you. I guess I didn't want you to think of me… like that.'

He brought her chin up so her gaze came back to his. 'Hey.' His eyes were as dark as sapphires, his voice low and deep as a bass chord. 'I could never think of you like that and nor should you think of yourself that way. You're a beautiful person who had an ugly thing happen to her. Don't keep punishing yourself.'

Violet had spent years berating herself for being in the wrong place at the wrong time with the wrong personality. If she'd been less reserved, less trusting, more able to stand up for herself, then maybe it wouldn't have happened. For so long she had blamed herself for allowing herself to get into such a situation. But now that she had opened up to Cam, she could see how futile that blame game was. It was time to let it go and accept that it could have happened to anyone. She had been that *anyone* that fateful day.

Violet looked into his dark, caring eyes. Did this mean it was still hands-off? She still wanted him to kiss her. She wanted to be free from her past and experience being in a relationship with a man who respected her and treated her as an equal. Why couldn't Cam be that man? Cam who listened to her as if she were the only person in the world he wanted to hear talk. Cam, whom she'd trusted enough to tell her most shameful secret to, which, strangely enough, didn't feel so shameful now that she had shared it with him.

Cam's phone started ringing and he took it out of his pocket and grimaced when he saw the caller ID. 'Fraser.' He pressed the mute button. 'I'll call him later.'

Violet bit down on her lip. Fraser wouldn't give up in a hurry. She had yet to talk to him and her sisters. How soon before one of her family began to suspect things weren't quite as they seemed? What if it jeopardised Cam's contract? She didn't want to be responsible for ruining that for him, but nor did she want to be responsible for wrecking everyone's Christmas. 'This situation between us is getting awfully complicated… I'm not a very good liar. What if someone guesses this isn't for real?'

His hand cupped one side of her face, his touch gentle fire licking at her flesh. 'No one will guess. You're doing a great job so far.'

That's because I'm not sure I'm still pretending.

CHAPTER FOUR

CAM DROVE VIOLET back to her flat half an hour later. He was still getting his head around what she'd told him earlier. He'd had trouble containing his rage at what had happened to her. The frustrated anger at the way she had been treated gnawed at him. He had the deepest respect for women and felt sickened to his gut that there were men out there who would act so unconscionably. For all these years since, Violet had lived with the shame of being in the wrong place at the wrong time with the wrong people. It saddened him to think she blamed herself. *Still* blamed herself. No wonder she had no dating life to speak of. Why would she want to fraternise with men if she didn't know if she could trust them?

He didn't trust himself around her. Not that he would ever do anything she didn't want, but still. The attraction that had flared up between them was something he was doing his best to ignore. It was all very well pretending to be engaged for a couple of weeks. Kissing and holding hands and stuff was fine to add a little authenticity. More than fine. But taking it any further?

Not a good idea.

A dumb idea.

An idea that had unfortunately taken root in his brain and was winding its tentacles throughout his body like a rampant vine. He had only to look at Violet and those tentacles of lust coiled and tightened in his groin.

But how could he act on it? Even if it was what she wanted? It wouldn't be fair to her to get her hopes up that he could offer her anything more than a casual relationship. He hated hurting people. If he broke Violet's heart he would never forgive himself. Her family would never forgive him either.

Engaged via social media.

What a nightmare. How had he got himself into such a complicated mess?

Cam walked Violet to the door of her flat but when they got there it was slightly ajar. She stopped dead, cannoning back against his body standing just behind her. 'Oh, no…' Her voice came out as a shocked gasp.

Cam put his hands on her shoulders. 'What's wrong?' And then he saw what she had seen. The lock had been jemmied open, the woodwork around it splintered. 'Don't touch anything,' he said, moving her out of the way. 'I'll call the police.'

Within a few minutes the police arrived and investigated the scene. The police told Cam and Violet that several flats in the area had been targeted that night in the hunt for drugs and cash. Once they were allowed inside, Cam held Violet's hand as she inspected the mess.

And it was a mess. Clothes, shoes, books, kitchen items and even food thrown around and ground into the carpet as if the intruders were intent on causing as much mayhem as possible.

Cam could sense Violet's distress even though she was putting on a brave face. Her bottom lip was quivering and her brown eyes were moving from one scattered item to the next as if wondering how on earth she would ever restore order to the place. He was wondering that himself. 'I… I've got to call Amy and Stef,' she said in a distracted tone, fumbling for her phone in her purse and almost dropping it when she found it.

Cam would have led her to the sofa to sit down but it had been slashed with a sharp object, presumably one of the kitchen knives the police had since bagged and taken away for fingerprinting. He shuddered at the thought of what might have happened if Violet had been alone inside the flat when the intruders broke in. Who knew what this new class of criminals were capable of these days? It didn't bear thinking about. He picked up an overturned chair instead and set it down, making sure it was clean first. 'Here, sweetie. Come and sit down and I'll call the girls for you.'

Violet's expression was a mixture of residual fear and gratitude. 'Would you? I'm not sure I can think straight, let alone talk to anyone just now.'

Cam spoke to both of Violet's flatmates, telling them what had happened and that everything was under control now as he was organising an emergency locksmith to repair the lock. 'And don't worry about Violet,' he added. 'I'm taking her back to my place.'

Of course he would have to take her home with him. There was no question about it. He couldn't leave her in the trashed flat to lie awake all night in terror of being invaded again. Or worse. It was the right thing to do to take her home with him. What friend wouldn't offer a bed for a night or two? He wasn't one for sleepovers. He liked his space too much. But this was Violet. A friend from way back.

It was a pity his body wasn't so clear on the friend factor, but still. His hormones would have to get control of themselves.

While the locksmith was working on the lock, one of Violet's elderly neighbours shuffled along the corridor to speak to her. 'Are you all right, Violet?' the wizened old man said. 'I didn't hear a thing. The sleeping pills the doctor gave me knock me out for most of the night.'

Violet gave the old man a reassuring smile. 'I'm fine, Mr Yates. I'm glad you weren't disturbed. How's your chest feeling? Is your bronchitis better?'

Cam thought it typical of Violet to be more concerned about her elderly neighbour than herself. The old man gave her a sheepish look. 'The doc reckons I should give up smoking but at my age what other pleasures are there?' He turned his rheumy gaze to Cam. 'And who might you be, young man?'

'I'm Violet's—'

'Friend,' Violet said before Cam could finish his sentence.

Mr Yates's bushy brows waggled. 'Boyfriend?'

'Fiancé, actually,' Cam said with a ridiculous sense of pride he couldn't account for or explain. He knew it was beneath him to be beating his chest in front of an elderly man like some sort of Tarzan figure but he couldn't help it. *Boyfriend* sounded so…juvenile, and *lover*, well, that was even worse. Violet wasn't the sort of girl to take a lover.

Mr Yates smiled a nicotine-stained smile. 'Congratulations. You've got a keeper there in Violet. She's the nicest of the girls who live here. Never could understand why she hasn't been snapped up well before now. You're a lucky man.'

'I know.'

Once the locksmith had finished and Mr Yates had shuffled back to his flat, Cam led Violet back out to his car with a small collection of her belongings to see her through for a few days. Not that she could bring much as most of it had been thrown about the flat. The thought of putting on clothes that some stranger had touched would be horrifying for her. It was horrifying to him.

He glanced at her once they were on their way. She was sitting with a hunched posture, her fingers plucking at her evening bag, her face white and pinched. 'How are you doing?'

'I don't know how to thank you…' She gave a little hiccupping sound as if she was fighting back a sob. 'You've been so amazing tonight. I really don't know what I would've done without you.'

Cam reached for her hand and placed it on top of his thigh. 'That's what friends—or rather, fake fiancés—are for.' His attempt at humour didn't quite hit the mark. Her teeth sank into her lower lip so hard he was worried she would puncture the skin. She looked so tiny and vulnerable it made his chest sting. It made him think of how she must have been after that wretched party—alone, terrified, shocked, with no one she felt she could turn to. If only he had known. If only he had been there that night, he could have done something to protect her. Violet was the sort of girl who made him want to rush off for a white horse and a suit of armour. Her trust in him made him feel…conflicted, truth be told.

He wanted to protect her, sure, but he wanted her, period. Which was a whole lot of capital *T* trouble he could do without right now. Bringing her home with him was the right thing to do. Of course it was. Sure, he could have set her up in a hotel but he sensed she needed company. Her parents were too far away in Scotland to get to her in a hurry, so too were her brother and sisters, who lived in various parts of the country.

Cam was on knight duty so it was up to him to hold her hand.

As long as that's all you hold.

Violet had held off tears only because Cam had done everything that needed to be done. He'd taken charge in a way that made her feel supported and safe. The horror of finding all her possessions strewn around the flat had been such a shock. She felt so violated. Someone—

more than one someone, it seemed—had broken in and rifled through her and her roommates' things. They had seen her photo with the girls at Stef's last birthday celebration stuck on the kitchen door, which meant she might one day pass them in the street and they would know who she was but she would have no idea who they were. It was like being back on the university campus after that party. She didn't know who the enemy was. They had touched her clothing, her underwear. Invaded her private sanctuary and now it was defiled, just as her body had been defiled all those years ago.

Cam kept glancing at her and gently squeezing and stroking her hand. It was enormously comforting. Violet could see the concern, and the anger he was doing his best to suppress on her behalf. Was he thinking of what might have happened if she'd been in that flat alone? She was thinking about it and it was terrifying. How fortunate that he had walked her to the door. But then, of course he would do that. It was the type of man he was. Strong, capable, with old-fashioned values that resonated with hers.

His offer to have her stay with him at his house was perfectly reasonable given their friendship and yet… she wondered if he was entirely comfortable with it. Would it make it harder for him to keep things platonic between them?

Once they were back at his house, Cam carried her small bag of belongings—those she could stomach enough to bring with her—to one of the spare bedrooms. But at least her embroidery basket had been left intact. She was halfway through making a baby blanket for Lily's unborn baby and couldn't bear the thought of anyone destroying that.

'I'm only a door away over there.' Cam pointed to the master bedroom on the other side of the wide hallway. 'I'll leave my door open in case you need me during the night.'

I need you now.

'Thanks…for everything.'

He gave her one of those lopsided smiles of his that made her heart contract. 'You're welcome.'

Violet shifted her weight. 'Do you mind if I have a hot drink? I'm not sure I'm going to be able to sleep. Maybe a hot milk or something will help.'

'Of course.'

Violet followed him back down to the spacious kitchen and perched on one of the breakfast-bar stools while he went about preparing a hot chocolate for both of them. It was a strange feeling to be alone with him in his house, knowing she would be sleeping in one of his beds. Not *his* bed. He'd made that inordinately clear. But the possibility he could change his mind made her feel a thrill of excitement like someone had injected champagne bubbles into her bloodstream. She couldn't stop looking at his hands, couldn't stop imagining how they would feel touching her, stroking her. He had broad hands with long fingers with neat square nails. Capable hands. Careful hands. Hands that healed instead of hurt. Every time he touched her she felt her body glow with warmth. It was like she was coming out of cold storage. His touch awakened the sensuality that had been frozen by fear all those years ago.

He slid the hot chocolate towards her with a spoon and the sugar bowl. 'There you go.'

Violet took a restorative sip and observed him while he stirred his chocolate. He still had a two-fold crease between his eyes as if his mind was still back at her flat thinking up a whole lot of nasty scenarios, similar to the ones she was trying her best not to think about. 'I'll only stay tonight,' she said into the silence. 'Once the girls and I tidy up, I'll go back.'

His frown wasn't letting up any. 'Is that such a good idea? What if you get broken into again? The security there is crap. You don't even have a security chain on the door. Your landlord should be ashamed of himself.'

'It's actually a woman.'

'Same goes.'

Violet cradled her drink between her hands, looking at him over the rim of her cup when she took another sip. He had abandoned his drink as if his mind was too preoccupied. There were lines of tension running down either side of his mouth. 'I know this must be awkward for you…having me here…' she said. 'You know, after our conversation earlier about…only kissing.'

His gaze went to her mouth as if he couldn't help himself. 'It's not awkward.' His voice came out so husky it sounded like it had been dragged along a rough surface.

'I could go to a hotel or stay with a—'

'No.' The word was delivered with such implacability it made Violet blink. 'You'll stay here as long as you need to.'

How about for the rest of my life? Violet took another sip of her chocolate before setting the mug down. She had to stop this ridiculous habit of imagining a future with him. She was being a silly romantic fool, conjuring up a happy ending because she was almost thirty and Cam was the first man to treat her the way she'd always longed to be treated. It was her hormones...or something. 'I guess it kind of makes sense, me being here, since we're supposed to be engaged.'

'Yes, well, there's that, of course.'

Violet slipped off the stool and took her mug over to the sink, rinsing it first before putting it in the dishwasher. She turned and found Cam looking at her with a frowning expression. 'I'm...erm...going to bed now,' she said. 'Thanks again for everything.'

He gave her a semblance of a smile that softened the frown a smidgen. 'No problem. Hope you can get some sleep.'

Violet was about to turn for the door when, on an impulse she couldn't explain let alone stop, she stepped up to where Cam was standing and, rising on tiptoe, pressed a soft kiss to his stubble-roughened cheek. His hands went to her hips as if he too couldn't stop himself, drawing her that little bit closer so her body was flush against his. His eyes searched hers for a long moment before dipping to her mouth. 'We really shouldn't be doing this, Violet. It only makes things more—'

'More what?' Violet said, pressing herself closer,

feeling the hardened ridge of him against her belly. 'Exciting?'

His hands tightened on her hips but, instead of drawing her closer, he put her from him, dropping his hold as if her body was scorching hot. His frown was severe but she got the feeling it was directed more at himself than at her.

'You're upset after the break-in,' he said. 'Your emotions are shot to pieces. It would be wrong of me to take advantage of you when you're feeling so vulnerable.'

Take advantage! Take advantage! Violet knew he was being the sensible and considerate man she knew him to be, but the fledging flirt in her felt hurt by his rejection. Why shouldn't they have a fling? It was the perfect chance for her to let go of her past and explore her sensuality without shame, without fear, with a man she not only trusted but admired and cared about. Why couldn't he see how much she needed him to help wipe away the past? 'I'm sorry for misreading the signals. Of course you wouldn't want to sleep with me. No one wants to sleep with me unless I'm coma-drunk. Why am I so hopeless at this?'

Cam took her by the shoulders this time, locking his gaze on hers. 'You're not hopeless at anything, sweetheart. You're a beautiful and talented young woman who deserves to be happy. I'm trying for damage control here. If we take this further, it will blur the boundaries. For both of us.'

Violet planted her hands on his chest, feeling the thud-pitty-thud-pitty-thud of his heart beneath her palm. The battle was played out on his features: the push of pulsating desire and the pull away of his sense of duty. Push. Pull. Push. Pull. It was mirrored in the rhythm of a muscle flicking in his jaw. 'But you want me…don't you?' she said.

He brought her up against his body, pelvis to pelvis, his eyes holding hers. 'I want you, but—'

'Let's leave the "but" out of it,' Violet said. 'If I were anyone else, you'd have a fling with me, wouldn't you?'

He let out a short breath. 'You're not a fling type of girl so—'

'But what if I was? What if I wanted to have a fling with you because I'm so darn tired of being the girl without a date, the girl who hasn't had proper consensual sex? I'm sick of being that girl, Cam. I'm turning thirty in January. I want to find the courage to embrace my sexuality and who better with than you? Someone I trust and feel safe with.'

It was clear she had created a dilemma for him. His expression was a picture of conflict. His hands tightened on the tops of her shoulders, as if torn between wanting to bring her closer and pushing her away. 'I don't want to hurt you,' he said. 'That's the last thing I want.'

'How will you hurt me?' Violet asked. 'I'm not asking you to commit to anything permanent. I know that's not what you want and I'm fine with that.' *Not exactly true, but still.* 'We can have a fling for as long as our pretend engagement lasts. It will make it appear more authentic.'

He cupped her face with the broad span of his hand while his thumb stroked back and forth on her cheek. 'Looks like you've thought all of this through.'

'I have and it's what I want. It's what you want too, isn't it?'

His frown hadn't gone away but was pulling his brow into deep vertical lines between his eyes. 'What about your family?'

'What about them?' Violet said. 'They already think we're…together. Why shouldn't we therefore actually be together?'

'There's something a little off with your logic but I'm not sure what it is.'

'What's logical about lust?'

His frown was back. 'Is that all this is?'

'Of course.' Violet suspected she might have answered a little too quickly. 'I love you but I'm not *in* love with you.'

His eyes did that back and forth thing that made her feel as if he was looking for the truth behind the screen of her gaze. 'The thing is…good sex can make people fall in love with each other.'

Violet cocked her head. 'So, I'm presuming you've had plenty of good sex. Have you ever fallen in love?'

'No, but that doesn't—'

'Then what makes you think you will this time?'

He blinked as if he was confused about her line of argument. 'I'm not worried about me falling in love, I'm worried about you.'

Violet raised her brows. 'What makes you think you'll be immune to falling in love?'

He opened and closed his mouth, seemingly lost for an answer. 'Sex for me is a physical thing. I never allow my emotions to become involved.'

'Sounds like heaps of fun, just getting it on with someone's body without connecting with them on any other level.'

His brows snapped together and he dropped his hands from her hips. 'Damn it. It's not like that. At least I know their names and make sure they've given full and proper consent and are conscious.'

Violet wasn't going to apologise for her straight talking. In her opinion he was short-changing himself if he stuck to relationships that were based on mutual lust and nothing else. What about sharing someone's life with them? What about growing old together? What about being fully present in a relationship that made you grow as a person?

All the things she wished for but hadn't so far been able to find.

'You remind me of Fraser before he met Zoe. He was always saying he'd never fall in love. Look what happened to him. A chance meeting with Zoe and now he's married with twins and he couldn't be happier.'

Cam blew out a frustrated-sounding breath. 'It's different for your brother. He's had the great example your parents have set. He's had that since he was a baby—all of you have. I had a completely different example, one I wouldn't wish on a partner and certainly not on any children.'

Violet studied his tense expression, his even more rigidly set body and the way his eyes glittered with bitterness. And the way he had put some distance between their bodies as if he didn't trust himself not to reach for her. 'What exactly happened between your parents that you're so against marriage?'

It was a moment or two before he spoke. 'They only got married because my mother got pregnant with me. They were pressured into it by both of their families, although to be fair my mother was in love with my father, but unfortunately he didn't feel the same. It was a disaster from the word go. The earliest memories I have are of my parents fighting. They're the only memories I have, really.'

'But that doesn't mean you'd conduct a relationship like that,' Violet said. 'You're not that type of person.'

He gave a short laugh that had a note of cynicism to it. 'Thanks for the character reference but it won't be needed. I'm fine with how my life is now. I don't have to check in with anyone. I'm free to do what I want, when I want, with whomever I want.'

'As long as they're not married to your richest client or are your best friend's kid sister,' Violet said with a pointed look.

He pressed his lips together as if checking a retort. 'Violet…'

'It's fine.' Violet turned away with an airy wave of one hand. 'I get the message. You don't want to complicate things by sleeping with me. I'm not going to beg. I'll find someone else. After our engagement is over, of course.'

It was a great exit line.

And it would have been even better if she hadn't stumbled over the rug on her way out.

CHAPTER FIVE

CAM SWORE AND raked his hand through his hair until he thought he'd draw blood. Or make himself bald. What was he doing even *thinking* of taking her up on her offer of a fling? Violet was the last girl he should be thinking about. Tempted by. Lusting over. She was so innocent. So vulnerable. So adorable.

Yes, adorable, which was why he had to be sensible about this. She wasn't someone he could walk away from once the fling was over and never see or think of again. He would see her every time he was at a Drummond family gathering. He could avoid them, of course, but that would be punishing her family as well as himself.

Not that he didn't deserve to be punished for dragging her into this farce. If he hadn't asked her to that wretched dinner, none of this would have happened.

But if the dinner and the Christmas party tomorrow night weren't bad enough, now he had her under his roof in one of the spare bedrooms. Now he would spend the night, or however many nights she would be here, in a heightened state of arousal. Forget about cold showers, he would have to pump in water from the North Sea to deal with this level of attraction.

What was wrong with him?

Where was his self-control?

Why had he kissed her? That had been his first mistake. The second was to keep touching her. But he couldn't seem to keep his hands off her. As soon as she came within touching distance, he was at it again.

He had to stop thinking about making love to her. Stop picturing it. Stop aching for it. Just stop.

But truth was it was *all* Cam had been thinking about since running into Violet at that café. Which was damned annoying, as he'd never seen her that way before last Easter. For years she'd been one of the Drummond girls, just like Rose and Lily—a sister to him in every way other than blood. But it had all changed that last time he'd visited Drummond Brae. He could sense the exact moment when she turned her gaze on him. His body picked up her presence like a radar signal. His stomach rolled over and begged when she smiled at him. His skin tingled if she so much as brushed past him in a doorway. When his knees bumped hers under the table in the café he'd felt the shockwave travel all the way to his groin.

Even though she was safely in the spare room, he couldn't get her out of his mind. Her neat little ballerina-like figure, gorgeous brown eyes the colour of caramel, wavy chestnut hair that always smelled of flowers, a mouth that was shaped in a perfect Cupid's bow that drew his gaze more than he wanted it to. He had fantasies about that mouth. X-rated fantasies. Fantasies he shouldn't be having because she was like a sister to him.

Like hell she is.

Was that why he'd offered to bring her back here? Had some dark corner of his subconscious leapt at the opportunity to have her under his roof so he could take things to the next level? The level Violet wanted? The level that would change everything between them? Permanently. Irrevocably. How would he ever look at her in the future and not remember how her mouth felt under his? He was having enough trouble now getting it out of his mind. He could think of nothing else but how her mouth responded to his. How her lips had been as soft as down, her tongue both playful and shy. How her body felt when she'd brushed up against him. How her dainty little curves made him want to crush her to him so he could ease this relentless ache of need. How he wanted to explore every inch of her body and claim it, nurture it, release it from its prison of fear.

But how could he do that, knowing she had so much more invested in their relationship? She was after the fairytale he was avoiding because loving someone to that degree had the potential to ruin lives. If—and it was a big if—he ever settled down with a partner, he would go for a companionable relationship that was based on similar interests rather than the fickleness of love that could fade after its first flush of heat. His mother had paid the price—was still paying it—for loving without caution. It hadn't just ruined her life but that of several others along the way, as well. He didn't want that sort of emotional carnage. He already had feelings for Violet. Feelings that could slip into the danger zone if he wasn't careful. Having her here under his roof was only intensifying those feelings. The thought of her being only a few doors away was a form of torture. Making love with Violet would be exactly that: making love. Encouraging love, feeding love, nurturing it to grow and blossom. Sex was easy to deal with if he kept his feelings out of it. But having sex with Violet would be all about feelings. Emotions. Bonding. Commitment. All the things he shied away from because they had the potential to disrupt the neat and controlled order of his life.

He had to be strong. Determined. Resolute. Violet was looking for someone to give her heart to. She was vulnerable and it would be wrong of him to give her the impression an affair between them could go anywhere.

Why couldn't it?

Cam slapped the thought away like he was swatting away a fly. But it kept coming back, buzzing around the edges of his resolve, making him think of how it would be day after day, week after week, month after month, year after year with Violet in his life. Having her not just as a temporary houseguest but as a permanent partner. He wasn't so cynical that he couldn't see the benefits of a long-term marriage. He had only to look at Violet's parents to see how well a good marriage could work.

But how could he guarantee his would work? There were no guarantees, which was what scared him the most.

Violet didn't expect to sleep after the evening's disturbance. She thought she'd have nightmares about her flat being invaded but the only dreams she had were of Cam kissing her, touching her, making her feel things she'd never expected to feel. With time to reflect on it, she understood his caution about getting involved with her sexually. Of course it would be a risk. It would change everything about their relationship. Every single dynamic would be altered. You couldn't undo something like that. Every time she saw him at family gatherings in the future it would be there between them—their sensual history. He had only kissed her and held her and yet she was going to have a task ahead of her to forget about it. It was like his touch had seeped through every pore of her skin, tunnelling its way into her body so deep she instinctively knew she would never feel like that with anyone else. How could she? His touch was like a code breaker to her frozen sensuality. It unlocked the primal urges she had hidden away out of shame. He'd awoken those sleeping urges and now they were jumping up and down in her body like hyperactive kids on a trampoline.

Violet threw off the bedcovers and showered but when she looked at her overnight bag of belongings she'd hastily packed last night she knew she could never bring herself to touch them, let alone wear them. How could she know for sure if the intruders had touched them? What if she wore them and then out on the street the burglars recognised them as the ones they had rifled through last night? She had only the clothes she'd been wearing for the dinner last night. She didn't fancy putting them on again after her shower and, besides, the velvet cocktail dress was hardly Saturday morning wear. It was way too dressed up. If she went out in that get-up, she would look like she had been out all night. She rinsed out her knickers and dried them with the hairdryer she found in one of the drawers in the bathroom. There was a plush bathrobe hanging on the back of the bathroom door so she slipped it on over her underwear.

Cam was in the kitchen pouring cereal into a bowl when she came in. He looked up and Violet saw the way his eyes automatically scanned her body as if he was imagining what she looked like underneath the bathrobe. He cleared his throat and turned back to his cereal, making rather a business of sealing the inside packet and folding down the flaps on top of the box. 'Sleep okay?'

'Not bad…'

He took a spoon out of one of the drawers and then turned and opened the fridge for the milk. Violet drank in the image of him dressed in dark blue jeans and a black finely woven cashmere sweater with a white T-shirt underneath. There should be a law against a man looking so good in casual clothes. The denim hugged his trim and toned buttocks; the close-fitting sweater showcased the superb musculature of his upper body. His hair was still damp from a shower and it looked like his fingers had been its most recent combing tool, for she could see the finger-spaced grooves between the dark brown strands.

'What would you like for breakfast?' he said, turning from the fridge. 'I'm afraid I can't match your mother's famous breakfast spreads but I can do cereal, toast and fruit and yoghurt.'

'Sounds lovely.' Violet perched on the stool opposite him. 'Can I ask a favour?'

His gaze met hers. 'Look, we had this discussion last night and the answer is—'

'It's not about…that.' Violet captured her lip between her teeth. Did he have to rub it in? So he didn't want to sleep with her. Fine. She wasn't going to drag him kicking and screaming to the nearest bedroom. 'It's about my clothes. I need to get new ones. I can't bear wearing any of mine from the flat, not even the ones I brought with me, and I don't want to wear my cocktail dress because I'll look like I've been out all night.'

A frown pulled at his forehead. 'You want me to go…shopping for you?'

Did he have to make it sound like she'd asked him to dance naked in Trafalgar Square? 'I'll give you my credit card. I just need some basics and then I can do the rest myself once you bring those couple of things back.'

He blew out a breath and reached for a pen and a slip of paper, pushing it across the bench. 'Write me a list.'

* * *

Cam had never shopped for women's clothing before. Who knew there was so much to choose from? But choosing a pair of jeans and a warm sweater wasn't too much of a problem. The problem was he kept looking at the lingerie section and imagining Violet in the sexy little lacy numbers. He had to walk out before he was tempted to buy her the black lace teddy with the hot pink feathers. Or the red corset one with black silk lacing. Once he'd completed his mission, he was making his way back to his house when he walked past a jewellery store. He'd walked past that store hundreds, if not thousands, of times and never looked in the window, let alone gone in. But for some reason he found himself pushing the door open, going inside and standing next to the ring counter.

It's just a prop.

Violet's office party was tonight and what sort of cheap fiancé would he look if he hadn't bought her a decent ring? No need to mortgage the house on a diamond but that one at the back there looked perfect for Violet's hand. He didn't have too much trouble guessing her ring size; he had thought of her hands—holding them, feeling them on his skin—enough times to know the exact dimensions. Actually, he knew pretty much the exact dimensions of her whole body. They were imprinted on his brain and kept him awake at night.

Cam paid for the ring, placed it in his pocket and walked out of the store. Just as he was about to turn the corner for home, he got a call from Fraser. He couldn't avoid the conversation any longer, but something about lying to his best mate didn't sit too comfortably. 'Hey, sorry I haven't returned your calls,' he said. 'Things have been happening so fast I—'

Fraser gave a light laugh. 'You don't have to apologise to me, buddy. I saw the way you were looking at Vivi at Easter. Is that why you skived off to Greece? So you wouldn't be tempted to act on it?'

Maybe it had been, now that he thought about it. Cam often had to travel abroad at short notice in order to meet with a client, but the chance to go to Greece for a few months had been exactly the escape hatch he'd needed. He'd felt the need to clear his head, to get some perspective, to have a little talk to himself about stepping over boundaries that couldn't be undone. But the whole time he'd been away, Violet had been on his mind. 'Yeah, well, now that you mention it.'

'Great news, man,' Fraser said. 'Couldn't be more delighted. Zoe reckons this is going to be the best Christmas ever. Did you hear about Grandad? Talk about a turnaround. He's so excited for your wedding.'

The wedding that wasn't going to happen… Cam sidestepped the thought like someone avoiding a puddle. 'Yeah, your mum told me. It's great he's feeling better.'

'So when's the big day? Am I going to be best man? No pressure or anything.'

Cam affected a light laugh. 'I've got to get my father's fifth wedding out of the way first. We'll set a date after that.'

'What's your new stepmother like?'

'Don't ask.'

'Like that, huh?'

'Yep,' Cam said. 'Like that.'

Violet looked around Cam's house while he was out. It was a stunningly beautiful home with gorgeous touches everywhere but on closer inspection it didn't have a personal touch, nothing to hint at the private life of its only occupant. There were no family photos or childhood memorabilia. Unlike her family home in Scotland, where her mother had framed and documented and scrapbooked each of her children's milestones, Cam's house was bare of anything to do with his childhood. There were no photos of him with his parents. None of him as a child. It was as if he didn't want to be reminded of that part of his life.

Violet turned from looking at one of the paintings on the wall in the study when Cam came in carrying shopping bags. 'You've been ages,' she said. 'Was it frightfully busy? The shops can be a nightmare at this time of year. I shouldn't have asked you. I'm sorry but I—'

'It was fine.' He handed her the bags. 'You'd better check I've got the right size.'

Violet took the bags and set them on the cedar desk. She took out the tissue-wrapped sweater and held it against her body. It was the most gorgeous baby-blue cashmere and felt soft as a cloud. The other wrapped parcel was a pair of jeans. But there was another tiny parcel at the bottom of the second shopping bag. Her heart gave a stumble when she picked it up and saw the high-end jewellery store label on the ribbon that was tied in a neat bow on top. 'What's this?'

'An engagement ring.'

Violet's eyes rounded. Her heart pounded. Her hopes sounded. *Did this mean...? Was he...?* 'You bought a ring? For me?'

His expression was as blank as his house was of his past. 'It's just for show. I figured everyone would be asking to see it at your office party tonight.'

Violet carefully unpeeled the ribbon, her heart feeling like a hummingbird was trapped in one of its chambers. She opened the velvet box to find a beautiful diamond in a classic setting in a white gold ring. It was more than beautiful—it was perfect. How had he known she wasn't the big flashy diamond sort? She took it out of the box and pushed it onto her ring finger. It winked up at her as if in conspiracy. *I might be just a prop but don't I look fabulous on your hand?* She looked up at Cam's unreadable expression. 'It's gorgeous. But I'll give it back after Christmas, okay?'

'No.' There was a note of implacability to his tone. 'I want you to keep it. Think of it as a gift for your help with the Nicolaides contract.'

Violet held up her hand, looking at the light dancing off the diamond. She didn't like to think it might be the only engagement ring she ever got. She lowered her hand and looked at him again. 'It's very generous of you, Cam. It's beautiful. I couldn't have chosen better myself. Thank you.'

'No problem.'

Violet gathered up her new clothes and the packaging. 'I'm going to get dressed and head out to replenish my wardrobe. What are your plans?'

'Work.'

'On the weekend?'

He gave her a *that's how it is* look. 'I'll catch up with you later this evening. What time is your office party?'

'Eight.'

'I'll be back in time to take you. Make yourself at home.' He reached past her to open the drawer of the desk and took out a key on a security remote. He handed it to her. 'Here's the key to the house.'

Violet took the key and a rush of heat coursed from her fingers to her core when her hand came into contact with his. He must have felt it too for his gaze meshed with hers in a sizzling tether that made her wonder if he was only going to work to remove himself from the temptation of spending time with her. Doing…things. Wicked things. Things that made her blood heat and her stomach do cartwheels of excitement. 'Cam?' Her voice came out croaky and soft.

His eyes went to her mouth and she saw the way his throat moved up and down over a tight swallow. 'Don't make this any harder than it already is.' His tone was two parts gravel, one part honey, and one part man on the edge of control.

With courage she had no idea she possessed, Violet moved closer, planting her hands on his chest, bringing her hips in contact with his. 'Don't I get to kiss you for buying me such a gorgeous ring?'

His eyes darkened until it was impossible to tell where his pupils began and ended. His body stirred against hers, the swell of his erection calling out to her. Desire burned through every lonely corridor of her body, every network of nerves, every circuit of her blood. She became aware of her breasts pushed up against the fabric of her bathrobe, the nipples already tight, her flesh aching for human touch—Cam's touch. Her courage increased with every pound of his heart she could feel thundering under her palm.

His head came down at the same time she stepped up on tiptoe, their mouths meeting in the middle in an explosion of lust that sent a shockwave through Violet's body. It sent it through Cam's, too, for he grabbed her by the hips and pulled her hard against him, smothering a groan as his mouth plundered hers.

His tongue didn't ask for entry but demanded it, tangling with hers in a sexy combat that mimicked the intimacy both of them craved. This wasn't a chaste kiss between old friends. This was a kiss of urgency, of frustration, of long-built-up needs that could wait no longer for satiation.

Cam's mouth continued its thrilling exploration of hers while his hands slipped beneath the opening of her bathrobe, exposing her breasts. Violet shivered as the feel of his hand shaping her, cupping her, caressing her threatened to heat her blood to boiling. She'd had no idea her breasts were that sensitive. No idea how wonderful it felt to have a man's hand cradle her shape while his thumb moved back and forth across her nipple.

But it wasn't enough. Her body wanted more. More contact, more friction, more of the sensual heat his body promised. She pushed her lower body against his, relishing the delicious thrill it gave her to feel the potency of his arousal. She had done that to him. Her body stirred his as his stirred hers. It was a combustible energy neither of them could deny nor ignore any longer.

'This is madness,' Cam said just above her mouth.

Violet didn't give him a chance to pull away any further. She pressed closer, stroking her tongue over his lips, the top one and then the lower one, a shiver coursing through her when he gave another rough groan and covered her mouth in a fiery kiss. His hands gripped her by the hips, holding her to his rigid heat, the contact making Violet's inner core tingle and tighten with anticipation. How had she survived so long without this magical energy rushing through her body? Cam's touch made every nerve in her body cry out for more.

He pulled his mouth away, his breathing a little unsteady. 'Not here, not like this.'

Violet kept her arms around his waist, reluctant to give him the opportunity to break the intimate contact. 'Don't say you don't want me because I know you do.'

He gave her a rueful look. 'Not much chance of hiding it, is there? But I want you to be comfortable and making love on a desk or the floor is not my idea of comfortable.'

Before Violet could say anything, he scooped her up

in his arms. She gave a startled gasp and held on, secretly delighted he was taking charge like a romantic hero out of an old black and white movie.

They came to his bedroom door and he shouldered it open and carried her to the end of the bed, lowering her to the floor, but not before trailing her body down the length of his, leaving her in no doubt of his erotic intentions. He pressed another lingering kiss to her lips, exploring the depths of her mouth with a beguiling mix of gentleness and urgency. Sensations rippled through her body in tiny waves, making her skin sensitive to his touch like he had cast a sensual spell on her. But then he had. From the moment he had walked into that café, she had been under the heady spell of sexual attraction.

Violet pulled up his sweater and T-shirt so she could glide her hands over his naked skin. Warm, hard male flesh met the skin of her palms; a light smattering of masculine hair grazed her fingertips, the scent of his cologne teased her nostrils. She explored the tiny pebbles of his nipples, and then the flat plane of his stomach with its washboard ridges that marked him as man who enjoyed hard physical exercise.

Cam untied the waist strap of her bathrobe and sent his hands on their own sensual journey. Violet shuddered when his hands glided around her ribcage, not quite touching her breasts but close enough for her to feel she would die if he didn't. He brought his mouth to the upper curve of her right breast. He didn't seem in a hurry, but maybe he was giving her time to get used to this level of intimacy. He brushed his thumb over her nipple, a back and forth movement that made her body contract with want.

Rather than undress her any further, he set to work on his own clothes, taking each item off while his gaze was trained on hers.

Finally, he was in nothing but black underpants, and then and only then did he remove her bathrobe. Violet's belly did a somersault an Olympic gymnast would have been proud of when she saw the way his eyes feasted on her breasts. He cupped them in his hands with exquisite care, rolling his thumb over each nipple before lowering his mouth to subject her to an intimate torture that made her senses spin in dizzying delight.

He lifted his mouth off her breast and, kneeling in front of her, continued to kiss his way from her sternum to her belly button. Violet sucked in a breath, her hands on his shoulders, not sure she could handle what he was planning.

'Relax, sweetheart.'

Easy for you to say. Violet held her breath while he peeled away her knickers. The warmth of his breath on her intimate flesh made her spine weaken as if someone had unbolted her vertebrae. His mouth came to her softly, a light as air touch that made her knees tremble. He gently parted her, stroking her with his tongue, the sensation so powerful she pulled away. 'I—I can't…'

His hands were gentle but firm on her hips. 'Yes, you can. Don't be frightened of it. Trust me.'

Violet glanced down at him worshipping her body, his touch so tender, so respectful it made her see her body differently, not as something to be ashamed of and hidden away, but as something that was not only beautiful and capable of receiving pleasure, but also of giving it too. The rhythmic strokes of his tongue sent a torrent of tingles through her body, concentrating on that one point—the heart of her femininity. The tension grew to a crescendo until she was finally catapulted into a vortex that scattered her thoughts until all she could do was feel. Feel the power of an orgasm that swept through her like a hot wave, rolling through every inch of her flesh, trickling over every nerve ending, sending showers of goose bumps over her body, leaving no part of her immune. She was limbless, dazed, out of her mind as the aftershocks pulsed through her.

Cam brought his mouth back up over her stomach and ribcage, then her breasts, leaving a blistering trail of kisses on her tingling skin. He stood upright, drawing her closer, his mouth settling back on hers in a mind-altering kiss, the eroticism of it heightened by the fact she could taste her own essence on his lips and tongue.

Violet had thought herself too shy to draw his briefs from his body but somehow her hands reached for the elastic edge of the waistband and slid them away from his body. She took him into her hand—hot, hard, and quintessentially male. She stroked him with experimental caresses, her fingers drawing down from the base to the head and back again. It was so empowering to be an active part of a sexual encounter. The deep guttural noises he made added to her sense of agency.

She was doing this to him. She was the one he wanted. She was the one exciting him, pushing him to the limit of control.

Cam gently moved her hand away and guided her to the mattress behind her, coming down over her in a tangle of limbs, balancing his weight on his arms so as not to crush her. 'Comfortable?'

'Yes.' Violet was surprised she was capable of thought, let alone speech. The way he made her feel, so safe, so treasured, made the shame she had carried for so long slip further out of reach, like an old garment stuffed at the back of the wardrobe. It was still there but she could no longer see it.

Cam stroked her face with his fingertip, his eyes dark and lustrous. 'We don't have to go any further if you're not ready.'

I'm ready! I'm ready! Violet touched the flat of her palm to his stubbly jaw, looking into his eyes without reserve. 'I want you inside me.'

A flash of delight went through his gaze. 'I won't rush you and you can stop me at any point.'

He reached for a condom in the bedside drawer and deftly applied it before coming back to her. The choreography of their bodies aligning themselves for that ultimate physical connection was simple and yet complex. It was like learning the steps to a dance, one leg this way, the other that, her breasts pressing against the wall of his chest, her arms winding around his body to anchor herself. He gently probed her entrance, allowing her time to adjust to him just…being there. She felt the weight and heft of him waiting there but it wasn't threatening in any way.

He slowly entered her, waiting for her to relax before going any further. Violet welcomed him inside her body with soft little gasps as the sensation of him stretching her, filling her, tantalising her gained momentum. He began a slow rhythm that sent shivers of delight through her body, the friction of male against female making her aware of her body in a way she had never been before. Nerves she hadn't known existed were firing up. Muscles that had been inactive for most of her life were now being activated in a deeply pleasurable workout that had one sure goal. She could feel that goal dangling just out of reach, the thrill of her flesh building and building but unable to go any further. It was a frustrating ache, a restless urging for more. But, as if Cam could read her silent pleas for release, he brought his hand down between their bodies and sought the heart of her arousal. The stroking of his fingers against her tipped her into a free fall of spinning, whirling, dizzying sensations. They ricocheted through her in giant shudders, making her lose her grasp on conscious thought. She was in the middle of a vortex, vivid colours bursting like thousands of tiny fireworks behind her squeezed-shut eyelids.

Then the slow wash of a wave of lassitude… She was drifting, drifting, drifting…

But then she became aware of the increasing pace of Cam's thrusts as his own release powered down on him. She experienced every second of it through the sensitised walls of her body, his tension building to a final crucial point before he pitched forwards against her, his deep primal cry making something in her belly shiver like a light wind whispering over the surface of a lake.

Violet lay in his embrace, her fingertips moving up and down his spine while his breathing gradually slowed. She couldn't find the words to express what her body had just experienced. She felt reborn. As if the old her had been sloughed away like a tired skin. Her new skin felt alive, energised, and sensitive to every movement of Cam's breathing as his chest rose and fell against hers.

Should she say something? What? *How was it for you?* That seemed a little trite and clichéd somehow. How many times had he lain here like this with other women? How many other women? He might not be the fastest living playboy on the planet but he wasn't without a sex life. He just kept it a little more private than other men in his position. How many women had lain here in his arms and felt the same as her? Was what she had experienced with him run-of-the-mill sex? Or was it different? More special? More intense?

Violet knew she was being a fool for allowing her feelings to get involved. But this was Cam. Not just some hot guy she happened to fancy. Cam was a friend. Someone she had known for years and years and always admired.

They had stepped into new territory and it felt… weird, but not horribly weird. Nicely weird. Excitingly weird. Would he make love to her again? How soon? Would he get so hooked on having sex with her he would extend their 'engagement'? What if he fell in love with her? What if he decided marriage and kids wasn't such a bad idea? What if—?

Cam dealt with disposing of the condom and then looked down at her with a soft smile that made his eyes seem even darker. 'Hey.'

Violet hoped he wasn't as good at reading her mind as he was at reading her body. Her thoughts were running like ticker tape in her head. *Please fall in love with me. Please.*

'Hey…'

He brushed some stray strands of hair back from her face, his smile fading as a frowning concern took up residence instead. 'Did I hurt you?'

Violet had trouble speaking for the sudden lump in her throat. 'N-not at all.'

He picked up another strand of hair and gently anchored it behind her ear, holding her gaze with his. 'Sure?'

How was she supposed to keep her feelings out of this when he looked at her like that? When his hands touched her as if she were something so eminently precious to him he would rather die than hurt her? 'I'm sure.'

He leaned down to press a soft kiss to her mouth. 'You were wonderful.'

Violet traced the line of his mouth with her fingertip. 'This won't…change things between us, will it? I mean, no matter what happens, we'll always be friends, won't we?'

A flicker of something moved through his gaze like a passing thought leaving a shadow in its wake. 'Of course we will.' He took her hand and quickly kissed the ends of her fingertips before releasing it. 'Nothing will ever change that.'

Violet wasn't so sure. What if she couldn't cope with going back to normal? He might be able to go back to relating to her as he had always done, but she wasn't confident she would be able to do the same to him. How could she look at him and not think of how his mouth felt against her own? How could she not think of how his hands had stroked her most intimate flesh? How could she not think of how his body had awakened hers and made her feel things she hadn't thought were possible to feel?

Not just physical things, but emotional things.

Things that might not be so easily set aside once their fling was over.

CHAPTER SIX

CAM WAITED WHILE Violet had a shower and got changed. He would have joined her but he was conscious of allowing her time to recover. God, *he* needed time to recover. So much for keeping his distance. So much for his self-control. Where had that gone? He hadn't been able to resist the temptation of making love to her. So apparently they were having a fling. It didn't feel like any fling he'd ever had before. He had never known a partner the way he knew Violet. Her trust in him had heightened the experience. Every touch, every kiss, every stroke, every whimper or gasp of hers had made his pleasure intensify. It was like having sex for the first time but not in a clumsy, awkward way, but in a magical, mutually satisfying way that left his body humming like a plucked string.

Somehow the thought of spending the afternoon working didn't hold its usual appeal. Even a yuletide cynic like him had to agree there was no greater place to be before Christmas than in London. He wasn't much of a shopper but Violet needed a new wardrobe and he would rather spend the time with her than chained to his desk.

Violet came down the stairs wearing the jeans and baby-blue sweater he'd bought her. Cam had trouble keeping his hands to himself. He ached to slide his hands under the sweater and cradle the perfection of her breasts. To feel those pink nipples embed themselves into his palm. To feel her body quake with pleasure when he touched her.

She smiled at him shyly, her cheeks going a faint shade of pink as if she too were recalling their earlier intimacy. 'I thought you were going to work?'

Cam shrugged. 'It can wait.' He took her hand and brought it up to his mouth. 'I probably should warn you I'm not the world's best shopper but I'm pretty handy with carrying bags.'

Her eyes shone as if the thought of him accompanying her pleased her as much as it pleased him. 'Are you sure you're not too busy? I know how much men loathe shopping. Dad and Fraser are such pains when we try to get them through a department store door.'

Cam looped her arm through his. 'I have a vested interest in this expedition. I have to make sure Cinderella is dressed appropriately for the ball tonight.'

A flicker of worry passed through her gaze. 'I never know what to wear to the office party. There's a theme this year… *A Star-Struck Christmas*. Last year it was *White Christmas*. The year before it was *Christmas on the Titanic*.'

'You could turn up in a bin liner and still outshine everyone else.'

Her smile made something in his chest slip sideways. 'I really appreciate you coming with me. I can't tell you how much I hate going alone.'

Cam bent down to press a kiss to her forehead. 'You're not alone this year. You're with me.'

Cam wasn't much of a party animal but even he had to admit Violet's firm put on a Christmas extravaganza that was impossible not to enjoy. It occupied the ballroom of one of London's premier hotels and the decorations alone would have funded a developing nation for a year. Giant green and gold and red Christmas bells hung from silken threads just above head height. Great swathes of tinsel adorned the walls. A fresh Christmas tree was positioned to one side of the room, covered with baubles that looked like they had been dipped in gold. Maybe they had. There was an angel on the top whose white gown glittered with Swarovski crystals. The music was lively and fun. The food was fabulous. The champagne was top-shelf and free flowing.

Or maybe he was having a good time because he was with the most beautiful girl at the party. The shimmery dress he'd helped Violet choose skimmed her delicate curves so lovingly his hands twitched in jealousy. The heels she was wearing put his mind straight in the gutter. He couldn't stop imagining her wearing nothing but those glossy black spikes and a sexy come-and-get-me smile.

Cam had been ruminating all afternoon over whether he had done the right thing in making love to Violet. Who was he kidding? He was *still* ruminating. It was like a loop going round and round in his head. *What have I done?*

It was fine to put it down to hormones, but he wasn't some immature teenager who didn't know the meaning of the word self-control. He was a fully grown adult and yet he hadn't been able to walk away.

Had he done the wrong thing?

His body said *Yes.*

His mind said *Yes, but.*

The *buts* were always going to be the kicker. Violet wasn't like any other casual lover he'd met. She'd been in his life for what seemed like for ever. He'd seen her grow from a gangly and shy teenage girl to a beautiful young woman. She was still shy but some of that reserve had eased away when they'd made love. Sharing that experience with her, being the one to guide her through her first experience of pleasure with a partner had been special. More than special. A sacred privilege he would remember for the rest of his life. Her trust in him had touched him, honoured him, and made him feel more of a man than he had ever felt before.

But...

How could he give her what she wanted when it was the opposite of what he wanted right now? Violet came from a family where marriage was a tradition that was celebrated and treasured and believed in. She wanted the fairytale her parents and siblings had.

It wasn't that Cam was so cynical he didn't think marriage could work. It did work. It worked brilliantly, as Margie and Gavin Drummond demonstrated and their parents before them. But Cam's parents' example had made him see the other side of the order of service: the stonewalling, the bitter fights, the disharmony, the petty paybacks, the affairs and then the divorce lawyers, not to mention years of estrangement where the very mention of the other person's name would bring on an explosive fit of temper.

While Cam didn't think he was the type of person to walk out on a commitment as important as marriage, how could he be sure life wouldn't throw up something that would challenge the standards he upheld? The promises people made so earnestly in church didn't always ring with the same conviction when life tossed in a curve ball or two.

It was all well and good to be confident he would stand by his commitment, but it wasn't just about his commitment. The other person would have to be equally committed. How could he be sure Violet, as gorgeous and sweet as she was, would feel the same about him in ten weeks, let alone ten years or five times that? Watching his parents go through their acrimonious divorce when he was a young child had made him wary about rushing into the institution.

He had never had any reason to question his decision before now. It had always seemed the safest way to handle his relationships—being open and honest about what he could and couldn't give. Yes, some lovers might have been disappointed there was no promise of a future. But at least he hadn't misled them.

But sleeping with Violet had changed things. Changed *him*. Made him more aware of the things he would be missing out on rather than the things he was avoiding. Things like walking into a party hand in hand, knowing he was going to leave with that hand still in his. Knowing the smile she turned his way was for him and no one else. Recognising the secret look she gave him that told him she was remembering every second of his lovemaking and she couldn't wait to experience it again. Feeling the frisson of awareness when she brushed against him, how his body was so finely tuned to hers he could sense her presence even when she was metres away.

Had he ever felt like that with anyone else? No. Never. Which wasn't to say he wouldn't with someone else…someone other than Violet. His gut swerved at the thought of making love to someone else. He couldn't imagine it. Couldn't even picture it. Couldn't think of a single person who would excite him the way she excited him.

It will pass. It always does.

Lust for him was a candle not a coal ember. It would flare for a time and then snuff out. Sometimes gradually, sometimes overnight.

But when he looked at Violet, he couldn't imagine his desire for her ever fading. Because his desire for her wasn't just physical. There was another quality to it, a quality he had never felt with anyone else. When he'd made love to her it had felt like an act of worship rather than just sex. Her response to him had been a gift rather than a given. The fact she trusted him enough to feel able to express herself sexually was the biggest compliment—and turn on—he had ever experienced.

But...

How was he going to explain the end of their 'engagement' to her family? How was he going to go back to being just friends? How would he be able to look at her and not remember the way her mouth had felt when she'd opened it for him that first time? How her shy little tongue had tangled with his until his blood had pounded so hard he'd thought his veins would explode? How would he be able to be in the same room as her without wanting to draw her into his arms? To feel her slim body press against his need until he was crazy with it?

Maybe he was crazy. Maybe that was the problem. Making love to her was the craziest thing he'd done in a long time.

But...

He wanted to make love to her again. And again and again.

God help him.

Violet was coming back from a trip to the ladies' room when she was intercepted by three of her workmates, including Lorna.

'Congratulations, Violet,' Lorna said, eyeing her engagement ring. 'Gracious me, that man of yours was quick off the mark.' Her gaze flicked to Violet's abdomen. 'You're not pregnant, are you?'

If there was one time in her life Violet wished she didn't have the propensity to blush, this was it. Could Lorna tell the engagement wasn't real? After all, Violet hadn't mentioned anything about dating anyone, not that she talked about her private life that much at work. But women working together for a long time tended to pick up on those things. Besides, conversations around the water cooler tended to show how boring her life was compared to everyone else's. 'No, not yet but it's definitely on the to-do list.' *Why did you say that?*

Lorna's smile didn't involve her eyes. 'When's the big day?'

'Erm...we haven't decided on a date yet,' Violet said. 'But some time next year.' *I wish.*

'So how did he propose?'

Violet wished she'd talked this through a little more with Cam. They hadn't firmed up any details of their story apart from the fact—which was indeed a fact—they had met via her older brother. How would Cam propose if he were going to ask her to marry him? He wasn't the bells and whistles type. There wouldn't be any skywritten proposals or football-stadium audiences while he got down on bended knee. That was the sort of thing his father did, even on one memorable occasion making the evening news. Cam would choose somewhere quiet and romantic and tell her he loved her and wanted to spend the rest of his life with her. Her heart squeezed. *If only!* 'It was really romantic and—'

'Ah, here's Prince Charming himself,' Lorna said as Cam approached. 'Violet's been telling me how you proposed.'

Cam's smile never faltered but Violet knew him well enough to notice the flicker of tension he was trying to disguise near his mouth. He slipped an arm around Violet's waist and drew her close against him. 'Have you, darling?'

Violet's smile had a hint of *help me* about it. 'Yes, I was saying it was terribly romantic…with all the roses and…stuff.'

'What colour?' Lorna asked.

'White,' Violet said.

'Red,' Cam said at exactly the same time.

Lorna's artfully groomed brows rose ever so slightly. But then she smiled and winked at Cam. 'You have good taste. Violet's a lucky girl to land a man who knows his way around a diamond dealer.'

'She deserves the very best,' Cam said.

'Yes, well, she's waited long enough for it,' Lorna said and with a fingertip wave moved on to return to the party.

Violet released a long jagged breath. 'She suspects something. I know she does. We should've talked about the proposal.' She spun around so her back was to the party room. 'I feel such an idiot. And, for the record, I hate red roses.'

'I'll make a note of it.'

Violet searched his expression but he had his blank-wall mask on. 'So how would you propose if you were going to?'

His brows moved together over his eyes. 'Is that a trick question?'

'No, it's a serious one,' Violet said. 'If, and I know it's a very big "if", but if you were to ask someone to marry you how would you go about it?'

Cam glanced about him. 'Is this the right venue to talk about this?'

Violet wasn't going to risk being cornered by another workmate for details of their engagement. Nothing would out a charade faster than someone cottoning on to a clash of accounts of an event from witnesses. 'We're out of earshot out here. Come on, tell me. What would you do?'

He blew out a short breath. 'I'd make sure I knew what the girl would like.'

'Like what colour roses?'

He gave her a droll look. 'What have you got against red roses?'

Violet gave a lip shrug. 'I don't know… I guess because they're so obvious.'

'Right, then I'd make sure we were alone because I don't believe in putting a woman under pressure from an audience.'

'Like your father did with wife number three?'

'Number two and three.' Cam's eyes gave a half roll.

'So no TV cameras and news crews?'

'Absolutely not.'

Violet looked back at the party in the next room. 'We should probably go and mingle…'

'What's your dream proposal?' Cam asked.

She met his gaze but there was nothing to suggest he was asking the question for any other reason than mild interest. 'I know this sounds a bit silly and ridiculously sentimental, but I've always wanted to be proposed to at Drummond Brae. Ever since I was a little girl, I dreamed of standing by the loch near the forest with the house in the distance and my lover going down on bended knee, just as my father did with my mum and my grandfather did with my grandmother.'

'Your would-be fiancé would have to have a meteorological degree to predict the best time to do it.' Cam's tone was dry. 'Nothing too romantic about being proposed to in sleet or snow.'

Violet's smile was wistful. 'If I was in love I probably wouldn't even notice.'

Half an hour later, Violet turned back to Cam after listening to a boring anecdote from one of her co-workers who'd had one too many drinks. Cam was staring into space and had a frown etched on his brow. 'Are you okay?' she said, touching him on the arm.

He blinked as if she'd startled him but then he seemed to gather himself and smiled down at her. 'Sure.' He slipped an arm around her waist and drew her closer. 'Did I tell you you're the most beautiful woman in the room?'

Violet could feel a blush staining her cheeks. Did

he mean it or was he just saying it in case other people were listening? She felt beautiful when she was with him. What woman wouldn't when he looked at her like that? As if he was remembering every moment of making love to her. The glint in his dark eyes saying he couldn't wait to do it again. 'Don't you feel a little… compromised?'

'In what way?'

She glanced around at the partying crowd before returning her gaze to his, saying sotto voce, 'You know… pretending. Lying all the time.'

He picked up her left hand and pressed a kiss to the diamond while his eyes stayed focused on hers. 'I'm not pretending to want you. I do and badly. How long do we have to stay?'

Violet's inner core tingled in anticipation. 'Not much longer. Maybe five, ten minutes?'

He dropped a kiss to her forehead. 'I'm going to get a mineral water. Want one?'

'Yes, please.'

'Hey, Violet.' Kenneth from Corporate Finance came up behind her and placed a heavy hand on her shoulder. 'Come and dance with me.'

Violet rolled her eyes. She went through the same routine with Kenneth every year at the Christmas party. He always had too much to drink and always asked her to dance. But, while she didn't want to encourage him in any way, she knew Christmas for him was a difficult time. His wife had left him just before Christmas a few years ago and he hadn't coped well with the divorce.

Violet turned and gently extricated herself from his beefy paw. 'Not tonight, thanks. I'm with my…fiancé.'

Kenneth looked at her myopically, swaying on his feet like his body couldn't decide whether to stand or fall. 'Yeah, I heard about that. Congrats and all that. When's the big day?'

'We haven't got around to settling on that just yet.'

He grabbed her left hand and held it up to the light. 'Nice one. Must've cost a packet.'

Violet didn't care for the clammy heat of his hand against hers. But neither did she want to make a scene. The firm had strict guidelines on sexual harassment in the workplace but she felt sorry for Kenneth and knew he would be mortified by his behaviour if he were sober. 'Please let me go, Kenneth.'

He lurched forwards. 'How about a Christmas kiss?'

'How about you get your hands off my fiancée?' Cam said in a tone as cold as steel.

Kenneth turned around and almost toppled over and had to grab hold of the Christmas tree next to him. Violet watched in horror as the tree with all its tinsel and baubles came crashing down, the snow-white angel on the top landing with a thud at Violet's feet, her porcelain skull shattering.

The room was suddenly skin-crawlingly quiet.

But then Kenneth dropped to his knees and picked up the broken angel and held it against his heaving chest. His sobs were quiet sobs. The worst sort of sobs because what they lacked in volume they made up for in silent anguish.

Violet went down beside him and placed a comforting hand on his shoulder. 'It's all right, Kenneth. No one cares about the tree. Do you want us to give you a lift home?'

To her surprise Cam bent down on Kenneth's other side and place his hand on the man's other shoulder. 'Hey, buddy. Let's get you home, okay?'

Kenneth's eyes were streaming tears like someone had turned on a tap inside him. He was still clutching the angel, his hands shaking so much the tiny bits of glitter and crystals from her dress were falling like silver snow. 'She's having a baby… My ex, Jane, is having the baby we were supposed to h-have…'

Violet had trouble keeping her own tears in check. How gut-wrenchingly sad it must be for poor Kenneth to hear his ex-wife was moving on with her life when clearly he hadn't stopped loving her. She exchanged an agonised glance with Cam before leaning in to one-arm-hug Kenneth. She didn't bother trying to search for a platitude. What could she say to help him recover from a broken heart? It was obvious the poor man wasn't over his divorce. He was lonely and desperately sad, and being at a party where everyone was having fun with their partners was ripping that wound open all over again.

After a while, the music restarted and the crowd went on partying. Cam helped Kenneth to his feet while some other men helped put the tree back up.

Violet collected their coats and followed Cam and Kenneth out to the foyer of the hotel where the party was being held. She waited with Kenneth while Cam brought the car to the door and within a few minutes they were on their way to the address Kenneth gave her.

He lived in a nice house in Kensington, not unlike Cam's house, but Violet couldn't help thinking how terribly painful it must be for Kenneth to go home to that empty shell where love had once dwelled, where plans had been made and dreams dreamt.

Once they were sure Kenneth was settled inside, Cam led Violet back to his car. 'Sad.'

'I know…'

'Did you see all the photos of his ex everywhere?' Cam said. 'The place is like a shrine to her. He needs to find a way to move on.'

'I know, but it must be so hard for him at Christmas especially.'

He gave her hand a light squeeze. 'Sorry for being a jerk about him touching you.'

'That's okay, you weren't to know.' She let out a sigh. 'It must be terrible for him, seeing everyone else having a good time while he comes back here to what? An empty house.'

'Does he have any other family? Parents? Siblings?'

'I don't know…but even if he did, wouldn't being with them just remind him of what he's lost? It's hard when you're the only one without a partner.' Violet knew that better than anyone.

Cam nodded grimly. 'Yeah, well, divorce is harder on some people than others.'

Violet glanced at him. 'Your mother took it hard?'

The line around his mouth tightened. 'I was six years old when they finally split up. A week or two after my father moved out to live with his new partner, I came downstairs one morning to find her unconscious on the sofa with an empty bottle of pills and an empty wine bottle beside her. I rang Emergency and thankfully they arrived in time to save her.'

No wonder he was so nervous about commitment. Seeing the devastation of a breakup at close quarters and at such a tender age would have been nothing short of terrifying. 'That must have been so scary for you as a little kid.'

'Yeah, it was.' He waited a beat before continuing. 'Every time I went back to boarding school after the holidays I was worried sick about her. But she started seeing another guy, more to send a message to my father than out of genuine love. It was a payback relationship—one of many.'

'No wonder you break out in a rash every time someone mentions the word marriage,' Violet said.

'Divorce is the word I hate more. But you can never know if it's going to happen or not. No one can guarantee their relationship will last.'

Violet wanted to disagree but deep down she knew what he said was true. There were no guarantees. Life could change in a heartbeat and love could be taken away by disease or death or divorce. Just because you were in love didn't mean the other person would remain committed. She knew many women and men who'd been devastated by their partners straying. But she believed in love and commitment and knew she would do her best when she fell in love to nurture that love and keep it healthy and sustained.

What do you mean—when you fall in love? Haven't you already?

Violet waited until they'd gone a few blocks before speaking again. 'Cam? I have to do something about my flat tomorrow. I really should have done something about it today but I couldn't bring myself to face it. But I can't leave that mess for the girls to clean up on their own.'

'Do you have to go back there?'

Violet glanced at him again. 'What do you mean? It's where I live.'

'You could live somewhere else. Somewhere safer, more secure.'

'Yeah.' Violet sighed. 'Somewhere heaps more expensive too.'

There was a silence broken only by the swishing of the windscreen wipers going back and forth.

'You could stay with me for as long as you like,' Cam said. 'Until you find somewhere more suitable, I mean. There's no rush.'

Violet wondered what was behind the invitation. Was it solely out of consideration for her safety or was he thinking about extending their relationship until who knew when? 'That's a very generous offer but what if you want to start seeing someone else after we break up after Christmas? Could be awkward.'

'Everything about this situation is awkward.'

Violet looked at the tight set of his features. 'Are you regretting…what happened this morning?'

He relaxed his expression and reached across the gear console and captured her hand, bringing it over to rest on top of his thigh. 'No. Maybe I should, but I don't.'

'I don't regret it either.'

His eyes met hers when he parked the car. 'Your family is going to be hurt when we…end this.'

Why had he hesitated over the word 'end'? Who would end it? Would it be a mutual decision or would he suddenly announce it was over?

'Yes, I feel bad about that. But at least it's not for long,' Violet said. 'Once Christmas is over we'll say we made a mistake…or something and go back to normal.'

He studied her for a long moment. 'Will you be okay with that?'

Violet gave him a super-confident smile. 'Of course. Why wouldn't I be? It's what we agreed on. A short-term fling to get me back on my dating feet.'

His expression clouded. 'You have to be careful when you're dating guys these days. You can't go out with just anyone. It's not safe when there are so many creeps on the prowl. And don't do online dating. Some of those guys lie about their backgrounds. Anyone can use a false identity. You could end up with someone with a criminal past.'

Violet wondered if he was cautioning her out of concern or jealousy or both. 'You sound like you don't want me to date anyone else.'

He paused before responding. 'I care about you, Violet, that's all. I don't want you to become a crime statistic.'

'I'm sure I'll manage to meet and fall in love with some perfectly lovely guy, just like my sisters have done,' Violet said. 'I'm just taking a little longer than they did to get around to it.'

He opened his car door and came around to hers but, instead of tension, this time there was a self-deprecating tilt to his mouth. 'Sorry about the lecture.'

Violet smiled and patted his hand where it was resting on the top of the doorframe. 'You can lecture me but only if I can lecture you right on back. Deal?'

He bent down to press a kiss to the end of her nose. 'Deal.'

CHAPTER SEVEN

CAM WOKE FROM a fitful sleep to find the space next to him in the bed was empty. He sat bolt upright, his chest seizing with panic. Where was Violet? When he'd drifted asleep she had been lying in his arms.

Calm down, man. She's probably gone to the bathroom.

He threw off the bedcovers and, snatching up a towel, wrapped it around his hips and padded through his house, checking each room and bathroom upstairs but there was no sign of her.

'Violet?' His voice rang out hollowly. His blood chugged through his veins like chunks of ice. His skin shrank away from his skeleton. He was annoyed at his reaction. What did it say about him? That he was so hooked on her he couldn't let her out of his sight? Ridiculous. She had a right to move about the house without asking permission first. Maybe she'd had trouble sleeping with him in the bed beside her. After all, she'd never been in a proper relationship before. Sharing a bed with someone took some getting used to, which was why he generally avoided it.

'Violet?'

Where could she be? Had she gone outside? He tugged the curtains aside but the back garden was as quiet and deserted as a graveyard. It was three in the morning and it was bitterly cold. Had she gone back to her flat? No. She wouldn't go there without backup. He flung open the sitting room door, then the study.

All empty.

'Are you looking for me?' Violet appeared like a ghost in the doorway of the study.

Relief flooded through Cam like the shot of a potent drug. 'Where were you?'

Her eyes did a double blink at the edginess of his tone. 'I was reading in the breakfast room.'

Cam frowned so hard his forehead pinched. 'Reading?'

Her tongue snaked out and left a layer of moisture over her lips. 'I was…having trouble sleeping. I didn't want to disturb you. You seemed restless enough without me putting on the light and rustling pages.'

Cam forked a hand through his already tousled hair. 'You should've woken me if I was disturbing you. Was I snoring?'

'No, you were just…restless like you were having a bad dream or something.'

He had been having a bad dream. It was coming back to him now in vivid detail. He had been alone in a run-down castle. The drawbridge was up and there was no way in or out. Loneliness crept out from every dark corner, prodding him with tomb-cold fingers. The yawning emptiness he felt was what he had seen on Kenneth's face when they'd returned him to his home last night: the absence of hope, the presence of despair, the bitter sting of regret.

But it was a dream. It didn't mean anything. It was just his mind making up a narrative while his body rested. It didn't mean he was worried about ending up alone in a castle with nothing but cobwebs and shadows to keep him company. It didn't mean he was subconsciously regretting his stance on marriage and commitment. It meant he was dog-tired and working too hard. That was what it meant. That. Was. All. 'Sorry for wrecking your beauty sleep. Next time just give me a jab in the ribs, okay?'

Violet's shy smile tugged like strings stitched on to his heart. 'It was probably my fault more than yours. I've never spent the night with anyone before.'

Of course she hadn't. She might have felt all sorts of uncomfortable about sharing the night with him in his bed. Cam put his hands on her hips and brought her closer. 'I'm not much of a sleep-over person myself.'

A flicker of concern appeared in her gaze. 'Oh… well, then, I can sleep in one of the spare rooms if you'd—'

'No.' Cam brought his mouth down to within an inch of hers. 'I like having you in my bed.' *More than I want to admit.*

Her hint of vanilla danced over his mouth. 'I like it too.'

Cam covered her mouth with his, a shockwave of need rushing through him as her lips opened beneath his. He moved his lips against hers, a gentle massage to prove to himself he could control his response to her. But within seconds the heat got to him, the flicker of her tongue against his lower lip unravelling his self-control like a dropped ball of string. He splayed his fingers through her silky hair, holding her face so he could deepen the kiss. She gave a soft whimper of approval that made his body shudder in delight.

Her body pressed against his, her breasts free behind the bathrobe she was wearing. Knowing she was naked underneath that robe made him wild with need. He untied the waistband, still with his mouth on hers, letting it fall to her feet. He glided his hands over her breasts and then he brought his mouth to each one in turn, caressing the erect pink nipples with his tongue, gently taking them between his teeth in a soft nibble. She smelt of flowers and sleep and sex and he couldn't get enough of her.

He brought his mouth back to hers, his hands holding her by the hips so she could feel what she was doing to him. The ache of need pounded through his body, the primal need to mate driving every other thought out of his brain.

He should have taken her upstairs to the bed but he wanted her now. *Now.*

The hunger was in time with his racing pulse. He

wanted her on the floor. On the desk. On the sofa. Wherever he could have her. He dragged his mouth off hers. 'I want you here. Now.'

Violet's eyes shone with excitement. She didn't say anything but her actions spoke for her. She stroked her hands down his chest to his abdomen, deftly unhooking the towel from around his waist and taking him in her hands. Her touch wreaked havoc on his control. Red-hot pleasure shot through his body, luring him to the abyss where the dark magic of oblivion beckoned.

Cam had to stop her from taking him over the edge. He drew her hand away and guided her to the floor. He kissed his way down from her breasts to her belly, lingering over her mound, ramping up her anticipation for what was to come. She squirmed and whimpered when he claimed his prize, her body bucking within seconds of his tongue moving against her. Her cries of pleasure made him want her all the more. Her passion was so unfettered, so unrestrained it made him wonder if she would find the same freedom to express her sexuality with someone else.

Someone else...

Cam tried to push the thought aside but it was impossible. It was ugly, grotesque thinking of Violet with some other guy. Someone who might not appreciate her sensitivity and shyness. Someone who might pressure her into doing things she wasn't comfortable with doing. Someone who wouldn't protect her at all times and in all places.

That's rich coming from the guy who hasn't got a condom handy.

Violet must have sensed Cam's shift in mood for she propped herself up on her elbows to look at him. 'Is something wrong? Did I do something wrong?'

Cam took her by the hand and helped her to stand. 'It's not you, sweetheart. It's me.' He handed her the bathrobe before picking up his towel and hitching it around his waist. 'I didn't bring a condom with me.'

'Oh…'

'Unlike other men, I don't have them strategically planted in every room of the house.' *But maybe I should.*

Her lips flickered with a smile. 'That's kind of nice to know…'

'I'm selective when it comes to choosing partners.' He only ever chose women he knew he wouldn't fall in love with: safe, no-strings women who were out for a bit of fun and a tearless goodbye at the end of it. Women who didn't look at him with big soulful brown eyes and pretend they didn't feel things they clearly felt.

How was he going to end this?

Do you even want to?

Cam played with the idea of extending their affair. But how long was too long and how short was too short? Either way, it still left him with the task of facing her family and saying the happy ever after they were hanging out for wasn't going to happen.

And that wasn't even the half of it. What about what Violet felt? No matter how much she said she was only after a short fling, he knew her well enough to know she was only saying that to please him. Would it be fair to continue this, knowing she was probably falling in love with him? God knew he was having enough trouble keeping his own feelings in check. Feelings he couldn't explain. Feelings that crept up on him at odd moments, like when Violet looked at him a certain way, or when she smiled, or when she touched him and it sent a lightning zap of electricity through him. Feelings he couldn't dismiss because Violet wasn't a temporary fixture in his life.

The longer he continued their affair, the harder it would be to end it. He knew it and yet…and yet…he couldn't bring himself to do it. Not until after Christmas. Grandad Archie surely deserved to have his last Christmas wish?

Violet made a business of tying the bathrobe back around her waist. 'I suppose you're careful to choose partners you're not likely to fall in love with.'

'It's easier that way.' Maybe that was why he never felt fully satisfied after an encounter even when the sex was good. Something always felt a little off centre. Out of balance, like only wearing one shoe. He never let a relationship drag on for too long. A month or two maximum. It made him look like a bit of a player but that was the price he was prepared to pay for his freedom.

Violet gave him a smile that didn't quite make the grade. 'Lucky me.'

Cam frowned. 'Hey, I didn't mean I chose you for that reason. You're different, you know you are.'

'Not different enough that you'll fall in love with me.'

'Violet—'

She held up her hand. 'It's okay, I don't need the lecture.'

Cam took her by the shoulders again. 'Are you saying you're in love with me? Is that what you're saying?'

Her eyes did everything they could to avoid his. 'No, I'm not saying that.' Her voice was hardly more than a thread of sound.

Cam tipped up her chin, locking her gaze with his. 'This is all I can give you. You have to accept it, Violet. Even if we continued our relationship past Christmas, it would still come down to this. I'm not going to get married to you or to anyone just now.'

Her shoulders went down on a sigh. 'I know. I'm being silly. Sorry.'

He brought her head against his chest, stroking her silky hair with his hand. 'You're not being silly. You're being normal. I'm the one with the commitment issues, not you.'

Her arms snaked around his waist. 'Can we go back to bed now?'

Cam lifted her in his arms. 'What a great idea.'

Violet had arranged with Cam to take her back to her flat on Sunday afternoon to help Amy and Stef with the clean-up, but while she was getting breakfast ready while Cam checked some emails, Amy phoned.

'You're not going to believe this,' Amy said. 'But last night old Mr Yates in twenty-five was smoking in bed and started a fire—'

'Is he all right?' Violet asked.

'Just a bit of smoke inhalation but both our flats are uninhabitable from the water damage,' Amy said. 'The landlady is furious and poor Mr Yates won't want to face her in a hurry.'

'So what will we do?' Violet asked. 'Are we expected to clean it up or will a professional cleaning service do that?'

'Cleaning service,' Amy said. 'I'm not going in there until the building's secure. The ceiling might come down or something. Stef's going to move back in with her mum and I'm going to move in with Heath. We've talked about moving in together for ages so this nails it. What about you? Will you stay with Cam now that you're officially engaged?'

'I… Yes, that's what I'll do,' Violet said. What else could she say? *No, Cam doesn't want to live with anyone*?

Cam came in at that point and smiled. It never failed to make her shiver when he looked at her like that. He stroked a hand down her back while he reached past her to take a mug out of the cupboard next to her. It was the lightest touch but it sent a tremor of longing through her flesh until her legs threatened to buckle.

Violet said goodbye to Amy and put her phone on the bench. 'I have a slight problem…'

'What's wrong?'

She explained about the fire and the water damage. 'So, I have to find somewhere else to live.'

It was hard to read his expression beyond the concern it showed while she had related the events of last night's fire. He turned to one side to take out a tea bag from a box inside the pantry. 'You can stay here as long as you need to. I told you that the other day.'

'Yes, but—'

'It's fine, Violet, really.'

'No, it's not fine,' Violet said. 'A couple of weeks is okay, but any longer than that and things will get complicated.' *More complicated than they already were.*

'What if I help you find a place?'

'You don't have to do that.'

'I'd like to,' he said. 'It'll mean I can give the security a once-over.'

Violet gave him a grateful smile. 'That would be great, thanks.' She waited a beat before adding, 'What's happening with the contract with Nicolaides? Is it secure yet?'

'Not yet.' Cam pulled out one of the breakfast-bar stools. 'I have some drawings to finalise. Sophia keeps altering the design, I suspect because she wants to drag out the process.'

'Has she sent you any more texts?'

'A couple.'

Jealousy surged in Violet's gut. 'When's she going to get the message? What is wrong with her?'

He gave a loose shrug. 'Some women don't know the meaning of the word no.'

Violet would have to learn it herself and in a hurry. 'I think it's disgusting how she openly lusts over you while her husband is watching. Why does he put up with it?'

'He's too frightened to lose her,' Cam said. 'She's twenty years younger than him. And she brings a lot of money to the relationship. Her father left her his empire. It's worth a lot of money.'

'I wouldn't care how much money someone had. If I couldn't trust them, then that would be it. Goodbye. Have a good life.'

He stroked a fingertip down her cheek, his smile gently teasing. 'If you think Sophia's bad, wait till you meet my father's fiancée.'

Violet frowned. 'You want me to meet her?'

'My dad's organised drinks on Wednesday night,' Cam said. 'If you'd rather not go, then—'

'No, it's okay. Of course I'll go. You went to my boring old office party, the least I can do is come with you for drinks with your father.'

Cam's father, Ross, had arranged to meet them at a boutique hotel in the centre of London. Violet hadn't met Ross McKinnon before but she had seen photos of him in the press. He was not quite as tall as Cam and his figure showed signs of the overly indulgent life he led. His features had none of the sharply chiselled definition of Cam's, and while he still had a full head of thick hair, it was liberally sprinkled with grey. His eyes, however, were the same dark blue but without the healthy clarity of Cam's. And they had a tendency to wander to Violet's breasts with rather annoying frequency.

'So this is the girl who's stolen my son's hard heart,' Ross said. 'Congratulations and welcome to the family.'

'Thank you,' Violet said.

Ross pushed his fiancée forward. 'This is Tatiana, my wife as of next weekend. We should have made it a double wedding, eh, Cameron?'

Cam looked like he was in some sort of gastric pain. 'Wouldn't want to steal your thunder.'

Violet took the young woman's hand and smiled. 'Lovely to meet you.'

Tatiana's smile came with a don't-mess-with-me warning. 'Likewise.'

Cam was doing his best to be polite but Violet could tell he was uncomfortable being around his father and new partner. Ross dominated the conversation with occasional interjections from Tatiana, followed by numerous public displays of affection that made Violet feel she was on the set of a B-grade porn movie. Clearly she wasn't the only one as several heads kept turning at the bar, followed by snickers.

Ross showed no interest in Cam's life. It shocked Violet that his father could sit for an hour and a half in his son's company and not once ask a single question about his work or anything to do with his private life. It made her feel sad for Cam to have had such a selfish parent who acted like a narcissistic teenager instead of an adult.

Violet was relieved when Cam got to his feet and said they had to leave.

'But we haven't told you what we've got planned for the honeymoon,' Ross said.

'Isn't that supposed to be bad luck?' Cam said with a pointed look.

Ross's face darkened. 'You can't help yourself, can you? But Tatiana is the one. I know it as sure as I'm standing here.'

'Good for you.' Cam's tone had a hint of cynicism to it and Violet wondered how many times he had heard exactly the same thing from his father. Ross was the sort of man who treated women as trophies to be draped on his arm and summarily dismissed when they ceased to pander to his bloated ego.

Violet quickly offered her hand to Ross and Tatiana. 'It was lovely to meet you. I hope the wedding goes well.'

Ross frowned. 'But aren't you coming with Cameron?'

Violet realised her gaffe too late. 'Erm...yes, of course, if that's what you'd like.'

'You're part of the family now,' Ross said. 'We'd be delighted to have you share in our special day, wouldn't we, babe?'

Tatiana's smile was cool. 'But of course. I'll aim the bouquet in your direction, shall I?'

Violet's smile felt like it was stitched in place. 'That'd be great.'

Cam took her by the hand and led her out of the hotel. 'I did warn you.'

'How on earth do you stand him?' Violet said. 'He's impossibly self-centred. He didn't ask you a single thing about your work or anything to do with you. It was all about him. How amazing he is and how successful and rich. And Tatiana looks like she's young enough to be his daughter. What on earth does she see in him?'

'He paid for her boob job.'

Violet rolled her eyes. She walked a few more paces with him before adding, 'I'm sorry about the wedding gaffe. I didn't think. Do you think they suspected anything was amiss?'

'Probably not,' Cam said. 'They're too focused on themselves.'

'Poor you,' Violet said.

He gave a soft smile. 'You want to grab a bite to eat before we go home?'

Go home. How…permanent and cosy that sounded. 'Sure. Where did you have in mind?'

'Somewhere on the other side of the city so there's no chance my father and Tatiana will chance upon us.'

Violet gave him a sympathetic look. 'I swear I am never going to complain about my family ever again.'

'There's no such thing as a perfect family,' he said. 'But I have to admit yours comes pretty close.'

Violet adored her family. They were supportive and loving and always there for her. But the pressure to live up to the standards her parents had modelled for her always made her feel as if she wasn't quite good enough, that she would never be able to do as brilliant a job as they had of finding love and keeping it. It was one of the reasons she had never told her mother or her sisters about what had happened at that party. Although she knew they would be nothing but supportive and concerned, she'd always worried they would see her differently…as damaged in some way.

'I know, but it's hard to live up to, you know? What if I don't find someone as perfect as my dad is for my mum? They're such a great team. I don't want to settle for less but I'm worried I might miss out. I want to have kids. That makes me feel under even more pressure. It's all right for guys; you can have kids when you're ninety. It's different for women.'

'If it's going to happen it'll happen,' he said. 'You can't force these things.'

'Easy for you to say. You have a queue of women waiting to hook up with you.'

He gave her hand a tiny squeeze. 'I'm only interested in one woman at the moment.'

At the moment.

How could she forget the clock ticking on their relationship? It was front and centre in her mind. Each day that passed was another day closer to when they would go back to being friends. Friends *without* benefits. It would be torture to be around Cam without being able to touch him, to kiss him, to wrap her arms around him and feel his body stir against her. It would be torture to see him date other women, knowing they were experiencing the explosive passion and pleasure of being in his arms.

What if she never found someone as perfect for her as Cam? What if she ended up alone and had to be satisfied with being an aunty or godmother instead of the mother she longed to be? She had been embroidering baby clothes since she was a teenager. She'd made them for her sisters and brother's wife Zoe each time they were expecting but she had her own private stash of clothes. It was her version of a hope chest. Every time she looked at those little vests and booties and bibs she felt an ache of longing. But it wasn't just about having a baby, she realised with a jolt. She wanted to have *Cam's* baby. She couldn't think of anything she wanted more than to be with him, not just for Christmas but for ever.

After dinner they walked hand in hand through the Christmas wonderland of London's streets. Violet had always loved Christmas in her adopted city but being with Cam made the lights seem all the brighter, the colours all the more vivid, the hype of the festive season all the more exciting. When they walked past the Somerset House ice-skating rink, Cam stopped and looked down at her with a twinkling look. 'Fancy a quick twirl to work off dinner?'

Violet looked at the gloriously lit rink with the beautifully decorated Christmas tree at one end. She had skated there a couple of times with Stef and Amy but she'd felt awkward because they had brought their boyfriends. The boys had offered to partner her but she'd felt so uncomfortable she'd pretended to have a sore ankle rather than take them up on their offer. 'I'm not very good at it…' she said. 'And I'm not wearing the right clothes.'

'Excuses, excuses,' Cam said. 'It won't take long to go home and change.'

Within a little while they were back at the rink dressed in jeans and jackets and hats and gloves. Violet felt like a foal on stilts until Cam took her by the hand and led her around until she felt more secure. He looked like he'd been skating all his life, his balance and agility making her attempts look rather paltry in comparison.

'You're doing great,' he said, wrapping one arm around her waist. 'Let's do a complete circuit. Ready?'

Violet leaned into his body and went with him in graceful sweeps and swishes that made the cold air rush past her face. It was exhilarating to be moving so quickly and with his steady support she gained more and more confidence, even letting go of his hand at one point to do a twirl in front of him.

Cam took her hand again, smiling broadly. 'What did I tell you? You're a natural.'

'Only with you.' *And not just with skating.* How would she ever make love with someone else and feel the same level of pleasure? It didn't seem possible. It wasn't possible because there was no way she could ever feel the same about someone else.

Once they had given back their skates, they walked to the London Eye, where Cam paid for them to go on to look at the Christmas lights all over London. Violet had been on the giant Ferris wheel a couple of times but it was so much more special doing it with Cam. The city was a massive grid of twinkling lights, a wonderland of festive cheer that made all the children and most of the adults on board exclaim with wonder.

Violet turned in the circle of Cam's arms to smile at him. 'It's amazing, isn't it? It makes me get all excited about Christmas when usually I'm dreading it.'

A slight frown appeared on his brow. 'Why do you dread it? I thought you loved spending Christmas with your family.'

Violet shifted her gaze to look at the fairyland below. 'I do love it…mostly, it's just I'm always the odd one out. The one without a partner. Apart from Grandad, of course.'

His hand stroked the small of her back. 'You won't be without a partner this year.'

But what about next year? Violet had to press her lips together to stop from saying it out loud. Once Christmas was over so too would their relationship come to an end. All the colour and sparkle and excitement and joy would be snuffed out, just like someone turning off the Christmas lights.

'No one knows what the next year will bring,' Cam

said as if he had read her thoughts. 'You could be married and pregnant by then.'

I wish...but only if it were to you. 'I can't see that happening.' Violet waited a moment before adding, 'Would you come to my wedding if I were to get married?'

Something flashed across his face as if pain had gripped him somewhere deep inside his body. 'Would I be invited?' His tone was light, almost teasing, but she could sense an undercurrent of something else. Something darker. Brooding.

'Of course,' Violet said. 'You're part of the family. It wouldn't be a Drummond wedding if you weren't there.'

'As long as you don't ask me to be the best man,' he said with a grim look. 'My father's asked me to be his and that'll be four times in a row.'

'Wow, you must be an expert at best man speeches by now.'

'Yeah, well, I hope this is the last time but I seriously doubt it.'

Violet thought of her parents and how loving and committed they were to each other and had been from the moment they'd met. They renewed their wedding vows every ten years and went back to the same cottage on the Isle of Skye where they'd spent their honeymoon on each and every anniversary. How had Cam dealt with his father's casual approach to marriage? Ross McKinnon changed wives faster than a sports car changed gears. How embarrassing it must be for Cam to have to go through yet another wedding ceremony knowing it would probably end in divorce. 'Maybe this time will be different,' she said. 'Maybe your dad is really in love this time.'

Cam's expression was a picture of cynicism. 'He doesn't know the meaning of the word.'

CHAPTER EIGHT

THE NEXT DAY Cam came home from work with the news that his contract with Nick Nicolaides had been signed that afternoon.

'Let's go out to celebrate.' He bent down to kiss Violet on the mouth. 'How was your day?'

Violet looped her arms around his neck. 'My day was fine. You must be feeling enormously relieved. Was Sophia there at the meeting?'

'Yes, but she was surprisingly subdued,' he said. 'I think she might've been feeling unwell or something. She got up to leave a couple of times and came back in looking a bit green about the gills. Too much to drink the night before, probably.'

Violet's brow furrowed. 'Could she be pregnant?'

He gave a light shrug. 'I wouldn't know, although, now that I think of it, Nick was looking pretty pleased with himself. But I thought that was because we finally finalised the contract.'

'Maybe being pregnant will help her settle down with Nick instead of eyeing up other men all the time,' Violet said.

Cam stepped away to shrug off his coat, laying it over the back of a chair. His expression had a cloaked look about it, shadowed and closed off. 'A Band-Aid baby is never a good idea.'

Violet knew he was bitter about his parents and the way they had handled his arrival in the world. Did he blame himself for how things had turned out? How could he think it was his fault? His parents were both selfish individuals who ran away from problems when things got the slightest bit difficult. They moved from relationship to relationship, collecting collateral damage along the way. How many lives had each of them ruined so far? And it was likely to continue with Ross McKinnon's next marriage. No wonder Cam wanted no part of the type of marriage modelled by his parents. It was nothing short of farcical. 'True,' she said. 'But a baby doesn't ask to be born and once it arrives it deserves to be treasured and loved unconditionally.'

A frown pulled at Cam's forehead. 'We haven't discussed this before but are you taking any form of oral contraception?'

Violet felt her cheeks heat up. It was something she had thought about doing but she hadn't got around to making an appointment with her doctor to get a prescription. There hadn't seemed much point when she wasn't dating regularly. But now…now it was imperative she kept from getting pregnant. The last thing Cam would want was a baby to complicate things further, even though she could think of nothing more wonderful than falling pregnant with his child. 'I'm not but I'm sure it won't be a problem—'

'Condoms are not one hundred per cent reliable,' he said, still frowning.

Violet felt intimidated by his steely glare. Why did he have to make her feel as if she was deliberately trying to get pregnant? There were worse things in the world than falling pregnant by the man you loved. Much worse things. Like not getting pregnant at all. Ever. 'I'm not pregnant, Cam, so you can relax, okay?'

A muscle tapped in his cheek. 'I'm sorry but this is a big issue for me. I don't want any mishaps we can't walk away from.'

Violet cast him a speaking look. 'You'd be the one walking away, not me.'

His frown deepened. 'Is that what you think? Really? Then you're wrong. I would do whatever I could to support you and the baby.'

'But you wouldn't marry me.' It was a statement, not a question.

For once his eyes had trouble meeting hers. 'Not under those circumstances. It wouldn't be fair to the child.'

Violet moved away to fold the tea towels she had taken out of the clothes dryer earlier. 'This is a pointless discussion because I'm not pregnant.' *And I wouldn't marry you if I were because you don't love me the way I long to be loved.*

'When will you know for sure?'

'Christmas Day or thereabouts.'

A silence ticked past.

Cam picked up his jacket and slung it over his arm. 'I'm going to have a shower.' He paused for a beat to rub at his temple as if he was fighting a tension headache. 'By the way, thanks for doing the washing. You didn't need to do that. My housekeeper will be back after Christmas.'

'I had to do some of my own so it was no bother.'

He gave her a tired-looking smile. 'Thanks. You're a darling.'

Violet disguised a despondent sigh. *But not* your *darling.*

Cam couldn't take his eyes off Violet all evening. They had gone to one of his favourite haunts, a piano bar where the music was reflective and calming. She was wearing a new emerald-green dress that made her creamy skin glow and her brown eyes pop. Her hair was loose about her shoulders, falling in soft fragrant waves he couldn't wait to go home and bury his head in.

But there was something about her expression that made him realise he had touched on a sensitive subject earlier. Babies. Of course he'd had to mention contraception. He had the conversation with every partner. It was the responsible thing to do. A baby—*he*—had ruined his mother's life. It had changed the direction of her life, her career plans, her happiness—everything. A thing she unfortunately reminded him of when she was feeling particularly down about yet another broken relationship.

But Violet wanted a baby. And why wouldn't she? Her siblings were growing their young families and she was the only one left single.

Not quite single...

Cam picked up his glass and took a measured sip. Weird how he felt…so committed and yet this was supposed to be temporary.

Violet raised her glass, a smile curving her lips. 'Congratulations, Cam. I'm so happy for you about the contract.'

'Thanks.' He couldn't think of a single person he would rather celebrate his contract with. It wasn't as if either of his parents were interested, and while Fraser was always thrilled for him when he won an award or landed a big contract, it wasn't the same as having someone who wanted your success more than their own.

'About our conversation earlier…' Cam said.

'It's fine, Cam,' Violet said. 'I understand completely.'

'It's tough on women when they get pregnant. I realise that,' Cam said. 'Even today when there is so much more support around. It's a life-changing decision to keep a baby.'

'Did your mother ever consider…?' Violet seemed unable to complete the sentence.

'Yes and no.' Cam leaned forward to put his glass down. 'She kept me because by doing so she thought she'd be able to keep my father. But when that turned sour, she decided she wished she'd got rid of me so she could have continued her studies.'

Violet frowned. 'She told you that?'

He gave an I'm-over-it shrug. 'Once or twice.'

'But that's awful! No child, no matter how young or old, should hear something like that from a parent.'

'Yes, well, I was an eight-pound spanner in the works for my mother's aspirations. But I blame my father for not supporting her. He got on with his career without a thought about hers.' Cam passed Violet the bowl of nuts before he was tempted to scoff the lot. 'Have you ever thought of going back and finishing your degree?'

Her mouth froze over her bite into a Brazil nut. She took it away from her mouth and placed it on the tiny, square Christmas-themed napkin on the table between them. 'No… I'm not interested in studying now.'

'But you were doing English Literature and History, weren't you?' Cam said. 'Didn't you always want to be a teacher?'

Her eyes fell away from his and she dusted the salt off her fingers with another napkin. 'I'm not cut out for teaching. I'd get too flustered with having to handle difficult kids, not to mention their parents. I'm happy where I'm working.'

'Are you?'

Her eyes slowly met his. 'No, not really, but I'm good at it.'

'Just because you're good at something doesn't mean you should spend your life doing it if it bores you,' Cam said. 'Why don't you study online? Even if you don't teach, it will give you some closure.'

Violet pushed her glass away even though she had

only taken a couple of sips. Her cheeks were a bright shade of pink and her mouth was pinched around the edges. 'Can we talk about something else?'

Cam leaned forwards, resting his forearms on his thighs. 'Hey, don't go all prickly on me. I'm just trying to help you sort out your life.'

Her eyes flashed with uncharacteristic heat. 'I don't need my life sorting out. My life is just fine, thank you very much. Anyway, you need to sort out your own life.'

He sat back and picked up his glass. 'There's nothing wrong with my life.'

Her chin came up. 'So says the man who only dates women who won't connect with him emotionally. What's that about, Cam? What's so terrifying about feeling something for someone?'

Losing them.

Like his mother had lost his father and gone on to lose every other partner since in a pattern she couldn't break because the one person she had loved the most hadn't wanted her any more.

Cam didn't want to be that person. The person left behind. The person who gave everything to the relationship only to have it thrown away like trash when someone else more exciting came along.

He was the one in control in his relationships.

He started one when he wanted one.

He left when it was time to go.

'We're not talking about me,' Cam said. 'We're talking about you. About how you're letting a bad thing that happened to you rob you of reaching your full potential.'

'But isn't that what you're doing? You're letting your parents' horrible divorce rob you of the chance of long-term happiness because you're worried you might not be able to hang on to the one you love.'

So what if he was? He was fine with that. It wasn't as if he was in love with anyone anyway. *You sure about that?* Cam blinked the thought away. Of course he loved Violet. He had always loved her. But it didn't mean he was *in* love with her.

Yes, you are.

No, I'm not.

The battle went back and forth in his head like two boxing opponents trying to get the upper hand. He was confusing lust with love. The sex was great—better than great—the best he'd ever had. But it didn't mean he wanted to tie himself down to domesticity. He was a free agent. Marriage and kids were not on his radar. Violet was born to be a mother. Any fool could see that. She went dewy-eyed at the sight of a baby. She embroidered baby clothes for a hobby, for goodness' sake. Even puppies and kittens turned her to mush. She had planned her wedding day since she was a kid. He had seen photos and home videos of her and her sisters playing weddings. Violet had looked adorable wearing her mother's veil and high heels when she was barely four years old.

How could he ask her to sacrifice that dream for him?

Violet began chewing at her lip. 'Are you angry at me?'

Cam reached across and took her hand. 'No, of course not.' He gave her hand a gentle squeeze. 'Would you like to dance?'

Her eyes lit up. 'You want to dance?'

'Sure, why not?' He drew her to her feet. 'I might not be too flash with a Highland fling but I can do a mean waltz or samba.'

Her arms linked around his neck, bringing her lower body close to the need already stirring there. 'I didn't mean to lecture you, Cam. I hate it when people do that to me.'

Cam pressed a soft kiss to her mouth. 'I'm sorry too.'

Violet had always been a bit of a wallflower at her home town's country dances. She stood at the back of the room and silently envied her parents, who twirled about the dance floor as if they were one person, not two. But somehow in Cam's arms she found her dancing feet and moved about the floor while the piano played a heartstring-pulling ballad as if she was born to it. His arms supported her, his body guided her and his smile delighted her. 'If you tell your brother about this I'll have to kill you,' Cam said.

Violet laughed. 'Someone should be videoing this because no one's going to believe I've got through three songs without doing you an injur— Oops! Spoke too soon.' She glanced down at his feet. 'Did I hurt you?'

'Not a bit.' He guided her around the other way, drawing her even closer to his body.

Violet loved the feel of his arms around her, but

the slow rhythm of the haunting melody of lost love reminded her of the time in the not too distant future when those words would apply to her. How long had she been in love with him? It wasn't something she could pin an exact time or date to. She had always thought falling in love would be a light bulb moment, a flash of realisation that this was *The One*. But with Cam it had been more of a slow build, a gradual awareness the feelings she had towards him were no longer the platonic ones she had felt before. It was an awakening of her mind and body. Every moment she spent with him she loved him more. Which would make the end of their affair all the more difficult to deal with. Had she made a mistake in letting it go this far? But then she would never have known this magic. She would never have known the depth of pleasure her body was capable of giving and receiving.

The song ended and Cam led her back to their table in the corner to collect their coats. Violet suppressed a shiver when his hands pulled her hair out from the back of her collar when he helped her into her coat. She turned back around to face him and her belly did a flip at the smouldering look in his eyes. 'Time to go home?' she asked.

His mouth tilted in a sexy smile. 'If I make it that far.'

They barely made it through the door. Violet slipped out of her coat and walked into Cam's arms, his head coming down to connect his mouth with hers in a hungry kiss that made her whole body tingle. His tongue entered her mouth with a determined thrust that mimicked the intention of his body. She sent her tongue into combat with his, stroking and darting away in turn, ramping up the heat firing between them.

His hands went to the zipper at the back of her dress, sending it down her back, his hand sliding beneath the sagging fabric to bring her closer to the hardened length of him. His mouth continued its passionate assault on her senses, his teeth taking playful nips of her lower lip, pulling it out and releasing it, salving it with his tongue and then doing it all over again.

Desire roared through Violet's body with a force that was almost frightening in its intensity. She clawed at his clothing like a woman possessed, popping buttons off his shirt but beyond caring. She had to feel his hot male skin under her hands. *Now.* She unzipped him and dragged down his underwear, taking him in one hand, massaging, stroking up and down until he was fighting for the control they'd lost as soon as they'd stepped through the door. She sank to her knees in front of him, ignoring his token protest and put her mouth to him.

He allowed her a few moments of torturing him but finally hauled her upright, pushing her back against the wall, ruthlessly stripping her dress from her, leaving her in nothing but her tights and knickers and heels. He cupped her mound, grinding the heel of his hand against her ache of longing, his mouth back on hers, hard, insistent, desperate.

Violet fed off his mouth, her hands grasping him by the buttocks, holding him to the throb of her female flesh. 'Please...*please...*' She didn't care that she was begging. She needed him like she had never needed him before.

Cam pulled off her tights, taking her knickers with them. He left her hanging there while he sourced a condom, swiftly applying it and then coming back to her, entering her in one deep thrust that made her senses go wild. He set a furious pace, unlike anything he had done before. It was like a force had taken over his body, a force he couldn't control. The same force that was thundering through her body, making her gasp and whimper and arch her spine and roll her hips to get the friction where she needed it most.

He hooked one of her legs over his hip and caressed her with his fingers, triggering an earthquake in her body. It threw her into a tailspin, into a wild maelstrom of sensations that powered through her from head to toe. Even the hairs on her head felt like they were spinning at the roots.

Cam followed with his own release in three hard thrusts that brought a harsh cry out from between his lips.

Violet's legs were threatening to send her to a puddle of limbs on the floor at his feet. She grasped at the edges of his opened shirt, which she hadn't managed to get off his body in time. 'Wow, we should go dancing more often.'

He gave a soft laugh, his breathing not quite back to normal. 'We should.'

Violet pulled her clothes back on while he dealt with

the condom and his own clothes. If anyone had told her she would have acted with such wanton abandon even a week ago, she would have been shocked. But with Cam everything felt…right. She had the confidence to express herself sexually with him because she knew he would never ask her to do something she wasn't comfortable with. He always put her pleasure ahead of his own. He worshipped her body instead of using it to satisfy himself.

'We'll have an opportunity to dance at my father's wedding on Saturday,' Cam said once they had gone upstairs to prepare for bed.

Violet stalled in the process of unzipping her dress. 'You're not really expecting me to go with you, are you?'

He was sitting on the end of the bed, reaching down to untie his shoelaces, but looked up with a partial frown. 'Of course I want you there. We can fly up to Drummond Brae that evening. The wedding's in the morning so we should make it plenty of time for Christmas.'

Violet sank her teeth into her lip. 'I don't know…'

'What's wrong?'

'Your father won't mind if I don't show up. He won't even notice.'

'Maybe not, but I want you there. I'm the best man. Dad's arranged to have you with me at the top table.'

Violet thought about the wedding photos that would be taken. How she would be in all the family shots that for years later everyone would look at and say, *'There's the girl who was engaged to Cam for two weeks.'* It was bad enough with it being all over social media. But at least everyone would forget about it after a while. But a wedding album wasn't the same as cyberspace. It would be a concrete reminder of a charade she should never have agreed to in the first place.

However, it wasn't just the fallout from social media that had her feeling so conflicted about his father's wedding. It was the wedding ceremony itself, the sanctity of it. How she felt she would be compromising someone else's special day by pretending to be something she was not. How could she cheapen a ceremony she held in such high esteem? It would be nothing short of sacrilege. 'I don't think I belong at your father's wedding.'

He got up from the bed and tossed his loosened tie to the chest of drawers. 'You do belong there. You belong by my side as my fiancée.'

Violet pointedly raised her brow. 'Don't you mean your *fake* fiancée?'

A flicker of annoyance passed over his features. 'You didn't have any problem with lying to your workmates and your family. Why not stretch it to my family as well?'

'I'm not going, Cam. You can't make me.'

Cam came up to her and placed his hands on her shoulders. 'We're in this together, Violet. It's only till after Christmas. Surely it's not too much to ask you to come with me.'

Violet held his gaze. 'Why do you want me there? It's your father's fifth marriage, for pity's sake. It'll be a farcical version of what marriage is supposed to represent. I can't bear to be part of it. It would make me feel as if I'm poking fun at the institution I hold in the highest possible regard. Why is it so important to you that I be there?'

He dropped his hands and stepped away, his expression getting that boxed up look about it. 'Fine. Don't go. I don't blame you. I wish I didn't have to go either.'

Violet realised then how much he was dreading his father's wedding. Just like he had dreaded meeting his father for drinks. If she didn't go to the wedding then he would have to face it alone. Surely it was the least she could do to go with him and support him? He'd supported her at her office Christmas party. He'd supported her through the ordeal of her flat being broken in to. He'd been there for her every step of the way. It was a big compromise for her but wasn't that what all good relationships were about? She came up behind him and linked her arms around his waist. 'All right, I'll go with you but only because I care about you and hate the thought of you going through it alone.'

He turned and touched her gently on the cheek with his fingertip. 'I hate putting you through it. If it's anything like his last one it will be excruciating. But it'll be over by mid-afternoon and then we can fly up to Scotland to be with your family.'

Violet stepped up on tiptoe to plant a kiss to his lips. 'I can't wait.'

* * *

The church was full of flowers; every pew had a posy of blooms with a satin ribbon holding it in place. On each side of the altar was an enormous arrangement of red roses and another two at the back of the church. Violet sat in the pew and looked at Cam standing up at the altar with his father. Ross was joking and bantering with the other two groomsmen and, even though Violet was sitting a few rows back, she wondered if he was already a little drunk. His cheeks were ruddy and his movements were a little uncoordinated. Or perhaps it was wedding nerves? No. Ross McKinnon wasn't the type of man to get nervous about anything. He was enjoying being the centre of attention. He was relishing it. It was jarring for Violet, being such a romantic. She loved weddings where the groom looked nervous but excited waiting for his bride to arrive. Like her brother Fraser, who had kept checking his watch and swallowing deeply as the minutes ticked on. It had been such a beautiful wedding and Cam had been a brilliant best man.

Violet looked at Cam again. He looked composed. Too composed. Cardboard cut-out composed. He met her gaze and smiled. How she loved that smile. He only did it for her. It was *her* smile. The way his eyes lit up as if seeing her made him happy. She was glad she'd come to the wedding. It was the right thing to do even if the wedding was every type of wrong.

The organ started playing the 'Wedding March' and every head turned to the back of the church. There were three bridesmaids who were dressed in skimpy gowns that didn't suit their rather generous figures. Had Tatiana deliberately chosen friends who wouldn't upstage her? Not that anyone could upstage Tatiana. Violet heard the collective indrawn breath of the congregation when the bride appeared. Tatiana's white satin gown was slashed almost to the waist, with her cleavage on show as well as the slight bulge of her pregnancy. Violet looked on in horror as Tatiana's right breast threatened to pop out as she walked—strutted would be a more accurate description—up the aisle. The back of Tatiana's dress was similarly slashed, this time to the top of her buttocks, which her veil was not doing a particularly good job of hiding.

Ross looked like he couldn't wait to get his hands on his bride and made some joking aside to Cam that made Cam's jaw visibly tighten. Violet felt angry on his behalf. What a disgusting display of inappropriateness and poor Cam had to witness every second of it.

It got worse.

Ross and Tatiana had written the vows but they weren't romantic and heartfelt declarations but rather a travesty of what a marriage ceremony should be. Finally they were declared man and wife and Ross and Tatiana kissed for so long, with Ross's hand wandering all over his new bride's body, that several members of the congregation snickered.

The reception was little more than a drunken party. How Cam managed to get through his speech while his father cracked inappropriate jokes and drank copious amounts of champagne was anybody's guess.

When Cam sat back down beside her, she took his hand under the table and gave it a squeeze. 'This must be killing you,' she said.

'It'll be over soon.' He gave her a soft smile. 'How are you holding up?'

Violet curled her fingers around his. 'I'm fine, although I feel a bit silly up here at the top table. Tatiana doesn't like it. She keeps giving me the evil eye.'

'That's because you outshine her,' Cam said.

Violet could feel herself glowing at his compliment. His look warmed her blood. The look that said *I want you*. 'I'm going to powder my nose. Can we leave after that, do you think, or will we have to wait until your father and Tatiana leave?'

He glanced at his watch. 'Let's give it another hour and then we'll go.'

On her way back from the ladies' room, Violet saw Cam's father leading one of the bridesmaids by the hand to a corner behind a large arrangement of flowers. The bridesmaid was giggling and Ross was leering at her and groping her. Violet was so shocked she stood there with her mouth hanging open. Did Ross have no shame? He'd only been married a matter of hours and he was already straying. Did the commitment of marriage mean nothing to him?

Violet swung away and went back to where Cam was waiting for her. She couldn't stay another minute at this wretched farce of a wedding. Not. One. Minute.

She felt tainted by it. Sullied. Defiled by listening to people mouthing words they didn't mean and watching them behaving like out of control teenagers. No wonder Cam was so against marriage. Apart from her brother and sisters' weddings, all he had seen was the repeated drunken mockery of what was supposed to be the most important day in a couple's life. No wonder he was cynical. No wonder he couldn't picture himself getting married in the near future.

'What's wrong?' Cam said when she snatched up her wrap from the back of the chair.

'I can't stay here another minute,' Violet said. 'Your father is feeling up one of the bridesmaids out in the foyer.'

Cam's expression showed little surprise about his father's behaviour. 'Yes, well, that's my father for you. A class act at all times and in all places.'

Violet tugged his arm. 'Come on. Let's get out of here. My flesh is crawling. Oh, God, look at Tatiana. She's got her tongue in the groomsman's ear. She's practically doing a lap dance on him.'

Cam took Violet's hand and led her out of the reception room. 'Sorry you had to witness all that craziness. But I'm glad you came. It would've been unbearable without you there.'

Violet was still seething about his father's and Tatiana's behaviour when they got home to change and collect their bags for their evening flight to Scotland. 'I can't believe you share any of your father's DNA. You're nothing like him. You're decent and caring and principled. I'm sure if you were to get married one day in the future you won't be off canoodling with one of the bridesmaids within an hour or two of the ceremony. What is wrong with him?'

Cam paused in the action of slipping off his coat. But then he resumed the process of shrugging it off and hanging it on the hallstand with what seemed to Violet somewhat exaggerated precision. 'We've had this conversation a number of times before,' he said. 'I don't want to get married.'

Violet felt his words like a rusty stake to her heart. Not married? *Ever?* She had heard him say it before but hadn't things been changing between them? Hadn't *she* changed things for him? He cared about her. He talked to her. *Really* talked. About things he'd not spoken of to anyone else. He had invited her into his home. Was his heart really still so off-limits? How could he make love to her the way he had and not have felt anything? He'd bought her an engagement ring, for goodness' sake. He could have bought something cheap but he'd chosen something so special, so perfect, it surely meant he cared more than he wanted to admit.

Violet understood now why he was so wary of marriage. But deep down she had harboured hope that he would see how a marriage between them would be just like the marriage between her parents: respectful and loving and lasting. 'You don't really mean that, Cam. Deep down you want what I want. What my parents and siblings have. You've seen how a good marriage is conducted. You can't let your father's atrocious behaviour influence you like this. You're not living his life, you're living yours.'

Cam's expression went into lockdown. Violet knew him well enough to know he felt cornered. A frown formed between his eyes, his mouth tightened and a muscle ticked in his lean cheek. 'Violet.'

'Don't *do* that,' Violet said, frustrated beyond measure. 'Don't use that schoolmaster tone with me as if I'm too stupid to know what I'm talking about. You're not facing what's right in front of you. I know you care about me. You care about me much more than you want to admit. I can't go on pretending to be engaged to you when all I want is for it to be for real.'

The tenseness around his mouth travelled all the way up to his eyes. They were hard as flint. 'Then you'll be waiting a long time because I'm not going to change my mind.'

Violet knew it was time for a line to be drawn. How long could she go on hoping he would come to see things her way? What if she stayed in a relationship with him for months and months, maybe even years, and he still wouldn't budge? All her dreams of a beautiful wedding day with her whole family there would be destroyed. All her hopes for a family of her own would be shattered. She couldn't give that up. She loved him. She loved him desperately but she wouldn't be true to herself if she drifted along in a going nowhere relationship with him. She had to make a stand. She couldn't go on living in this excruciating limbo of will-he-or-won't-he? She had to make him see there was no future without a proper commitment.

No fling.

No temporary arrangement.

No pretend engagement.

Violet drew in a carefully measured breath, garnering her resolve. 'Then I don't want you to come home to Drummond Brae with me. I'd rather go alone.'

It was hard to tell if her statement affected him for hardly a muscle moved on his face. 'Fine.'

Fine? Violet's heart gave a painful spasm. How could he be so calm and clinical about this? Didn't he feel anything for her? Maybe he didn't love her after all. Maybe all this had been a convenient affair that had a use-by date. *Be strong. Be strong. Be strong.* She knew he was expecting her to cave in. It was what she did all the time. She over-adapted. She compromised. She hated hurting people's feelings so she ended up saying yes when she meant no. It had to stop. It had to stop now. It was time to grow a backbone. 'Is that your final decision?' she said.

'Violet, you're being unreasonable about—'

'*I'm* being unreasonable?' Violet said. 'What's unreasonable about wanting to be happy? I can't be happy with you if you're not one hundred per cent committed to me. I can't live like that. I don't want to miss out on all the things I've dreamt about since I was a little girl. If you don't want the same things then it's time to call it quits before we end up hurting each other too much.'

'It was never my intention to hurt you,' Cam said.

You just did. 'I have to go now or I'll miss the flight.' Violet moved past him to collect her bag from his room upstairs. Would he follow her and try and talk her out of it? Would he tell her how much he loved her? She listened for the sound of his tread on the stairs but there was nothing but silence.

When she came back downstairs with her overnight bag he was still standing in the hall with that blank expression. 'I'll drive you to the airport,' he said, barely moving his lips as he spoke.

'That won't be necessary,' Violet said. 'I've already called a cab.' She took off her engagement ring and handed it to him. 'I won't be needing this any more.'

He ignored her outstretched hand. 'Keep it.'

'I don't want to keep it.'

'Sell it and give the money to charity.'

Violet placed the ring on the table next to his keys. Did it have to end like this? With them acting like stiff strangers at the end of the affair? She'd taken a gamble and it hadn't paid off. It was supposed to pay off! Why wasn't he putting his hands on her shoulders and turning her around and smiling at her with that tender smile he reserved only for her? She turned back to face him but if he were feeling even half of the heartache she was, he showed no sign of it. 'Goodbye, Cam. I guess I'll see you when I see you.'

'I guess you will.'

Violet put on her gloves and rewound her scarf around her neck. *Do* not *cry.*

'Right, that's it then. I'll have to collect the rest of

my things when I get back. I hope it's okay to leave them here until then?'

'Of course it is.'

Another silence passed.

Violet heard the telltale beep of the taxi outside. Cam took her bag for her and opened the front door and helped her into the taxi. He couldn't have given her a clearer message that he was 'fine' with her decision to leave without him.

Violet slipped into the back of the taxi without kissing him goodbye. There was only so much heartbreak she could cope with. Touching him one last time would be her undoing. She didn't want to turn into a mess to add insult to injury. If it was over then it was over. Better to be quick and clean about it. Apparently he felt the same way because he simply closed the door of the taxi and stood back from the kerb as if he couldn't wait for it to take her away.

'Going home for Christmas?' the cabbie asked.

Violet swallowed as Cam's statue-like figure gradually disappeared from view. 'Yes,' she said on a sigh. 'I'm going home.'

CHAPTER NINE

CAM STOOD WATCHING the taxi until it disappeared around the corner. *What are you doing?* Being sensible, that was what he was doing. If he chased after her and begged her to stay then what would it achieve? A few weeks, a few months of a relationship that was the best he'd ever had but could go no further. That was what he would have.

He walked back into his house and picked up the engagement ring off the table. It was still warm from being on Violet's finger. Why was he feeling so… numb? Like the world had dropped out from under him.

Violet had blindsided him with her ultimatum. He was already feeling raw from his father's ridiculous sham of a wedding. She couldn't have picked a worse time to discuss the future of their relationship. Seeing his father act like a horny teenager all through that farce of a service, and then to hear via Violet he had been feeling up one of the bridesmaids at the reception had made Cam deeply ashamed. So ashamed he'd wanted to distance himself from anything to do with weddings. The word was enough to make him want to be ill. Why had she done that? Why push him when they'd already discussed it? He had been honest and upfront about it. He hadn't told her any lies, made any false commitments, allowed her to believe there was a pot of gold at the end of the rainbow. They hadn't been together long enough to be talking of marriage even if he was the marrying type. If he were going to propose for real—*if*—then he would do it in his own good time, not because it was demanded of him.

Go after her.

Cam took one step towards the door but then stopped. Of course he had to let her go. What was the point in dragging this out till after Christmas? It wasn't fair to her and it wasn't fair to her family. She wanted more than he was prepared to give. She wanted the fairytale. Damn it, she *deserved* the fairytale. All her life she had been waiting for Mr Right and Cam was only getting in the way of her finding him.

He paced the floor, torn between wanting to chase after her and staying put where his life was under his control. He blew out a long breath and went through to the sitting room. He sat on one of the sofas and cradled his head in his hands. His chest felt like someone had dragged his heart from his body, leaving a gaping hole.

If this was the right thing to do then why did it feel so goddamn painful?

Violet hadn't worked up the courage to tell her parents she and Cam were finished when her mother texted to ask what time they would be arriving. She told her mother they would be arriving separately due to his father's wedding commitments. She knew it was cowardly but she couldn't cope with their disappointment when hers was still so raw and painful. Checking into that flight at Heathrow had been one of the loneliest moments of her life. Even as she'd boarded the plane, she had hoped Cam would come rushing up behind her and spin her around to face him, saying he had made the biggest mistake of his life to let her leave.

But he hadn't turned up. He hadn't even texted or phoned. Didn't that prove how relieved he was that their relationship was over? By delivering an ultimatum she had given him a get-out-of-jail-free card. No wonder he hadn't argued the point or asked for more time on their relationship. He had grabbed the opportunity to end it.

Violet's mother met her at the airport and swept her into a bone-crushing hug. 'Poppet! I'm so happy to see you. Your father's at home making mince pies. Yes, mince pies! Isn't he a sweetheart trying to help? But you should see the mess he's making in the kitchen. We'll be cleaning up flour for weeks. Now, what time is Cam coming? There are only two more flights this evening. I've already checked. I hope he doesn't miss whichever one he's on. I've made up the suite in the east wing for you both. It's like a honeymoon suite.'

Violet let her mother's cheerful chatter wash over her. It reminded her of the time when she'd come home after quitting university. She had kept her pain and shame hidden rather than burst her mother's bubble of happiness at having her youngest child back home. It wasn't that her mother wasn't sensitive, but rather Violet was adept at concealing her emotions.

Her father was at the front door of Drummond Brae wearing a flour-covered apron when Violet and her mother arrived. He came rushing down the steps and gathered her in a hug that made her feet come off the ground. 'Welcome home, wee one,' he said. 'Come away inside out of the cold. It's going to snow for Christmas. We've already had a flurry or two.'

Violet stepped over the threshold and came face to face with a colourful banner hanging across the foyer that said: *Congratulations Cam and Violet*. Helium balloons with her and Cam's names on them danced in the draught of cold air from the open door, their tinsel strings hanging like silver tails.

Her grandfather came shuffling in on his walking frame, his wrinkled face beaming from ear to ear. 'Let's see that ring of yours, little Vivi,' he said.

Violet swallowed a knot that felt as big as a pine cone off the Christmas tree towering in the hall in all its festive glory. She kept her gloves on, too embarrassed to show her empty ring finger. How on earth was she going to tell them? The rest of the family came bursting in, Fraser and Zoe with their twins Ben and Mia and then Rose and Alex with their boys Jack and Jonathon. And, of course, Gertie the elderly golden retriever who looked like the canine version of Grandad with her creaky gait and whitened snout.

'Aunty Violet! Did you bring me a present?' Ben

asked with a cheeky grin, so like her brother Fraser it made Violet's heart contract.

'Can I be your flower girl?' Mia asked, hugging Violet around the waist.

Rose and Lily greeted her with big smiles and even bigger hugs. 'We've already started on the champagne,' Rose said. 'Well, not Lily, of course, but I'm drinking her share.'

'When's Cam arriving?' Lily asked.

'Erm…' Violet felt tears burning like acid behind her eyes. 'He's…hoping to make it in time for Christmas dinner.' *Coward.*

Her brother Fraser came forward and gave her a big hug. 'So pleased for you guys. Always knew Cam had a thing for you.'

'I thought so too,' Rose said, grinning. 'He wasn't himself at Easter, do you remember, Lil? Remember when I asked him to take in a hot cross bun to Vivi and he got all flustered and said he had to make a call? Classic. Absolutely classic.'

Lily's smile made her eyes dance. 'I'm so thrilled for you, Vivi. All three of us will be married. How soon will you start a family? It'd be so cool to have our kids close in age.'

Gertie came up to Violet and slowly wagged her tail and gave a soft whine as if to say, *What's wrong?*

Violet could stand it no longer. 'I—I have something to tell you…'

Rose's eyes lit up as bright as the lights on the Christmas tree she was standing near. 'You're pregnant?'

Violet bit her lip so hard she thought she would break the skin. 'Cam and I are…not engaged.'

The stunned silence was so profound no one moved. Not even the children. Even the tinsel and baubles on the Christmas tree seemed to be holding themselves stock-still. Everyone was looking at her as if she had just told them she had a disease and it was contagious.

'Oh, poppet.' Her mother came to her and gathered her in her arms, rocking her from side to side as if she were still a baby. 'I'm so sorry.'

Her father joined in the hug, gently patting her on the back with soothing 'there, there's' that made Violet sob all the harder.

Rose and Lily ushered the children away and Fraser helped Grandad back into the sitting room near the fire. Lily's husband Cooper and Rose's husband Alex came in late and, taking one look at the scene, promptly walked back out.

'What happened?' Violet's mother asked. 'Did he break it off?'

'No, I did. But we weren't even engaged. We were pretending.'

Her mother frowned. 'Pretending?'

Violet explained the situation through a series of hiccupping sobs. 'It's my fault for being so pathetic about going to the office Christmas party on my own. I should've just gone alone and not been such a stupid baby. Now I've hurt everyone and ruined my friendship with Cam and spoilt Christmas for everyone too.'

'You haven't spoilt anything, poppet,' her mother

said. 'Take the banner down, Gavin. And get the kids to pop the balloons. I'll take Violet upstairs.'

Violet followed her mother upstairs, not to the suite prepared for her and Cam but to her old bedroom. All her childhood toys were neatly arranged on top of the dresser and some on her bed. Violet's books were in the bookshelves, waiting for her like old friends. It was like stepping back in time but feeling out of place. She wasn't a child any more. She was an adult with adult needs. Needs Cam had awakened and then walked away from as if they meant nothing to him.

As if *she* meant nothing to him.

Her mother sat on the edge of the bed beside Violet. 'Are you in love with him?'

'Yes, but he doesn't love me. Well, he does but not like that.'

'Did you tell him you loved him?'

Violet gave a despondent sigh. 'What would be the point? He never wants to get married. He doesn't want kids either.'

'I expect that's because of his parents,' her mother said. 'But he might change his mind.'

'He won't.'

Her mother hugged her again. 'My poor baby. I wish there was something I could do or say to help you feel better.'

Violet wiped at her eyes with her sleeve. 'I love him so much but he's so cynical about getting married. Deep down, I don't really blame him after attending his father's fifth wedding today. It was awful. So awful you wouldn't believe.' She described some of what went on and her mother made tut-tutting noises and shook her head in disgust.

'Did you press him for a commitment after you came back from the wedding?' her mother asked.

Violet looked at her mum's frowning expression. 'You think I should've waited?'

Her mother squeezed her hand. 'What's done is done. At least you were honest with him. No point pretending you're happy when you're not.'

Violet's bottom lip quivered. 'He's the only one for me, Mum. I know I won't be happy with anyone else. I just know it.'

Her mother gave her a sad smile. 'For your sake, poppet, I hope that's not true.'

Cam packed up Violet's things for when she was ready to collect them. He could have done it any time between Christmas and New Year because she wouldn't be back till the second of January as they had planned to spend the week with her family. But he was feeling restless and on edge. He kept telling himself it was better this way. That it was wrong to drag things out when he couldn't give her what she wanted.

But when he came to her embroidery basket, his heart gave a painful spasm. He opened the lid and took out the creamy baby blanket Violet was in the process of embroidering with tiny flowers. He held it to his face, its softness reminding him of her skin. He could even smell her on the blanket—that sweet flowery scent that made him think of spring. He put the blanket back inside the basket and took out a pair of booties. They were so tiny he couldn't imagine a baby's foot small enough to fit them. He started to picture a baby…one he and Violet might make together: a little squirming body with dimpled hands and feet, a downy dark head with eyes bright and clear and a little rosebud mouth.

What if Violet were pregnant? They had been careful but accidents could happen. Should he call her? No. Too soon. He needed more time. Time to get his head together. He wasn't used to feeling this level of emotion. This sense of…loss. The sense of loss was so acute it felt like a giant hole, leaving him empty and raw.

Cam picked up a tiny jacket that had sailing boats embroidered around the collar. He rubbed his thumb over the meticulous stitches, wondering what it would be like to have a son. His father hadn't been an active father in any sense of the word, but Cam couldn't imagine not wanting to be involved in your child's life. How could you not be interested in your own flesh and blood? Being there for every milestone, watching them grow and develop, reading to them at bedtime—all the things Violet's parents had done and were now doing for each of their grandchildren when they came to stay.

He put the sailing boat jacket down and picked up a pink cardigan that was so small it would have looked at home on a doll. There were tiny rosebuds around the collar and the cuffs of the sleeves. What would it be like to have a daughter? To watch her grow from babyhood to womanhood. To be there for her first smile, her first tooth, her first steps. *Gulp*. Her first date. Walking her down the aisle. One day becoming a grandfather…

Cam had never thought about having his own children. Well, he had thought about it but just as quickly dismissed it. Like when he had walked into the sitting room at Drummond Brae at Easter and seen Violet curled up on the sofa with a baby's bonnet in her hands. It had been a jarring reminder of the responsibility he'd spent his adult life actively avoiding.

But now he wondered why he was working so hard when he had no one to share it with. What was the point? Would he end up some lonely old man living out his end days alone? Not surrounded by a loving family like Grandad Archie in the winter of his life. No one to tell him they loved him, no one to be there in sickness and in health and everything in between. No laughter-filled Christmases with all the family gathered around the tree exchanging gifts and smiles and love.

Cam put the pink cardigan back inside the basket and closed the lid. What was he doing? It was best this way. Violet was better off without him and his crazy family who would do nothing but stir up trouble between them if given half a chance. He wasn't cut out for marriage and commitment. He was too driven by his career, by achieving, by the next task waiting on his desk. He didn't have the time to invest in a long-term relationship.

Cam had been to three of his father's previous weddings and never once taken much notice of the vows. But when he'd heard his father make all those promises earlier that day it had made Cam's gut churn to realise his father didn't mean a word of them. They were just words, empty, meaningless words because his father had no intention of committing to his new wife other than in an outward way by standing up in church in front of family and friends. His father didn't mean them on the inside, in his heart where it counted. Anyone could say they would love someone for the rest of their life but how many people actually meant it? Violet's parents obviously had. So had her grandad Archie and Maisie Drummond when they had married sixty-five years ago.

Cam knew if it were him up there saying those words with Violet by his side, he would make sure he meant them. His heart gave a kick as the realisation dawned. This was why he had avoided marriage and commitment all this time—because he had never been able to picture himself saying those words with any sincerity. But with Violet they meant everything. He loved her with all his heart and mind and soul. He worshipped her with his body, he wanted to protect her and stand by her in sickness and in health, in pregnancy and childbirth.

What a damn fool he had been. Letting her walk away when he loved her so much. Loved her more than anything, more than his freedom, which wasn't such a great thing anyway. True freedom was in your ability to love someone without fear, without conditions, loving without restraint.

The love he felt for Violet was bigger than his fear of abandonment. It was bigger than the need to protect himself from hurt. He couldn't control life and all its vagaries. Life happened, no matter how carefully you laid plans. He thought of Violet's poor workmate Kenneth, so hung up on his ex-wife he was unable to move on with his life. Cam didn't want to be like that. Too afraid to love in case he lost it.

He loved Violet and he would make sure nothing and no one destroyed that love. They would face the future together, a dedicated team who had each other's backs no matter what.

Cam glanced at his watch. He would have to hot-foot it but he could make the last flight if he was lucky.

Violet was determined her family's Christmas would not suffer any more disturbance after her tearful confession. She joined in with the family board games—a Drummond tradition late at night on Christmas Eve while everyone drank eggnog—and laughed at her father's corny jokes and patiently repeated everything for Grandad, who was hard of hearing. Her mother kept a watchful eye on her, but Violet did her best to assure her mum she was doing just fine, even though on the inside she felt a cavern of emptiness.

She couldn't stop wondering what Cam was doing. Was he spending Christmas with his mother or alone? Or had he hooked up with someone new? It wasn't like him to do something like that but what if he wanted to press home a point? He wanted his freedom, otherwise wouldn't he have come after her by now? Called her? Texted her? Given her a fragment of hope? No. He hadn't. It didn't seem fair that she was up here in the Highlands of Scotland nursing a broken heart while he was in London living the life of a playboy. Did he miss her? Was he thinking about her?

'Well, we're off to bed,' Fraser announced, taking Zoe's hand. 'The kids will be up at four, looking for their presents.'

Zoe gave Violet a sad look. 'Are you okay, Vivi?'

Violet put on a brave smile. 'Rose and I are going to work on that bottle of champagne over there, aren't we, Rose?'

Rose gave her an apologetic look and reached for her husband Alex's hand. 'Sorry, Vivi, but I've had too much already.'

'Don't look at me,' Lily said, placing a protective hand over her belly. 'I'm knackered in any case.'

'Will you take Gertie out for a wee walk, poppet?' her mother asked. 'Your father and I have to stuff the turkey.'

Violet shrugged on her coat and put on her gloves and took the dog outside into the crisp night air. There were light flurries of snow but it wasn't settling. So much for a magical white Christmas. Maybe it was going to be one of those miserable grey and gloomy ones, which would be rather fitting for her current state of mind.

Gertie wasn't content with waddling about the garden and instead put her nose down to follow a scent leading down to the loch. Violet grabbed a torch from the hall table drawer and followed the dog. The loch was a silver shape in the moonlight, the forest behind it a dense dark fringe.

Violet stood at the water's edge, feeling the biting cold coming off the sheet of water while Gertie bustled about in the shadows. An owl hooted, a vixen called out for a mate.

A twig snapped under someone's foot.

Violet spun around, shining the torch in the direction of the sound. 'Who's there?'

Cam stepped into the beam of light. 'It's me.'

Violet's heart gave an almighty lurch. 'Cam?'

He shielded his eyes with his arm. 'Will you stop shining that thing in my face?'

'Sorry.' She lowered the torch. 'You scared the heck out of me.'

He came up closer, the moonlight casting his features into ghostly relief. Gertie padded over and gave him an enthusiastic greeting as if she had suddenly turned into a puppy instead of the fifteen-year-old dog she was. Cam leaned down to scratch at the dog's ears before straightening. 'I'm sorry about earlier today. I was wrong to let you leave like that. I got flooded with feelings I didn't want to acknowledge. But I'm acknowledging them now. I love you, Violet. I love you and want to spend the rest of my life with you. Will you marry me?'

Violet stared at him, wondering if she was hearing things. 'Did you just ask me to marry you?'

He smiled so tenderly it made her heart skip a beat. Her smile. The one he only used for her. 'I did and I want to have babies with you. We can be a family like your family. We can do it because we're a team who are batting for each other, not against each other.'

Violet stepped into his waiting arms, nestling her head against his chest. 'I love you so much. It tore my heart out to leave you but I had to. I wasn't being true to myself or to you. Your father's wedding brought it home to me. I couldn't go on pretending.'

'After you left I started thinking about my father and that ridiculous sham of a wedding,' Cam said. 'He doesn't love Tatiana enough to die for her. He's using her as a trophy to prove his diminishing potency. He uses every woman he's ever been with like that. I know I won't do that to you. I couldn't. You mean the world to me. I couldn't possibly love anyone more than I love you.'

Violet gazed up at him. Was this really happening? Cam was here. In person. Asking her to marry him. Telling her he loved her more than anyone else in the world. 'It was a bit mean of me to push you on commitment so close to your father's wedding,' she said. 'No wonder you backed away. The mere mention of the word *wedding* after that debacle of a ceremony would've been enough to make you run for cover.'

He gave her a rueful smile. 'Your timing was a little off but I got there eventually. I'm sorry you had to go through an awful few hours thinking we were over. After you left I sat in numb shock. Normally when a relationship of mine comes to an end I feel relieved.

Not this time. Can you forgive me for being so blockheaded?'

Violet linked her arms around his neck. 'I'm never leaving again. Not ever. You've made all my dreams come true. You've even proposed to me by the loch.'

He grinned and drew her closer. 'I reckon we've got about sixty seconds before your family come down here to check if there's a reason to celebrate Christmas with a bang or we both freeze to death. Will you marry me, my darling?'

Violet smiled so widely her face ached. 'Yes. A million times yes.'

'Once will be more than enough,' Cam said. 'From here on I'm a one-woman man.'

She stroked his lean jaw, now dark and rough with stubble. 'I've been a one-man woman for a lot longer. I think that's probably why I never dated with any enthusiasm. I was subconsciously waiting for you.'

His eyes became shadowed for a moment as if he was recalling how close to losing her he had come. 'How could I have been so stupid not to see how perfect you are for me all this time?'

Violet smiled. 'Mum saw it. She's going to be beside herself when she hears you're here. Did anyone see you coming up the driveway?'

'I'm not sure. When I pulled up I caught a glimpse of you heading towards the lake with Gertie so I came straight down here.'

'They made a banner for us,' Violet said. 'It was a

bad moment when I saw it hanging in the hall. I hadn't told them we were over at that point.'

He winced. 'Poor you. Well, we'd better tell them the good news. Ready?'

Violet drew his head down to hers. 'Not yet. Let's treasure this moment for our kids. I want to tell them how you kissed me in the moonlight, just like Grandad did to my grandmother in exactly this spot.'

'Hang on, I'm forgetting something.' He took out the ring from his pocket and slipped it on her finger. 'I don't want to see that come off again.'

Violet smiled as she twirled the ring on her finger. Her hand had felt so strange without it there. Like someone else's hand. The diamond winked at her as if to say, *I'm back!* 'I can't believe this is happening. I felt so lonely and lost without you.'

'Me too,' he said. 'I was so afraid of losing you that I ended up losing you. I will regret to the day I die not following you out of my house and bringing you back. I wanted to but I kept thinking you were better off without me.'

There was the sound of twigs snapping and a few hushed whispers. Cam's eyes twinkled. 'Looks like the family has arrived. Shall we make an announcement?'

Violet drew his head down to hers. 'Let's show them instead.'

EPILOGUE

Christmas Eve the following year...

CAM LOOKED AROUND the sitting room at Drummond Brae where all Violet's family were gathered. Correction. *His* and Violet's family. The last few months since his and Violet's wedding in June had shown him more than ever how important family was and how much he had missed out on having a proper one growing up. But he was more than making up for it now. He glanced at Violet where she was sitting almost bursting to tell the family her good news. *Their* good news. He still couldn't believe they were having a baby. Violet was just past the twelve-week mark and there could be no better Christmas present for her parents than to tell them they were about to have another grandchild.

He smiled when Violet's gaze met his. He never tired of looking at her; she was glowing but not just because of being pregnant. She had completed her first semester of an English Literature degree. He couldn't have been prouder of her. Of course she topped her class.

Grandad Archie was sitting with a blanket over his legs and a glass of whisky in his hand and looking at Violet with a smile on his face. That was another miracle Cam felt grateful for. Grandad Archie, while certainly not robust in health, was at least enjoying life surrounded by his beloved family. Even Kenneth, Violet's workmate, had started dating again. Cam had introduced him to a young widow who worked part-time in his office and they'd hit it off and had been seeing each other ever since.

Poor old Gertie, the golden retriever, hadn't been so lucky; her ashes were spread out by the loch not far from where Cam had proposed to Violet. But there was a new addition to the family, a ten-week-old puppy called Nessie who was currently chewing on one of Cam's shoelaces.

'Vivi, why aren't you drinking your eggnog?' Grandad Archie asked with a twinkle in his eyes. 'Is there something you have to tell us?'

Cam took Violet's hand just as she reached for his. He squeezed it gently, his heart so full of love he could feel his chest swelling like bread dough. 'We have an announcement to make,' he said. 'We're having a baby.'

'Ach, now I'll have to live another year so I can wet the wee one's head,' Grandad said, grinning from ear to ear.

Violet's mother grasped her husband's hand and blinked back happy tears. 'We're so thrilled for you both. It's just the most wonderful news.'

Violet placed Cam's hand on the tiny swell of her

belly and smiled up at him with her beautiful brown eyes brimming with happiness. 'I love you.'

Cam bent down and kissed her tenderly. 'I love you too. Happy Christmas, my darling.'

'Okay, knock it off you two,' Fraser said with a cheeky grin. 'The honeymoon's been over for six months.'

Cam grinned back. 'Not this honeymoon.' He gathered Violet closer. 'This one's going to last for ever.'

* * * * *

THE SHEIKH'S PREGNANT PRISONER

TARA PAMMI

For my lovely and wonderful editor, Pippa—
for these ten books and many, many more to come.

CHAPTER ONE

COULD HE BE DEAD? Could someone as larger than life as Zafir be truly gone? Could someone she had known for two months, someone she had laughed with, someone she had shared the deepest intimacies with, be gone in the blink of an eye?

Lauren Hamby pressed her hand to her stomach as dread weighed it down.

It had been the same for the past two days. The more she saw of the colorful capital city of Behraat and the destruction the recent riots had wreaked, the more she saw Zafir everywhere.

But now, staring at the centuries-old trade center building, every nerve in her vibrated. The answer she had been seeking for six weeks was here, she could feel it in her bones. All she had was his name and description but she was desperate to find out what had happened to him.

Desperate to find out about the man who had somehow come to mean more than just a lover. More than a friend, even.

The richly kept grounds were a lush contrast to the stark silence in the city. The glittering rectangular shallow pool of water lined on either side by mosaic tiles and flanked by palm trees showed her strained reflection. She walked the concrete-tiled path laid out between the pool's edge and the perfectly cut lush lawn, her heart hammering against her rib cage.

Marble steps led to the enormous foyer with glinting

mosaic floors, soaring, circular ceiling and, she couldn't help smiling, palm trees in giant pots.

There was so much to look at, so much to breathe in that the sights and sounds around her dulled the edge during the day. But at night, the grief pushed in with vehemence, pressing images of *him* growing up in this country.

She saw him in every tall, stunning man, remembered the pride and love with which he'd painted a picture of Behraat to her.

"You coming, Lauren?"

Her friend David had spent the past few days capturing footage about the recent riots in the city.

She looked up and averted her face as he pointed his camcorder at her. "Stop filming me, David. Is my asking to see the records of people who died in the riots so necessary to your documentary on Behraat?"

Her gaze moved past the reception area, taking in the spectacular fountain in the middle of the hall, the water shimmering golden against the light shed by the orange, filigreed dome.

A hum of activity went on behind the gleaming marble reception area.

Her rubber soles made no sound as she walked past the fountain toward the reception desk. The glass elevator pinged down, a group of men exiting.

A quiet hush descended over the activity. Her nape prickling, Lauren turned, the sudden shift in the very air around her raising goose bumps on her skin. Six men stood in a circle in front of the elevator, all dressed in the traditional long robes. One man, the tallest among the group, addressed the rest in Arabic.

His words washed over Lauren, the tenor of his tone harsh and unyielding. It whispered over her skin like a familiar caress.

Rubbing her palms over her midriff, she tried to quell

the sudden shiver. She turned back toward David, who was filming the group of men with arrested attention. The tall man turned, bringing himself directly into her line of vision.

Lauren stilled, her heartbeat deafening to her ears.

Zafir.

The red-and-white headdress covered his hair, rendering his features starker than usual. His words resonated with authority, power, his mouth set into a hard line.

He was not dead.

Relief was like a storm, rippling and cascading over her. She wanted to throw her arms around him, touch the sharp angles of his face. She wanted to…

A cold chill seeped into her very bones even though she was wearing a long-sleeved T-shirt and loose trousers to respect the cultural norms of Behraat.

Zafir was unharmed.

In fact, he'd never looked more in his element. Yet she hadn't heard a word from him in six weeks.

She moved toward the group, an incessant pounding in her head driving away every sane thought. Adrenaline laced with fury pumped through her. The man standing closest to her turned around, alerting her presence to the group. One by one, they all turned.

Her breath suspended in her throat, her hands shook. The few seconds stretched interminably. A hysteric bubble launched into her throat.

Zafir's gold-flecked gaze met hers, the sheer force of his personality slamming into her.

Everything else around her dulled as the explosive chemistry that had punctuated every moment of their affair sparked into life, a live wire yanking her closer.

There wasn't a trace of pleasure in his gaze.

No shock in it.

But there was no guilt either.

The fact that he felt no remorse whatsoever fueled her fury. She'd shed tears over him, she'd reduced herself to a shadow of worry over him and he didn't even feel guilt.

The men stared with interest as he stepped toward her. Two guards flanked him at a little distance.

Why did Zafir have guards?

The question shot through her and fell into nothingness like dust. His dark sensuality swathed her. Her skin shivered with awareness, her stomach churned with every step that they took toward each other.

The intoxicating power of his masculinity, her intimate knowledge of that leanly honed body, everything coiled around her, binding her immobile under his scrutiny. He stopped at arm's reach, his mouth a hard slash in that stunning face, the burnished, coppery skin a tight mask over his features.

A regal movement of his head, his nod was barely an acknowledgment and so much a dismissal. "Ms. Hamby, what brings you to Behraat?"

Chilling cold filled her veins.

Ms. Hamby? He was calling her Ms. Hamby? After everything they had shared, he spoke to her as if she was a stranger?

Every little hurt Lauren had patched over since she'd been a little girl ripped open at that indifference. "After the way you left, that's what you have to say to me?"

A taut nerve throbbed in his temple but that golden gaze remained infuriatingly sedate. He looked so impossibly remote, as harsh and bleak as the desert she'd heard so much about. "If you have a complaint to register with me," he said, as now a thread of temper flashed into his perfectly polite tone, "you need an appointment, Ms. Hamby. Like the rest of the world."

His dismissal scraped her raw with its politeness but she

held on to her temper. *Somehow.* "An appointment? You're kidding me, right?"

"No. I do not...*kid*." A step closer and she could see something beneath that calm. Shock? Displeasure? Indifference? "Do not make a spectacle of yourself, Lauren."

A shard of pain ricocheted inside her, stealing her breath.

"Don't make a scene, Lauren."

"Grow up and understand that your parents have important careers, Lauren."

"Swallow your tears, Lauren."

Her heart beating a wild tattoo inside her chest, memories and voices swirling through her head like some miniature ghosts, Lauren covered the last step between her and Zafir and slapped him.

His jaw jerked back, the crack of the slap shattering the silence like a clap of thunder.

The sound of quick footsteps pierced the haze of her fury, her hand jarring painfully at the impact, her breathing rough. Angry commands spoken in Arabic rang around them.

But she...it was as if she was functioning in a world of her own.

Something ferocious gleamed in his eyes then.

Oh, God, what had she done?

Caught in that flare, Lauren shivered, something hot twisting low in her belly. His long fingers dug into her forearms as he jerked her toward him, the scent of sandalwood and musk drenching her. "Of all the—"

An urgent whisper spoken in rapid Arabic rattled behind them. Zafir's fingers instantly relented. His gaze raked her, before the fire of his emotions slowly seeped out, settling that indifferent mask into that lethal face.

When those golden eyes met hers again, it was like looking at a stranger—a forbidding, dangerous, contemptuous stranger.

"Your Highness…let security deal with the woman."

Your Highness? Security?

The adrenaline ebbed away, leaving her cold.

Zafir barked out a command, something short and hard in Arabic and then stepped back.

Cold sweat trickled down her back as she looked around. The most unholy silence enveloped her, and everyone watched her with curiosity and contempt.

Two men with discreet-looking guns flanked her. "Zafir, wait," she called out, but he'd already turned his back on her.

Her gaze followed the elevator's ascent, but he didn't look at her, not once. She tried to step back, only to find her every move blocked.

What nightmare had she walked into? Where was David?

Trying to stem the panic bubbling inside her, she turned and noticed an older man who spoke to the guard. "What the hell is going on?"

The man's eyes chilled. "You're under arrest for attacking the Sheikh of Behraat."

Zafir Al Masood stalked out of the meeting with the High Council. His displeasure must have been evident in his face because even the most audacious members quickly shuffled out of his way.

For the first time in six weeks, the outrageous complaints from the council pricked him.

Who was the woman? How could a woman, a Western woman, an American at that, have such familiarity with him as to strike him? Was he going to bring the Western world's wrath on Behraat?

Was he going to doom Behraat for a woman like his father had done?

He entered the elevator, hit the button to hold it there.

Fury and frustration pumped in his veins as he sought to control his temper.

The glass walls around him reflected his image back at him, forcing him to take stock. Forcing him to swallow his bitterness, as he had done for the past six years.

Did they see a glimpse of his father, the great Rashid Al Masood, the man who had brought Behraat out of the dark ages, in him?

Would he be never allowed to forget that his father had only acknowledged him as his son when he had needed a different crown prince, thanks to his corrupted half brother Tariq?

Once upon a time, he would have been glad to hear that his father's blood flowed in his veins. But now…now that he was spending his life paying for his mistake…

He cursed the wretched High Council and its power to elect the High Sheikh. Maybe if the bunch of corrupt cowards had spoken up during Tariq's regime, Behraat wouldn't be in this state now.

But with Rashid's strict regulations blown apart, they had been busy stuffing their pockets with Tariq's bribes while he had ruined relations with neighboring countries, destroyed peace treaties and violated trade agreements…

Yet they used any reason to doubt *his* rule over Behraat, harped on and on about the separation of tribes from the state.

As if it was his mistake and not his father's.

Zafir headed straight to the situation room, determined to stomp them out. Much as he hated his father for bringing him up as a favored orphan, he couldn't turn a blind eye to Behraat. Even before he had learned about his birth, duty had been filled in his very blood.

This was his father's legacy to him.

Not love, not pride, not even the knowledge of his mother, but this infernal sense of duty toward Behraat.

Lauren's face on the huge plasma screen monitor brought him to a sudden halt.

Something twisted deep and hard in his gut…a hard thrum in his very muscle, an echo of a primal need that he couldn't fathom to this day…

That plump bottom lip caught between her teeth, her complexion paler than usual. Blue shadows marred the beauty of wide-set black eyes. The scarf she had used earlier to cover her hair loosely was gone, her black hair cut to fall over her forehead, once again hiding her entire face from him.

The long-sleeved cotton T-shirt molded the curve of her breasts. She sat with her fingers entwined on top of the table, her posture straight, reckless defiance in every line.

Defiant and honest, sensuous and wary, from the moment he had set eyes on her, Lauren had ensnared him.

At his command, his special security force had locked her up, confiscated everything from her. Punishment meted out to anyone who was suspected of being a threat to his new rule. And all the evidence they had gathered since didn't bode well for her either.

But he couldn't shake off the betrayal, the hurt that had glittered when she had looked at him. He had wanted to kiss her. He'd wanted to plunder her mouth until the betrayal etched into her face turned into arousal.

"She planned the charade," Arif said in his matter-of-fact tone. "She clearly means to exploit your weakness in indulging in an affair with her. You should have mentioned her to me after you returned so that I—"

"No."

Still transfixed by the sight of her, Zafir scrubbed a hand over his face.

There was no place for regret. There was no place for softness, in his feelings or in his actions. There was no choice to be anyone but himself.

Already he'd made a mistake, somehow he'd let her get too close.

"What would be her motivation, Arif?" he asked the older man. His father's oldest friend, Arif was now his biggest ally.

"She walks around the trade center with a journalist friend who knew you would be present, Zafir. It's all planned," Arif spat out, with a vehemence that had been nurtured over a lifetime for women, foreign or otherwise.

Zafir remained quiet, giving the doubts that polluted his thoughts free rein.

The few members of staff present at the trade center had already been pledged into silence. He had offered an explanation to the High Council—to keep the peace for Behraat's sake.

Her bow-shaped mouth was pinched, her shoulders strained under the weight of her feigned defiance. "Did they find him?"

The older man's disquiet was answer enough.

Zafir switched off the monitor, taking away the temptation messing with his head.

"We need to contain this as soon as possible. If that video falls into the hands of the media…" Arif continued, letting his silence speak for the consequences.

"We might have a full-scale riot on our hands again," Zafir finished. Tariq had used too many women, bloated with power and Zafir couldn't be seen in the same light.

If they didn't find the video and contain it, what little trust he had gained of the people of Behraat could be blown to smithereens.

Already, the High Council was questioning his proposals for change, looking for ways to skew public perception of him. "I'll talk to her. No one else," he said, wondering if he had misjudged the first woman to mess with his head in…ever.

* * *

How dare he lock her up?

Lauren eyed the camera in the top corner of the room. She wanted to march toward it, stick her face in it and demand they release her. But it would only waste her dwindling energy.

The sheer fury she had been running on was crashing already. Misery gnawed at her.

She turned her attention to the small room with its austere white walls and concrete floor. The sterile smell of the room made her empty stomach heave. A window boarded shut with cheap plastic and a faded plastic chair and table graced the room. The other end of the spectrum from the magnificent foyer and reception hall where she'd stood in awe only a couple of hours ago.

Even if she wanted to delude herself that it was all some ghastly mistake, the gritty reality of the room stopped her.

She held her shoulders rigid. But each passing minute filled her with increasing dread and confusion. The old man's words rang in her ears.

Zafir, the Sheikh of Behraat?

It sounded straight out of a nightmare, yet how else could she explain all this?

She rubbed her eyes and swallowed, her throat dry and scratchy like sandpaper. They had taken her backpack, her cell phone. She thought longingly of the bottle of water in there and even the granola bar she usually hated.

The knob turned as the door was fiddled with on the outside.

Her muscles tensed up, her lungs expanding on a huge breath.

Zafir stepped into the room. She sagged against the chair, saw the tight line of his mouth and instantly pulled herself back up.

He had ordered his minions to lock her up. Just because he was here didn't mean *anything*, she told herself sternly.

He cast a look at the camera at the top wall. The tiny orange flicker went out.

Apparently, all it took was a blink of an eye from him and the world rearranged itself.

He closed the door behind him, and leaned against it.

His gaze swept over her, noting everything about her with a chilling thoroughness.

The traditional attire was gone yet he felt no more familiar than the cold stranger she had slapped so foolishly. A white cotton shirt folded back at the cuffs revealed strong forearms, the burnished bronze of his skin a startlingly stunning contrast against it.

Black jeans outlined the hard strength of those muscular legs, legs that had pinned and anchored her in the most intimate of acts, a mere couple of hours before he had stepped out of her life.

The Zafir she had known in New York had still been a mystery, but he'd been a kind, caring man. Not friendly but she'd felt safe with him, even after knowing him for only an hour.

Not straightway approachable after the way she'd ripped into him at the ER, but he'd still been a gentleman.

Not exactly the boy-next-door type and yet he'd laughed with her.

Had all that been just a mask to get her into bed?

He prowled into the room and leaned against the opposite wall, forcing her to raise her gaze. Her stomach was tied up in knots, but she refused to let him intimidate her.

Standing up, she moved behind the chair and mirrored his stance.

He folded his hands and pinned her with that hard gaze. "Why are you here, Lauren?"

"Ask your thugs that question." She gripped the back of

the chair with shaking hands, and tilted her chin up. "*Sorry*, I mean, your guards."

He raised a brow, quiet arrogance dripping from every pore. *How had she not seen this cloak of power he wore so effortlessly?* "This is not the time to play with the truth."

"Look who's talking about truth," she said, anger replacing the dread. "Is it true? What that man said?"

An eternity passed while his gaze trapped hers. But she saw the truth in it.

In fact, the truth or a shadow of it had been present all along.

In his tortured words whenever he spoke of Behraat, in the anguish in his eyes when they had watched a TV segment about the old sheikh still in coma, in the pride that resonated in his voice when he spoke of how Behraat had emerged as a developing country under the sheikh's regime.

Even in that sense of stasis she had sensed in him, as though he was biding his time.

His very presence was a ticking powerhouse in the small room. He shrugged. Such a casual gesture for something that shook her world upside down. "Yes."

The single word grew in the space between them, bearing down upon her the consequences of her own actions.

Her throat dried up, every muscle in her quivered. All the stories she had heard from a fascinated David about Behraat, of the ruling family, they coalesced in her mind, shaking loose everything she had believed of Zafir.

She stared at him anew. "If you're the new sheikh, that means you're…"

"The man who ordered the arrest of his brother so that he can rule Behraat. The man who celebrated victory on the eve of his brother's death." His words echoed with a razor-sharp edge. "But be very careful. You've already committed one mistake. I might not be so lenient again."

CHAPTER TWO

"LENIENT?" LAUREN GLARED at him, hating the tremor she couldn't contain at the casual power in his words. "You had your thugs throw me here without hearing a word I had to say."

"If you were anyone else…the punishment would have been much worse."

"I slapped you. It's not a capital crime."

"You slapped me in front of the High Council who thinks women should stay at home, that women need to be protected from the world, and from their own weaknesses."

There was no smoothness to his words now. They reverberated with cutting hostility. "That's archaic."

"Fortunately for you, I agree. Women are just as capable of deception, of manipulation as any man I've known."

Lauren stared at him. "So you're a misogynist as well as being a sheikh? I don't know how much more of this I can handle."

Something entered his gaze. "This is not New York, Lauren. Nor am I an average Joe."

"No, you're not," she whispered. Even in New York, she hadn't made the mistake of thinking he was an average man.

A small-scale exporter, he'd told her, struggling to keep his place in Behraat because of the changing political clime. The gleam of interest in his eyes—six feet of stunning, sexy, jaw-droppingly arrogant man's interest in her, averagely attractive ER nurse, who'd long ago chosen a life of non-adventure and boring normalcy, because it was safe—it had gone straight to her head.

She'd swallowed his lies all too willingly.

Instead, he *was* the ruler of a nation and, if the media was to be believed, one who had seized power from the previous sheikh. He was the very embodiment of power and ambition she despised, far from the rootless man she had thought him to be.

The black-and-white tiles swam in front of her eyes. She slid into the chair in a boneless heap, tucked her head down between her knees and forced herself to breathe.

The fine hairs on her neck prickled, the air coated with an exotic scent that her traitorous body craved all too easily. Standing over her, his presence was a dark shadow stealing every bit of warmth from her.

His long fingers landed on her nape and her skin zinged. "Lauren?"

The concern edging into those words tugged at her, but she resisted its dangerous quality. Because it was reluctant at best. "Don't pretend you care."

Shock flared in his gaze. At least, that's what her foolish mind told her. But when she looked back at him, it was gone. Before she could move, he trapped her behind the table, his arms on either side of her head. "Did you know already?"

"Know what?" Her answer croaked out of her, every cell in her pulsing with awareness at his proximity.

Her gaze fell on the thin scar that stretched from the corner of his mouth to his ear, on the left side. The memory of tracing the scar with her tongue, the taste of his skin, the powerful shudder that had gone through him, it all came back to her in a heated rush.

"Look at me when I'm speaking to you," he said, his tone dark and gravelly.

More than impatience colored his tone. She pulled her

gaze upward, her stomach doing a funny flip. His nostrils flared. The same memory danced in his eyes, making the irises a darkly burnished gold.

With a curse that reverberated around them, he clamped his jaw, until the memory and the gold fire was purged from those eyes.

The ruthlessness of his will was a slap.

She was tired, hungry, and her composure was hanging by a very fine thread. All she wanted to do was crawl into her bed and never look at the world again.

"What did I know, Zafir?"

"Did you know who I was? Is that why you slapped me and had your friend record the whole thing?"

Her sluggish brain took several seconds to react. When it did, it destroyed the barrage of unwanted memories and their effect on her. "What the hell does that mean?"

He bent down toward her, swallowing her personal space. Until their noses were almost touching and his breath fanned over her heated skin. "Your journalist friend David had a tiny camcorder and shot the whole...*incident*."

"So? Which part of the word *journalist* confuses you?" she said, confusion swirling within her. "He was running that thing all day..."

"Did he know what you were about to do? Did you plan it?"

His voice was no more than a raspy whisper yet each word dripped with menace.

Shredded everything she'd ever felt for him. "Is that how much you know me?"

Zafir ruthlessly tuned out the hurt resonating in Lauren's words.

The feel of her soft, warm flesh under his fingers was already disturbing his equilibrium.

His muscles tightened, his blood became sluggish and

the spiraling desire to kiss her mouth was a relentless hum in his veins.

He closed his eyes, and let the pictures of Behraat from six weeks ago swim in front of his eyes…the people who had died in the riots, the destruction Tariq had wrought on it. The mindless carnage instantly took the edge off his physical hunger.

A sense of balance returned to him, a cruel but efficient tether to control his body. He swept his gaze over her, letting the harsh reality of his life creep into his words. "Do we really know each other, Lauren? Except for what we like in—"

Pink seeped into her cheeks, her fiery gaze shooting daggers at him. "Stop it, Zafir."

"We knew each other for two months. I brought Huma to the ER. She told you I was…rich and you pursued me for a donation. You recklessly challenged me and I…rose to it. Against my better instincts, I started an affair. The fact that I hadn't been with a woman in a few months could have been one factor."

He continued like the ruthless bastard he was, refusing to let her pale face, the way she retreated from him, the way she shrank into the wall as though she couldn't bear to be touched by even his shadow, thwart him. "And we continued to sleep with each other because it suited us both."

He tucked away a distracting lock of hair from her cheek and she flinched. "So no, I don't know what you're capable of.

"What I do know is that you were always, what is the word, *chummy* with the press. That reporter friend David, that lawyer, Alicia and you…"

She ran long, trembling fingers over her forehead. "To set up an abuse shelter in Queens. I have nothing to gain by exposing your true colors to the world."

Frustration made his words harder. "I need that video, Lauren. The current political climate of Behraat is volatile. Even something as simple as a lover's tiff can be interpreted in so many different ways. My…predecessor abused his power, toyed with women as if they were his personal playthings. Your *act* questions my credibility, paints me in the same mold as him."

She shot her hand out, her slender fingers spread out, defiance shining out of her gleaming gaze as she ticked off her fingers. "Abuse of power? *Check.* Toys with women as though they were personal playthings? *Check.* It seems you're the perfect man for the job, Zafir."

His skin crawled to think she would cast him in the same mold as Tariq. "I've never treated you with anything other than respect."

"*Respect*?" The words boomeranged in the sterile room, mocking him. "If you respected me, you wouldn't be treating me like a criminal, questioning my actions, you wouldn't have walked out in the middle of the night and disappeared.

"The only thing missing was a bunch of cash on the nightstand and a recommendation to your friends."

"*Enough.* How dare you speak as if you sold yourself to me?"

"Because that's what *you're* implying, Zafir," Lauren shouted back at him. With an increasing sense of emptiness, she fell against the wall.

He trapped her against it, his hot gaze burning, his body a seething cauldron of aggression and sensual intent. There was no control now, only a sense of possession. She had truly angered him and still, Lauren didn't feel fear. Not when he stood close like that.

Silly, stupid Lauren.

"Is that why you did it? Because you're angry with me, you thought to teach me a lesson?"

"You know nothing about me. And I'm realizing how little I know you."

"You have no idea what you have done, Lauren. Are you ready to face the consequences? To take responsibility when another riot begins?"

She'd already learned enough about the atrocities suffered by the people of Behraat. And the sooner this nightmare was over, the sooner she would be able to leave.

She clutched on to the thought like a mantra. "Even though it isn't something I should have to explain, I will. Your claim that David and I planned…this whole thing is ridiculous. He doesn't even know about our affair."

"Then why did he run, Lauren? Why not wait to find out what happened to you?"

"Maybe because against your claims to the contrary, you seem to be walking exactly the same path as the old sheikh. You had your men seize me for a mere slap, Zafir. Can you blame him? What would he do with that video anyway? Put it on YouTube?"

His gaze hardened and she realized it was exactly the thing he wanted to avoid. He pulled her cell phone out of his pocket and slid it into her hand. "Call him. Ask him to meet you in the front lobby and bring his camcorder."

"Why?"

He glared at her. "So that we can delete that video."

"I told you. Even if David recorded it, it would be by accident. He would never do anything to hurt me. I know him."

A vein stretched taut at his temple, something hot and indecent uncoiling in his eyes. "Is that as well as you knew me or even better?"

There were so many things wrong with that question that she couldn't sift through the nuances for a minute. "What…does that mean?"

"You fell into my bed three days after we met. You traveled halfway round the world to see a man who walked out on you. I will not put much stock in your judgment right now."

A soft whimper fell from her mouth and Lauren hated herself just as much as she hated him.

Her judgment? He was using their weakness, their utter lack of control when it came to each other against her?

"You're manipulative too, great." She whispered the words softly, slowly, as though she needed to believe them herself.

A headache was beginning to blur her vision. "David isn't even aware of our…liaison," she said, intent on making him understand. "When he told me he was traveling to Behraat, I persuaded him to let me join him, made him wait until my visa was through. He didn't even know why I was coming."

"Why?"

"Why what, Zafir?"

"Why *did* you come to Behraat?"

Because I'm a silly, sentimental fool. Because, even after all these years, I still didn't learn.

He was right. Her usual common sense had taken a hike from the minute she had woken that morning six weeks ago and found him gone. But she'd acted the fool enough.

"I thought you were dead, Zafir." The hollow ache she had battled for six weeks resonated around them. "I came to see the Behraat that you told me so much about. I came to Behraat to mourn you."

He flinched and took a step back. Shock radiated from him.

"I saw the news coverage of the riots. When I didn't hear anything from you, when they reported the number of civilian casualties, I thought you had died fighting for your country and its people," she paused to breathe, to pull air past the lump that seemed to have wedged in her throat like a rock. She rubbed her fingers over her eyes, feeling incredibly tired. "But I'm such a fool, aren't I? If you had cared, you could have picked up the phone, *no wait*, you could have barked a command like you did before, and one of your thugs could have informed me that you were alive. That you were through with me."

He didn't blink, didn't move, just stared at her. Had he thought it meant nothing to her? *Had she meant nothing to him?*

"I never promised you anything, Lauren."

She nodded and the movement cost her everything she had. "As you pointed out so clearly a few minutes ago, it was an affair at best, an exchange of sex." She laughed through the tears edging into her eyes, through the haze of something clouding her eyes. All of a sudden, she felt woozy, as if there wasn't enough oxygen in the room to breathe. "I've realized that the man I came to mourn doesn't exist.

"Or if he did, he's truly dead."

Her words hit Zafir like a fist to his gut, rendering everything inside him still. The man he'd been with her, he had been neither the orphan nor the ruler.

He'd been just Zafir, free to pursue whatever he wanted.

But not anymore. Never again.

She licked her lips and swallowed visibly, her skin losing the little color she had. "Now, unless your plan is to torture me, in which case I demand a lawyer, please order one of your thugs to bring me some water. My throat feels like it's on fire."

Her gaze unfocused, she swayed on her feet and slid down the wall in a tangle of limbs.

Zafir caught her before she hit the floor, his heart pounding.

Propping her up, he tugged her close, pushed the silky

strands of her hair away from her forehead. She was burning up and dehydrated.

It could happen to anyone visiting such a hot clime for the first time, but her fainting was a direct result of his actions. Because she had been locked up the whole morning without water. On his command.

With her body slumped against his, he pulled his phone out and called Arif.

He traced the stubborn angle of her jaw with his finger, mesmerized by the contrast of his rough, brown hand over her delicate soft skin. That was it.

She had *mesmerized* him the moment he had set eyes upon her. Stunning features, alabaster skin and a sensuous mouth that could make a man forget he wasn't allowed something as frivolous as a blazing hot affair.

And even if he had somehow resisted her beauty, her biting tongue and no-nonsense attitude had won him over.

He had never met a woman like her before.

But she'd been a distraction, a respite, all that he could ever have. So he had walked away when it was time for him to return to Behraat.

But, why hadn't he, as she'd so recklessly demanded, told her he was through with her? A simple phone call would have done it…why hadn't he been able to let go?

As the door opened behind him, he lifted her in his arms and laid her on the stretcher brought in by his personal medical staff. He shook his head as Arif opened his mouth. They waited in silence as the two paramedics checked her vitals.

He couldn't let her go, not until he found the video footage. But he refused to lock her up.

"Put her in the extra suite in my wing. Plant someone from my personal guard outside her suite and ask Dr. Farrah to give her a thorough checkup."

All three men froze around him. His command went

against one of the traditional customs of Behraat. No unmarried woman strayed near the edges, even by mistake, of a man's quarters.

Arif said, "We can send her to the women's clinic in the city and still have a guard there."

"No."

Letting Lauren wake up in some unknown clinic amid strangers when this was all his fault, that was inexcusable, even for him.

He wanted her close, somewhere she could be watched without causing a fuss and curiosity, which she undoubtedly would anywhere else.

And he was no normal man like he had told her. He was not the favored orphan anymore either. He was the sheikh, and he was damned well going to use, or abuse—he didn't care which—his power in this.

"Do as I command, Arif."

Stealing one last look at her, he turned and headed toward the elevator, Lauren's words echoing in his ears.

"The man I mourned doesn't exist. Or if he did, he's truly dead."

How close she'd come to the truth. That carefree, reckless, indulgent man he'd been in New York, he truly didn't exist.

CHAPTER THREE

LAUREN OPENED HER eyes slowly, feeling a sharp tug at her wrist. Her mouth felt woolly as if she had fallen asleep with cotton stuffed into it. It took her a moment to focus around the strange room. Feeling a little frayed, she propped herself on her elbows and scooted into a sitting position.

She was lying on a huge bed on the softest scented cotton sheets. The subtle scent of roses tickled her nostrils. A dark red tapestry hung on the opposite wall while sheer silk curtains fluttered at the breeze. Her whole apartment in Queens could fit into the suite, she thought, awed by the magnificence of the surroundings.

"It is nice to see some color in your cheeks," said a voice near the foot of the bed in heavily accented English.

The IV tube tugged at her wrist as Lauren moved.

A woman laid a cool hand against Lauren's forehead and nodded. She wore a bright red tunic with a collar and long sleeves, and black trousers underneath it. Her hair was tied into a ponytail at the back. Her skin, a shade lighter than Zafir's rich copper tone, shone with a vibrancy that made Lauren feel like a pale ghost.

"The fever is gone. Would you like something to drink?"

When Lauren nodded, instead of handing the glass to her, the woman tucked one hand at Lauren's neck and held it to her mouth with the other. The cool liquid slid against her throat, bringing back feeling into her mouth. Feeling infinitely better, Lauren looked at her. "Where am I?"

A little line appeared in the woman's smooth forehead. "The royal palace."

Holding her growing anxiety at bay, Lauren studied the suite again. Rich, vibrant furnishings with hints of gold greeted her eyes. A high archway lighted with bronze torches led into the balcony on her right, from which she could see the turrets and domes of the palace.

First, he had her locked up accusing her of conspiracy, and now he had staff waiting on her?

She ran a finger over her dry, cracked lips. Her blouse was creased and her cream trousers looked dirty. "I've never fainted in my life before. If you remove the IV, I'd like to wash up. And then leave."

The woman shook her head. "That's not possible."

After the day she'd had, Lauren was in no mood to be ordered around. "Excuse me, but who are you?"

"I'm one of the palace physicians, the only female one. His Highness ordered that I attend to you personally," she said, her words ringing with pride.

It took Lauren a moment to realize who she meant. She was still a prisoner then, upgraded from that stark…*cell* to the sumptuous palace. "Well… *His Highness* can screw himself for all I care," she muttered, emotions batting at her from all directions.

The woman's mouth fell open, and she looked at Lauren as though she had grown two heads. Lauren felt like an ass. It wasn't really the woman's fault.

"I'm sorry…."

"Dr. Farrah Hasan."

"Dr. Hasan, I have to leave. In fact, if you can just hand me my phone." She pointed to her gray metallic handbag—the funky bag looked as out of place on the red velvet settee as she felt in the grandiose palace. "I'll call the airport and reschedule my flight."

"You can't leave, Ms. Hamby. Besides the fact that His Highness has forbidden it," she rushed over her words as if afraid that Lauren would lose it again, "given your condition, you're very weak. I recommend that you spend at least a week in bed and wait two weeks before you fly long-distance."

"My condition?" Lauren said, her heart beginning a strange thump-thump loud enough to reach her ears. "Nothing's wrong with me except the effects of dehydration." *Which was really His Highness's fault.* But she managed to keep the words to herself this time.

"Your pregnancy," Dr. Hasan said with a frown. "You're not aware of it?"

Lauren felt as if she'd been physically slapped. She shook her head, huffed a laugh at the ridiculousness of the suggestion. The doctor's eyes remained serious.

She couldn't be. "But that's not..."

She collapsed against the bed, shaking uncontrollably from head to toe. Her breaths became shaky, and a vicious churn started in her stomach. *Pregnant? How was that possible?* She took her pill without missing it a single day. She clutched the sheets with her hands, tears leaking out of the corner of her eyes.

Fear and shock vied with each other, a heaviness gathering in her belly.

She couldn't be pregnant. A child needed unconditional love, stability, two parents who loved it, who would put it before anything else, before their own ambitions and duties.

Zafir and she couldn't even bear to look at each other without distrust.

Panic unfurled its fangs, and she felt woozy again.

"Just breathe, Ms. Hamby," the doctor said, and Lauren let that crisp tone wash over her, glad to have someone tell her what to do.

As her breathing became normal again, a little flicker of something else crept in. She shoved her top away under the cotton sheets and splayed her fingers on her stomach.

A tiny life was breathing inside her, and it felt as though it breathed courage into her.

A baby.

Her job as an ER nurse at an inner-city hospital in Brooklyn consumed every ounce of her energy, both physical and emotional. Christ, she had never even had a normal boyfriend.

She saw and dealt with unwed, single mothers and their difficulties on a day-to-day to basis. That gritty reality coupled with her own childhood had made at least one thing clear in her head. She'd never wanted to bring a child into the world that couldn't have the love of both parents.

"Is everything okay with the…baby?" she said, her thoughts steering in another direction suddenly.

Dr. Hasan smiled, as though reassured of Lauren's mental state. "It is very early in the pregnancy, I'm assuming. As far as your health, you're fine. But you're dehydrated and I suspect your iron content is low. Nothing that a week's rest and nutritious food wouldn't cure, though."

Lauren nodded, feeling a little calm. As much as she hated staying within a ten-mile radius of Zafir, she wasn't going to take any chances. She'd stay a week and then fly back to New York on her originally scheduled flight.

She needed to sort out her life, and she couldn't do that here. Once she was back in her own city, adjusted to this new change, then she would tell him.

"Are you friends with Zafir?"

Deep pride filled the doctor's eyes. "Yes, Zafir… I mean, *His Highness* and I have known each other since childhood."

So Farrah was not only his staff but one of his friends. A week was a long time surrounded by people who worshipped the ground Zafir walked on. "But as your patient, I have your discretion?"

She frowned. "Yes, of course, Ms. Hamby."

"Please call me Lauren." She tugged the sheet up and clasped her hands on top of it. "I need you to keep…*this,*" she said, as her fingers fluttered over her stomach, "between you and me, Dr. Hasan." A part of her flinched at the lie she was spouting with such little effort. "It doesn't concern Zafir and I would like to keep it that way."

A frown furrowed the doctor's forehead. "Of course, it's not something I will disclose to anyone. But if—"

Lauren turned away from her questions. It was better for everyone concerned if she said very little right then.

Zafir signed the last file with satisfaction and pushed it into the pile for his assistant. This was one of his pet projects, a plan sanctioning the money to upgrade the existing women's clinic on the outskirts of the city for the tribes that still resided in the desert and constantly faced the challenge of bringing their women into the city for medical care.

He stood up from the massive oak table and walked toward the liquor cabinet. He poured himself a glass of whiskey and drank it straight. It burned a fiery path through his throat and gut but did nothing to curb the seething mass of frustration. Knowing that Lauren was in the palace, just in reach, was messing with his self-control.

Tariq's death had put an end to their affair, but he had not forgotten the mindless pleasure he had found in her arms.

The man he was in Behraat couldn't have an affair without courting undue scrutiny from the High Council and more importantly, the wronged people of his country. He needed to create a different image, put distance between him and the scandalous life led by Tariq. Yet…

Arif stepped into his office, a tiny camcorder in his hand. "We found the man."

Zafir's heart pumped faster, as if he was on a stallion racing against a desert storm. "And?"

"He gave us the footage, said he didn't want to do anything to upset the balance of power in Behraat. As long as you give him an exclusive one-on-one."

Perversely, her friend's indifference toward Lauren's safety riled Zafir while she had refused to betray him in any way. "He did not inquire after Lauren?"

"He did. I took him to speak to the woman. He was satisfied about her safety and a little curious about her stay in the royal palace," Arif said, a little hint of his own dissatisfaction thrown in for good measure.

Excitement pulsed through Zafir. He pushed his chair back and stood up. "Say it, Arif."

"Send her away, immediately."

No other man would have dared to suggest what Arif had said. But his old mentor was nothing if not ruthlessly loyal to Behraat.

"Why?"

"That woman," Arif continued, showing his distaste by not mentioning Lauren by name, "is trouble. Only two days and she has already…unsettled you."

Zafir shook his head. "I walked away, in the middle of the night, without looking back. Hid my identity from her."

All he cared about now, or ever, was Behraat. Yet, the same thought plagued him. Did that mean he was not entitled to even the little pleasures he wanted?

"She's due a little anger."

His gaze steady, Arif shook his head. "You cannot let anything distract you from your path."

And what Arif didn't say was that he already had. Frustration and anger mixed in with a healthy dose of unsatisfied libido swirled through him.

All he had ever done was to give of himself to his father, even though he hadn't known it then, and to Behraat. And yet, in return, he would be denied such a small thing as the one woman that tempted him no end.

No!

"Should I live my life like a monk?" It was a question he'd already asked himself. And with Lauren within reach, the answer was becoming blurry to him.

"The best thing for your future, for the future of Behraat would be to find a suitable young woman, one who knows her place in your life and marry her. Cement your position in front of the High Council."

A pleasant, traditional, biddable Behraati woman would never talk back to him, would definitely not even think of striking him.

That's what the future held for him. But he was in no hurry to embrace it just yet.

Tariq's wife, Johara's portrait caught his attention.

Johara was delicate, stunningly beautiful, shy, the daughter of a member of a powerful High Council member. Someone like her was what he needed for a future wife.

Lauren, on the other hand, was the exact opposite of Johara. Tall and lithe, hardworking, tough, prickly, and unflinchingly honest.

She asked for nothing, made no demands of him, and had nearly killed herself with flu instead of asking for help once. She had few friends outside of her work at the inner-city ER, no personal life. They had been like two perfectly matched ships crossing each other at a port.

Yet she had come looking for him, had cared enough to mourn for him.

A dangerous temptation for a man who rarely allowed himself any personal attachments…

"My life is, always will be, about Behraat, Arif. No woman will change that. Or change me into something I never could be."

But, for once in his life, he wanted to indulge himself.

She had made the choice to come, hadn't she? After the

brutal reality of the past few weeks, maybe Lauren arriving in Behraat was his prize.

Just the thought of her was enough to tighten every muscle in his body with need.

But first, he needed to make it right with her. And he knew how to do just that.

After all, there had to be some perks to being the ruler of a nation.

Lauren pushed the French doors aside and stepped onto the private balcony. Dusk was an hour away and it painted the sky crimson. She tugged the edges of a cashmere sweater tighter around her shoulders, feeling the chill in the air.

It was something that amazed her even after a week in Behraat. As hot as it got during the day, with sunset, chill permeated the air.

She couldn't believe she was in the royal palace, home to the royalty of Behraat, with its various turrets and domes.

Landscaped gardens, water fountains, meandering pathways amid tiled courtyards, everywhere she looked, old-world charm, sheer opulence and unprecedented luxury greeted her. It was a setting straight out of a princess tale her aunt had read to her years ago from a book her parents had gifted her after another diplomatic stint in some far-off, exotic country, just like Behraat.

The quarters she'd been given boasted a large antique bed with the softest cotton sheets spun with threads of gold, satin drapes and the en suite bathroom with a marble bathtub was fit for a princess. Plush, colorful rugs snuggled against her bare feet, a vanity mirror framed with intricate gold filigree…everywhere she turned, the opulence of Zafir's wealth, the sheer differences in their worlds mocked her.

Even when she lay down on her bed, there was the soaring ceiling inlaid with an intricate mural that cast a golden glow over the room. As though she needed a reminder of where she was or who she was dealing with.

She turned around and walked back into the suite. Restlessness and uncertainty gnawed at her, even though it had been a full day since she had learned of her pregnancy. "You're a fully qualified doctor?" she shot at Farrah who hadn't left except for a couple of hours.

Farrah looked up from her journal and nodded.

"It doesn't bother you that he's ordered you to play nursemaid to me?"

"It's a small request from a man who saved me at my lowest without judgment, when...even my family had forsaken me." She put the journal aside. "And it is clear that you are important to him."

Lauren ignored the obvious question in Farrah's words and shot one of her own. "Because he has jailed me *here* rather than one of those underground cells?"

"You misunderstand. You're in Zafir's private wing. Women are not allowed here. If imprisoning you was what he intended, he could have put you anywhere." She paused as though waiting for the import of her words to sink in. "Here, he can be absolutely certain of your safety."

Lauren refused to attach any meaning to Farrah's revelation.

She walked toward the dark side table laden with exotic fruits and pastries. She picked up the elegant silver jug and poured sherbet into the gleaming silver tumbler and took a sip. Apparently, in Zafir's world, silverware meant actual *silverware.*

The smooth fruity liquid slid down her parched throat blissfully. "The only person posing a problem to my safety is *His Arrogant Highness.*"

"There have been two attempts on his life since he returned to Behraat, Lauren."

The tumbler slid from Lauren's grasp, soundlessly spreading a stain on the thick Persian rug at her feet.

Lauren gripped the wooden surface, an image of Zafir dead instantly pressed upon her by her overactive mind. Nausea rose up through her, turning the sweet taste of the sherbet into bitterness.

That he might be dead was a reality she had accepted a few days ago. Yet having seen him, she couldn't bear the thought of anything happening to him. She picked up a napkin and knelt to soak up the stain from the rug. "Why would—"

A knock at the door to the suite cut off her question.

A woman, dressed in a maroon kaftan and head robes that covered her hair, entered the suite. She had a silver tray in her hand, the contents of it covered by a red velvet cloth lined with gold threads.

Kohl-rimmed eyes stole glances at her as the woman spoke to Farrah. Her eyes wide, Farrah stared at Lauren and back at the woman. "His Highness wants to see you in an hour on the rooftop garden," Farrah said, her gaze tellingly blank of any expression.

The woman stepped forward and stretched her arms. Lauren took a step back, unease settling low in her belly.

Her heart going thump-thump, she pulled the velvet cloth and bit back a gasp. With shaking hands, she took the precious emerald silk gown from the tray and unfolded it, the soft crunch of tissue wrapped in its folds puncturing the silence.

Thousands of tiny crystals, sewn along the demure neckline and the tight bodice, winked at her. A pencil line skirt flared from the waist with a knee-high slit in the back.

A dress fit for a princess, a sheikha, or a rich man's plaything.

It would fit her like a glove, Lauren realized. Her gaze caught Farrah's for a second, and the same knowledge lingered there. Her temper rising, she dropped the gown, feeling more dirty than she had ever felt.

The curiosity with which the two women watched her every move, every nuance in her expression, scraped at her nerves.

Were they coming to the same conclusion as her? A female *guest* tucked away in the High Sheikh's quarters, on whom he bestowed gifts of the most intimate kind.

What kind of a game was he playing?

A sick feeling coursed through Lauren, settling in her stomach. She showed the velvet case no such care as she had done the dress. She yanked it open and stared at its contents.

A diamond necklace, with matching earrings and bracelet. The name of the top designer in gold threading on the velvet case was redundant to Lauren. She knew this particular design too well. Tears that she dare not shed choked up her throat.

He remembered her obsession with diamonds.

Every surface in her apartment in Queens was littered with brochures and catalogs from the top diamond galleries of the world. It was her guilty pleasure to spend a lazy evening in her recliner, going through the catalogs, marking the ones she liked, while in reality, she didn't own a tiny pendant.

The diamonds glittered and winked at her as she closed the lid, struggling to keep a check on her unraveling temper.

Did he think she would be softened by this blatant display of wealth, that she would forget everything that had happened? That he could buy her off with expensive gifts?

The fact that he remembered her obsession plunged the stab of his betrayal a little deeper. Whatever he said now, whatever he did, she had to remember that he'd made the choice to cut her out of his life with little regret. That he'd suspected her of the worst.

She dropped the velvet case onto the tray on the bed. "Please instruct her to take it back, Farrah, and to inform His Highness that I don't intend to see him. Not today, not tomorrow, not ever again."

CHAPTER FOUR

LAUREN TIED THE sash on the plush thigh-length robe and walked into the sitting area of her suite. With another plush towel, she rubbed the wetness out of her hair. She would have lingered another hour in the marble tub, playing and luxuriating in the innumerable jets and settings, if she wasn't scared she would turn into a prune. "That marble tub is decadent, Farrah."

"I'm glad something in my palace gives you pleasure, Lauren."

Husky, honeyed—his tone sent waves of sensation rollicking over her already tingly flesh. Her knees wobbled. She pulled her towel off her face, her cheeks tightening with heat.

Uncurling himself from the velvet armchair, Zafir cut a direct path toward her, his gaze traveling over her with a thoroughness that instantly put her on edge. Flaring with shock, Farrah's gaze volleyed between them.

"Leave us, Farrah." He threw the command without turning his thoroughly disconcerting gaze from Lauren.

"I have nothing to say to you that Farrah can't—"

"I have," he said, stopping a few inches from her. Farrah had already gathered her things and quietly exited the room.

His hair still wet, he smelled so good that her stomach did a funny flip.

In a light brown V-neck T-shirt and tight blue jeans, he looked sexy and approachable. Like delicious dark chocolate that she wanted to sink her teeth into. The shirt exposed the strong column of his throat, hugged the hard contours of his chest and muscled abdomen.

Her throat dry, Lauren tucked her hands at her sides and tugged her gaze up.

His tawny gaze glinted with incinerating warmth, a hint of mockery in the grooves around his mouth. It swept over her with invasive familiarity, lingering far too long over the opening in her robe.

Her pulse went haywire, a new kind of oxygen deprivation drying her mouth now.

She tugged at the sash holding it together, the soft silk burning against her overheated skin. His hand shot out to her cheek in a quick movement, too fast for her hazy senses to grasp. Every cell in her being pushed her into leaning into his touch and she resisted it. Just.

When he touched her, his movements were gentle, tracing the circles she sported under her eyes. "You look awful." He said this in a tone that spoke of regret. As if it hadn't been in his power to not hurt her. As if he hadn't made that choice himself.

She stepped back. "Thanks for noticing, *Your Highness*, and for deigning to see me," she drawled. "I should curtsy, but seeing that you had me locked up here for two days, I'm not in the mood. Instruct your staff to release me. I want to leave, at once."

A frown twisted his brows and then smoothed down. Her hands instantly went to her midriff and that incisive gaze followed. She pretended to secure the knot of her robe, her fingers shaking. Heat flushed her from within when he moved closer again, triggering every nerve into a hyper-aware state, stealing rational thought.

"Stop that," she said softly, suddenly wishing the dark stranger from that afternoon back. She wanted to be angry with him, *she was*, yet her body seemed disjointed from her mind.

He raised his hands like shields, a butter-won't-melt expression on his face. "Stop what?"

"Looking at me like that," she croaked.

"It gives me pleasure to look at you."

She rolled her eyes, hoping that he couldn't hear the thudding of her heart. "I fell for that line six weeks ago. Fool me once—"

His finger on her lips cut her off. She trembled all over, the simple contact breathing a firestorm of need all over. "Choosing that gown and the jewelry was the most pleasure I've had in six weeks."

He had picked the gown himself? Her heart, if possible, skipped a beat, his words falling over her like sparkly, magic dust, ensnaring her senses into a web of intoxicated desire. How else could she explain the gooey mass in the center of her stomach?

"If you had worn it and accepted my invitation for dinner, I would have been even more pleased."

"*I...me...my pleasure*, self-absorbed much, Zafir?" she mocked him. Something uncoiled in his gaze but her bitter words were the only things she had to fight him with. "Your gifts don't mean anything to me except that you think you can buy your way out of anything. You locked me up here. Dinner with you is the last thing I want."

"I wanted to make sure Farrah could take proper care of you. What is bothering you?" he said, steel creeping into his words.

"You're kidding, right? Should I fall at your feet because you moved me here, because you threw some gifts at me? Three days ago, you accused me of conspiring against you and now..." She vibrated with anger and hurt, barely getting words out. "You talk to me as if nothing happened. I've had quite enough of you and this...place."

"I would like to apologize for that. I knew that you weren't capable of scheming like that."

"And you came to this realization after getting concrete proof from David and not a second before?"

His mouth hardened and Lauren realized she hated this version of him. Every time he spoke or thought of Behraat, he became someone she didn't know, someone she didn't want to know. "I needed that video, Lauren. I have to be ruthless from time to time. Consider it one of the hazards of being the ruler."

"More like the effect of being drunk on your own power."

Instead of the anger she had expected, his mouth curved into a smile. His gaze moved to her mouth and she felt his perusal like a tingle. "Surrounded by my people, I've forgotten how outspoken you are." He pushed a lock of hair from her forehead. "It was the first thing I noticed about you."

Whatever she had been about to say flitted away. Pure sensation skittered over her skin. He cupped her jaw and pulled her close, the rough pad of his thumb rubbing her skin. "I brought Huma to the ER, you took one look at her, and demanded if I was the one who had given her those bruises. The way you looked at me with fire burning in your eyes…" His Adam's apple bobbed up and down.

"You reminded me of a lioness I once saw in the zoo… ferocious and breathtaking." His tone became molten, honeyed on those last words, a fire burning in his eyes.

"I have never in my life become so hard just by looking at a woman, *ya habeebti*."

Wet warmth pooled at her core and she clutched her thighs together.

Torture, that's what it was. And worse than being locked up. Because when he accused her of nefarious intentions, she could fight him, and despise him.

But when he spoke like that, with desire, with honesty, with nothing but that warmth, she stood no chance.

She tried to let her body go slack, but she had no control over her own muscles. All she wanted was to drop the robe and let him ease the ache between her legs. *God,* and he would…with those clever fingers, he would unravel so easily and efficiently…until there was only her and him and that fire between them.

"Stop touching me," she finally managed, sounding breathless and shivery.

Forcing her back until the back of her legs hit the bed, he crowded her. His thumb moved over her lower lip, the heat from his body swathing her. "You love it when I touch you. In fact, while we were together, we couldn't get enough of each other."

"I used to." She somehow pulled her sanity together finally. "Now all I want is to put several thousand miles between us."

His gaze became hard, a muscle jumping in his jaw. "I thought you would have cooled off by now." He spread his hands around, and the lack of economy in that movement betrayed his rising temper that his even tone hid. "Seeing that you assumed I was dead and I'm clearly not, I thought you would get over your shock and be happy to see me."

"And that we would take up where we left off six weeks ago?" she yelled the words, masking the lump in her throat. The incredible arrogance in his assumption left her shaking, dousing her desire with the efficiency of an ice-cold bath. "I'm never going to get over it, Zafir.

"If I weren't a…*sentimental fool* who jumped on a plane, we wouldn't have seen each other again…*ever.* You made a deliberate choice to walk out of my life that night. Don't act as though you care now."

Her legs quaked beneath her when she meant to move away from him. She felt light-headed.

His arms forming a steel cage, Zafir picked her up instantly and laid her down on the settee. His forehead wreathed in concern as he studied her face. "*Ya Allah*, you were about to faint again. What the hell is going on with you, Lauren?"

She had let herself get upset by his gifts this morning and barely touched her lunch. No wonder she felt so weak, so vulnerable. She couldn't do this again and again. She couldn't let her child pay the price for her weakness.

Moving back on the chaise, she wrapped her hands around her legs. "I'm just hungry," she whispered. He immediately picked up the intercom and ordered enough food to feed an army.

When he reached for her, she shook her head. "Leave, before the staff arrives."

"Why?"

"Because you've already given them enough to gossip about. I would like to not become another dirty spectacle of your palace, Zafir."

His jaw tight, he glared at her. "You are awful at taking care of yourself. I will wait until I'm sure you're not going to collapse again," he said, the frustrated anger in his voice snaring her again.

After everything that had happened that day, it was the last thing she wanted to hear. "What the hell is that supposed to mean?"

"You had the most virulent flu two weeks before I left, remember? And it's obvious you've not recovered from it. When Huma found you on the bathroom floor and called me, you looked like you were about to die. I literally carried you to the clinic. And here you are again looking like a ghost. What have you been doing, starving yourself?"

Shying her gaze away from him, Lauren drank a glass of ice-cold water.

She had been worried over *him*. But there was no point in reiterating what a fool she had been.

Instead, her thoughts moved to that evening he had taken her to the clinic. For a week, he and Huma had taken shifts, nursing her back to health, not leaving her alone even for a few minutes. By the time her friend Alicia had heard about her illness and arrived with chicken soup, Lauren had been halfway to recovering.

And when she had gotten better, he had come to her that evening, and dismissed Huma, a wild light in his eyes…

It was the last time she had seen him, the only time he had actually stayed over at her apartment in two months…

Her gaze flew open, her stomach twisting at the final nail in the coffin.

Zafir laid his hand on her forehead, frowning. “Do you feel faint again?”

She shook her head, dislodging his hand. “Huma knew, didn’t she?”

A stillness crept into his face. “Knew what?”

“She knew about us…that we were…” she forced the words out, killing any tender thought she had ever indulged in, “having sex?”

His expression became distasteful. “I do not discuss my sex life with Huma. But yes.”

“Did she also know you were leaving the next morning?”

He looked as though he was weighing his response and she wondered why when he had given her the absolute truth earlier. “Huma’s the daughter of an old friend whose life was in danger here. She was under my care in New York. I had to tell her that I was leaving, that I had made plans for her.”

Huma had left a week after he had. With a hug and something muttered in Arabic that Lauren couldn’t understand to her question about Zafir.

“Did she tell you that I had been worried?”

“Yes.”

She bolted from the chaise, fury finally, *mercifully* coming to her rescue. All this could have been avoided. It could have all ended in New York just as he'd intended.

She turned back to him, one last question gnawing at her gut.

Leave it alone, Lauren, a part of her whispered, the part that preferred to cling to delusion.

No.

Knowing the bitter, eviscerating truth was better than driving herself crazy for years to come with speculation. She'd learned early on, with her parents' indifference, that hope was toxic, gnawing away at one's self.

"Were you *ever* going to call, Zafir?"

Silence stretched between them, its cruel fingers shredding her patched up nerves.

"Leave," she whispered.

He turned her around, his fingers gripping her tight. "It was a decision I made. But I did…*regret* the necessity of making it. It doesn't mean I didn't think about you in these last few weeks." Arrogant features softened. "Stay in Behraat for a while, as my guest."

She stared at him, her mouth hanging open for several seconds. They were mere words but she could already feel herself softening, traitorous desire whispering sweet temptations in her ears.

It seemed nothing had changed in how she reacted to his magnetic presence. After everything she had gone through in the past few weeks, she was ashamed to feel the thrum of excitement his words incited.

"No," she forced the word out.

He trapped her again. Rock-hard thighs pressed into hers. Molten gaze hovered over her mouth and a low hum began to vibrate over her skin. "Why not?"

She licked her lips and straightened, fisting her hands. It was either that or touch him. God, how she wanted to run her fingers over his sensual mouth, lean into him and relish the heat of his body.

His hands crept into her hair and tugged her closer, his long fingers encircling her nape. Awareness shot through her like a surge of current. "You're a workaholic and haven't taken a vacation in forever. Besides, I've missed our Friday, what did you call them, *movie and...make out* sessions."

"You're serious?" she said.

He didn't answer her question, only pulled her closer. It went straight to her head, making her light-headed with longing, shooting need to the apex of her thighs, drenching her in liquid heat.

How she wanted to close her eyes and let him take her to ecstasy once again. How she wanted to delude herself that physical pleasure was intimacy…that lust was caring…that she mattered and not just as a willing woman.

Fears and insecurities she had repressed for so long festered in that void. And she detested herself for feeling so much. "I can't. In fact, if I never lay eyes on you again after tonight, it'll be too soon for me."

A vein fluttered at his temple, his grip tight in her hair. Her pulse hammered, her insides feeling as though she had taken a vertical leap.

"You're a liar." His mouth hovered mere inches from her, his breath brushed her skin in a featherlight touch, teasing. "Do you have any idea how I long to possess you again? How much I need you, Lauren?" His gaze came alive, his words low and husky. "And if I kiss your luscious mouth, can you honestly say you'll stop me? Can you deny us both the pleasure we want so much?"

Lauren shook her head, knowing everything she felt was reflected in her eyes. A grim satisfaction shadowed over his face, its razor edge mocking her feeble defenses.

"No. I'll admit that I'll enjoy the sex as much as you do.

I'll go as far as to say you're the best lay I've ever had," she said, hungry to see his smooth charade fracture.

Thunder danced in his gaze, his razor-sharp cheekbones streaked with color. Even as he knew that she had had one lover before him, a boyfriend in college who had been more into his military career than into her.

"The best lay you've ever had?" he inquired silkily, the force of his anger all the more fierce for the leash with which he reined it.

"Yes," she said, tilting her chin up with a recklessness she was far from feeling. "You're extremely skilled and generous when it comes to sex."

Reducing their affair to the crudest terms was the only thing that would save her. From him and herself.

"But I have to resist the attraction, the lure of self-delusion this time. Your power and the ruthlessness with which you wield it, the reckless indifference it affords you of other's feelings, especially someone like me who's all too willing to fall into your bed…

"How long before you decide that you've had enough of me, before you decide I don't belong in your world? How long before, once again, you walk out of my bed in the middle of the night and have one of your guards throw me out without so much as a goodbye?"

An immense stillness came over him. Her breath hitching in her throat, Lauren waited. For something—for refusal, for anger, anything that refuted her accusation.

But nothing came.

His silence plunged her deep into a vortex of painful memories.

Discarded in the name of ambition and lofty goals, picked back up with no thought to her feelings, and discarded again. She couldn't count the number of times her parents had hurt her.

The insecurity, the fear that she didn't somehow measure up, her resolution to make no demands—a vicious circle of pain that stole every ounce of joy from her. That's what she would bring upon herself if she succumbed.

Stepping back from him when every inch of her thrummed to be with him, it was the hardest thing she had ever done.

Her heart stuttered anew at the dark beauty of the man.

God, he was the father of her child, the first man who had made her feel so much…the first man for whom she had forgotten herself. And she…she had to walk away.

"If you truly respect me, leave now, Zafir. Let me leave Behraat."

Even now, a fragment of hope flickered inside her, waiting for him to persuade her otherwise.

He stepped back, slowly, irrevocably and Lauren's knees gave out under her.

"As you wish, Lauren." That dark gaze swept over her face with a thoroughly hungry appraisal before he turned and marched out of the suite.

Without looking back once.

Lauren sank against the bed, struggling to pull air into her lungs, squeezing her eyes to keep the wet heat at bay.

She would never amount to more than a willing woman to Zafir. And maybe she had been okay with that status quo in New York, but not anymore.

Not when it was her child's well-being in question.

A playful giggle echoed somewhere and she turned toward the balcony looking out onto the vast courtyard below. A boy, somewhere between five and nine—she couldn't tell any closer than that—ran on the cobbled stones, his dark hair shining under the light of bronze torches, a mischievous smile on his face, chased by a man around the fountain.

The man let him run around two more circles before he caught up with him and slung him on his shoulder.

She felt as if a fist was squeezing her heart as she realized the magnitude of her decision.

Zafir was the ruler of a nation, a man who had a long list of priorities in which she didn't feature, a man who could set aside everything else quite ruthlessly when it came to Behraat. And she and her child would only be complications in that path.

After what she had suffered at her parents' hands, she would never put her child through it.

It had been the longest week of Lauren's life. She felt as though she was sitting on shifting sands with no tether.

More than once, she had picked up the phone, eager to blurt out the news to Zafir. She just wasn't programmed to lie or hide the truth as she was doing.

Zafir refused to let her go back to the hotel, so she spent her days locked up in the palace. Scared of weakening, she cut herself off from everything. And when life intruded, it only brought a truth that crystallized her decision.

Having learned that Lauren was the sheikh's *scandalous female guest*, Huma had come calling. Hugged Lauren and chattered on and on about how decent life was in Behraat now, about how she had enrolled herself in a women's college to study nursing.

"Just like you," Huma had whispered with a proud smile.

And in the same innocent way she did everything else, she informed Lauren of the rumors about the sheikh's upcoming wedding and the celebrations that would ensue.

Nausea filled her throat as Huma continued merrily.

Childhood friends, reunited after several years, daughter of a High Council member, born to be a sheikha and so on…

The excruciating doubts she had had about hiding the

pregnancy from him, the conflict that had eroded her from within, everything evaporated at the bitter news.

Not even a little regret pricked her as she packed that night.

Her child would be secondary to neither duty nor a new bride in his father's life. She would make sure of that.

CHAPTER FIVE

LAUREN STARED AROUND the terminal, the beautiful architecture of the private airport building filling her with awe. The same soaring circular ceilings, grand archways and a colorfully hued marble stretched as far as she could see, a far cry from the commercial airport she and David had flown into.

On learning that she'd been scheduled on a privately chartered flight, Lauren had called it a huge wastage of resources. But as Farrah had pointed out with a lingering question in her eyes, the sheikh had decreed that she be sent off in style.

And no one could defy the mighty sheikh's word.

Whose withdrawal had been absolute and chilling.

When her stomach grumbled, Lauren opened her energy bar and took a bite. After the elaborate, mouthwatering meals of the past week, the granola bar tasted foul in her mouth but she forced herself to chew.

"We're ready to board you," announced the flight attendant, carefully shying away his gaze from Lauren.

From gleaming dark wood paneling to supple wide leather seats sitting on priceless Persian rugs constituted the decor. A flat-screen plasma television faced the seats.

Despite the disparity in their lifestyles and cultures, there had been a connection between them from the first moment. A connection that now had a permanent consequence…

Her throat felt thick with an emotion she refused to name.

A woman, dressed in traditional tunic and trousers with her hair concealed in a loose scarf, approached her, a glass of sparkling water in her hand. "Hello, Ms. Hamby," she said deferentially. "I'm a qualified nurse, so please let me know if you feel faint."

Had he informed his whole staff that she was incapable of looking after herself? "I'm a nurse too, so I would know," she added a little sharply.

Sighing, Lauren peered through the window and saw the jagged outline of the capital city set against sprawling desert land in the distance. Turreted domes and spires stood out against the sky and she hungrily clutched the sight to herself.

"Aren't you leaving?" she asked the woman.

"I accompany you to New York," she said demurely, "and then, return to Behraat."

Lauren set her glass on the table so fast that the cold water spilled on her fingers.

This was going too far. She'd decided to tolerate the jet because she didn't want to draw Zafir's attention by complaining about it. But she drew the line at wasting a qualified nurse's time.

She had learned from Farrah that women qualified in the medical field were just not enough for the growing demand in the outlying villages of the city where families still refused to let the women see male doctors.

"Please ask whoever's in charge to take me back to the commercial airport."

"But the sheikh himself—"

"If he has a problem with this," Lauren replied, as she stood up and grabbed her handbag, "he can come see me himself."

The woman gasped.

"You have your wish, *habeebti*," came the sudden, soft reply behind her.

Lauren whirled so fast that she was dizzy.

Zafir. The sheer force of his presence was like a blast of toe-curling heat. Her insides plummeted alarmingly.

"You're also going to wish," his tone was silky smooth, like velvet cloaking a knife's edge as he dismissed the nurse with a flick of his head, "we had never met by the time I'm through with you."

With that veiled threat, he threw a file at her. The contents scattered with a soft whisper that nevertheless felt like a thudding roar. As though even the flimsy paper didn't dare disobey his command, a sheet flew toward her.

Goose bumps broke out on her skin. She didn't need to read the paper to know what it said. The red file with her name in capital letters, the small insignia, the seal of the palace physician, was enough.

"Tongue-tied, Lauren?"

Now his voice rang with power, cold ferocity, absolute disgust. Her stomach churned fiercely, her heart racing far too fast and far too loud.

He knew. God, he knew, and he looked so angry. Why? Why was he so angry?

She picked up the papers from the floor, one by one, her movements slow and shaky, her thoughts in a whirl. Slowly, she stood up and faced him.

A white cotton tunic with a Nehru collar hung carelessly over his broad chest, dark hair on golden brown skin peeking through its opening. The very unassuming, casual way of his dressing only served to emphasize how easily he wore his power.

Molten heat uncoiled low in her belly, as instinctual as her breathing.

He gripped her elbow and pulled her toward him. "Explain that file."

Was his fury because of the truth she had hidden or the

fact that she had dared to? Was that a shadow of hurt beneath his anger?

Doubts piled upon her, weakening her. His nearness wrecked her balance, her mind, compelling little pinpricks of guilt.

No, it had been the hardest decision she'd ever made in her life.

She looked into the sharp planes of his aristocratic face, forced herself to keep her tone light—a herculean task with his gaze peeling layers off her. "It goes something like this. A man and a woman have fantastic, mind-blowing sex thinking they are protected by her pill, but the pill fails because the woman is on antibiotics, *annndd…*" she made a singsong sound, her throat drying up at the lick of molten fury in his gaze, turning the tawny irises to scorching flames "…a few weeks later, the woman is pregnant. Your basic biology in action."

A curse fell from his mouth—something she had no hope of understanding except that it was nasty and aimed at her, his long fingers digging into her arm.

"Learn to curb that tongue of yours, *ya habeebti*, or I'll put it to a more pleasurable activity next time."

Something hot and twisty and unbearably achy gripped her lower belly, her cheeks burning up. Their gazes met and held, his meaning clear in the dark heat in it. "I'm not going to acknowledge that with a refusal."

He laughed then and while it etched gorgeous grooves into his cheeks, it lacked any warmth. The luxurious cabin felt chilly. "You think I cannot command you to do my bidding, Lauren? All that lacked until now was intention on my behalf."

"You're trying to frighten me."

"Try me then, *habeebti*. Try and see how far I can go when I'm pushed, when I'm denied what's mine."

She swallowed and took a deep breath. Angering him

was not, had never been, her objective. "How did you find out? Did—"

"No, the dedicated doctor that she is, Farrah kept her silence and faces my wrath."

Her heart sank to her toes. "I told her this had nothing to do with you, Zafir. Don't punish her because you're angry with me."

"Worry about your own fate."

Beating down the fear that swamped her, she tried to be rational. "I don't understand your reaction, Zafir."

"No? Then let me explain it to you. You found out that you were pregnant *with my child,* and decided to flee Behraat without a word." He ran a shaky hand over his face, the starkness of the gesture contrasting sharply with the fury in his words. "And to think I was honoring your wish, that I was being respectful… How dare you hide something so important from me?"

Something so important. Was it?

Suddenly she had springboarded into a category that merited his precious time and attention? That more than anything pierced her, robbing her of her innate decency, turned her bloodthirsty. "Are you so sure that it is yours then, Zafir?"

An icy mask fell over his face, and he loosened his grip on her and thrust her back from him with infinite care. He studied her with a detached coldness that turned the blood in her veins into ice. "No, I don't know that, do I?"

Plucking the phone from the wall, he barked a command to be connected to Farrah. Ordered a DNA test and slammed the handset into the wall without waiting for a response. It dangled by the cord, back and forth, the rubbery sound of it reverberating in the silence.

Lauren gripped her forehead, all fight deflating out of her. She had pushed him until the veneer of his civility was ripped at her feet. She had no one to blame except herself.

And she wondered, with an instinct she didn't understand if she had hurt him with her callous words.

Her throat was like sandpaper when she spoke. "It is yours, Zafir."

His back to her, he remained dangerously silent.

Despite all the disappointments she'd faced, she had never been a spiteful person. She hadn't intended her departure as a malicious move. She simply refused to let her child endure the same uncertainty, the same gut-wrenching pain of learning that he or she didn't feature highly in its parents' life.

"It's not possible to perform a DNA test so soon in the pregnancy," she whispered. "I will get one done as soon as it is safe and send you the results."

When he turned and looked down at her, she realized she was pathetic, imagining things that weren't possible, still so weak where he was concerned.

Because there was no hurt in his gaze. A smile, if the cruel curve of his mouth could be called that, bared his teeth, the triumphant light in his stance letting butterflies loose into her stomach.

Cold calculation glinted in his gaze, as though he was devising ways to punish her and having fun while doing it. "You're not going anywhere, not until you give birth to my child. After that, you can disappear into the sands of the desert for all I care."

Zafir watched as Lauren paled, held his gaze defiantly, realized he was serious and then fell back into her seat with a soft thud.

Instinct and something else, something shameful and useless and weakening like honor maybe, something the *great Rashid Al Masood* had taught him when he had been a boy, kicked in, and he found himself shooting out of his seat to help her.

No.

He shoved away the chivalry, crushed the very code of honor he had embraced early in his life after hearing whispered taunts about his parentage.

He'd always been discreet about how he'd indulged his lust, had cautiously distanced himself from Tariq and his wild, orgiastic parties.

All because he had been determined to not be the cause of some woman's distress.

The only time he had weakened, the only time he had forgotten that he could never let any personal attachment distract him was with Lauren. And her betrayal plunged the dagger the deepest because he had thought her above it.

If she had left, if she had disappeared…he would be unaware of the existence of his child. Just as he hadn't known of his parentage until just a few years back.

She tucked herself into the leather seat, retreating as far back as possible, *as though she didn't trust him*. The irony of it would have amused him if he wasn't seething with the need to punish her.

And he knew how to punish that independent, strong mind of hers, knew her weakness. An insidious thrill shot through him, cooling the edge of his anger.

"You're bluffing," she finally said, trying for defiance but failing.

He stretched his legs, settled into the seat opposite her and took his own sweet time answering.

Let her stew in fear, he thought with a bitterness that spread like an infection. Let her wonder what the powerful, arrogant sheikh would do with her now.

He had her where he wanted, he realized, excitement pulsing in his blood. And there was a freedom in knowing that she was like any other woman.

"Try to leave Behraat and see."

Little beads of moisture pearled over her upper lip, despite the air-conditioning.

"You're angry, I get that. But consider reality, Zafir. We're talking about a child here. You can't decide you want it now and then put it away when *something more important* comes along."

"You dare to preach to me of the intricacies of parenthood? Let us not delude ourselves of what this is really about.

"The fact that I walked away from you. I didn't pander to what you wanted, so you pay me back by robbing me of my child."

"It. Is. Not," she whispered, her long legs uncoiling from under her. "I was furious with you, yes, but I've accepted that our…*relationship* meant nothing to you. I—"

"Your actions speak otherwise." He moved toward her, his mind reeling with infinite questions. "What would you have told my child? That his father didn't want her or him, that he rejected him?"

She bolted from the seat, her arms around her midriff, her breasts rising and falling. "I would never lie to my child."

"Only its father then."

"I didn't lie to you. And I… I would have let you know eventually."

"*Eventually*?" He shot up from the seat, his temper seething again. "It was not your decision to make."

Her lithe form bristling with emotion, she poked him in the chest. "You're accusing me? You're the ruler of a nation, Zafir.

"You ruthlessly bury anything if it clashes with your rule. Can you blame me in thinking this baby would only be an unwanted complication? That its well-being, even its mere existence would be so far down the list for a man whose first priority will always be Behraat, a man who's on the verge of getting married to another woman?"

A smile teased the edges of his mouth, and he let it.

He took another step forward, forcing her to step back until her back hit the wood-paneled wall of the craft. He slapped his palms on either side of her, his gaze dropping to her mouth. She bristled with energy yet her breath was slow, chunky.

Striking flame to oil, that's what it would be if he touched her. That's what it had been from the second he had laid eyes on her.

"Now I see how your mind works. You heard rumors about my wedding and thought '*here he is propositioning me and getting ready to marry another woman*'?

"So I'll rob him of the knowledge of his child. You pride yourself on being a smart, educated woman, yes? Didn't it occur to you to talk to me once?"

Her breathing becoming raspier. "This was not payback, Zafir."

"No? Although in a twisted way, it shows that you were jealous at the thought of my wedding."

Something very much like a growl erupted from her. Her hands fell to his chest, fisted tight and pushed him back. He tucked them into his own and held his footing, her knuckles digging into his palms. "I've no desire to feature in a man's life for whom my only value is the pleasure I can provide in his bed. One who will discard me at a whim."

Tension turned those high cheekbones into tight angles, her mouth quivering and fighting.

"I've been lied to, dropped off like a pet at a relative's door, got picked up for a summer, got dropped off again by my own parents so many times in the name of duty, ambition and whatnot. I don't want my child to feel like that, okay?

"I won't allow you to do that.

"Will he or she ever come first with you, Zafir? Over anything else, over Behraat, over your precious duty? Because that's what this child means to me."

He stilled, her words striking him like a whip.

She was right. A child deserved better than lies and excuses, better than being used as a pawn. His own childhood had been a lie and he couldn't tolerate it.

He wanted to brush her concerns away, but the stark pain in her gaze wouldn't let him. "Whatever else I'm unable to give this child, it will know that I love it. And I will use everything within my power before I let you corrupt its mind against me."

Lauren swayed at the coldness of Zafir's threat.

His resentment was like a force field she couldn't penetrate. His anger, she was beginning to understand barely, but there was a glimmer of pain in it that disconcerted her. "If you care about the welfare of the baby, then let me go, Zafir. I would never deny your rights."

"No," he said, his voice raised enough to reverberate around them. "Get this into your mind, Lauren, for once and for all. I will never let a child of mine grow up without knowing me," he said, "nor will I agree to be a stranger who lives a million miles away."

She slackened against the wall. "Then we have a problem."

"I do not see one."

Her stomach tightened into a knot. He was too calm, too sure of his own mind, which sent panic rippling along her nerves. "I live in New York, you live here. I'd call that a *major* problem."

"Your life in New York is over."

His will was like an immovable, invisible wall. And still, she tried to bang away at it, because the alternative was unthinkable. "You can't dictate what my life is, force me to turn it upside down. I'm not one of your minions."

His gaze became hard, his tone relentlessly resolute. "If you want to be a mother to my child, you do it in Behraat."

"You've got to be..." But no, he was not joking. Lauren's gut knotted so hard she couldn't speak for a few seconds. "I don't see you prepared to give up anything. How about it, Zafir?"

He smiled, the bitterness in it sharp enough to cut her.

She could see the axis of her world tilting, every preconception she'd ever harbored about Zafir crushed by the autocratic man in front of her. There was nothing civil or kind about him anymore.

There was nothing but a chilling frost.

"Can you give the baby the best care by yourself in New York, living in that little dingy studio while working night shifts six days a week? You have no family to help and your friends...other single women who work just as hard as you do.

"Who will watch the baby while you work round-the-clock shifts? Who will help you when you walk in the door barely able to stand on your own feet?"

His words rang with logic, piercing holes in her plans, shredding her armor to pieces. "And if I don't agree?"

He shrugged and she fisted her hands, filled with the urge to hit him, to do anything to shake that cold mask so strong that it frightened her. "Then you will be free to leave Behraat once you give birth, to your hassle-free life."

His gaze moved to her midriff, and she hugged herself tighter. "My child will have everything it requires except a mother. And who knows? It's even possible that it might be better off without its deceitful mother. What is the guarantee that you will be a good one?"

Her shoulders shook, bile rose through her. She swallowed to push it back, to hold back the scream clawing its way up her throat. And yet, he stood there, staring at her, no concern or any other emotion in those golden eyes, the true man behind the stranger she'd known in New York. "You're doing this to punish me."

"You decided to leave without giving me a choice, but I'm generous. It's your choice whether you want to be a part of the baby's life."

"That's not a choice, that's an ultimatum."

"No, Lauren. My decision would have been the same had you come to me." There was a resigned finality to his tone. "Our child would have had two parents who respected each other, trusted each other. You would have had a say in the child's future. Now, you're only a glorified babysitter. I will never again trust you.

"How I intend to punish you…"

That voice became molten honey, naked hunger dancing in his gaze as it slowly flitted to her mouth. To her eternal shame, she felt it like an incinerating spark all across her skin.

No, God, no, she screamed inside her head, struggling to control her skittered breath, her tightening cheeks. *Hate him, resist him*, she begged of herself.

If her body was ever going to let go of the strange hold he had on it, it would be this moment.

Instead, amid the growing panic and helplessness that surged within her, heat and need vied viciously for space. So she latched on to the one thing that perversely grounded her. "You despise me, I see it shining in your eyes."

He tilted that powerful frame forward and the tips of her breasts grazed his hard chest. Need knotted her nipples and she whimpered. Half entreaty, half retreat. "I can see the loathing for me in your eyes, too." His hoarse voice caressed the rim of her ear. "But if I run my hand over—"

She slammed her palm over his mouth and then he was

whispering into her skin, his words a searing promise. “This time, I’m going to take what I want, Lauren.”

Self-loathing lent her courage she wouldn’t have had otherwise. “An experienced, disposable mistress on the side while you take a biddable, virginal wife and spawn heirs for your great country?”

He laughed, the tendons in his neck stretching with the movement. But something moved in the glittering depths of his eyes. Loathing? Fear? “That would complete your picture of me as a monster and justify your own appalling actions, yes?”

“I won’t be willing this time, Zafir.”

His hand curling around her nape, he pulled her closer. Languorous heat exploded as he whispered the words at the corner of her mouth. “I shall ensure you surrender that very will and I shall enjoy taking it from you.”

A soundless scream left her mouth, a sliver snaking down Lauren’s spine. Even then, instead of protest, she said “And then?”

“And then, it’s only a matter of time before the fire between us burns out.” Resignation danced in his gaze as he stepped back from her. “You will be one of the ex-mistresses of the Sheikh of Behraat, languishing somewhere in the palace and the woman who bore his first child.”

For days after he had left Lauren at the airstrip—barely containing his ragged temper, because he was sure, for all his threats, he would have despised himself for the rest of his life if he had taken her right there while he turned into exactly the monster she thought him to be—he hadn’t been able to concentrate on any of the numerous tasks awaiting his attention.

“It is yours, Zafir.”

Much as he despised what she had intended, he didn’t need a DNA test to know she spoke truth.

Once he had acknowledged that beneath his simmering anger came the realization that ate away at him—mind and heart and soul.

His child would be a bastard, just like him, if he didn't marry her.

His child would question his place in society, in the royal hierarchy, would know that keening gnawing of rejection, just like Zafir had known for years.

At his desk, he opened the file Farrah had given him that morning and looked at the pregnancy report.

Lauren would hate it, he knew instinctively, to be tied to him. She would hate a life of traditions and customs, hate the curbed freedom in the spotlight and personal sacrifices. The depth of her pain about her childhood had been a revelation in so many ways.

She would hate to bend to his will in and out of the bedroom, taking a third or fourth or tenth place in his life, to limit herself to the narrow confines of being his wife, the mother of his children.

Because Lauren demanded just as fiercely as she gave, something he should have realized long ago.

What stunned him to the depth of his core was how perversely amenable he was to the idea of making her his wife, of conquering that infuriatingly strong will of hers, of reveling in her thrilling sexuality night after night, of having someone in his life whose passions and strength and will ran as deep as his.

But he was not just Zafir.

He was Zafir Al Masood.

With the High Council still bitter about his rule and the perceived instability of the royal house in the minds of his people, Lauren was the last woman he could marry, the worst choice for his sheikha.

Which meant his child would be born out of wedlock

and face everything it ensued. Just as he had because his mother had been his father's mistress.

With a growl that ripped out of him, he grabbed the priceless, gold-embossed seal of generations of Al Masoods and threw it at the wall.

The weight of Behraat pressed at him from all sides. For a man who was supposed to be powerful, at that moment he felt anything but.

His life was not his own. It had never been.

CHAPTER SIX

LAUREN DIDN'T SEE Zafir again over the next three weeks.

Only a hazy recollection remained of how she had arrived at the palace again.

His ruthless words, the press of those hard thighs against hers, the caressing heat of his words against her skin...*that* she remembered with a vivid intensity and with an alarming frequency.

Maybe if she had something to do other than being his pampered, very pregnant captive. Even her leave of absence at the clinic had been handled with super efficiency at the request of the sheikh's administrative office.

She had never been so well looked after, not even when she had been a child.

There was a woman whose primary duty was to help her bathe—a fact she had learned when *said woman* had walked into the bath one day while Lauren was lounging in the tub, after which Lauren never forgot to lock the door behind her—a personal chef and a nutritionist who stopped by every morning asking after her appetite, a yoga instructor—which Farrah had informed her had been difficult to find, but Zafir remembered that she did yoga—and then, there was Farrah checking on her every evening, though she always seemed exhausted.

And even with the very minimal understanding she was trying to gain of Arabic—because her child was going to be half Arab—she grasped one thing.

They all knew that she was carrying the child of the High Sheikh of Behraat. The numerous staff that waited on her hand and foot was perfectly courteous, but she saw the curiosity in their eyes. Caught the word *Nikah* bandied about.

When she'd realized it meant wedding, which painted an image of Zafir with a young, biddable bride, it felt as if her heart would be ripped out of her chest. Until she realized what the staff *was* speculating about.

Lauren was carrying the sheikh's child but there was to be no wedding. Because, *of course,* a Westerner like her could never be a proper sheikha. She was only suitable for one thing.

"This time, I will take what I want."

Those words haunted her in the pitch-dark of the night when she lay in her luxurious bed, restless in her overheated skin. When she couldn't lie to herself anymore. When she admitted that, if he came to her, if his powerfully naked body joined her on the cool sheets, that compelling gaze captivating hers, she would beg him for his wicked words, his rough hands, his utter possession.

But the glimpse of pain before he had become cruelly cold again—it haunted her, made her curious about him.

Her only source, however, was Farrah, who had begrudgingly begun uttering monosyllabic responses to Lauren's questions, a vast improvement over the glares and silent nods of the past two weeks.

Lauren took the bull by the horns as Farrah checked her pulse. "How long will you be angry with me?"

Farrah sighed, her forehead creased in a delicate frown. "It was your decision to make. But I failed Zafir. I've known him all my life, I know what he..." She studied Lauren, weighing her words. "But I've never seen him like this. The palace staff are afraid to look him in the eye, some won't even enter the same room. Even Arif finds Zafir hard to handle nowadays, I hear."

Lauren felt a perverse satisfaction at the thought of upsetting Zafir's old mentor. It was Arif who had discovered the truth of her pregnancy. With hindsight, she resented him less for telling the truth and more for knowing her private affairs. "Good. Everyone is learning what a jerk your sheikh is."

She thought Farrah would explode at her, instead, a grin split her mouth, and relief shuddered through Lauren. Farrah had come to mean so much to her already and not because she was the only one who spoke her mind. "You should talk to him, get to know him. It might relieve the tension between you two, and the staff, too."

"How?" The word rang around them with all her frustration packed into it. "How will I ask him anything if he doesn't even see me? For all his proclamations about wanting the best for the baby, he hasn't inquired once."

"I report to him every night, with orders to contact him immediately if you even feel a twinge of discomfort."

Okay, so he was keeping tabs on her. "Can you help me convince the guards to escort me to his suite?"

Even before she completed the sentence, Farrah shook her head. "That's forbidden and…scandalous."

"Because there's no scandal surrounding me already?" she said, unable to staunch the bitterness that crept into her words. "Because all of Behraat hasn't already decided that I'm the sheikh's Western plaything?"

Except he hadn't *played* with her, despite the threats he had made. God, how much more twisted and perverse could she get about him?

The tightening of Farrah's mouth was enough to confirm Lauren's suspicions. "No one who has seen Zafir with you would assume anything, but…" Sighing, Farrah looked at her. "The Zafir I know would never take away a woman's freedom. If you'd known Tariq, you would see how different Zafir is, especially, when it comes to women."

But only she'd hidden an important truth from him.

Lauren slid down into the velvet recliner. Little niggles of doubt shaking her will lose.

Had she fallen into the very trap she had been intent on avoiding? Put herself first and not her child? Had she reacted only out of hurt and jealousy?

Had Zafir been right, after all?

Burying her head in her hands, she groaned. It had been wrong to take away his right to know.

She had to apologize, make him understand she had never meant to cut him out of the child's life. She had to swallow her insecurities, move past her vulnerability when it came to him.

And accept that Zafir wanted to be a part of her child's life. Much as she wished she never had to lay eyes on him ever again.

That evening, Lauren felt refreshed after a brisk walk in the lush private gardens, sealed off from the outer world by an eight-foot red brick wall.

Two guards always flanked her, even over the little distance she went. And she didn't believe it was for protection as Farrah had tried to convince her, as if Lauren was of value to anyone.

More like surveillance, because His Royal Highness didn't trust her.

She entered the sitting area and stilled.

Zafir was lounging on the velvet-lined couch, his head tilted back and his eyes closed.

She pulled the tall twin doors that weighed a ton with a vicious tug, intending to slam them but holding on to her frustration took more than she had.

Her heart beating noticeably faster at his mere presence, she studied him greedily. The setting sun behind him cast an orange glow that lovingly caressed the angles and planes of his face. His long legs sprawled out carelessly in front of him drawing her attention to the sinewy strength of his thighs. A white dress shirt, with gold cuff links and unbuttoned halfway emphasized that raw masculinity of his arms. The leanly muscled expanse of bronzed chest underneath sent tingles to places she'd rather not think about in his presence.

The more she saw Zafir in his natural element, the more she couldn't believe that he'd been attracted to her in the first place.

She wasn't plain-looking, she admitted that much. But he…he was magnificently masculine, starkly sensual, like the harshly beautiful elements of the very desert had come together to mold him. Even in that dormant state, a pulse of energy radiated from him.

"Are you quite done with your perusal, *habeebti*?"

Husky, low, his voice touched her skin like a charge of electricity. To occupy her hands, she unwound the silk scarf she had wrapped around her neck.

"I've been rendered mute that you remember my existence."

Her hands not quite steady, she poured herself a glass of water.

The water slid down her throat coolly. She pressed the glass to her face and groaned, hoping he would put down the heat in her cheeks to the weather.

His gaze flew open and traveled over her with a thorough possessiveness that wound her up even tighter. Hands clasped behind his head, the action pulling his shirt tighter across his chest, the dark shadow of his skin was a visual feast.

"Farrah was right, you did miss me. If I had known you were so *hungry* for the sight of me, I would have come sooner."

Her mouth fell open and she just stared, unable to even mumble a token retort. Even seething with the knowledge that he was turning her life upside down, she was starved for the sight of him.

She walked around the couch to the opposite side, needing the distance between them. Extremely conscious, she tugged the flimsy edge of her sheer yellow cotton blouse.

Which was absolutely the wrong thing to do, because his smoldering gaze moved slowly over her mouth to her throat and her chest.

He tilted forward suddenly with a contained violence. She jerked back instantly and the back of her knees hit the couch. "What are you walking around in?"

She remained resolutely mute.

"No snarky response?" he goaded, and she had a feeling he was looking for a fight. Or something else, a voice whispered, stretching her nerves unbearably tight. For all his smooth tone, there was an edge of something darker at play.

"I…was too hot," she replied softly, striving to rid her voice of that mutinous tone. "The guards, they barely look at me, much as they're equally fascinated and disgusted by what I represent within these palace walls."

He leveled a look of pure disbelief at her. But she would behave like an adult if it killed her, she decided. "All of Behraat is fascinated with you right now, and plotting about how best to use you to damage me."

"Am I in danger then?"

Hard and unrelenting, his gaze held hers. "Yes. But the only kind that would actually get to you is from me."

"Even my love for this baby won't make it tolerable to be confined to these palace walls for the rest of my life, Zafir. I need—"

"I don't have any other role for you." *Which is why I walked out*, his unsaid explanation fluttered in the silence between them.

There it was, the answer to the question that had plagued her since he had locked her up.

"I'm not asking for one." Throat thick with something she couldn't even name, she looked at her hands. "I wasn't supposed to be in Behraat, I wasn't supposed to know your real identity and I definitely wasn't supposed to get pregnant, was I?"

"No, you were not." The statement was matter-of-fact, no bitterness, no regret, no blame. She wished she had his flair for that acceptance.

"I had control over this attraction when you devoured me with those big eyes on that night in the ER. Or that minute the next morning when I kissed you at the end of your shift. Or the next night when I returned to your apartment after I dropped off Huma and you opened the door and invited me in. Or when I, even knowing what awaited me, came back to you again and again. Not now."

"Easy for you to accept it, because nothing changes in your life."

"Believe that if it helps you hate me." His head fell back against the couch, and his eyes closed again. "Don't drive that fruit knife into me while I rest. It will plunge Behraat into chaos."

"I'll control my murderous urges for now," she quipped, noting the blue shadows under his eyes, the gaunt look to his features.

He was king of the palace and he wanted to rest here?

Sighing, she uncoiled her legs to move away from him.

Instantly, his hand shot out and clasped her wrist. Streaks of heat from his thumb on her veins. "No, stay.

"I like having you next to me, your heart beating rapidly, your nerves stretched to the hilt, your head saying no and your body saying yes, while you wonder whether I will touch you or not, kiss you or not. Whether this will be the day when you surrender your will to me.

"It relaxes me, unlike the myriad delights the palace offers."

A gasp escaped her, half outraged, half laughing. "You're a sadist."

"Hmm."

She settled back against the chaise, her hand trapped still in his.

"Maybe keeping a *helpless, pregnant woman captive—*" A bark of disbelieving laughter escaped him and it was a dart shot straight to her heart "—is haunting you at night and you can't sleep?" Her hand reached out to push a lock of hair from his forehead.

Only when she saw her pale fingers against the backdrop of that high forehead did she realize what she was doing. Snatching it back, she fisted it in her lap. "You look awful." And because she couldn't bear for him to think she was concerned, she added, "Is the world not bowing and scraping enough to Your Highness?"

Uncomfortable silence lingered as he slowly opened his eyes. Studied her. She saw him hesitate and then sigh. A wealth of emotion reverberated in that soft exhale. "It's more likely due to a couple of nights spent by my comatose father's bed because the doctors think he might have moved a finger."

Lauren finally identified the emotion radiating from him.

Grief.

He was grieving and he'd come to her. Somehow, Lauren couldn't stop thinking they were connected, couldn't stop her mind from jumping to a thousand different conclusions. Curiosity trampled her every effort to keep him at a distance, shattered the safety net of her hatred.

"Every couple of weeks, I'm told that consciousness is within his grasp. So I wait by his bedside to tell him that my brother, his firstborn, is dead, so that I can push him that last step to his death, and put both of us out of our misery."

The pain in his voice gutted Lauren, the resignation in it so unlike the man she knew.

"I'm the man who ordered the death of his brother so that he can rule Behraat."

Those words slammed into her. How easily she had buried her head in her own fears and insecurities, how egotistic to believe that she was the center of his world?

His father was in a coma, his brother recently dead…to take up the rule of Behraat in such a volatile climate, she couldn't imagine what he was going through.

"I'm sorry for your loss."

"Hmm?" he said absentmindedly, his gaze lingering on her neck. She fought to sit still under the scrutiny.

"If his chopper hadn't been caught in that desert sandstorm and led to his death, Tariq would have been captured and…executed. Under my order.

"If he were here, I would pick up a gun and shoot him again for what he did to Behraat, for what he did to…" He flexed his fingers as though he could feel the gun in his hand. "Do you still feel sorry for me?"

Guilt and grief reverberated in each word he spoke. She held on to his gaze steadily while her insides quivered. He didn't want her sympathy, in fact, his words were tinged with warning.

She ran a hand over her tummy, more to distract him than to calm herself. "I'm actually wondering how I'd explain all this family history to the baby without sounding like we're a couple of nutcases, y'know? Murdering father, untrustworthy mother…"

A light came on in those golden eyes, chasing away the shadows. His grin tugged at her. "We have annihilated any chance of normality the poor child had, yes?"

She laughed, the tightness in her chest loosening. They could hate each other all they wanted, but they shared a bond through this child. And it filled her with immense joy and sadness. "Definitely. But then normal is overrated, don't you think?"

She loved it when she could laugh with him like this, when she could bring that warm light to his eyes.

"Is there anything I can do to help, Zafir?"

That gaze, amused and fiery, jerked to hers and she instantly wanted to snatch her words back. He turned his neck this way and that. "Work those magical fingers over my neck."

The last time she had touched him for that so-called massage… *Casablanca* had been forgotten, their pizza had gotten cold…

The same knowledge glittered in his languorous gaze, stoked over her, a whisper of sinful promises and sensual delights. She ran a hand over her neck, feeling wound up pretty tight.

"Find yourself a damn masseuse, Zafir. Isn't Behraat crawling with women ready to serve His Royal Highness?"

He grinned. His uncut hair falling over his forehead, he looked like a carefree rogue. But he wasn't. The more she learned of him, the more she realized that New York had been a taste of the forbidden for both her and him.

"I did have two proposals of marriage this past week from the fathers of two beautiful, young, traditional Behraati girls. Every man's dream."

And just like that, any goodwill she had cultivated vanished, the very thought of Zafir with his bride scouring her in a place she desperately wanted to erase.

She leveled a breezy smile at him while she felt brittle inside. "They sound perfect for you, Zafir.

"Women ready to do your bidding without a word of protest, ready to please you in bed when you want to get laid, willing to fade into the background when you forget their existence," she said bitchily, offering up a silent apology to the women in question, "why not take one of them up on their offer and let me be?"

He was next to her in two seconds, his rock-hard thigh wedged sinfully against hers.

She strove to hold herself still, but with his hand behind her, she had nowhere to go on the couch.

He pushed a lock of hair from her forehead, the simple touch evoking a fierce need within her. His breath caressed her lips, the scent of him, rich musk breathing under exotic sandalwood, drugged the very air she breathed.

"It would make life easy for me. But I don't want any of them." His hands kneaded the stiff muscles in her shoulders turning them into liquid mush. "I want you, the one I shouldn't want. The High Council fears it right, I think."

"What do they fear?"

"That somehow you have bewitched me."

She closed her eyes to shut out the image of him, digging deep within herself to find the strength to fight. There was none.

Only memories lingered, memories that shifted and shaped themselves into coherence now. As though she needed to look through this lens to understand the full significance of her relationship with Zafir.

She caught his hand with hers, intending to push him away, instead, he linked his fingers with hers, the little hairs on his forearm rubbing against hers.

Her gaze drifted downward to the bulge in his trousers and she was on instant, incinerating fire. "You ignored me for three weeks. You're stressed again now and you want sex. Just like in New York." There it was, the common denominator. "So you decided to pay me a visit. Like I was a hooker who knows your special needs. Like you were a junkie and I your fix."

A growl fell from his mouth. "You're determined to cheapen yourself, aren't you?"

She shrugged. "Calling it like I see it."

Gripping her arms, he forced her to look at him. "Yes, every time, I received news about another atrocity committed by Tariq, every time I felt rage run feral in my veins, every time I thought I would die a little more inside if I didn't seize Behraat from him, every time I thought I wouldn't see my father again… I came to you…

"I came to you and I lost myself in you until my sanity was back, until I had control over myself again, until that powerless rage cleared.

"But it was not cheap."

Hoarse and powerful, his words demolished her fragile defenses in one fell swoop. "Zafir," she protested, sinking sinuously deep into his spell.

One long finger traced the seam of her lower lip, pressed it, sending fresh shivers spewing into her skin. He lifted her toward him until she sat astride him. The soft silk of his trousers or her cotton leggings were no barrier to the hard length of his arousal fitting so perfectly against her core.

She was like putty in his arms, her will nonexistent.

A whimper wrenched from her and he caught it with his mouth, his lean frame shuddering around her.

If he had used that honed body to seduce her, if he had used those skillful hands to wrench her response, she would have resisted him, somehow. But instead, his gaze blazing with such depth of hunger, he pulled her down to meet his mouth.

Jagged and desperate, his words were a lash against her senses. "Do not deny us this, Lauren…"

It was the closest he'd ever come to saying please and the most *she would ever amount* to in his life.

She turned away at the last second, need and agony twisted together into a rope that bound her to him.

He dragged his mouth against her throat, open and

searing, infusing her skin with delirious need, whispering words she couldn't understand. Sharp, spiraling pleasure forked through her lower belly.

Ripped of even a semblance of sanity or control, she moved up over him in an age-old instinct, rubbing the crease of her aching core against his hardness. One large hand stayed on her hip, kneading possessively while the other cupped her breast.

Wet heat from his roving mouth branded the skin at her neck, her nipple tightening boldly against his palm.

Shivering and shaking, she sank her fingers into his hair, draped herself over him like a clinging vine.

"Too long, I've needed this for too long, *habeebti…*"

Then he was whispering words of reverent praise into the valley of her breasts, his hands running over her arms in soothing strokes as if she was a filly he had to calm and then he was sinking his hands under her blouse, and his big, rough palm came to rest on her not-so-flat-anymore midriff…

And the world froze. Their gazes collided while their breaths huffed noisily around them.

Heavy and abrasive, the weight of his palm scorched her. "Your body is…" he sounded stunned as his gaze ate her up "…different already?"

Lauren jerked back so hard that she fell out of his lap, onto the floor. The edge of the coffee table hit the back of her head and she gasped as pain thudded through the back of her head and to the front.

And then she was scrambling away from him, so afraid that he would catch her, so afraid that she had no defense left. So afraid that he would want no more from her than sex, that he would never give more of himself to her, that one day, he would be done with her and walk away.

And to wonder why he had, it would become the vicious cycle of her life.

But there had been such longing in his gaze when he had gentled his hand on her abdomen, such a deep hunger in that unguarded moment.

It was like handing her a grenade in the middle of a war.

If she had to admit defeat, if she had to give in, she would make sure he paid a price, too.

Yes, something inside her roared.

Make him pay for your surrender.

His obsession with her was becoming dangerous, Zafir realized as he panted hard. The scent of her swirled around him like a net, ensnaring his senses, obliterating rationality.

Swollen and pink, her mouth was tempting enough to give his soul over. Her breasts fell and rose fast, her lithe body bristling with emotion.

She looked like a wild deer, cornered but defiant.

All he'd wanted was to bury himself in her willing body, escape the relentless fury, the powerless grief that continued to ravage him as he sat by his father.

All he'd wanted while the politics and power plays continued around him was her. Only this sensuous creature that pierced the loneliness, the only one who had seen the real him. And wanted him.

"Come back here, Lauren," he said smoothly. "I want to confirm you're not hurt," he said, gritting his jaw when she stepped back again.

Something chased across her angular face. Not need, not fear, but challenge.

He felt like the wild thing in her eyes had electrocuted him.

"You don't have to chase me, Your Highness," she said while she grabbed the small opening of her blouse with both hands. The rip of the thin cotton was like a tribal drum in the silence. "I surrender," she said so softly and yet in a voice that carved through him.

The edges of her blouse fell away, exposing the curves of her plump breasts cupped in white silk, the dainty dip of her waist, flaring into hips he had anchored himself on so many times. The shadow of her dark nipples was barely hidden by the silk. Color streaked her cheeks, and her neck.

Slowly, he brought his gaze to her face, something in her stance dousing cold water on his need.

"You win," she declared, and his ire rose slowly.

He didn't want her like this, like spoils of a war he'd won. "What the hell are you talking about?" he said cornering her.

But this time, she didn't step back. Stubborn chin held high, she stood her ground.

She pushed the blouse off her shoulders and reached for the hem of her skirt. "Should I shower and ready myself for you or do you need instant gratification? You want to have me here or on the bed?"

The breath knocked out of him as if someone had jammed a fist in his throat.

"Enough, Lauren."

"No. This is what you are turning me into. Tucked away in this palace, cut off from the world, waiting on tenterhooks, wondering if you'll see me again...wondering what my child's place is going to be in your world..."

"I would love her or him more than anything in the world." He heard the words after he spoke them, realizing the truth.

Something flashed in her gaze before she drove it away. "But you will treat his mother as if she were disposable?

"It was wrong to hide the truth from you, I admit it.

"But you...you decided, from the beginning, that this is all I'm good for. So let's do it the proper way."

She moved toward the chaise longue and pushed away the myriad of colorful pillows from it. "Do you want me to face you or the other way around? Or would you prefer me on my knees?"

He flinched. "Cover yourself."

When she stood like that brazenly, he picked up a velvet throw.

She trembled at his touch, so stiff and tensed like a stretched bow, teetering on the edge, and yet determined to fight this. Determined to fight him and herself.

Dirty, was that what this was? Was that what he had made of them?

In that moment, he fought that loneliness, that craving for her body, that yearning to lose himself in her arms, this struggle his father must have fought with himself and lost, turning his mother into a whore in the eyes of her family, her tribe and the world, turning Zafir into an orphan.

And Zafir won.

He would never become a slave to his body's needs. He would not ruin Lauren's life, the mother of his child's life, simply because he wanted something he couldn't have.

Without another glance at her, he walked away.

CHAPTER SEVEN

Bear with the prison until the baby is here, until I can ensure your safety. We will discuss it again. I will not give up on my child, however.
—Zafir

LAUREN STARED AT the careless scrawl on the softest paper printed with the seal of the Al Masood house for the thousandth time. Farrah's voice across the sitting room sounded far away as she pushed out a shaky breath.

Only one thought lingered since she'd seen him a week ago.

If she had saved herself from a fate she loathed—becoming his mistress—why did it feel as if she had lost him all over again?

At least, he was willing to reevaluate, the first sign of which had been when she'd been informed that she could visit the famous open bazaar that she'd been dying to go to since day one.

She'd stupidly assumed Zafir was coming.

Foolish Lauren.

Instead, armed with a maid and three guards, she'd set off, eager to be out of the palace.

It had been dusty, crowded, hot and a glorious sensory whir of spices and sounds, unlike anything she had ever seen.

Colorful, sprawling tents and shops set up on both sides of a long, winding street sold handwoven scarves, authentic handicrafts, antique hookahs, thick syrupy dates that Lauren had washed down with cold mint sherbet, set against the backdrop of the redbrick buildings that were centuries old.

Every step she took, she wished Zafir was there, showing her the sights, mocking her when she refused to try a new dish.

Laughing, she had haggled for five minutes over an intricately designed antique silver bracelet, aware that she was being fleeced as a foreigner.

Until the youngest and the nicest of her guards, Ahmed, had chivalrously interfered and it became obvious to the street vendor and the crowd around her that she wasn't just any tourist.

The sudden silence that had emerged amid the ruckus had been so unnerving.

She was the sheikh's mistress, an instant spectacle drawing curiosity, disgust and even pity in some generous eyes. In the blink of an eye, she'd understood why Zafir confined her to the palace.

Noticing Farrah's worried face, Lauren got up from the recliner. "What's going on?"

"There are two women going into labor right now. One family is high powered and I'll have to attend her at her house. The other one's in a village that borders the city. The other ob-gyn is out of town and her husband won't let her see male doctors."

She pulled her phone from her handbag and made another call.

"Any luck?" Lauren asked.

Farrah shook her head.

It was as simple as her next breath for Lauren. "I'll attend the other one."

Farrah's gaze flew to Lauren, relief dancing in it. Until she was shaking her head again. "Zafir would never allow it. And I can't even ask because he left this morning to visit the States. I—"

"That's absurd. We're talking about a woman who needs medical attention. Are you going to let your fear of Zafir dictate her fate? I'll take Ahmed with me and hopefully will be back tomorrow morning at the worst. Come on, Farrah. I'll lose my mind sitting here, knowing I could help."

Farrah studied her for several heart-stopping seconds. "Have you delivered before?"

"Yes."

"Fine," Farrah said with a sigh. "But please, please be careful, yes? She's had a smooth pregnancy so far, so there shouldn't be any complications." She tugged Lauren's hands into hers. "Lauren, this woman, the tribe to which she belongs to, they don't…consider themselves part of Behraat, her husband—he's been defying their rules to bring her to the clinic—"

"Doesn't mean they don't deserve medical attention."

"No, it doesn't." Farrah smiled. "Just be careful. Zafir will skin me alive if anything happens to you." But it was clear that her mind was already on the task in hand. "The moment I'm free, I'll be at the clinic."

Adrenaline spurring her into action, Lauren nodded. For the first time in so many weeks, she felt a sense of purpose.

While Farrah made another call, Lauren crammed energy bars and bottles of water, and a loose cardigan into her backpack. Then she changed into a freshly laundered white kaftan and loose cotton trousers, also in white, as it was the best fabric for the heat. She braided her hair tightly and wrapped a silk scarf loosely around her hair and neck. Catching Farrah's curious gaze, she stilled. "I don't want to draw attention to myself." She patted her hand over her not-so-flat tummy. "Do I look—?"

"Yes." Farrah answered without hesitation. "But pregnant or not, American or not, you're not average. No wonder Zafir lost his head over you."

Something in her tone tugged at Lauren.

Within minutes, they were walking out of Zafir's private quarters, through the marble-tiled corridors. A state-of-the-art elevator brought them to the underground parking lot where a man in uniform was waiting next to a rugged jeep that she only saw in *Survivor*-type shows.

Checking to see that the medical file Farrah had emailed downloaded onto her phone, she climbed into the jeep.

"No wonder he lost his head over you." She clutched Farrah's words to her heart foolishly and waited for the envoy to leave.

Zafir closed the door to his office, bone-tired after his four-day trip to the United States to discuss a new treaty regarding Behraat's oil supply to the Western nation.

His first official trip abroad and all he had heard was: stability in their region of the world, and Behraat's particular lack of it in the past three years. About all the feathers Tariq had ruffled since his father's coma.

For a blistering cowardly moment, Zafir had indulged in not returning. And just as soon discarded the fanciful notion.

He needed to pick a side in the divisive High Council, needed to pick one of their daughters they paraded like horses under his nose for his bride and be done with it.

Behraat needed it. He as the High Sheikh needed to show stability, his commitment as a ruler to both his people and the outside world.

But all he thought of was Lauren, her soft mouth and her mewling moans and her trembling body. The tears on her proud face, the regret in her expression when she had admitted that she'd been wrong…

The door to his office burst open. He bit back the scathing words that rose to his lips at the sight of Farrah, fear etched into her unlined face. Followed closely by a stone-faced Arif.

Unknown dread fisted his throat.

"Zafir," Farrah said, "Lauren…she has been kidnapped."

His chest felt as if there was a vise clamping it. "She…*what*?" he mumbled, his voice barely recognizable to his own ears. "How?"

"*She*," Arif still wouldn't utter Lauren's name, "convinced Farrah to let her help the Dahab tribe woman who went into labor just as Farrah was getting ready to attend another woman."

The mere mention of the Dahab made his heart thud.

"And?" he exploded.

"By the time I got there…" Farrah was distraught. "No one knew where Lauren was. The Dahab woman, her baby, her husband, even Ahmed, were all gone."

"When was this?"

"Three days ago."

With a growl, Zafir pushed at his chair.

The revolving chair crashed into the chest behind him, scattering the contents—a flower vase, and a framed photo of his father that fell to the rug with a soft thump.

Lauren's face swam into his vision, fear stealing his very thoughts. If something happened to her all because he had selfishly involved her in his life…

He ran a hand over his forehead, the headache that had been coming on all day crystallizing into a pounding behind his eyes.

Farrah stepped toward him, her hands clasped together in front of her. "I'm so sorry, Zafir."

But knowing Lauren's stubborn will, he couldn't blame Farrah.

"I sent a message to the Dahab in your name," Arif said, "but as usual, they have ignored any communication. The palace guard reports them traveling east into the desert."

Had they taken her because she was carrying his child? As revenge against his father?

Dahab didn't care for the ways of the outside world including Behraat.

But they had good reason to hate his family. If his father had brought shame on them, Tariq had hunted them across the desert. Every instinct clamored to order his Special Forces Air Team, to use his might to pluck Lauren from their midst.

But he couldn't.

Even if it was a huge risk to Lauren and his unborn child, he had to do it the peaceful way.

"Arrange transportation for me, alone." If he descended on them with men and weapons, the rift would only widen and become something he couldn't resolve in his lifetime. "If they harm her in any way, they'll face my wrath," he said, knowing that he would destroy everything in his path if she even had a scratch.

Lauren shot up from the worn-out divan, a sound hurling her from the hazy edges of her afternoon nap into wide-eyed alertness in the space of a breath.

The chief of the tribe had ensured her that she'd be safe with them, that no one would harm her, when they'd asked her to accompany them three days ago. But the pitch-black of the night outside the tent, the thick silence that descended when the encampment settled for the night, had unnerved Lauren.

Yet she'd learned she'd been right to trust him. Even though he had accompanied her, she hadn't seen Ahmed once they had reached the Dahab's encampment though. Nor had there had been any word from Farrah, which worried her the most.

Then she realized what had woken her up. She saw the

long shadow, clearly male, over the silk partition that curtained the room off from the rest of the tent.

She was rubbing her eyes when Zafir marched inside, his broad frame shrinking the tent. Greedy for the sight of him, she drank him in.

There were dark shadows under his eyes. His jet-black hair was rumpled in a sexy, inviting, run-your-fingers-through-me way, as if he had already done that numerous times. His white cotton shirt and light blue jeans did nothing to dampen the effect of his masculinity.

She'd barely drawn a breath when she was ensconced against a hard chest. Hands anchored on his hips, she shuddered. Rough hands moved over her back urgently, the upper curve of her bottom, her hips, her stomach…and stilled. Heart slamming hard against her rib cage, Lauren held herself still while the scent of desert and pure, intoxicating male filled her nostrils.

A soundless whimper ricocheted through her as her body adjusted against his hard muscles.

Soft pressure on her nape tilted her head up. A scowl pulled his brows together, his eyes shimmering golden with emotion she'd never glimpsed before.

Mouth groggy, belly knotted, she squeaked out his name. "Zafir?"

Seconds passed before he responded but it felt like an eternity. Tenderness flew from his fingers where he clasped her cheeks. "You look tired."

Her throat hoarse, she nodded, sinking into his embrace foolishly.

Just one minute, she told herself. Just one minute before she reminded herself why this wasn't a good idea.

But that minute was barely done before she was released.

Blinking, she looked up at him.

Hard edges, inscrutable expression, thinned mouth, everything she didn't like about him was back.

"Pack your things. We're leaving," he said dismissively, his gaze taking in her tent.

Stuffing her few things into her backpack, Lauren turned and found the tent ominously empty.

Ahmed stood outside, a paleness under his tanned skin, his gaze dutifully shied away from her.

Zafir, his gaze not leaving her, listened with his head bowed to the chief of the tribe. Lauren nodded and smiled when the new mom Salma pressed a silk scarf into her hands and hugged her.

A small crowd of women and children waved at her while men surrounded Zafir and the chief, but at a distance. But Lauren could feel the distrust and animosity that surrounded him.

Had she caused trouble for him again?

Coffee-colored dunes stretched toward the horizon in front of her while the Dahab encampments lay behind her. The same 4x4 was idling on the road.

When Ahmed, without touching her, nodded for her to move toward the vehicle, she searched for Zafir.

His thundering presence beside her robbed her words. "Do me the small courtesy of pretending I can control you, yes?" he gritted through his teeth. A low vibration raced along her lower back.

Instantly, his hold loosened. Swallowing her flippant "thank you" for his condescending tone, she nodded.

Within minutes, Zafir and she hurtled along the rough track, hugging narrow paths through the dunes.

"Aren't we returning to the city?" she asked and got a sharp "no" in answer.

Pulling her gaze away from that chiseled profile, she kept her hands in her lap.

Zafir's mind raced like the sand that flew from dune to dune shifting the very landscape of the harsh desert.

His anxiety about Lauren had lasted two minutes after he had entered the chief's tent.

Shame had his fingers tighten over the steering wheel as he remembered the chief's disbelief at Zarif's accusations.

"Your father and you have forgotten tradition, our roots, the very fabric that makes the Bedouin life."

Every word, spoken in a soft yet steely tone, was true.

To assume that they would have harmed a hair on Lauren, on any woman, pregnant or otherwise, had been pure ignorance and blind prejudice.

The tribes were known for their hospitality, their generosity to even an enemy requesting shelter, legendary.

"We give our women protection, a respectable place in life. Not keep them as prisoners or mistresses."

That statement lashed against his sense of honor.

Knowing the route to the oasis like the back of his hand, he chanced a glance at Lauren. Her head tilted back against the seat, and her eyes closed, he saw the resolute tilt of her chin, the long line of her throat, her fingers laced tightly in her lap.

Still, there was a knot in his chest, a leftover from his fear for her and the baby.

"This woman carrying your child is brave, kind, strong..." the chief had said. *"Marry her, Zafir. Make her your sheikha and we will end this enmity between the tribes and the state. We will forget what your father did to one of our daughters."*

Bringing the tribes back into the fold would be the advantage he needed. Not even the High Council could fault his power, or his reign then. For he would be fixing a fracture in the very fabric of their nation.

Behraat would be strong and one again, after three decades of being torn apart by his father's selfish and scandalous pursuit of a young, innocent woman from the tribes.

All he had to do was marry the woman carrying his

child, the woman that set fire to his blood, the woman who…

Might hate to be used as a pawn in his game for power, his conscience piped up.

It is a gift, Zafir, some devil inside his head said. *It's the one gift you have received in your hard, betrayed, duty-bound, cursed life*, it whispered.

Lauren and this child and the ability to finally unite Behraat and rule it, it was all a gift.

She had always wanted his commitment, a definition to their relationship, hadn't she?

Here it was. The biggest commitment he had ever made, except to Behraat.

He couldn't squander this gift.

Not if it would bring legitimacy to his child and his power.

CHAPTER EIGHT

THEY TRAVELED ON for what seemed like the better part of an hour. Lauren fidgeted in her seat, trying to work out a kink in her shoulder.

"Are you uncomfortable?" Came the instant question from Zafir.

"I'm fine."

The track vanished halfway through, until it seemed as if they climbed hundreds of feet up a giant ocher sand mound that offered panoramic views of the desert floor and then suddenly evened out again.

Her eyes wide, Lauren took in the landscape as the jeep came to a halt.

Miles and miles of rippled, undulating dunes rose in all four directions, the harsh beauty of it stealing her breath. Against the backdrop of the desolate sands lay a lush encampment, eons away in scale and quality from the Dahab's tents, a stark contrast to the stretching emptiness.

Tall palms behind the two curved tents formed a dense circular perimeter as far as she could see. The early evening sun streaked everything reddish orange.

It was breathtaking, tremendous, and it made her concerns seem so small.

She pulled out her cell phone. But remembered her battery had drained a few hours after she had arrived at the Dahab camp.

Hearing Zafir's tread, she turned around. "Do you have your phone?"

He looked at her outstretched hand, beating a path up

her arm, her neck and then settling on her face. Something shimmered in his eyes then. A possessive glint. A triumphant light that sent goose bumps over her skin even under the relentless heat. "It's a little late to call for help." But he pulled his phone out.

Grabbing the phone from his hand, she turned around to click a selfie with the dazzling encampment behind her. She knew she was acting a little juvenile and a lot irreverent tourist but after that glimpse of fire in his eyes and the absence of another soul around for as far as she could see, she wasn't eager to go into the tent.

"Is there no one else here?"

Something gleamed in his eyes. "The servants are trained to be not seen or heard."

Which didn't help her any. "Could you take a pic for me?"

"*A pic*?" he repeated with quiet murder in his tone.

"Yes." She placed her hands on her hips. "And no, I won't sell pictures of the Sheikh of Behraat's oasis hideaway in the desert even if I was paid a million dollars." She swiped a trickle of sweat from her forehead. "As far as I can see, there's no interrogation room here either, so come on."

With a sudden movement that made her heart crawl to her throat, he grabbed the phone from her hand, and marched to the entrance and held the flap open.

Do not poke the grumpy bear, Lauren.

She entered the tent.

A burst of rich color, deep purples and sheer violets, greeted her everywhere she looked. Brass tables set with more lanterns and tea lights, handcrafted rugs strewed around, it was a sight to behold. Two veiled areas separated away from the lounge where they stood.

One had a myriad of dishes laid out on low tables guessing by the delicious aroma wafting toward her and the other contained a low but vast bed with a million pillows of all shapes and sizes on it. Bed big enough for two. A thick fur rug lay neatly folded at the bottom while a small brass-legged washstand with a basin stood against the far corner.

Swallowing the sudden tension, she faced the silent six-foot-two-inch male staring at her. His very silence sent her nerves thrumming. "I like it. Which tent is yours?" she said with a cheer that hurt her own head.

"This."

Thud went her heart against her rib cage. "The other one's mine then?"

She moved to his side, or tried to. Viselike fingers clamped her arm and pulled her to the seating area behind them.

With precise movements that actually betrayed his ruffled temper, he poured water into a copper tumbler and handed it to her. "Drink before you expire from the heat."

She took the tumbler and drank the water without a word. Choosing the divan farthest from him, she sank onto it. The bed was soft and comfy so she tucked her legs beneath her and leaned against the tent wall.

Heart tattooing in her chest, she lifted her head and met his gaze. Before he could take the little place left next to her, she groaned and stretched her legs, tilting to the side.

Something like a curse fell from his mouth before he chose the divan perpendicular to hers. His long legs spread out before him, he sat straight unlike her. As if he suspected that she would run and he would need to pounce.

"Where do you think I'm going to run to," she said slowly.

His head jerked up, his entire frame unnaturally still. "You're the most infuriating, exhausting woman I've ever met."

Fury. Impatience. Worry. She frowned at the last.

"Are you hungry?"

She shook her head while casting her mind around to find any excuse to postpone the storm she could sense brewing between them. There was a sense of calculation, a sense of coiled energy about him, as if he was deciding what to do with her and it let loose panic in her tummy.

Looking down at her wrinkled tunic, she scrunched her nose. "I need a shower and an early night. I didn't get my turn to shower this evening before you stormed in there." She added a little sigh to that to convince him.

His eyes narrowed.

"I spent most of the last two nights by Salma's side helping her while she recuperated."

The muscles in his face relaxed, just enough to let her breathe fully. "Why you? Where were her mother and aunts?"

"Bashir's continual presence in the tent chased them off."

"Bashir?"

"Her husband. Salma lost a lot of blood and he's determined to help her with the night feedings, and changing the baby and burping her and so on... Apparently, the women in the camp thinks it's scandalous for him to be spending so much time with her when she's not up to her usual duties yet."

This time, he frowned. And she thought how cute he looked when he didn't understand something. Which was very rare. "What usual duties?"

"Really, Zafir... *Her wifely duties*," she said with an arch to her tone.

Understanding dawned in his golden gaze. He ran a hand through his hair and she wondered if he was trying not to look at her. He cleared his throat then, and Lauren knew, just knew, that he didn't want to hear any more.

So, of course, she elaborated.

"They seemed to think Bashir wanting to help his wife

when he couldn't get sex out of her was strange and shocking. Imagine that.

"Even Salma was shy at first but I convinced her that it was very important for the baby to bond with the father as well as the mother, for them as a family."

His gaze jerked to hers and held it. Challenge simmered there and her gut swooped. "What was she shy about?"

She shrugged, cursing herself inwardly for the heat rising up her neck. "I told Salma that feeding the baby in front of her husband is the most natural thing in the world and that she should be glad that she has a husband who wanted to pitch in and do the dirty work, not just strut around like a peacock and announce that his boys were good swimmers."

His long fingers pressed at his temple and then rubbed his face. But he couldn't quite hide the amusement in his eyes. "You did not say that."

"I did." The expression she'd seen on the couple's faces made her grin. "Bashir dropped a pile of baby clothes while Salma, with a blank face, said they didn't have boys. He wouldn't meet my gaze for the rest of the night. Once he left, she asked me to explain.

"When I did, she was both amazed and a little horrified, I think."

"Not all men strut around claiming that their…" A dark flush claimed his cheeks. "Whatever it is you said. I didn't strut."

"Well, you're not really the strutting kind."

"No?" His mouth twitched now. "I feel as though my machismo has been reduced. What kind am I?"

"Please. Like you don't know."

It was his turn to shrug now. "I would like to hear it in your words."

"Blatant sexuality oozes out of every pore in your body, Zafir." Warmth pooled below her skin at her own words.

"Six years of sexual drought and it took you three days. You made me feel as if I was the most attractive woman in the world. As if I was the only one to have shredded that tight control of yours. Hell of a trick that," she said, aware of how powerless her attraction to him always left her.

"It was not a trick. Whatever you felt, multiply it by ten times and you'll understand how I felt."

The divan shifted as Zafir's weight sank into it and every cell in her froze.

Golden eyes stared back at her. His elbows on his legs, he was leaning forward.

"So are you going to want help with night feedings and such when the baby comes? Is there a class we should be attending together to learn about these things?"

It was the cruelest thing he could have asked her. Like a mirage in the desert that could tempt and warp one's sense of reality. That promised to quench your unbearable thirst when there was not a drop.

He had no right to ask such things of her when they were anything but a married couple absolutely in love with each other.

Donning a smile that threatened to crack her face with its brittleness, she went for playfulness. No way would she ever betray how dismayed she felt. "There's going to be an army of maids and nannies at my command, right?" Her neck hurt at how stiffly she held herself.

She took his silence as a yes.

"Then you'll be excused. I'm sure you'll be super busy with state affairs to…" She shrugged the rest of her answer away.

The tent reverberated with something unsaid, yet Lauren didn't know what. Unless it was her brittle smile cracking into pieces.

Zafir stood to leave. Pausing at the entrance to the tent,

he looked back at her. "I will send a maid. You can wash in the oasis and rest. Is there anything you need?"

The moment she shook her head, he was gone.

Zafir heard the splash around the oasis while he walked the perimeter, like he had done since Rashid had brought him here a long time ago.

Once he had discovered his father's duplicity, he had not come here again. Loathed to mar this place with bitter reality, he realized now.

He had always felt great pride when he had visited here, pride that the High Sheikh had seen something in him to educate him alongside his son, that he trusted him, an orphan, with state affairs.

He felt no such pride today and thanks to the woman splashing in the pool, no peace either. All he needed to do was close his eyes and he could imagine her slender shoulders dipping into the cool waters, could imagine her hands pushing away that inky dark hair, could imagine her lithe legs kicking through the water.

A moment's fear stilled him at the deceptive depth of the oasis on one side. Did she know how to swim?

Cocking his head to a side, he listened but only heard the smooth swish of water and her clean strokes.

The sand shifted under him, but he pressed on, knowing the path very well. The sky was lit orange with the setting sun, but until the orange orb set, the heat would not relent.

Neither would the knot in his stomach.

He'd had the perfect moment to ensnare her earlier. There had been such desperate longing, such a raw need in her gaze before she had shied it away from him.

It was a vulnerability he had never seen in Lauren, not after that first day in the situation room. He realized he preferred her glaring at him, questioning him, rather than that shattered light in those eyes.

Because, somehow, it had made him feel responsible for her. And not just her physical well-being. He had wanted to crush her in his arms, he had wanted to tell her that he would do everything and more that Bashir had done for Salma. That he couldn't wait to see his child suckle at her breast.

Anything, he would have done anything to bring back the smile to her mouth.

And it was the very force of that need that had stayed his hand.

When he knew he couldn't have her as his wife, it was all he'd been able to think about.

And now, now that marriage to her offered him the reins of Behraat, the advantage he needed over the High Council, now he was hesitating.

Why?

He withdrew his sat phone from his jeans pocket and made a call, leaving himself no room to back out.

"Tell me how the Dahab treated you."

Lauren had just finished her dinner when Zafir came back into the tent.

One glimpse into his face told her he was serious. "I was brought meals and snacks at regular intervals, called when Salma needed attention."

"Did you agree to accompany them?"

"Yes. Salma...lost a lot of blood. Ahmed refused to leave my side so I said okay." His frown deepened and fresh anxiety trickled in to her veins. "I've been thinking about that. Didn't Farrah get their message?"

His jaw set like concrete, he shook his head. "There was no message. You vanished and there was nothing."

"Wait, why wouldn't they—" She paled. If they hadn't relayed her message, that means Farrah or Arif or Zafir hadn't known where she was. "Why wouldn't they tell you?"

"The Dahab hate me, Lauren. And what Dahab believes, the other tribes follow. They figured out who you were and brought you along to send a message to me."

Fear fisted her throat but she spoke through it. "They were nothing but courteous to me." Shaking inside, she realized why he'd been so angry back in the tent, why he had held her like that... *He'd been worried about her?*

No, she couldn't be foolish enough to think he'd been worried about her.

His unborn child was a different matter. "They hate you...why?"

"I represent their disgrace, their shame." He clutched his nape, a show of vulnerability she didn't think he was aware of. "My mother was from this very tribe. She defied their rules and lived with my father while he was married, became his mistress and bore me out of wedlock. Which turned all the tribes against the state.

"I spent the first twenty years of my life thinking I was a mutt the sheikh took pity on. Suddenly, Crown Prince Tariq, who had been my friend for as long as I could remember, hated the very sight of me."

"He'd discovered the truth?" she added, her chest aching. He sounded matter-of-fact yet she knew the scars were bone deep.

"Yes. But it took my brother's abuse of power, utter ruin of tradition and duty that finally forced the sheikh's hand." Bitterness carved lines into his beautiful face.

"Rashid, the sheikh, very cleverly, reared me into a faithful, dutiful pawn of his and there I was, to the shock of the nation, the new heir, blood of my father."

"Then why were you in New York?" She understood the truth the moment she asked. Finally understood his anguished wait.

"Because Tariq didn't like all the power being snatched away from him. He put Rashid in a coma, bought off half the High Council and exiled me under penalty of death. Attacked the Dahab again and again, making their very mode of life untenable. Threw the nation into civil war and riots.

"I was waiting for the right moment to take back control of the city."

"Your mother…did you know her?"

He shrugged, a hardness that she hated settling into those angles. His answer when it came sent a painful exhale through her, so unexpected it was. "I don't remember her, if I ever knew her. Apparently, she was weakened after I was born and died soon after.

"The Dahab didn't want me and my father, for reasons of his own, had Arif put it out that I was an orphan he picked up off the streets.

"And you…" He uttered something raw in Arabic. "You got in the middle of it all."

"All I did was…" Lauren searched for the right words, "do my duty. I might not be the ruler of a nation, but I owe it to anyone who needs medical attention."

The words came automatically, as the horrific reality of her actions dawned on her. He hadn't known his *mother or father* growing up and she had hidden the knowledge of his child from him.

Suddenly, Lauren could see beneath the power and duty that he wore like a second skin, to the loneliness, the dark anger, the self-imposed isolation around him. And the hard man he had become to overcome everything his childhood had imposed on him.

Would he ever forgive her?

She'd betrayed him at the deepest level with her ignorant actions. And that guilt made her raw, defensive, unbalanced. "How would I know, Zafir? How would I know what I'm stepping into if you treat me like a prisoner, a mistress, and *now a brood horse*? Unless you accept that I have a role in your life, as much as you'd like to put me in a box and lock me there?"

His gaze stayed on her, thoughtful, almost open.

She pressed on, feeling as if she was taking a step into some unknown, without seeing a way forward.

Her relationship with her parents had always been transactions. If Lauren was a good girl for the summer at her aunt's, they would let her visit them in Morocco. If Lauren got good grades, then she could spend Christmas break with them in Paris.

Even the friends she'd made at the hospital, she'd always kept them at a wary distance, afraid of letting anyone close. But now…one of them had to take that first step. One of them had to clean the slate and start over.

"Can we try to be friends, Zafir? For the sake of our child?"

Silence beat in tune with the thud of her heart.

Slow amusement dawned in those golden depths, sending her system into stunned shock. One tip of that sensuous mouth tipped up, carving a crease in his cheek. "Brood horse, Lauren?"

A strange sound—a combination of a horrified squeak and an outraged gasp fell from her lips. "That's what you get out of the whole speech I just gave you?"

"So do we have a *breeding program* in place after you deliver this one?"

"You did not just call…you've gone mad," she flushed as he folded his hands in exaggerated patience, his mouth twitching. "A breeding program? Really?"

His jaw was rough with stubble, there was tiredness in the lines of his face. All she wanted to do was wrap her arms around him, to tell him that she understood him a little better now, that she understood the pain he hid so very well. But he wouldn't welcome her sympathy or her gesture of affection.

All he'd ever wanted, could ever want, from her was only one thing.

"If you're the brood horse, that makes me what? Your stud?"

The twitch of his mouth was infectious, the light in his eyes irresistible. "My very own Arabian stallion?" she said. He raised a brow in that infuriating way that he did.

His mouth finally curved into a full, breathtaking smile while her nerves thrummed at the sudden change in his demeanor. She understood why he had been worried and angry even, but now he was joking…

No, he was flirting with her. How? Why? Was he seducing her with that smile and those awful puns?

"I asked for that, yes?"

She exhaled long. "I seem to cause you—"

"I understand why you jumped in to help this time," he said, cutting her off. "I'm also willing to accept that you made an ill-informed and wrong decision with the right intentions. But you have to promise me that you won't take any more unnecessary risks."

Her ire rose at his autocratic tone. But since her new motto was to set aside her needs and insecurities for the sake of her unborn child, she said, "Anything else that Your Highness is willing to cede?"

"Behraat's political clime is changing. If I curb your freedom, it's because your safety—" He raised a hand when she opened her mouth, and continued, "and not just because you carry my child, is important to me. I would not have you hurt in any way, Lauren. Ever."

She folded her hands, willing her heart to stop racing. Never had she heard that raw emotion in his tone, never had such simple words held such sway over her. "Is your offer to reevaluate our situation after the baby's here still valid?"

"There will be no need."

Shaking her head, she glared at him. "You promised."

"Come here," he said in a curiously flat, nonthreatening tone.

He meant to touch her. That intent in his gaze was like a tug at her senses that she found herself swaying to the balls of her feet. "No."

Something hot and needy detonated in his gaze. And it took everything she had to not scuttle away like cornered prey.

He took one step toward her and she instantly sidestepped. "I think you have a subconscious fantasy of me chasing and capturing you, Lauren."

Heat tightened her cheeks. Being chased by Zafir, being wanted by him, needed by him…it was a crazy fantasy she'd already indulged in, all right. That messed with her head far too often. "Zafir, I…" She faced him, ignoring her racing pulse. "I don't want to fight with you."

Another step closer. "No, *habeebti*, we won't fight."

"I don't want you to touch me either. There's only so many times I can pull the 'do what you will with me' routine."

Something almost like amusement glinted deep in his eyes. "All I said was to come closer. I'd like to see the changes my child is making in your body," he said in an exaggeratedly patient voice.

"And then, we can talk? Like adults," she rushed over her words as he loomed over her, "adults who're going to share a huge, life-changing responsibility," his hands covered hers and tugged her, their legs banging each other before he steadied her, his scent luring her in, as she continued speaking, "who both want the best for their child and…" soundless pants fell from her mouth as his hot gaze seared wherever it fell, "who would never, *ever*, force their child to pick sides."

And then she was shaking from holding herself back and his hands moved down her shoulders gently, whispering something in his native language, something tender. Oh, how she wished she could understand the words falling from his lips before he gathered her to him, his palm resting at the base of her back.

Warmth uncoiled in her lower belly.

Finally, after what seemed like a lifetime of waiting on the edge of a knife, one hand moved to her hip and the other to her abdomen.

His chin dropped to her forehead, her heart thumping so loud in her ears. She hid her face in his chest, felt the beat of his heart under her cheek. A harsh breath fell out of his lips and she felt his powerful frame shudder all around her while his palm moved softly. "This is the most precious thing I've ever experienced in my life," he finally said in a hushed, husky tone that sent shivers down her spine.

At least, that was not a lie, Zafir thought, his heart bursting with emotion.

"Please, Zafir, let me go," came Lauren's hoarse whisper. "I can't… I can't breathe."

A muscle jumped in his cheek as he looked down at her, but he leashed the possessive need that flared through him.

She looked tired and sleepy, her wild hair only half-dry. He wanted to burrow deep under her skin and never emerge.

"Dealing with you is like trying to contain a sandstorm."

"I'll not say or be sorry for upsetting your life. Not when—"

"Not when the result is this baby, yes?"

His hand moved up her back, traced the line of her shoulders, settled at her nape in a possessive hold.

Now that she was going to be his, he realized he couldn't

contain his excitement. And not because of the languorous desire that hummed through his veins. But for the first time in his life, he felt something different, something tender and yet equally disconcerting.

"You love the baby so much already?"

"Yes." Her hands tightened around his middle. And he swallowed the tight fist in his throat. "More than I've ever loved anyone."

Stark and beautiful like the desert, the truth of her words resonated around him, filling him with a joy like no other. "I apologize for my harsh words to you."

He heard her breath catch, and then even out. She knew what he was talking about.

He would give her everything he possibly could, he decided in that instant. For everything he couldn't, didn't know, how to give.

Finally, the stiffness in her shoulders eased and he could feel her relaxing against him. The brush of her slight belly against his abdomen sent his breath hurtling through his throat. "I'll forgive you if you forgive me."

"Already done."

"Zafir, whatever the future—"

"Become my wife, Lauren."

Shock propelled Lauren out of his arms. "You're..."

Joking...she'd been about to say but the word disappeared as she looked at him.

Without a hint of shadow, his gaze gleamed golden. Every line of his face said he'd made up his mind.

He wanted to marry her. God, he would be her husband...

The very word felt strangely exciting in her mind, so possessive, and so irrevocably final. For she knew in her very bones that Zafir didn't make the decision lightly.

Shivers spewed in her muscles. And they were as much out of excitement as they were out of fear.

"I would not joke. My anger from the past clouded my judgment until now."

"Because you don't want the same fate as you suffered for our child?" Of course, that's why.

Clasping her hand with his, he pulled her close. "That's what made me think of marriage, yes. But it was just the spark that ignited it. It is right for us in so many ways.

"If I had acknowledged my disturbing propensity to forget all rationale and judgment when it comes to you, I'd have realized where this was heading long ago."

Her heart threatened to shove out of her chest, so hard and loud it thumped. She didn't need love. She herself barely knew it. But that he would make this commitment to her, it made her blood pound in her veins. "Somehow, I don't think it's a compliment to be associated with low judgment."

"That is all you will get out of me," he quipped and her mouth went dry.

"What about Behraat? About me being an American and not fitting in your world... What about all that virgin bride stuff and alliances that will bring..."

What about you and me, the question came unbidden to her lips.

But there was no *just them*, she told herself.

Those two months in New York, that had been stolen time.

Until it had changed both their lives forever.

Clasping her hand tight in his, Zafir said, "You pay too much attention to the palace gossip, Lauren. I thought you above that kind of thing." Her pulse raced under his thumb. "Have you ever heard any of that from my mouth?" When she shook her head, he nodded. "The Sheikha cannot be susceptible to rumors for there will be many who'll want to sway you to their side," he said, arrogant confidence dripping from his pores. "In any case, I will train you in our ways."

She scrunched her nose at him. "I'm not a pet to be sent off to training. Nothing will make me into the kind of wife or the woman Behraat will expect me to be, Zafir."

His large hands were now on her shoulders, his breath feathering her face. "Your life will change in a number of ways, but I'm confident that you will handle it all. Independence is one thing, Lauren. Marrying the Sheikh of Behraat, another."

Hand tucked under her chin, he lifted her head up until she looked at him. Pressed his mouth to her temple, "I need you, Lauren. Unlike anything or anyone else in the world."

Everything within her, every urge she had ever repressed came out to play when it was this man who looked at her as if she was his sanity, as if she could calm him, as if she could rebalance his world.

That he needed her had always been her downfall.

She took his hand in hers. "This will work only if you promise me one thing, Zafir."

Don't ask me for the truth, Zafir thought.

Don't force me to lie even more, the ones he'd already told scouring him.

Something resolute filled her face, chasing away the hesitation that came before it. And he braced himself and suddenly he knew why he had hesitated so much.

This incredibly delicate, infinitely fragile slip of a woman had power over him.

He'd already indulged himself for far too much when it came to her.

She made him want to be a better man, to risk things he didn't possess while his duty chained him, forever weighed on his soul. She made him wonder and speculate about, for the first time, life outside of being the sheikh's favorite orphan, beyond Rashid's son, beyond Behraat even.

She made him want to reach for the impossible.

"I need your fidelity, Zafir. I'll face anything if you—"

His breath shuddered out of him. This was a promise he could give and keep with no effort. He wanted no other woman like he wanted her. Once they were married, he would have Behraat, he would have the woman he wanted with an insanity and he would have his child.

For once in his life, he would have everything he could ever want. As long as he could forget that it was all built on a very small lie.

"I have not touched another woman since I came to your apartment that night, Lauren. And I will not touch another ever again." He didn't like that she needed his reassurance in it. That she didn't know what kind of man he was.

But like she had rightly said, he hadn't let her know him.

He saw the relief in her gaze and traced her cheeks with his knuckles.

A warm smile curved her lush mouth. Stepping onto her toes, she anchored herself on his shoulders and pressed her mouth to his stubbled cheek. The effect of that soft mouth was instantaneous—a searing brand.

Her words whispered at his ear felt like both a blessing and a curse, a vow that he felt to his very soul. "Then yes. I'll marry you, Zafir." She smiled against his cheek. "And I'll try, to the best of my ability, to be an…interesting wife."

Laughter bubbled up out of his chest. His hands sunk into her hair, he turned her to him.

The minx was laughing. Tightening his fingers, he buried his mouth in her neck and licked the fluttering pulse. Just the way that drove her crazy.

She smelled like sun and desert and warmth and desire, all rolled into one.

Too weak to resist, he pulled her to him until every inch of her thrummed against him. Hard and insistent, his erection pressed against her belly. "I see that you're not promising to be a biddable wife."

Her low gasp, the way her hands sank into his hair, his control barely held on. "That would be a lie, wouldn't it? We both know I won't be a *good little wife.* And I'd hate to start our marriage with lies."

He jerked up and released her. Her smile dimmed and he shuttered his expression.

With light movements, he touched her lips, pressed a quick kiss to her cheek and wished her good-night.

He'd almost stepped out when she called his name.

A frown tied her brow and wariness clouded her dark eyes. And in that moment, Zafir knew he was taking a momentous step, one he could never erase. A strange kind of weight settled on his chest.

"You're leaving?"

"I promised myself I would never make you feel cheap ever again. That means staying out of your bed until you're my wife and I have every right under the desert sun to be there."

He left without waiting for her response. Little time, he had very little time to get over this strange anxiety in his gut.

Little time to indulge in the foolish notion that he was committing a wrong.

He was marrying a woman carrying his child and bringing his country together again. He should be celebrating with a primal roar.

CHAPTER NINE

A MERE TWO weeks later, in which she saw her fiancé one single time for the space of one measly hour, Lauren Hamby married Zafir ibn Rashid Al Masood, the High Sheikh of Behraat in an outrageously extravagant but traditional ceremony in the great hall of the Behraati palace with guests ranging from distinguished state members from all over the world to stone-faced, bearded High Council members who wore their disapproval like a shield to any number of Behraatis, all of whom viewed her with a tangible curiosity.

The flowing, turquoise creation made of satiny silk that had been picked for her fell to her ankles in a traditional, not-hugging fit and hid her bump quite well. For which she would be forever grateful.

"The Sheikh of Behraat, Lauren? What about your scorn for a life that's only about ambition and power? In the face of that lifestyle, you've forgotten your petty complaints?" her mother had said over the phone, throwing Lauren's old words back in her face.

"It's not like that, Mom," she had said, for her own benefit as much as her mother's.

Then she heard the muted whisper of her father's voice and then her mother was saying, "Wait, he's marrying you because you got pregnant? Did you get the *nikah* contract checked out by a lawyer, Lauren? If he marries another woman later, because, *believe me*, these fantastic cross-cultural marriages burn out in a blaze as soon as the lust dies down…and their council, whatever it's called in Behraat, will want a Behraati sheikha, what does your child get? If he's a boy, is he going to be named heir?" She had continued in that vein while Lauren had felt nauseous.

Nothing about what her feelings for Zafir were or his for her, if he treated her well or if Lauren wanted her mom by her side for the first time in years.

Of course, they were too busy on diplomatic assignment to attend the wedding even though she told them of Zafir's offer to fly them back and forth within days in his private jet. And even after years of hardening herself against their disinterest, it still hurt that when the wedding organizer inquired about her family and friends attending, Lauren had nothing to say.

It had been the same evening that she had seen him in the ensuing two weeks. And he had brought the very contract that her mother had gone on and on about, for her to sign.

Too stunned to string two words together, she had stared at him. And he had replied that it was a tradition.

Once the lawyer had begun explaining what it entailed—allowance money, enough for Lauren and three generations after her to live quite comfortably—and she had gotten over her shock, she had abruptly stopped him and requested that he leave.

Zafir, who'd been sitting in a corner of the room, his attention on the tablet in his hand, had jerked his head up, his gaze pinning her to the spot.

"You're not well?"

At her silence, he had walked to her. Tension had tightened the skin over his cheekbones. "Lauren?"

She had no idea why she'd mentioned it at all. Only that it had been eating away at her since her conversation with her mother.

Only that there was this infinitesimal, gnawing ache in the pit of her stomach every time she found herself alone.

Nerves, she had told herself. The very landscape of her life was changing, on top of the usual pregnancy hormones, Farrah had said when she had betrayed her worries.

"My mother asked if we were including anything about custody and such stuff…in the contract," she had said, her heart in her throat.

Sunlight filtered in through the high, vaulted ceilings, the stained glass puncturing it into a myriad of colors. And yet, Zafir was like the cold frost in the middle of it. "What other such stuff?"

Perfectly courteous his question might have been but there had been such a dangerous, almost forbidding quality to his gaze then. A hardness that had forcefully reminded her of how ruthless he could be when he set his mind to it. As if the seductive, easy charm he had worn that day in the desert had been a mask.

As if she had suddenly morphed into that stranger who was only good for one thing again in his life.

"I don't know," she had mumbled, her own words leaving a bad taste in her mouth. "Stuff like what would happen to my…" A muscle tightened in his cheek, she splayed a hand on her belly, seeking reassurance from the tiny life inside her, "—our child if you married again and had children by another woman. About where we would live and…"

"Are you saying you need these…" his mouth curled with disgust, "clauses included in the contract? That you wish to discuss such…things?"

Distant and distrustful, this version of Zafir made her feel as if she didn't know him at all, as if she was, once again, risking everything for this man. There was nothing of the man who had asked her so tenderly to marry him.

But she was the one who had started the…horrible discussion.

"I…just…"

The tension in the room became so thick that she couldn't even breathe, couldn't even get her thoughts to cohere. Couldn't understand why she was pushing this when it hurt her just as much as it disgusted him.

Though he stood close enough now to touch her, he very carefully didn't, which was a lash enough, because, even in anger, he'd always touched her. "If you require these things written in a contract, then there is—"

"No," she had finally said, finding the very thought of him with another woman bile-inducing. "I want trust. I want respect. I…hate thinking about it like this."

The hardness had relented in his gaze. "I'll not begin it by putting threatening terms and conditional clauses, with the assumption that it will fail. I intend for this marriage to last forever. This is the only time we will talk about such things, Lauren. Do you understand?"

Tears that had threatened all week had finally spilled over onto her cheeks.

Relief, shame, fear—too many emotions squeezed her chest tight. But she met his gaze square. "Yes. But if your council doesn't accept me and they force you to marry a Behraati girl…"

Determination pulsed in his very expression. "They will accept me and you and our child. I left them no other choice."

And in that moment, Lauren realized how many of his own demons this man had faced, still faced, every day. How honorably he did his duty by those very people who constantly questioned his rule.

The powerful arrogance in his words had unbalanced her, rubbed her raw more times than she could count but it was the only way he knew, the only way he could rule.

It was the only way he had taken what was his. And she understood it just as she understood the sense of isolation around him.

The light behind him outlined his wide shoulders, the leanly sculpted chest clad in dark blue, and tapered waist and those tough, hard legs encased in jeans. Lauren blinked at the swirling possessiveness, the almost atavistic urge that filled her to mark this proud man as hers.

To make sure the world knew that he was hers and hers alone.

One hand on her shoulder, he'd swiped a tear from her cheek. "You didn't want to have this conversation any more than I did, did you?"

There was no hesitation in her body's response to him even as her mind sometimes resisted him. She swayed toward him, seeking the cocoon of his embrace. He held her lightly, the warmth of his body a teasing caress.

She sniffled and swallowed her tears. "No."

Tipping her chin, he'd studied her. Then his frown turned into an outright scowl. "Your phone call with your mother…that's where this began."

She shrugged.

"Are they coming to the wedding?"

"No."

"That's what upset you?"

"No, I had a feeling that would be their answer." And she had known.

The disappointment, the loneliness, they were all lessons she had learned after years of silent tears and bitterness but in the end, she had learned to deal with it.

Had poured everything she had into caring for those who could barely afford medical care, to serve people who didn't call her needy, or emotional.

High school and college graduation, her twenty-first birthday, the day she had received her first job offer…she had done fine without her parents at all the milestones of her life. She would do fine this time, too.

Acknowledging that had always given her a sense of

control back and it did now. Forcing a smile, she met Zafir's gaze. "Let's just chalk up this episode to hormones, please."

Instead of being relieved that she was giving him an out, he had frowned. "You hide the fact that she hurt you? Just from me or yourself, too?"

Her spine straightened, a defensive gesture that was coded into her blood. "I'm not hiding anything. And it's true. It's the hormones and this huge wedding that have just made me more susceptible."

"So she's not only not coming for her daughter's wedding but she planted all that nonsense in your head, knowing of your condition and that you're all alone here?"

She nodded, awed at how easily he had surmised the situation. "Something like that. But it's not her fault, Zafir." She didn't even know why she was defending her mom. "She's always been the pragmatic type—"

"Of course, it is her fault, Lauren. I'm glad she's not coming to the wedding, or she would have numerous occasions to upset you.

"In fact, I think you should not see her ever again. I will order the state secretary to inform your parents that their invitation to visit Behraat has been rescinded."

"What?" Lauren didn't know where to begin. "First of all, you can't just rescind an invitation, Zafir. That smacks of arrogance."

"I'm the ruler of Behraat. I'm entitled to arrogance."

Her mouth twitched, her breath went all wonky from trying not to laugh. She wanted to kiss him for making her laugh so easily. And she had a feeling he had intended it. But she refused to be railroaded into anything, even though she was never going to discuss her marriage with her mother ever again.

She sighed, realizing she had to fight his autocratic dictate for the principle of it.

"Second, you can't just decide that I won't ever see her again. Or anyone else for that matter."

"Why would you want to? It is clear that they care little for your happiness and well-being. And you're not in a condition to deal with stress like this. Nor will you while I have something to say about it."

"They're still my parents, Zafir. Your father didn't even tell you you were his son until he needed a better crown prince. And yet, here you are, doing everything you can to hold Behraat together by its seams."

She thought he would get furious with her for bringing up that subject. At the least, tell her she wasn't allowed to bring it up. Or withdraw.

Instead, he seemed thoughtful. And that he let her in just that much made her miserable day a thousand times brighter.

"It's ingrained in me, in my very blood that I must do everything I can to ensure Behraat's prosperity. My father needed no big gestures or promises of wealth to earn my loyalty.

"He molded me into his weapon with mere words. I've never met another such great orator. I would attend classes during the day, train with the palace guard in the evenings, but the nights…they had always been my favorite part of the day.

"For he would summon me to his parlor when he was ready for dinner. He would tell me stories of great battles, tales of warrior men who gave up everything for their nation, for their tribe, of armies marching into battle for freedom. And a nine-year-old boy who has no family… he begins to breathe those stories. Begs to hear one more, swears his loyalty, his very blood in exchange for one more.

"To survive, he needs to believe that he's part of something much bigger than his concerns. In the end, there's nothing else left of him except trying to make the tale into reality."

A tremendous sadness filled Lauren for the boy he'd been, for the flash of raw longing she glimpsed in his eyes. And a burning rage for the man who'd so heartlessly turned him into this…this man who believed that there was nothing to him than serving Behraat.

That he was nothing more than a tool to be used for his country. That there was no reason or need for him to want for anything more.

"Zafir? Whatever you believed then, it's—"

"It's a conditioning I can't defeat in this life." Absolute, implacable, his gaze warned her to not try, his belief an impenetrable wall she couldn't breach.

And how she ached to reach him…

"But in your case, I'm here to change it. So I forbid you from even speaking to her."

"Forbid?" She should have been furious, yet Lauren could only laugh. Could only marvel at how easily he had turned the whole thing around on her again.

Walking around the sitting area, she poked him in the chest. "You can't *forbid me* from stuff. In fact, we must remove it from our marriage dictionary. I'm going to be your wife, Zafir, not your servant."

"Marriage dictionary?" His eyes had turned molten, humor lurking in their depths.

"Yes." She held out her fingers and counted them, "Forbid, order, train etc. Can't be in there."

His gaze swept over her face, her breasts barely hidden from that overpowering male gaze in a thin, cotton henley, already feeling heavy and achy. Settled on her mouth. "Do I get to add some words to it, too? Like things I've begged for but was denied in those two months? Like a—"

She swatted at him, laughing and giggling, knowing how his wicked mind worked.

He sighed dramatically and every cell in her sang with dizzy joy. "What is in this dictionary then?"

"Laughter."

She had no idea when he had moved close enough that her breasts rubbed against that hard chest. She shuddered just as a growl rumbled from his throat. "I like the sound of that, *habeebti*."

She placed one hand on his chest to feel his heart and clasped his cheek with the other. "Affection. Respect."

His arrogant head bowed as if in reverence, his shuddering exhale caressing her face. She had the strangest feeling that he was hiding his expression from her. Hard shoulders relaxed under her tentative touch. His fingers crawled around her nape then.

Finally, his molten gaze bore into her, lingering over her mouth. "Surrender?" he asked and she shook her head.

"No 'surrender'. Comfort. Care. Friendship."

Deep satisfaction glinting in his eyes, he rubbed his nose against hers. "Seduce?"

"No seduce. Cajole. Kiss. Need."

He rubbed his mouth over hers, and she moaned. "I think I'm getting the gist of it, *habeebti*," he whispered against her mouth.

Holding on to him because she was afraid she was melting on the inside, Lauren spoke against those soft yet thoroughly masculine lips. Evening stubble rasped her flesh, making her whimper with want. "Yeah? Try it then."

"Marriage. Commitment. Forever."

Just as he stole her breath with his words, so did his hot, hungry mouth on hers.

Resistance, imagined or real, was an alien concept. She might have squeaked at the influx of such delirious pleasure and he took that opportunity to swirl his wicked tongue around hers.

Her heart was still racing from the promise in his

words, her belly tightening with such fierce feeling she thought she might burst with it.

Every time she thought she had a measure of him, he went and toppled her all over again. Made her need him on such a visceral level that she came undone by his words, his smile, his touch. Joy made her want that much hotter, bone-deep affection made her need that much deeper.

She had never felt such heights of dizzying joy or such a deep hollow ache as she did with this man.

Moaning in the back of her throat, she clasped his neck and clung to him by her mouth.

Until he pulled her hands off his neck, and whispered, "Only one more week, *habeebti.*" Fire gleamed in his hungry gaze, his breath a harsh rhythm in her ears. "And if you get upset again because you didn't listen to me, I will put your mother in jail."

She sputtered and he pressed another hard, hasty kiss to her stinging lips. And then he was gone.

"Marriage. Commitment. Forever."

She had seen him only that once in the exhausting week and Lauren clutched those three words to her every time she felt as though she was sinking in the spotlight leading up to her fairy-tale, fantastic wedding that had Behraat and the rest of the world take notice of her.

She had never imagined her wedding day, having had only one disastrous relationship by twenty-six, much less on such a huge scale, and as the days blended into a flurry of activity, Lauren felt scared, isolated, inadequate and craving Zafir's company once again.

The palace staff in an upheaval over the upcoming wedding, even Farrah had kept their daily appointments to a minimum.

Exotic flowers and exquisite silks, diamond jewelry and

designer dresses, there was no end to the treasures Zafir bestowed upon her.

And in addition to the army of staff that catered to her every breath, she also now had a secretary whose job was to school her in everything social—mostly at what state ceremonies she could open her mouth and at what, which was 90 percent, she had to look poised and beautiful and ornamental for the sheikh.

"I will train you in our ways," he had told her arrogantly. And through those two weeks, she would have even taken his arrogant, imperious behavior if it meant she got to see more of him.

Abdul, her newly appointed secretary, she realized within two days, was adept at manipulating the truth to suit Behraat best. He had coached her intensively for an interview, the only one required of her, with a female journalist of a huge media channel. But when Lauren had sat down to watch it, her jaw had fallen to her chest.

The bits and pieces of responses that Abdul had fed her had been manipulated into a cohesive whole that told how Zafir and she had fallen in love with each other while he had been in exile, waiting to serve his country, how she had come in search of him thinking him dead, and how having found her again, the sheikh hadn't been able to wait to make her his sheikha.

It told of how a plain, hardworking nurse from Brooklyn, New York, had befriended their sheikh, fallen in love with him and now, had been transformed into the sheikha fit for him and his great country.

Lauren hadn't known whether to laugh or cry or take offense at being described as some kind of mouse who had unwittingly befriended a lion, and subsequently, transformed into an elegant deer?

Because levelheaded as she'd always been, even having been exposed to her parents' glittering, high-society life at an early age and turned her back on it, her wedding and all it ensued was on such a grand level that even her head could turn.

Could buy into the fantastical love story that the palace whispered it to be around her. Could delude herself that Zafir was marrying her because he couldn't bear to part with her rather than because it was the best thing for the situation they found themselves in.

But it was a commitment they had made and she was determined to give everything she could.

The morning of the wedding, minutes before she was due in the lavishly decorated great hall, she had seen Farrah and Huma standing in the corridor waiting to greet her. She'd barely embraced them when she saw David and a couple of her friends who had worked with her in the inner-city clinics.

Zafir had contacted David and the rest of them personally, Alicia had said with awe in her voice. Of course they had to come to see Lauren become the sheikha of her own nation.

Her chest ached as their words sunk in.

He had not only comforted her when she had been upset but had contacted her friends on her behalf. Domineering he might be, but Lauren was afraid he was slowly stealing bits and pieces of her very soul.

Beyond her friends from the States, another small group of men and women stood in the last hall. With Salma and Bashir at the front, Lauren realized it was the Dahab. Ahmed, standing close as always, had grinned at her stunned face, told her they had traveled to the city to stand witness to her wedding to their sheikh, to wish her happiness in her marriage.

Between Farrah's admonishments that they were getting late and Alicia's wicked whispers about Ahmed and the 'fine quality' of Behraati men in general, Lauren felt anything but alone.

In this strange country and between people she had only met for a few weeks, Lauren felt loved, cherished, and thanks to the dark, breathtaking man whose gaze swept over her with a possessive desire as she reached the great hall, utterly wanted.

Once she had repeated the vows that she had practiced, Zafir had nodded at the small group that had stood to the side of the hall. "Fans of yours, sheikha?"

Warmth filling her from the inside out, Lauren resisted the urge to plaster herself all over him. It was a losing battle, she realized as she studied his rough-hewn features, that generous mouth and the long bridge of his arrogant nose. "My tribe," she had finally said.

And he had smiled.

Before she knew it, they were joined together as man and wife in front of God and the people of Behraat and then she was whisked away to a feast unlike anything she had ever seen.

After two hours of raising sparkling water, picking at her food and thanking a host of dignitaries from around the world, her smile began to droop and her shoulders ached. The three-inch designer shoes that she had cooed over now felt like torture devices on her tired feet.

His hand around her, Zafir instantly held her as she toppled. Last she had looked, he had been walking around the room, greeting and meeting men she couldn't even remember the names of. That he had appeared by her side so fast…her breath shook.

Long fingers held her right below her breast and she felt branded, feeling his touch through her dress all the way to her skin. "You're ready to drop."

She saw the hunger in his golden gaze, felt the tight tension in his body, heard the hiss of his exhale as her hip brushed his front. Legs wobbling, belly tight with need, she said, "I'm sorry, it's just been a long day."

His finger landed on her mouth, while he signaled to someone behind her. "Don't apologize. I will see you tonight." He bent his head and whispered, "Get some rest, yes? It might be late but I'll be there."

Sparks of heat spreading to every limb, Lauren nodded.

She followed the contingent that seemed to be her shadow now.

No matter, she decided, because all she wanted right then was to escape from her own self, much less face the man who was slowly but inexorably imprinting himself on her very soul.

CHAPTER TEN

BY THE TIME Zafir had dealt with the numerous council members and state delegates, and the tribal chiefs led by the Dahab's chief, and arrived at the oasis, separately from Lauren, darkness had fallen like a thick cloak over the encampment.

He was glad he had sent her on earlier because his negotiations with the chiefs had gone on and on. And he had, eager to finalize the agreement he wanted to reach with them and loath to disturb the fragile peace, let half his wedding night pass by.

Not wanting to disturb her in case she was sleeping, he had the pilot land the chopper a mile or so from the camp.

The desert sky glittered with stars as he walked, the wild, crisp scent of the night driving his blood to pound faster in his veins.

Victory was his. For the first time in his life, he felt like he belonged to the Al Masoods, like the conquering warrior in those stories.

He had secured his rule of Behraat, had secured its return to a path of progress. Trade agreements could be renewed now that half its population wasn't trying to rip the other half apart. Excavation for oil could begin again in lands that had been occupied by the tribes.

He had done everything an orphan who had been thrust into power could have done.

And his prize was in that huge tent set just a little apart from the rest of the encampment, the path to the entrance flanked by a row of lanterns.

Tonight, he belonged in that tent, truly, with his wife. Even his father's wife, banished to the fortress in the old city could not contest his place here.

The wind whistling through the sands, the dark desert sky, and the harsh, unforgiving desert, he was a part of this land finally. And it filled every inch of him with a profound joy, an unquenchable fire.

He acknowledged Ahmed and another guard with a nod. She wouldn't like that they were so close by, the errant thought dropped into his head. Not for what he had on his mind, he thought with a smile.

But he wouldn't dismiss them. Not when her safety was paramount, not when he was hovering on the knife-edge of desire, his rationality and the civilized veneer like the slippery sand under his feet.

Before his next breath, he was standing inside the tent, at the foot of the vast bed. Numerous lanterns were lit all around the room and he wondered if she had been afraid of the pitch-darkness that was a desert night.

There she lay, *his wife*.

Still in the turquoise dress that had so lovingly hinted at those lithe curves. She slept on her side, the silk scrunched up to her knees, displaying toned calves.

Deep red henna swirled over her feet and hands. She was marked like that for him, he thought with a primal possessive urge like he had never known before.

His breath coming in short bursts, he devoured the sight of her. Her hair haphazardly framed her face, a mirror of the spirited, independent woman. The bodice of the dress dipped at her chest, her folded arms pushing up the globes of her breasts.

Need ripped through him, for the first time in his life, leaving him absolutely unraveled on a level he didn't understand.

Shedding his long tunic, he left his cotton trousers on. Much as he couldn't wait to feel her silken flesh against all of him, he didn't want to spook her when she was in such a deep sleep.

Slowly, he lowered his body onto the bed, shifted to his side and gathered her to him.

Mumbling something, she came to him, pliant and soft in a way she never was when she was awake, her dainty fingers drifting over his abdomen. His shaft tightened painfully and a groan burst deep from inside him.

Purring like a cat, she tucked herself against him, the scent of roses and her skin a sensory heaven. He hissed out a breath, the brush of her thigh against his sending shafts of heat through him.

Ya Allah, he had forgotten how fragile she had always been. Constantly pitted against that tough, self-sufficient exterior she presented, the delicate bones of her body and lithe curves made him feel like a hulking brute.

The remembered feel of her tight heat the first time he had gone to her apartment…desire was a roaring beast within him.

Yet, she had always stood toe-to-toe with him.

And now she was even more delicate, he thought, his gaze drifting over her curves, and going to the small, just-visible swell of her belly.

She was finally, irrevocably his. She carried his child in her womb, wore his ring on her finger.

His child and his wife, *his* in every way there was.

His, in a way no one had ever been.

His, in a way no one could ever take away from him.

The whisper of rustling clothes brought Lauren awake from the deep slumber she had fallen into. She blinked and sat up, the flickering light of lanterns illuminating her surroundings for her.

It took her a few seconds to realize she was at the desert hideaway, and that it was...*her wedding night.* Pushing her hair away from her face, she grimaced at the tangles. She had fallen asleep the moment her head touched the pillow, and had neglected to take her pins out. Wondering what time it was, she looked up.

Standing at the edge of the bed, his sparsely haired, lean chest bare, a white towel slung low around his hips, there was Zafir.

Her husband, hers to hold and obey and...love.

Her vows came back to her word by word, but panic was only a mild flutter in her chest now.

Faced with such potent masculinity, knowing that this powerful man had pledged his fidelity and respect and his body to her, everything else paled in significance.

This time, she was prepared for the burning flame of her own need, of the blast of heat that punched low in her belly.

Golden light bathed the musculature of his chest, delineating every ridge of tightly roped muscle and sinew. Droplets of water clung to his skin, skin that she knew would feel like rough velvet. Muscle and sinew, he was breathtakingly gorgeous and he had never been bared to her like this.

She must have made a sound—a needy whimper, because he turned around then.

Tawny eyes met hers and she gasped aloud.

A savage light filled those golden depths. He looked fierce, dark, like one of the warriors he had told her about, as if there was a well of some bright fire inside of him that lit him from the inside out. Power and confidence radiated from him in waves.

Fear of some unknown crashed through her, and she clasped her hands together to stop their shaking. This was ridiculous. She knew this man, but the reassurance rang hollow.

"Zafir?" His name was an entreaty on her lips, a soft intonation. As if she could tame whatever it was that clung to him like a second skin. As if she could call forth that veneer of civilized sophistication that she'd always known was only skin-deep.

The hand in his hair with a towel stilled and he looked up at her. A thoroughly possessive light glinted in his eyes as his gaze lingered over her brow, her nose and finally rested on her mouth.

"Did I wake you?"

Clutching the voluminous folds of her dress, she pushed her feet to the ground and stood up. "No. How long have you been back?"

Another rough tumble of his hair and then the towel went flying into the corner. "An hour, maybe." Catching her look around, he said, "It's almost dawn."

"It took so long?"

Powerful shoulders rose as he shrugged. "Go back to sleep, Lauren."

She licked her lips to moisten them. "No. I'm fine." An infinitesimal shudder racked the tense line of his shoulders. "You went for a swim in the oasis in the middle of the night? You must be freezing!"

"I needed to cool down."

That matter-of-fact statement hung in the room, sparking into life a simmering fire.

He was half-naked and she was drowning in silk and yet, she felt as if she was the one utterly bared to him.

Reaching him on barely steady legs, she stilled. The skirts of her dress fluttered against his legs. She thought his mouth must have twitched at how strange she was acting, but when she looked into his eyes, there was only that deeply disconcerting hunger again.

He was just as still as she was, waiting for what, she had no idea.

Breath hitching in her throat, she tried to smile. She had no idea where the sudden tension was springing from, why she felt as if she was meeting him for the first time. How a ceremony could drench them in a strange kind of intimacy. "Did everything go okay?"

He frowned.

"At your meeting with the High Council?"

"How do you know?"

"Ahmed said it was a meeting of all the tribal chiefs and the council members, a meeting unlike he had ever heard of or seen before." Hardness inched into his face until the planes jutted out starkly. "That none of the staff had any idea that they would even be arriving for the wedding. That they hadn't set foot in the palace, much less the city for so long. That you brought this all about. Is that true?"

"Yes. They will not contest my rule anymore."

Short, clipped and with a warning. That she didn't heed. "That's fantastic. Ahmed said—"

An edgy smile, more a snarl, touched his lips. "Ahmed, it seems, is a raging gossip and probably half in love with you, yes?" He seemed so utterly displeased that for a second it was like looking at a stranger in the same skin. "Maybe he needs a tougher assignment where he's not mooning over my beautiful wife and speculating on state matters?"

Heat tightened her cheeks as she strove to make light of his claim. But there it was again, that tinge of barely civilized hint to it. "Please don't do that. Ahmed's... *infatuation*," she said, and was relieved to see the tight set of his mouth relax a little, "is perfectly harmless and nothing I can't handle."

And then she was wondering why she had said please. Wondering what subconscious instinct made her want to appease him rather than argue like she had always done, what unnamed, wild thing inside him she recognized today, of all days.

At his raised brow, she flushed again. “I like him. He's young and friendly and—”

“You can't socialize with the guard, Lauren.”

If she didn't know such a thing was impossible, she would have thought him jealous. But jealous meant caring on a different level and speculating on his feelings or lack of them meant she'd have to face what she wanted them to be.

She injected steel into her voice. “And not prone to prejudice or judgment, like other members of your staff is what I mean,” she finished, thinking of his mentor, Arif. Although, for the first time since she had seen the older man in the trade center that day, his rigid features had relaxed when he had looked at her at the feast today.

Grudging acknowledgment, maybe.

“Tell me about the meeting, about their impression of me.”

“You don't need to concern yourself—”

“Don't say that. You don't have to protect me from… the worst.”

“As your husband, that is one of the job requirements, *habeebti*,” he added archly. “Whether they be old, distrustful council members or your mother or even yourself that I have to protect you from.”

She bit her lip, hating the insecurity that balled up in her throat. Normally, she would have closed herself off completely, barred any way she could hearing what some traditional, rooted-in-the-past old men thought of her. Not venturing where she wasn't needed, that had been her motto and her shield all her life.

Her parents didn't want her to tag along on a year-long assignment one year?

She'd made plans the next year before they could even reject her.

If she didn't give anything, there was no possibility of getting hurt.

But for the sake of her child, and for the sake of this man who had cared that she was upset, who had, while shouldering the burden of his volatile nation, still spared time to realize she must be feeling alone…

For him, she would face her fears.

She would not only face them, but she would never give him reason to be ashamed of her, she decided with a fierceness that was new to her.

"Why did they all show up in such force? To express their disapproval of me?"

"The Dahab approve of you and arrived to honor you. And the rest of the tribes follow where they lead." He shook his head, as if signaling to end the matter. "But I've had enough politics today to last me a lifetime, Lauren. I don't wish to discuss it anymore."

Commanding and absolute, his voice sent a shiver up her spine. It felt like dismissal. But something lingered in his face too, something that set a twisty feeling in her gut and she decided to let the matter drop. For now. "Okay."

Before she could turn around, one of his hands snaked up and caught around her nape, tugging her closer. The rasp of his hard chest against hers sent fire blasting into every nerve ending. Her lashes fell down and she dug her fingers into his shoulders. But even after his midnight swim, his skin was still hot.

"You're very submissive all of a sudden. Why?"

"Not submissive. Understanding," she corrected him, "and slowly learning to choose which battles to fight."

He pushed out a breath and his body seemed to tense up even more. "You're sure you've had enough rest?" he muttered against her temple. "I'll be gentle, I promise."

Low and deep, his words shot straight through to the core of her, leaving her writhing in her own skin.

"I fell asleep the moment—" The words barely left her before his mouth crashed down on hers.

She wanted to say she didn't need him to be gentle. She wanted to say that whatever it was that was burning inside him, she could see it. She wanted to say that she'd, *always*, want all of him—the tenderness and the passion, but also the harsher, tougher aspects of him.

The part that regretted a brother's death even though he'd made his life hell.

The part that hated the father just as much as the part that still, somehow, loved and grieved for him. Deeply.

The part that had been stunned that she'd come looking for him all the way to Behraat.

Even the part that had made him walk away from her as much as the part that admitted that what they'd shared hadn't been cheap.

All the parts that made him Zafir.

All of him. Always, she realized with a shiver.

But he didn't give her a chance to say any of that, and she was perversely glad because it was easier to surrender to the pleasure between them than face what she knew would change her entire life.

CHAPTER ELEVEN

HOT AND SLICK and expertly teasing, his wicked mouth was all she'd dreamed about in the past few weeks. The taste of him was erotic, the drag of his mouth righting her world, chasing away the silly anxiety, rocking through her with the force of an earthquake.

She wound her arms around his shoulders, hanging on as he drove her mindless with his desperate caresses.

The light in the room was only a soft glow yet she felt as if there was an explosion of color, sensation and dizzying excitement around her. Attar of roses and some wild fragrance from the desert and the scent of Zafir's masculinity, it was a cocktail she got drunk on.

Silk that had been soft when she had worn it this morning now rasped roughly against her knotting nipples. The lace of panties rubbed against her wet folds.

She knew him, her body screamed with a roar of delight.

She knew this mouth, knew those deep strokes of his tongue, knew the bite of teeth that grazed her lip, not so gently, knew the hoarse grunt that fell from him when she tangled her tongue with his. Knew the hunger and passion he kept buried beneath his isolation, knew the heart of him.

And then he was pushing her back with his large body, back toward the bed, all the while his mouth devoured hers with rough, almost desperate strokes.

With his hands on her hips, he braced her fall onto the bed. Stood at the edge and looked down at her with molten gaze. "Tell me what you're thinking."

"That I wish I could use telekinesis to make that towel drop," she drawled, pushing to her elbows.

"If my wife wishes it…" he said and then the towel was falling to the floor.

"Oh…" Fractured and desperate, the sound fell from her lips as she studied him to her heart's content.

Washboard abdomen, tapered hips, rock-hard thighs and the thick-veined length of his erection that rose up toward his belly…her womb tightened remembering the pleasure he could wield. She smoothed her hands down her belly as if she could calm the need clamoring inside of her. As if control of any sort wasn't a big, fat lie around him.

Powerful sheikh or not outside of this tent, here he was, quite simply, her man. Panty-meltingly gorgeous with a body honed to hard strength.

I will touch no woman ever again.

"You're all mine, Sheikh," she said, boldly raking a fingertip down one rock-hard thigh.

His hands drifted to her ankles and clasped one and softly slid her up the bed. He climbed up after her, pinning her to the bed by her dress, his hips snuggling between her legs, his weight on his elbows.

Muscles gleaming in the flickering light, copper-hued skin stretched tight over those pectorals, he leaned over her like some dark warrior claiming his prize.

He pulled back to his knees. One calloused hand found her ankle, moved up her leg, palm down. "Your mouth, that's what got us into this trouble in the first place, yes?"

The soft skin behind her knee, the sensitive skin of her inner thigh, from the line of her hip to the seam of her silk panties, those fingers learned all of her anew. It cost her several breaths to find her voice, unsteady and hoarse as it is. "So, what, this is all my fault?"

Her thighs squeezed as his big, callused palm pressed

farther. Gaze greedy and hot and all kinds of wicked, he watched her reaction. As if he enjoyed her coming apart as much as he enjoyed making her.

Head rolling back, shoulders coming away from the bed, she moaned as his palm covered her mound and pressed. All of her being pulsed under his hand, wet, and aching and desperate.

His other hand snuck under her dress and then he was pulling those wisps of lace down with one hand and pulling her down on the bed to straddle his legs.

While she watched hungrily, hanging upon the knife-edge of desire, he bared her lower body while her dress stayed snug over her aching breasts. Her legs, her thighs and the slick, drenched folds of her womanhood, all of her.

And looked at her.

"Beautiful," he muttered in a tight, clenched voice, the glow from the lanterns highlighting the sharp sweep of his cheekbones, the sensuality of his lower lip.

After all this time, Lauren felt the heat rushing and pooling under her skin, flushing her with color. She hadn't been a virgin, but nothing had prepared her for his brand of pulse-pounding, soul-baring kind of passion in New York. Without promises, without the usual, useless rituals of dating, without her knowledge even, he had stolen a part of her and imprinted himself on her.

No wonder she had followed him across the world.

"Zafir...please..."

His hand on her knee stopped her when she tried, too late but still, to shield her sex from his hungry gaze. And by the glint of masculine satisfaction in his gaze, he knew it. He liked that she trusted him, that she was putty in his hands while he did as he pleased.

He parted her sex with a possessive, intrusive, yet arousing touch and stroked her.

A hoarse moan left her mouth.

"Wet…you're so wet for me. How do I take this slow?" He sounded almost angry as if his loss of control was her fault. As if he didn't thoroughly relish having her drenched in the desire he created in her with one mere look.

Lauren saw the deft flick of his wrist before she felt his long fingers inside her.

A million nerve endings in her groin went ballistic.

Sobbing and moaning, Lauren gave in to the fire he set inside of her.

Her body arched off the bed as he slicked his fingers in and out while his thumb pressed down at the swollen nub crying for his attention. Again and again, he pressed on that bundle while she writhed under his touch.

And just when a tremor started in her lower belly, he withdrew his fingers.

She cried, so close to release and yet so far away again. Her fists landed on his shoulder, his chest as he knelt over her. Opening her eyes, she met the dark, male heat glittering in his.

A golden flame, an incinerating hunger.

"I can't wait any longer," he said, through clenched teeth, his hands roughly pushing the silk folds out of his way. Almost apologetic. "I should have known…"

Holding her hips down, he pushed into her wet heat with one firm stroke.

Their mingled groans ricocheted in the tent.

Twisting the sheets with her fists, Lauren let her legs go slack. Even having known this intimacy with him, her slick channel was still not prepared for how big he was.

After six years of celibacy, she had flinched when he had entered her that first evening in New York.

Again now, she had to breathe, short, panting bursts, through the invasion of his velvet heat, brace herself for the raw, mind-numbing friction in the walls of her sex.

Skin damp, clenched muscles rock hard beneath her fingers, he exhaled. Something almost like regret lingered around his mouth as he touched her damp brow. "You're fine?"

"Yes," Lauren breathed and wiggled her hips. A fist of need twisted her lower belly afresh.

"Come for me, *habeebti*," he said, his fingers once again finding the swollen button of her sex.

Lauren curled her legs around his back as he pulled out and thrust again. Excruciatingly slow, he let her feel every inch of him, his fingers relentless in their assault still.

She was sobbing and begging now, pressing his back with her legs, urging him to go faster. Going mindless at the release that hovered just beyond her reach.

Every muscle in his face pulled tight over his features, his jaw looked as if it was set in concrete. She knew his body, she knew what he liked when it came to sex, what drove him crazy. That he needed to go faster, deeper, rougher.

Heart murmuring to a halt, she realized that he leashed himself.

It was the only time she had him, the man in the center of the island he made around himself, the man he was beneath his dedication and duty to Behraat and she was damned if she gave that up because he thought she might break.

"You can't hurt me."

A vein flickered in his temple, his gaze filled with a feral hunger. Hunger that he denied himself.

She tried to shift under her him, but he locked her with his fingers on her hips. "Zafir…" she panted, furious that he would deny her. "I'm pregnant, not an invalid."

"I know that." She pushed a damp lock of hair from his forehead, something filling her chest. "But, do you know how fragile you feel to my rough hands?" Another slow thrust followed by their mingled groans.

She drew her nails down his back, the heated hiss of his breath goading her on. "Shield me, if you must, from the entire world, but not from you, Zafir. Never from you," she said, and then she traced the line of his rigid spine, dug her fingers into his taut buttocks. "I swear to God, if you treat me like this, ours will be the shortest marriage in the history of—"

His mouth took hers in such a carnal kiss that she felt thoroughly ravished. "You will learn to not threaten your husband, *habeebti*," he whispered, before he dipped his tongue into her mouth in actions mimicking his lower body. "And you'll definitely not talk of leaving me again, ever. Yes?"

"Harder, then, please," she murmured at his ear. His skin was rough silk as she licked his shoulder and then pushed her teeth in.

A hoarse grunt fell from his lips, before he clasped her jaw and crushed her mouth with a savage ferocity that burned her. There was no gentleness to him now, no semblance of control.

He was the man that had made her embrace insanity with a smile, that had made her wild with one kiss. That had made her leave safety behind and walk into fire.

Tilting her hips, he thrust deeper, faster, pushing her on and on… Until there was only him and her and the spiraling want between them…

Lauren screamed as she came in a shattering explosion of pleasure and sensation. Her lower belly quivered, her legs so much mush, her sex pulsing and shuddering with the waves.

With a guttural growl, Zafir followed her, keeping his weight off her even as his powerful body bucked and shuddered above her.

* * *

His breath coating his throat like a fire, Zafir looked at Lauren.

Brow damp, her breathing harsh, she was shaking.

His thighs still tightening and releasing from the aftermath of his explosive climax, he looked down the length of her. The scent of sweat and sex clung to the air they breathed, an explosive mix that he drew greedily into his lungs.

He saw the pink impressions his fingers had left on one hip and cursed. One layer of lace that fell over the turquoise silk beneath, he assumed, was ripped along the seam. Feeling himself harden again, he pulled the dress down all the way to her ankles.

A shuddering exhale left him, his chest feeling as if it was caving in on his heart.

Moving away from the bed, he found a washcloth, dunked it in a pitcher of water and came back to the bed. Gently, he snuck his hands again under the wreck he had made of her dress. She flinched when he separated her legs.

Ice filling his veins, he froze. Then he rolled his shoulders and searched for her gaze. "Lauren? You said—"

"Zafir!" Eyes, wide in her narrow face, locked on him. Her lashes cast shadows onto her cheeks, her skin damp. "I'm just…embarrassed, that's all."

Relief unlocked his wrist. Smoothing his palm over her belly, he continued again and gently cleaned her up.

Because they had never lingered like this after sex before, he realized. Because every time, after he had taken her, he had left.

The only time he had actually stayed at her apartment had been when she'd had the flu.

Because, every time, he had told himself it would be the last time.

Because, from the moment of his father's announcement to an outraged Tariq and a stunned council, he had not been just Zafir. Or was it even before that when his mother had given him birth.

The way Rashid had raised him, it seemed it had been inevitable.

But now, he needn't walk away.

Because she had helped him carve a small compartment in his life, for her.

He liked that—the permanence of something in his life, the freedom to be himself, even if it was in the very confines of this one relationship.

Freedom by binding him to her, that's what she had given him.

"You're smiling," she said then, and she was smiling, too. Lovely mouth trembling, dark black eyes glowing.

His heart crawled to his throat.

It was one of those perfect, precious, rare moments, he just knew it, even though there hadn't been very many in his life until then.

"I plan to be there when you give birth, Lauren. I plan to cut the cord and see my child enter this world. This," he said, gesturing to the cloth, "it's nothing, *habeebti.*"

"Yeah?" she said, something low and tender in her tone more than challenge.

"Yeah," he replied, with a smile. He thought he saw a flash of wetness but she blinked and looked away.

Getting off the bed, he cleaned himself and then washed up. He felt her gaze on his back and turned.

She looked utterly breathtaking on that vast bed, the bodice of her dress clinging to her breasts.

He hadn't even undressed her, he realized now. Just shoved her dress up and out of his way before plunging into her. Even the chilly waters of the oasis hadn't cooled him down.

He had been high on his victory, drunk on his own power, as she had blamed him once.

He had meant to take it slow, to savor the long night, but the moment he had touched her, found her ready for him, he had lost any semblance of will.

She wanted it just as much as you did, a part of him whispered. And she never pretended otherwise.

She had never feared him or his passion. Not before she knew who he was, not after.

Something inside him, something that feared that he would heap a world of hurt on this fragile woman, finally calmed.

This wild heat between them, Lauren wanted it.

Lauren always chose it, always chose him, he realized with a leaping feeling. And for the first time in his life, he could give back what little he could.

He returned to the bed and pulled a thick rug over their bodies. Traced the upper swell of her breasts and felt her shiver. "I'm a fool, *habeebti*, not that I would admit it to anyone but you."

"How so?"

"I ignored these glorious breasts."

"Hmmm…no arguments here," she said, sinking her fingers into his hair and pulling.

She didn't do it gently either. Then satisfied, she moved those long fingers down his forehead, over the bridge of his nose, his mouth, before settling over his shoulders again.

Then she petted him some more.

He lay still, silent, shuddering at the possessiveness in her touch, submitting to this woman who was slowly stealing into him. "Zafir?"

"Yes, Lauren?"

Her thickly fringed gaze fell on him, then shied away. She was hesitating, and instantly, he felt something in him twist and brace.

Against her? Against what she would say?

Was it fear, he wondered, trying to hold the curious feeling swirling through him. It was the same sensation that had shot through him when she had so boldly blurted out that their marriage would be short if he didn't…

Buried deep inside her, straining to not use her body roughly like he was used to, he had growled back at her.

He, who had finally achieved everything, could he fear what this mere slip of a woman could say to him? And what she could do?

She roughly pulled his chin up to meet his gaze. The uncertainty there pushed away his own jumbled thoughts. "What is it?"

The flush was receding from her cheeks, but her mouth was swollen. From his rough kisses. "Focus, will you?"

This time, he laughed. "I am focusing. You're the one hesitating. Which is as strange as a rainfall in a desert."

She didn't negate him. And his heart pounded harder in the thick silence.

"I've…you…" She sighed, licked her lips, rubbed one thumb over his stubbly jaw and began again. "I've been confused, overwhelmed and sometimes a little lonely these past weeks… But then…"

She pulled his hand to her cheek, and then kissed the center of his palm. The tenderness in her gaze unmanned him. "I would do anything to make this marriage work, Zafir. And not just for the baby. But for you and me."

He didn't know what to say in return.

It was what he had known she would give in return for his commitment, it was what he wanted of her for years to come, and yet the strength of her conviction, the courage it must have cost her to say it to him, shook him from within.

And because he didn't know how to stop it from shifting and splintering something inside of him, didn't know how to form a suitable response, because it was a promise the likes of which he had never known in his life, he bent and captured her mouth with his.

He worshipped her with his mouth, his hands and his body while her soft declaration took root in his veins, his cells, in his very blood. Like the roots of a gnarled tree that stood proudly in the courtyard of the palace, planting itself tight and deep within him.

The expression in her eyes, the joy in her smile, the tenderness in the way she touched him and kissed him, as if she couldn't contain it anymore, as if it was bursting out of her every breath, it haunted him long after she fell asleep and he extracted himself from the bed and watched the dawn coat the sky a myriad of oranges and pinks.

And then, just like that, in the space of one night, no, just a few hours, he felt as if he had lost it all. Before he had even grasped it properly yet.

As if all that he had achieved was so little next to that one small declaration from Lauren, which he hadn't earned.

Through the following four days that he allowed himself to spend with her, through his return to the palace, through every breath he took, her words haunted him.

It haunted him until he couldn't breathe for the weight of it, until every time he saw Lauren, it felt as if he deserved her, her open smile, her affection, less and less.

Until every word of hers felt like a small lash in his skin.

But this was the life he had wanted all along, wasn't it? The life in which he had everything?

CHAPTER TWELVE

AFTER FOUR DAYS of tasting paradise at the oasis, Lauren and Zafir returned to the city and the palace.

They had woken up before dawn one morning, and watched the sunrise together over the sand dunes. Swam in the pool while moonlight glinted off their skin. She had glutted on dates and figs and thick cakes, between feverish bouts of lovemaking during which she had, hopefully in a final way, proved to Zafir that having his wicked way with her was in no way harmful to either her or their growing child.

That it was very much what she needed.

They had exchanged college stories around a campfire in the evening. His, always working toward his goal of becoming a member of Behraat's state affairs, and hers, building a life that nurtured her need to help, away from the sphere of her parents' high-society life.

During the day, he'd been gone for a few hours, visiting different tribes before they migrated deeper into the desert, he'd informed her. Needing to recover from their long, busy, sweat-soaked nights, she was all too content to nap in the tent and stay away from the blistering heat.

It had been pure bliss and all Lauren wanted was to stay there forever with Zafir, cocooned away from the world.

But just like in New York, real life—full of schedules and meetings, and government and state dinners—awaited both of them this time.

She had barely showered, changed and inhaled more food when Abdul had appeared at the entrance to her suite, with a host of social appointments and a load of advice. Even before Farrah had appeared to check on her.

So Lauren fell into a routine, pushing back at Abdul at some things and bringing down Arif's stone-faced wrath on her head, sometimes letting them mold her into what they needed the sheikha to be. Refused point-blank on some issues.

She did miss her old life. But she knew that to be a symptom of her resistance to change, to teams of strangers taking over her life.

Her career, however, was a different matter.

She had put in years of hard work to get her nursing degree, and then long night shifts to gain experience and reputation.

All she did now was spend her days watching her team fight over which designer she should wear or which charity she should grace with her presence. It felt as though she, Lauren, got smaller and lost in the huge tsunami that was Zafir's life and Behraat.

To her shame, she'd even burst into tears a couple of times, but she decided to give herself a break and chalk it up to pregnancy hormones rather than call herself a coward.

Zafir, she decided, had paid enough all his life for Behraat. He wouldn't lose her to it too; whether he knew it or not, he had her.

And just like that, she felt a little in control of her life again.

So what if she chose the social engagements that were closer to her heart like women's issues and girls' education rather than spending another afternoon with the old shiekha and Johara—who wore a brittle smile on her face while the old woman bitterly complained about Zafir, short of calling him a murderer to Lauren's face.

Lauren however didn't mistake the older woman's hatred or the younger woman's veiled malice to be anything personal. That she had married the man who had usurped their son and husband respectively was bad enough. But that she was also an American and pregnant on top of it was a pill they just couldn't swallow.

When the old woman, however, began ranting about Zafir's mother, Lauren had walked to the door, called Ahmed to escort her guests out and returned to her bedroom.

That whole day, she had spent thinking of Zafir's mother, her defiance of her own tribe, cutting away every tie and living in shame with a man who hadn't even married her.

Had she loved Rashid so much then?

If only she could spend an evening with Zafir, just the two of them. Asking for one evening in two weeks was not petulant, she'd told Farrah who refused to stick her head into anything remotely marital.

The numerous public occasions and state dinners during which they saw each other and smiled and barely exchanged two words didn't count.

Neither did the nights when he came to her, sometimes at midnight, sometimes even at dawn.

The first night, three days after they had returned, Lauren had seen him earlier at a state dinner. She had worn a royal blue creation with long sleeves and a conservative cut that didn't declare her pregnancy blatantly. A Russian oligarch, who was interested in investing unholy amounts of money in Behraat, who apparently was very fond of New York City, was the guest of honor.

He had monopolized Lauren for most of the evening. The man's icy blue gaze lingered far too much over her body but Lauren had just smiled and nodded.

And none of it had escaped Zafir's notice.

It had been past midnight and Lauren had fallen into a sort of restless slumber after retiring to her quarters.

Hardness and heat, the wall of masculinity behind her had woken her up. Smiling, she had purred and stretched into him, her body already thrumming with anticipation.

That luscious mouth of his had kissed a blazing inferno down her spine, pulling away at her wispy nightgown. One hand snuck under her and played relentlessly with her breasts, pinching and stroking her already highly sensitive nipples.

He'd remained silent, which was strange in itself for she loved all the words he used to tell her how much he needed her. It was only after he had teased her to a fever pitch, hurtling her to the edge of climax, after commanding her to lift her leg and pushing into her from behind that he had finally spoken.

Teeth had dug into her shoulder, sending a spasm of sensation down her spine. "I don't like the way the Russian looks at you," he'd said, in a low voice that had been ripe with warning. "And I don't like that I don't like it."

Lauren had closed her eyes, breathing roughly, trying to sift through his words.

That she was not to make light of it, shouldn't argue with him on it, was clear. That it wasn't her that he doubted. That he felt so much at all. That he'd needed to claim her in the most carnal and intimate way before he could bring himself to mention it.

Tilting her head back, she'd sought his mouth, pulled the scent of him deep inside. "The investment and even more importantly, the exposure he brings to Behraat is not something you can turn your back on." The slight widening of his eyes made her glad she had read through the file her aide had prepared for her. "Neither can you hide me away because then it looks like you've noticed his interest and taken offense.

"The only remaining option, and the one that you despise is, pretending that you don't care, continuing to let him look at me like that until the deal with him is actually done.

"This is Behraat we're talking about, so there's not a choice, is there?"

He'd withdrawn and then thrust back into her slick heat, a darkness that scared her in his gaze. But even with her mind worried, still she had gasped at his skilled strokes and languorous kisses. Still, she succumbed to the need inside.

"Not only beautiful and smart, but such understanding too?"

She'd definitely known something was wrong then. Because his smile, it hadn't quite reached his eyes. And Lauren had a feeling that moment, that night hadn't been just about the Russian. "Really, Zafir, handling a few hours with one arrogant jerk who thinks he's God's gift to women is not that big of a deal," she'd somehow managed.

Something bleak had passed his eyes. He'd muttered something explosive in Arabic, pressed a kiss to her mouth and then began moving inside her again.

A couple of times, she imagined she'd glimpsed a shadow of pain in his gaze but then he would kiss her as though he couldn't breathe and she forgot all about it. Having learned so much about his childhood, she didn't expect some grand declaration of love from him.

His actions and his commitment to her and their child meant more than anything to her. The tenderness in his eyes when he glanced at her growing bump meant more than words.

But, her mind being the only place she had any sort of privacy left in her new life, she retreated to it often and there was no hiding from truth.

She had fallen in love with him. And the realization didn't come about like a flash of lightning like she had always imagined.

It crept up on her in the middle of a small gathering, one she'd had Abdul arrange, in cahoots with a reluctant Arif and Farrah, Ahmed and Huma and a few other staff that she'd been told had a friendly relationship with Zafir.

The small gathering waited in her quarters, both awkward and excited.

Please don't be distant, she'd been muttering to herself. *Please don't let this be a horrible idea that only pains him more.*

And then there he was pushing the wide doors open and striding inside with that prowling gait and they were all yelling, "Surprise!"

Thunder danced in his gaze.

The cheers they had practiced went from excited to a stunned silence as Zafir searched the crowd, his gaze still serious.

Finally, it fell on her.

Pulse thudding, somehow Lauren had covered the little distance between them.

Still, he stared at her, shock set into his features. "I was told you needed my attention urgently."

She didn't care for his tone. "I made sure it wasn't some super important meeting that we interrupted."

"But you made me think something had happened. To you."

"Oh…but, you can see, I'm fine." She rose up on her toes and kissed his unshaven cheek. Felt his lean frame tremble under her. "Happy birthday, Zafir."

His fingers snuck into her hair and pulled her closer.

Arabic fell from his mouth, like a clap of thunder. Within minutes, the room cleared out, leaving just them.

Stunned, Lauren turned back, swatted Zafir in the shoulder. "How could you?"

"Easily. I'm their sheikh."

She pouted. "They all wanted to wish you happy birthday and I'll have you know I went to a lot of trouble. It's not easy planning a surprise party for the man who has—"

She never finished her sentence because he picked her up. Her hands went around his nape, her heart thudded but she tried to keep the smile from her mouth.

"I wanted to be alone with my wife," he growled then.

Long strides carried her past the sitting area to the bedroom. He put her down on the bed with a tenderness that caught her breath. And then his hands were on her bodice. When the silk didn't cooperate, he ripped it with his hands, pushed away the silk of her bra and closed his abrasive palm against one plump breast.

"Zafir..." She threw her head back and moaned as he buried his mouth in her throat. Traced a searing path down her chest to her breast, licked the engorged tip. "Wait, I..."

"No, no waiting." Then his mouth closed over her nipple, licking and suckling, and then there were teeth. "Now, *habeebti*. I need this now."

A whimper fell from Lauren's mouth, her spine arching, her body bowing under the pleasure. Pulling her to the edge of the bed, he shoved her dress to her thighs, pulled her panties down and entered her in one long, smooth thrust.

Silk and steel, velvet hardness against wet heat, their bodies built up into a perfect rhythm, beautiful and raw, earthy and something out of this world, at the same time.

With soothing words, he bent her over his arm, and took her breast in his mouth.

Hands in his hair, Lauren rode him shamelessly, shuddering and splintering until they reached the peak together, and crashed down to earth again.

"I can't believe..." She flushed and hid her damp face in his chest, pulled in a much-needed breath and looked up again. "You were not supposed to do that."

His thumb brushing her cheek, he frowned down at her. "What? Not touch my lovely wife on my birthday?"

"No, turn the evening into…this. I mean, yes, but we could have waited."

"And you know when it comes to you and being inside of you," he said, nibbling at her throat again, "that I can never wait."

Looking down, she flushed, and held the edges of her torn bodice up. "I wanted to spend an evening with you. Outside of bed." It was hard to sound miffed when he looked at her with such hunger in his eyes. "Talk about what's going on with you and such. I know the weight of Behraat lies on your shoulders, but I…"

"What?"

"We see each other at those ghastly dinners, and then you make love to me in the dark of the night. It feels like… I'm trying so hard not be a petulant wife, Zafir… I… If there's something on your mind, *about us*, or anything else, I have a right to know."

Shielding his gaze away from her, Zafir tucked her head under his chin and held her tight. His heart still thudded from the fact that she'd arranged a party for him. "Lauren…you're so much more than I ever expected to have as a wife, *habeebti*." This, as he was learning every day with her, was the absolute truth. "As predictable as it sounds, I've just been busy, preoccupied."

"Okay," she said readily enough but Zafir wasn't sure she was convinced.

How had one small manipulation become such an impenetrable wall between them, he wondered. How had giving them both what they wanted turned into this ever-growing chasm?

What the hell was wrong with him that he had everything he had ever wanted and he was playing with it like this? He knew, even as he acted contrary to it, that Lauren would never let him put her in one safe compartment, just because he didn't like himself very much right now.

This wallowing was a weakness.

A weakness that made him look away from her, that made him shudder at what he spied in her eyes. That made him wish he was anything but who he was.

And that was the kind of useless, helpless thinking that he despised the most.

That made her doubt that he was not happy with her, when she was the one perfect thing he'd ever held in his life, was unacceptable.

He had no reason to be not happy.

Shoving away the lead weight in his gut, he moved back from her, grabbed a cashmere wrap from the bottom of the bed and slowly wrapped it around her.

When she looked down, she was frowning, thoughtful.

And he felt a flicker of fear unlike he had ever known. Not even when he'd thought Tariq would execute him had it clawed through him with such intensity.

He took her hands in his and pulled her off the bed. "I shouldn't have ruined your plans, yes. You have cake, I presume?" he said, smiling.

Whatever doubts she'd had earlier, her gaze was clear now. And a little naughty as she raised her brows. "I had it flown in from a bakery in New York. German chocolate." She laced her fingers with him and tugged him. "You might feel faint once you taste it, so hold on tight to me."

He burst out laughing and went willingly. "Now I get it. This whole party was a ruse. You just wanted cake from New York," he teased.

Eyes glinting like the brightest opals, she smiled. "Okay, you caught me. But believe me, you've not had cake like this, Zafir."

He let her voice wash over him as she extolled the life-affirming virtues of delicious cake. Joy and fear were both his in that moment.

This woman could calm him and excite him, drench

him in warmth just as easily as she undid him. And there was nothing he could do about it. He couldn't lose her and stay the same, he knew with a certainty that made his gut twist hard.

She hummed "Happy Birthday" while he cut the cake and then brought a small piece to his mouth. He licked at her finger, the action instinctive, his need for her as natural as breathing and ever-present.

Pink tinged her cheeks but she pulled away. She served two pieces, handed him silverware and ordered him to pour coffee for both of them.

Took one bite of the cake between those imperfectly wide lips and moaned so sensually that he was instantly hard.

He took a bite himself and smiled. "How do I compete with cake?"

Zafir and she had just finished their coffee when his phone rang. About to complain that he'd promised her an uninterrupted evening, she caught the words just in time when she saw his expression.

Pulling the cell phone out, he stared at it. And then he clicked it on.

She saw shuddering shock, and relief and such pain in it that she reached for him instantly.

So much emotion, such anguish cloaked his features that looked as if they'd been carved into that mold. "Zafir? What's wrong?"

Slowly, his gaze focused on her. As if he had been far, far away from her. "My father…he is awake. And asking for me." His tone had a tremor in it.

"Six years… The last time I saw him, he'd declared to the council that I was his heir. He and Tariq were arguing, *screaming, threatening each other*. And when Tariq left with a murderous glance at the both of us and my father turned to me, I told him I despised him. That I'd been better off as an orphan. And the next evening, he was found collapsed in his room. His food was poisoned."

"Oh… Zafir…"

She wrapped her hands around his nape and pulled him down to her level. Slowly, softly, she kissed him, pouring everything she felt for him. Leaning her forehead against his, Lauren clasped his cheeks. "Are you afraid?"

He laughed again, although it had a bitter tinge to it. He didn't push her away and she was unbelievably glad for that. "No. But I'm weak enough to wish I was anyone but who I am."

"No, Zafir. This…pain I see in your eyes, this grief, this love for a man whom you have every reason to hate, your courage to do the right thing by Behraat, by me, by your father, by everyone that falls in your sphere…this is what makes you you, Zafir. And why I love you so much."

His eyes widened, his chin jerked back. As though she had taken a swing at him. As though it was impossible, even unacceptable for her to feel such a thing for him. As if it was the worst fate he'd ever faced. "Lauren…"

"Why do you sound so shocked?" she said, determined to hold on to her flailing courage. That he was so stunned was not a bad thing, she reassured herself. "But this isn't the time, right? While your father's waiting. So go see him."

Zafir never returned the night he had gone to see his father. After waiting for a few hours, Lauren had fallen asleep, still worried about him.

About them.

A furor of activity took place once it had become known that the old sheikh was out of the coma. Not more than a day had gone by where he hadn't had numerous meetings with council members, Ahmed had told her when she'd begged him for information.

All with Zafir present, she'd learned. Even the tribal chiefs were there now.

In between those long meetings, she had gone to see Rashid, too. The unresolved animosity between father and son, mostly from Zafir had rattled her. When his father had asked Zafir to leave them alone, he'd point-blank refused.

To which, Rashid had leveled him a long look.

Rashid, his gaze incisively intelligent, had quizzed her about her family, her life in New York. But couldn't really say much with his son watching them like a hawk.

Two days later, Zafir found her in the library, one of her favorite rooms in the palace. Dressed in a gray silk suit that lovingly draped over his shoulders, he was all business.

A team of aides and the ever-present Arif stood outside the door.

"I have a three-week trip to Asia," he said regretfully, after kissing her, right in front of the library staff and Ahmed.

"Three weeks?" she sounded dismayed, and for once she didn't care. She was tired of seeing those shadows in his eyes. Tired of wondering if he was pulling away from her. Tired of the constant ache in her chest. "You're not doing this to avoid me, are you, Zafir?" She'd no idea where she had found the strength to pose that question, this courage to put herself out there when it was becoming more and more obvious that it was the last thing he wanted to hear.

His mouth flattened. "I'm trying to get these long trips out of the way so that I can have an easier schedule when the baby comes. We'll talk when I come back. I promise, Lauren."

She had held on to him tightly, curbing the words that rose to her mouth, wanting to be given voice again and again. Locked away the wet heat that pricked at her eyes.

The depth of her feelings for him, the longing for him, it wasn't something she was used to yet.

"I've told my father," he said, "that he's to leave you alone while I'm gone. Don't let him bully you in my absence."

The next couple of weeks passed in a blur. Just as Zafir had warned her, Rashid had summoned her twice but she had found excuses both times. Not that she was afraid of him. She was more worried she would rip into him for Zafir.

Her first ultrasound was due in a few days and Zafir and she had argued over the phone about whether they should learn the sex of the baby. And when he laughed like that, when he told her that he couldn't wait to kiss her, everything was perfect in her world.

She'd just finished her yoga class and showered when Ahmed informed her that Salma was in the city and wanted to visit with her.

Thrilled, Lauren welcomed Salma with a hug. She took the chubby infant from Salma, and cuddled her. Farrah, who had stayed on to see Salma, translated between them.

Laughing, they chatted together happily. But when Farrah repeated something Salma had said, Lauren was confused. "I'm sorry, what does she mean, she's happy I accepted the arrangement?"

Farrah asked Salma to elaborate. Salma's response, translated by Farrah, "She says that her grandfather, the chief of the Dahab, made a promise to Zafir. In return for you saving Salma's and the baby's life, he would bring the tribes together, help Zafir unite them with state. As long as Zafir stopped following in his father's footsteps and married the nurse. With the tribes back in the fold, the High Council finally had to accept his rule."

Lauren stilled where she stood, a kind of numbness

spreading through her limbs. He hadn't even wasted an evening before he had proposed to her. And this was why…

Like everyone else in her life, she had only been secondary to his actual goal. Like always.

She slid to the settee in a shaking heap, her chest so tight that she couldn't breathe.

"Head down, Lauren. Between your legs," Farrah's voice sounded sharp, as if it was rolling in through a fog.

Breath came rushing into her in huge gulps and with it the sound of her heart shattering. She heard Farrah rushing Salma out and closing the door. Heard her call her name, her face worried.

But as she raised her head, and scrunched her knees up, all Lauren could see, hear, feel was Zafir.

"I need you, Lauren. Unlike anything or anyone else in the world."

He'd so cleverly laid out a trap for her without really saying anything, let her spin a story with his teasing glances and caresses and words.

Manipulated her into believing what they had was more. When it was not even the mere marriage of convenience she had thought.

Used her guilt that she had hidden the truth from him. Used their unborn child. Used her growing feelings for him.

Played the part of the charming, teasing man who was beginning to feel something for her.

All for Behraat.

She hadn't asked for the fantasy of it. She hadn't asked for him to tease her, and charm her and pretend as if he cared about her.

You're the fool, Lauren, something nasty whispered inside her head. *You've always been a fool for him, since the beginning.*

Again and again, he'd proved that only Behraat counted for him. It was only Behraat that had his heart.

Pulling in a long breath, she got up from the settee and told Farrah that she wanted to lie down.

Behind her bedroom door, she crumpled onto the bed, every inch of her thrumming with fury.

She couldn't bear to be here another moment. Couldn't bear this ache in her chest. Couldn't bear to live the rest of her life with a man who had, again and again, not only showed her how little she meant to him, but used her and their situation.

How could she ever trust him again? How could she trust herself, when apparently, she could spin a fantasy out of nothing?

Afternoon gave way to evening and she shivered at the sudden chill coming in from the balcony.

She splashed water on her face, changed her clothes, called Abdul and instructed him to arrange a meeting for her. Only one person would help her leave the palace, the city and Behraat without notifying Zafir. Without caring about bringing down Zafir's wrath.

She had to leave before he was back. Or she would never leave.

Worse, she would live the rest of her life, knowing that she would never have his love but crave it anyway, caught in a misery of her own making.

And she would not be alone in her misery.

Zafir checked his watch, calculated the time difference and then dismissed his staff.

Picking up his phone, he walked to the balcony of his forty-fifth-floor suite and looked out at Beijing. It was a damp, cold night and he itched to be back in Behraat, in the palace, besides Lauren.

Every time he closed his eyes, he remembered the

stricken look in her gaze, the tremble of her lips as she asked him if he was avoiding her…

Always challenging him, always making him wonder what else was there to life, what else he hadn't known, what else, first Rashid and then Zafir himself, had deprived himself of in life…

Like that impromptu birthday party.

Her cell phone rang a few times before she picked up.

"Hello, Zafir." She sounded groggy, tired, hoarse.

His nape prickled. Something prowled inside of him then, a knowing, a feeling of fear, of loss, of a wide yearning chasm.

Something was very wrong.

Even her hello sounded distant, full of a weight he didn't understand. He shouldn't have left her, the first thought pounded into him. He shouldn't have been avoiding her. He shouldn't have…

Lost his head over her in the first place? Shouldn't have let her weaken him like this?

Shouldn't have fallen in love like this at all.

Because now, she made him want to defy the entire world for her, she made him want to do the impossible just so he could be worthy of her love. She made him want to damn himself just so he could be with her.

The murmur of a male voice in the background pulled his attention away from what it seemed had been as inevitable as breathing. He pressed his thumb at his temple, took a long breath.

Then he heard Lauren's low answer and then the door closed again.

Ahmed wouldn't come into her bedroom, even if Lauren considered him a friend…

He still couldn't believe how easily she had his staff eating out of her hand, how easily she had integrated herself into such a different, difficult life. And she had done it with barely any complaint.

"Lauren? Are you sick?"

"No. I'm fine. The baby's fine." He heard her hesitate, the rustle of clothes, and then she cleared her throat. "I was sleeping."

"But you never miss your yoga class. Did something upset you?"

He felt her amazement, and his own, stretch tautly in the silence, an incandescent flicker in the darkness that he could sense was coming at him. Among all the million things that ran through his brain on a given day, he'd remembered that and hadn't even known it.

"Lauren?" he prompted again, and this time, he knew what it was that pulsed through him.

Desperation. Panic. As though he was sinking in the middle of the vast, stark Behraati desert, swallowed up by its great jaws like every other ruler had before him. As though after all his struggle, after everything he'd learned from Rashid and everything he'd been forced to learn since being thrust into power, he was somehow still empty-handed.

"It's early morning here, Zafir." Clear, cutting, she was in control of herself again. "In New York."

His breath punched out of him and his hand fisted by his side. A great, big roar began in his chest, crashing everything inside him into pieces, thundering its way out. But he swallowed it away. Like he had always done any emotion, any impulse, anything that would be detrimental to his dream, his rule of Behraat.

"And why, *exactly*, are you in New York?" He sounded edgy, rough and he didn't care.

"I left. You and your beloved Behraat."

He exhaled, his breath stuck in his throat like cut glass, every inch of him shaking, as if he stood cold and naked.

As if every ounce of warmth had leeched out of his world, never to return.

"Why?" he still asked. As if it could be some small, mundane reason that had prompted her to flee when his back was turned. As if he had been finally rendered into this weak, pathetic shell of a man who hoped for impossible things.

Everything inside of him clenched tight, waiting for her answer.

"You don't know, Zafir?"

Now, she sounded like the Lauren he knew. Like the Lauren that had brought such joy and light into his life, the Lauren that had made him think of himself for the first time.

Like the Lauren that somehow kept wrenching parts of him away.

"God, you looked into my eyes, you held me in your arms and you told me this was for our child. While all along…it was to cement your rule of Behraat." She sounded so angry and yet her voice shuddered. "You…lied about everything."

"No. What I did was try to do right by everyone. Just like you said. When the opportunity came, I grabbed it with both hands. It was unbearable for me to know my child would not know his or her place, just like me. Untenable for me to walk away from Behraat. Unbearable for me to…

"And then you…you made it all possible. For once in my life, I had a chance to have everything I had ever wanted. And I took it."

"You'll always put Behraat first."

Pushing a hand through his hair, Zafir tried to breathe through the knot in his throat. And for the first time in his cursed life, he asked something for himself.

"Don't ask me to be someone else, Lauren. Don't walk

away when we have something so good. Do not call it love and then wreck what we have with its weakness and its exalted expectations of sacrifices and grand gestures.

"Don't ruin it all because it doesn't fit your vague notion of what love should be."

Lauren felt the dark anger in his words like a whip against her skin. "I threw myself into this marriage with everything I had and more. I…" Tears threatened to steal away her words, her very will. "I even told myself that your feelings for me didn't matter. Not when you…"

"Then come back."

"But I'll always wonder what could take you away from me. When Behraat will make you choose over me and our child.

"What new political alliance and promise of power would be the thing that makes you decide it's worth more than us? It'll kill me, Zafir."

"Then you do not know me at all, much less love me. And the kind of reassurance you ask for, it's not in me to give." He sounded like the crack of thunder, angry and cruel and final, and it seemed to suck away the breath from her very lungs. "Your vow, your grand declaration…they are nothing but empty words, lines from a fantasy you have of what love should be.

"And I…" it trembled then, his voice and Lauren shivered, "I am the fool that I believed you, that I tortured myself every minute that I didn't deserve this thing between us…and you, that I hoped at all," he said in such a tired, empty voice that Lauren could imagine that dullness that would dim his golden gaze, the weight that would pull at his sensuous mouth, the tightness that would descend on those broad shoulders.

Lauren stared at her phone for a full minute before she realized he'd hung up.

And then, she cried. Big, racking sobs that had David inquire outside the door, tears that burned her nose and eyes and throat, shook her body, and hurt her head.

This wouldn't be the end of it, she knew. Not this argument between them or the last she saw of him. Not the last of the fire he'd made her walk through from the first minute.

Zafir wouldn't give up on this child they'd created and that wasn't a bad thing, she told herself, as if that could cleanse away the misery that sat like a boulder on her chest.

CHAPTER THIRTEEN

LIFE, OF COURSE, didn't come to a standstill, just because you got your heart broken, Lauren realized painfully over the next month. Twenty hours after Zafir had ended their call, a real estate agent had arrived with keys for her old apartment and a very betrayed-looking Ahmed after him.

"He banished me here, after berating me and four generations of my ancestors for losing sight of you, over the phone. For letting you leave. And now I'm to guard you here, in this crowded, noisy city. He should have just killed me," he said, despair high in his voice.

Lauren, feeling emotional and lonely and heartsick for Zafir and anyone remotely related to him, threw her arms around him. Ahmed's thin frame froze at first, and then slowly he patted her back awkwardly. The expression in his eyes, like deer caught in headlights, made Lauren laugh in the middle of tears.

"I'm sorry, Ahmed," she'd said and he'd nodded, understanding in his gaze.

With Ahmed's help, Lauren settled back into her apartment. When she'd asked him where His Royal Highness thought Ahmed was supposed to stay, he'd told her an apartment had been arranged for him, on the same floor of her building.

Before she could even make a list, a delivery service stood at her door, with milk and juice and fruits and steaming hot meals. Since refusing would mean talking to Zafir again, Lauren let herself be pushed.

With Zafir arranging her life to the smallest detail, even

a continent away, she felt as if she was in limbo, waiting for some slick, high-powered law firm to start custody proceedings.

A month passed while she played with the idea of going back to work, yet didn't, a month in which she hid from Alicia, because she couldn't bear to tell her the truth and make it even more real, a month in which she heard not a word from Zafir.

Even Ahmed, who accompanied her on her long meandering walks through the parks and streets, and compared New York to Behraat incessantly, carefully veered away from anything related to Zafir.

And the more rational and in control of herself she became, the more Lauren went over every look, every word, every touch Zafir and she had shared. Faced her cowardice in running away without even waiting for him to return, forcing him to offer an explanation over the phone.

But he wouldn't choose her over Behraat. Ever.

Did she want him to, she wondered as winter approached and the days grew shorter and she became less and less sure of herself.

Would that be the same man she had fallen in love with if he did?

Like a toll he had to pay for being loved by her? Was that what her love was—a transaction?

On another gloomy, chilly day, which made Lauren wish for the sweltering heat of Behraat, not that she would ever admit it to Ahmed, she returned from her evening walk when she saw the sleek, armored limousine idling at the curb in front of her building.

Her pulse racing, she shied her gaze away and made it to her apartment on the first floor. She had pulled a bottle of water from the refrigerator, panic swirling through her, when there was a knock.

Bracing herself, she opened the door.

The bottle fell from her fingers and hit the floor with a swishy sound.

Rashid Al Masood stood there, the corridor shrinking several sizes by his height. That sunken, unhealthy pallor was gone and she felt more than a little awe at his commanding presence, unbalanced and off-kilter at his golden gaze, so much like Zafir's.

"May I come in?" he said in a papery voice and Lauren, too shocked still, signaled for him to come in. He held out his hand toward a shadow that materialized into a man, took a file from him and then stepped in.

Fear beat a tattoo in her chest as Lauren's gaze fell on the papers.

Maybe he was here to ensure the termination of their marriage? Maybe he'd already found a new, better suited, bride for Zafir? Maybe…

Stop it, Lauren.

Zafir wouldn't do it like this. He wouldn't send a messenger, his father of all people, to end this between them. Not after everything they had shared.

But you've told him that all that didn't matter. That it was all a lie. That the one small thing he hadn't told her minimized everything else he'd shared with her, felt for her, showed her.

She sank her fingers into her hair and pushed at it, a strange fear gripping her limbs all of a sudden.

Some sort of sound must have escaped her because Rashid peered down at her.

"Do you require medical assistance, Ms. Hamby?"

"*I'm not Miss Hamby anymore.*" Her response was instant, defensive, like a screech of wind in the silence.

"Yet you're here, thousands of miles away when your place is by my son." Dry and derisive, his voice scraped at her nerves. "For six years I've been in a coma and little has changed in Western society's perception of marriage."

"You've no idea what happened between us. Nor do I owe you an explanation."

"I can see why my son indulged in this nonsense with you." His gaze lingered on her face thoughtfully, then shifted to her belly for a fraction of a second. "But that he lets you have this reckless freedom in this dangerous city when every minute of every day, you court the media's eye or even harm. I reminded him that you're his wife, that he should command you to be back in—"

"I'm not a possession, Your Highness."

"Is it my grandson's safety that you're so careless about?"

Fury rattled along Lauren's nerves. "You've no right to speak to me that way. And that it's a…" She slapped a hand over her mouth and glared at him. "I won't share that with you. Not before I tell Zafir."

Because she had broken their agreement and asked the ultrasound technician to tell her.

She'd waited for him to call so that she could share the news. Had been dismayed that he hadn't. Instead, he'd had Farrah call her and confirm that everything was all right.

As if he was completely through with her.

"Is my son aware that you know then?"

Shocked at how easily he'd manipulated her, she tried to corral her thoughts. "My child will not be yours to mold, Your Highness. I won't allow it and neither will Zafir."

He bristled at her reckless statement.

"You seem to be certain of a lot of things about a husband you have fled. In secret, with a bitter old woman's support, a woman that wishes him no less than a painful death. Do you have any idea the risk you took in trusting her with your child, my grandchild's, safety? Or how it torments my son, night after night, as if your reckless actions were his fault?"

"Stop it, please," she whispered, sweat pooling over her. God, what had she done? What had she turned her back on? "Just…tell me why you're here. Or leave."

Arrogant pride filled the gaunt crevices of his face. "All of Behraat is at Zafir's feet today, as it always should have been. Yet there is no joy, no pride in his eyes. You…" His gaze seemed to spear her, and with doubts eating away at her, she struggled to hold it. "…have weakened him, crippled him in a way I can't seem to fix. My son will not be brought down by a selfish, spoiled, so-called independent *American* who doesn't understand the first thing about duty and—"

"Maybe it's you who did that to him," she attacked, loathing herself as much as he seemed to. Because, the galling thing, the bitter truth was that he was right.

For a moment, her words suspended there in the room, like bullets stilled on their way to the target in some 3-D action flick before shattering away.

His eyes widened in disbelief but she didn't care anymore. Not when every cell in her ached to see Zafir and hold him. "Maybe it's time to stop asking Zafir to give more of himself to you and Behraat. Maybe if someone, for once, thinks of him, instead of sucking him dry in the name of duty, he'll smile and laugh again. Maybe what he needs is someone who loves him unconditionally for the kind, honorable, generous man that he is, then he will…"

And in her own desperate, impassioned words, Lauren found the truth that she'd been so blind to see. As if it was there all along inside her, clawing to get out.

A whimper fell from her mouth.

It was herself she'd never believed in.

For all her promises, she'd been waiting for a reason to believe that Zafir would abandon her like her parents had done, waiting for it all to fall apart. And the moment their relationship had been tested, at the first hurdle, she'd run away.

As if life and love were a fantasy she'd could dabble at, just like Zafir had mocked her.

That he'd chosen to unite Behraat didn't cancel out all that he'd shown her. Didn't corrupt all the promises he'd made her.

She buried her face in her hands, the scope of the damage she had wreaked a lead weight on her chest.

Rashid stood up and looked at her, a smug little curve to his mouth. As if victory was finally his.

"It is clear you were never right for him with all the nonsense you just spouted. His sheikha would understand his destiny and would not distract him." With every wrong thing Rashid said, Lauren could see the right path.

Both she and this insufferable old man were wrong, too absolute, too rigid in their thinking. And Zafir…he'd been walking that tightrope all along. From the minute he had met her.

"I suggest you have your lawyers look at the papers I brought. My son needs to put this…*episode* behind him. As for my grandchild, I'll—"

"No," Lauren threw back, straightening from the couch. She'd face this bully and a thousand more like him for Zafir. She'd prove her love a thousand times over to Zafir if only he'd give her another chance. Mind made up, she said, "I'm not going to sign a thing and you can't make me. And I'll tell Zafir that you were trying to blackmail me into cutting all ties," she added for good measure.

Rashid's stare was flat, derisive. Could have scorched her into ashes, if she let it. "You think my son will believe your word over mine? If you still haven't learned your lesson—"

"If you care anything for Zafir, if there's even a little

regret inside that political heart of yours about what you denied him for so many years, you'll take me to Behraat," she demanded.

Warning glittered in his eyes. "There's nothing but misery for you in Behraat. Zafir does not forgive." And in that last sentence, there was a crack, a deep regret.

"I'll take my chances," she threw back and slammed the door.

She quickly dialed her ob-gyn for an appointment.

She'd beg if that's what it would take.

Lauren had to wait eleven hours and twenty minutes after setting foot in the dusty, blazing inferno that was Behraat before she saw Zafir.

Through the ride in the armored, dark-tinted limo, Lauren saw little villages en route to the city between long stretches of rough road in between. Her pulse thudded when the high walls of the palace came into sight.

This was home now, she reminded herself resolutely, even as she felt daunted by the task ahead.

Only to be told by Rashid's nasally aide that she'd have to wait.

She'd eaten, walked a path on the rug, fallen asleep out of sheer exhaustion and jet lag, wanted to scream at the silence, had even wondered if Rashid hadn't somehow imprisoned her with no intention of ever telling Zafir again. But she'd been shown into her old suite.

A day of administrative affairs cannot be disturbed for one emotionally weak woman, Rashid had said before leaving her to his staff, a grim smile to his mouth.

Not Farrah, not Huma, not even Arif, it seemed knew of her arrival. Only Ahmed waited outside in the lounge, as much a prisoner as she because he'd refused to leave her side. Even when Rashid had commanded it. Patted her shoulder in encouragement in that awkward way of his when he'd realized what she meant to do.

She'd showered and changed into a sleeveless tunic and loose, flowy cotton trousers and once again, fallen into a restless sleep. Inky black night cloaked the room in semi-darkness and she wondered what had woken her.

When she checked the time, she was shocked to see she had slept for more than three hours.

She sat up and whimpered as a cramp twisted her calf.

"Should I call for Farrah?"

The room lit up in a blaze of lights and Zafir stood at the foot of the bed. Tall. Dark. Impossibly gorgeous. Heart-wrenchingly remote.

"How long have you been here?"

He shrugged, as if he didn't care enough to answer. And in that casual tilt of his shoulders and the dull glow of his golden eyes, Lauren knew she was walking a very tight line.

Throat tight and limbs shaking, she looked at his face bathed in the light. A deep well of emotion clamped her chest.

His dark blue dress shirt and black trousers utterly failed at masking that barely civilized air around him. Thick stubble marked his jaw and her fingers itched to trace the proud angles of it. He'd let his hair grow longer and it made his face even more narrow and gaunt. Dark shadows hung under his eyes and she wondered how long he'd been up for if Rashid's words were to be believed.

Undiluted power clung to him, like a second skin, and she knew now that it was both his weapon and armor, as much to rule and right Behraat as it was to keep everyone out.

And yet, he'd let her in and she had thrown it all away.

Dismay swirled through her, threatening to break her, and she wondered if she'd already lost him.

When she tugged her gaze to his, something in it made her mouth dry. "It's just a cramp. I should have walked around more on the flight."

She pushed the throw away and got off the bed. She stumbled, her legs feeling like noodles but straightened herself.

While he stood there unmoving, his gaze cold, his demeanor utterly unapproachable. As though there was an impenetrable fortress around him and he'd allow nothing to touch it. As though he'd buried himself deep beneath those walls.

"Zafir, I—"

"Is it advisable for you to keep traveling back and forth on such long flights whenever you please?" Those golden eyes fell to her belly, and she saw his mouth flinch before he skewered her again. "Have I given you too much credit in this as well, Lauren?" Taunt and threat, his honeyed voice could cut her skin. "Will you make a monster of me yet by forcing me to imprison you, *habeebti*?"

She flushed and searched for the right words. Which mistake did she start apologizing for? "I made sure it was all right for me to travel. You know that I would never take an unnecessary risk."

"You have proved that I do not know you, Lauren. Inarguably. So indulge me." If his intention was to eviscerate her, he was succeeding. Lauren wanted to curl up and whimper.

"How long is this trip going to be for?"

She'd waited too long to answer because his voice cracked like thunder across the room again.

"Who let you through here without breathing so much as a word to even Arif? I don't know what shocked me more last time, that you had managed to flee or your cunning knack in making such a convenient alliance."

Lauren flinched, remembering Rashid's words. "I'm sorry for running away like that. For taking her help. For…"

"Who helped you return?"

"If you didn't know that I was here, what were you doing in this suite then?"

In that infinitesimal moment in which he hesitated, in the dark shadows under his eyes, in his reading glasses and papers and that fountain pen of his that sat on the coffee table, Lauren found her answer.

He sat here in the dark, in the suite she had stayed in, night after night.

God, she'd been such a fool, a thousand times she could call herself that and still, it wouldn't be enough.

"Answer my question, Lauren."

"Your father. He came to New York. Brought divorce papers with him. Told me he had to get me out of your life. That he wouldn't let me ruin your great destiny."

Shock flared in his eyes.

She covered the distance between them. Willed him to look at her, to give her one chance. "He was right, about me at least. I've been selfish, foolish, but I won't let you finish this because he—"

His hands clasped her wrists and he tugged her to look up at him. And that rough, not-so-together movement of his gave Lauren courage. "*My father…* Lauren, what the hell are you talking about? I forbade him from even mentioning your name to me. I told him that he wasn't to go near you.

"And yet he…" His golden gaze flared and then went flat again. "You're here because he threatened you about the baby…" Utter defeat and a helplessness she would have never associated with him filled his face. "You believed him," his voice was raw, shaky, "that I would take our child away from you. After everything we've been through."

It was the worst she could have believed about him, and yet she had.

And that's when Lauren realized how well Rashid had played his game. How well he had manipulated Lauren, tested her and then pushed her to the truth. How well he hid so much beneath the mask of an arrogant, insufferable old man.

How easily he had done it all for Zafir…

When Zafir turned away from her, Lauren waylaid him, her heart in her throat. "His threats were empty, his words designed to flay me, showed me what I truly was. I thought he was the most insufferable man I'd ever met.

"But I didn't believe the things he said about you, Zafir. In the end, it was that simple. Because I knew you."

Zafir turned away from Lauren, a crack inching its way through his already battered heart.

His father had flown all the way to New York? Why? He knew, Zafir had warned him, that he had to stay out of his personal affairs. That he wouldn't be manipulated for Behraat or any other reason.

That his child would not become some pawn of contention between Lauren and him…

Yet he had gone and now Lauren was here, because she…

Bracing himself, he allowed himself to look at her. To let himself believe that she stood there, and was not a figment of his nightly imagination, as it had been the past month. To breathe the air she filled with that wild, lavender scent of hers.

But he would not hope again.

He would not let her cripple him further. He would not become a fool like his father and risk everything. He would not give in to the savage urge to tie her up in this very room and ensure she never left him again.

That way, lay only madness.

But *Ya Allah*, she tempted him. She'd always tempted him into madness, into selfishness, into hoping for impossible things, into gut-wrenching love that threatened to make him lose his sense of himself.

Into almost letting it all go to hell—everything his father and he had built for Behraat.

Almost.

If he did, he would never forgive himself and he would come to resent her and it would be the utter ruin he'd always wished to avoid.

Not reaching for her now was like trying to avoid the harsh, beautiful, glittering sun while standing in the middle of the desert, however.

He clamped her chin with his fingers, a primal roar threatening to burst out of him. How many times would she test him, torment him? How much lower would she bring him?

"If you believed his threats to be empty, why are you here?"

"I didn't know then. But now…" She shook her head and when she looked up, a sheen coated her midnight-black eyes. Her mouth trembled. "I…came back for you, for us. I came back because I realized what a coward I've been, Zafir. I came back because I love you so much."

Zafir stiffened, even as her words chipped away at him. He released her and fisted his hands. "You have said that before, *habeebti*. And I believed you."

He pushed his hand through his hair, feeling as weak as a leaf. And she was the gust of wind that could forever blow him away.

Her shoulders rigid, her stubborn chin lifted, she nodded. Tears fell onto her cheeks and it was all Zafir could do to not take her in his arms. But he'd reached for everything she'd offered once, believed that he could have this light, this happiness that she brought him along with Behraat.

That he needn't be alone after all for the rest of his life, with nothing but the desert and Behraat stretched before him, that he was loved.

"I know how much I hurt you." She took a bracing breath, and wiped away her tears. And he could see her heart in those brilliant eyes of hers, her courage, her honesty and her love for him. He felt ragged then, at the battle within. And for once, he desperately wanted to lose.

"I'm so new to this whole thing," she was saying then, and each step she took toward him sent his pulse racing, crumbled his will, word by word. "It was myself I didn't believe in, Zafir, not you. But now I know myself. I believe in myself and that makes what you feel for me so much clearer. Makes this wildfire between us so gut-wrenchingly simple.

"I followed you before I even understood myself, Zafir. Now…now that I can trust myself, I would follow you to the end of the world."

She pressed her mouth to his, tentative and hot and a punch to his senses. Like a kick to his gut. Like pleasure so intense and shocking that it bordered on pain.

He fell apart then. Again and again as she anchored herself on his shoulders and took his mouth with such primitive, possessive passion. Claimed him. Marked him. Undid him all over again.

But this time, he welcomed the naked, raw, powerlessness that shuddered through him. Let it wash over him, knowing that it would be all right. Gave himself over to her soft nips and strokes.

"I love you, Zafir, so much. Mere words could not encompass it all. Tell me I haven't lost my chance with you. Please tell me—" she broke then, a catch in her throat, a tremble in those deceptively slender shoulders. And Zafir took over.

In the next breath, he was devouring her, tasting her. It was his will that took over then, his love for this courageous woman that kept feeding the fire.

He picked her up and brought her to the bed. Pushed all that wild, dark hair away from her face and tilted her chin up. Tasted her roughly, deeply, desperately. "You're my heart, Lauren. You bring such joy, such light to my life, *habeebti*." He traced the lush lower lip. "Trusting in this thing between us, allowing myself to love you, it's the most terrifying thing I have done.

"But I submit to it, I choose this, I choose you like I've chosen nothing else, Lauren. I willingly become weak for you."

Nodding, she threw her arms around him. And then she cried while he held her trembling body. Like he'd never seen her.

He knew it was fear leaving her body, that she needed it and he told her that there would be nothing but light after this, that he would never ever permit her to cry like this ever again. Because he couldn't take it.

She laughed then, and looked up at him. "Ever the powerful sheikh, Zafir?" But there was only tenderness in her gaze. She took his hands in hers and brought them to her face. Kissed the center of his palm, love shining in her eyes.

"I love you, Lauren."

"I love you, too." Then she directed his hands to her belly. And his heart felt as if it would rip out of his chest. "I know, Zafir."

His breath stilled. "We agreed that we would wait."

"We argued about it and you commanded me as if that was enough," she threw back. "I know you didn't want to know, so I won't force you—"

Her name was an entreaty on his lips as he begged her

to tell him. And the minx teased him. "You're going to be the death of me, *habeebti*."

She rubbed her finger over his lips, as if she couldn't bear to not touch him. "Only if you promise that you won't tell your father. This is the only way I can pay him back."

His smile slipping from his face, Zafir tried his hardest to not scowl. "I have no idea what you're talking about. But be assured, Lauren. He's not going to have a single say in our life, in our child's life."

So Zafir hadn't forgiven Rashid and yet, he had come for her.

"It's a boy, Zafir," she breathed against his mouth. Then she wrapped her arms around his middle and kissed his chest, held him through the tremor that shook him. "A son who'll be just as handsome as his father, I hope."

He kissed her temple reverently, his mouth curved into such a beautiful smile. "I love you, Lauren," he whispered again and again, against her mouth. "You're my heart, my friend, my family, everything."

"Zafir?"

"Yes?"

"Will you do something for me?"

"Anything, Lauren. I'm yours to command."

"Try to forgive your father. Please." When he began to retreat from her, she held his hands. "He…came for you, Zafir. He…pushed me and eviscerated me…just to see if I was worthy of you. He…he knew you'd do your duty by Behraat and still, he came…only for your happiness."

"He will only make our life hard, *habeebti*. Why do you ask this for him?"

Lauren traced that aquiline nose, his brow, his sensuous mouth with trembling fingers. "For you, Zafir. Forgive him for you. Forgive him for grabbing his happiness the only way he could with your mother.

"You know, amidst all this, I realized something. It was

her choice, wasn't it? To live with him, to love him, to make a life with him the only way she could. And as to why he didn't—"

"He told me why. He was afraid for my life. So he had it put out that I died along with her and then had Arif bring me back to him when I was four."

Lauren waited, the haunted expression in his eyes twisting her. "I wish I could bear this pain for you, Zafir. I… All I can do is tell you that I love you."

His forehead leaning against hers, he smiled. "That is not a small thing you give me, Lauren. Your love is everything to me, *habeebti*. With you by my side, I can take on the entire world. Even my father."

"You. Me. Forever," she said lightly and her reward was the look of utter joy in his gaze.

EPILOGUE

KAREEM ALEXANDER AL MASOOD was born four months later, a chubby, black-haired, golden-eyed bundle that gave his father, the magnificent High Sheikh Zafir Al Masood, the fright of his life when he'd balled up his cheeks for a full five seconds and bellowed at the top of his lungs when he'd held him.

The look in Zafir's eyes every time he held Kareem and that deep, visceral smile for Lauren, it filled her with joy and gratitude.

Over that first month, true to his promise, Zafir tried his level best to spend time with their son and Lauren. Most often than not, his visit got interrupted even with all the contingencies in place.

And Lauren told herself to have patience.

Six weeks after Kareem was born, Lauren had taken a bath, dismissed the maid who was watching Kareem and settled down to feed him. It was around four and suddenly the night stretched in front of her felt long and interminable.

And then there stood Zafir looking down at her, a content smile on his face.

Lauren pressed a kiss on his hand when he cupped her face and leaned against him as he silently settled on the armrest. "Hmm… I've forgotten how good you smell," she said, trying to swallow the rush of love gathered in her throat.

She'd barely seen him this past week. Even exhausted

as she was mostly with Kareem and sleep-deprived, she had missed him so much.

They sat in silence. When Lauren finished with Kareem, Zafir took him, cuddled his son for a little longer and then called back the maid and handed him over to her, before dismissing her once again.

"Your evening is mine," he declared, pulling her out of the recliner. When she looked at the retreating maid in question, he clasped her face, his golden gaze smiling. "He'll be close, Lauren. There is a number of staff that'll be watching him. They'll bring him to us when he needs you."

Surprised, Lauren smiled and tucked herself closer into Zafir's arms. Every day, their bond only deepened. And with a million matters that he managed, Zafir still somehow understood when she needed him.

He kissed her brow, her nose, her cheek and then finally found her mouth. She groaned and pushed herself into his touch, the fire always just there simmering, waiting to be stoked. Waiting to engulf them both.

"I've missed you so much," the words escaped her and then she hid her face in his neck.

He cradled her head with one hand, while the other settled on her hip, and nudged her closer to him. Languorous fire licked through Lauren's nerves. "No, *habeebti.* Never feel ashamed for missing me, or for needing me. Never stop loving me. I miss you every day, too, Lauren."

She flattened her palms on his chest, loving the thud of his heart under it. "So, Your Highness, what do you think we should do with three whole hours?"

He flicked his tongue over her ear, his hands sinking into her shoulders. "The whole night is ours, *habeebti.* And I'm yours."

Then his hungry gaze held hers. "I was wondering if you were ready to resume your wifely duties."

When Lauren remained silent, he tilted his head. "What is it, Lauren?"

Shuddering, Lauren ran her hands over him. The washboard abdomen, the narrow hips, the rock-hard thighs… every inch of him that she missed, that she hadn't touched in so many weeks. "No, I've missed you and… I'm more than ready. It's just that…"

"Whatever it is, you can tell me, Lauren."

"I… I look different, Zafir." He didn't let her shy her gaze away and Lauren flushed even more. "My body's different. I guess—"

Without letting her finish, Zafir picked her up and carried her to the bed. "You've given me such a beautiful and apparently ferocious son," he added laughing. "You even somehow forged a bond between me and my father. You've created the family that I'd always longed for, Lauren. Have you any idea how precious you are to me?"

With the flick of his hand, he pulled something out of his pocket and held it out for her.

The antique silver glinted in the muted light, a soft tinkle from the charm hanging against it.

It was the bracelet she had haggled over in the bazaar. "How did you know?" Tears filled her eyes. "How did you find it?"

"Ahmed told me how much you had loved it. That vendor traveled on with a tribe and it took me some time to have him tracked."

He put the bracelet on her hand, and slowly unbuttoned her blouse. Lauren heard the hiss of his breath as he cupped her breasts.

One look at the dark desire in his eyes and Lauren's doubts melted away. Desperate for him, she brought her hand down to his crotch.

He was hard, ready for her. As she was for him.

The same heat flickering wild between them, Lauren let Zafir take her to dizzying heights again.

And that particular, moonlit night, their forever continued in that room with fireworks and middle-of-the-night feedings and laughter and cuddles.

* * * * *

SNOWBOUND WITH HIS INNOCENT TEMPTATION

CATHY WILLIAMS

To my three wonderful daughters

CHAPTER ONE

'HONESTLY, ALI, I'M FINE!' Complete lie. Becky Shaw was far from fine.

Her job was on the line. The veterinary practice where she had been working for the last three years was in the process of being sold—and being turned into yet another quaint coffee shop to attract the onslaught of tourists who arrived punctually every spring and summer, snapping the gorgeous Cotswold scenery with their expensive cameras and buying up all the local art in a flurry of enthusiasm to take away a little bit of local flavour with them. Her friends Sarah and Delilah had got it right when they had decided to turn their cottage into a gallery and workshop. Not that they had had to in the end, considering they had both been swept off their feet by billionaires.

And then there was the roof, which had decided that it was no longer going to play ball and she was sure that right now, if she listened hard enough, she would be able to hear the unnerving sound of the steady leak drip-dripping its way into the bucket she had strategically placed in the corridor upstairs.

'I keep telling you that you're too young to be buried out there in the middle of nowhere! Why don't you come out to France? Visit us for a couple of weeks? Surely the practice can spare you for a fortnight…'

In three months' time, Becky thought glumly, the practice would be able to spare her for approximately the rest of her life.

Though there was no way that she was going to tell her sister this. Nor did she have any intention of going out to the south of France to see Alice and her husband, Freddy. Her heart squeezed tightly as it did every time she thought of Freddy and she forced herself to answer her sister lightly, voice betraying nothing.

'I'm hardly *buried out here*, Alice.'

'I've seen the weather reports, Becks. I always check what the weather's doing on my phone and the Cotswolds is due heavy snow by the weekend. You're going to be trapped there in the middle of March, when the rest of the country is looking forward to spring, for goodness' sake! *I worry about you.*'

'You mustn't.' She glanced out of the window and wondered how it was that she was still here, still in the family home, when this was supposed to have been a temporary retreat, somewhere to lick her wounds before carrying on with her life. That had been three years ago. Since then, in a fit of lethargy, she had accepted the job offer at the local vet's and persuaded her parents to put all plans to sell the cottage on hold. Just for a little while. Just until she got her act together. She would pay them a monthly rent and, once she'd got herself on a career ladder, she would leave the Cotswolds and head down to London.

And now here she was, with unemployment staring her in the face and a house that would have to be sold sooner rather than later because, with each day that passed, it became just a little more run down. How long before the small leak in the roof expanded into a full scale, no-holds-barred deluge? Did she really want to wake up in the middle of the night with her bed floating?

So far, she hadn't mentioned the problems with the house to her parents, who had left for France five years previously, shortly having been joined by Alice and her husband. She knew that if she did the entire family would up sticks and arrive on her doorstep with tea, sympathy and rescue plans afoot.

She didn't need rescuing.

She was an excellent vet. She would have a brilliant recommendation from Norman, the elderly family man who owned the practice and was now selling to emigrate to the other side of the world. She would be able to find work somewhere else without any problem at all.

And besides, twenty-seven-year-old women did not need rescuing. Least of all by their younger sibling and two frantically worried parents.

'Shouldn't *I* be the one worrying about *you*?'

'Because you're three years older?'

Becky heard that wonderful, tinkling laugh and pictured her beautiful, charming sister sitting in their glamorous French gîte with her legs tucked under her and her long, blonde hair tumbling over one shoulder.

Freddy would be doing something useful in the kitchen. Despite the fact that he, like her, was a hard-working vet, he enjoyed nothing more than getting back from the practice in which he was a partner, kicking off his shoes and relaxing with Alice in the kitchen, where he would usually be the one concocting the meals, because he was an excellent cook.

And he adored Alice. He had been swept off his feet from the very first second he had been introduced to her. At the time, she had been a high-flying model on the way to greatness and, whilst Becky would never have believed that Freddy—earnest and usually knee-deep in text books—could ever be attracted to her sister—who was cheerfully proud of her lack of academic success and hadn't read a book cover to cover in years—she had been proved wrong.

They were the most happily married couple anyone could have hoped to find.

'I'll be fine.' Becky decided to put off all awkward conversations about job losses and collapsing roofs for another day. 'I won't venture out in the middle of a snowstorm in my pyjamas, and if anyone out there is stupid enough to brave this weather on the lookout for what they can nick then they won't be heading for Lavender Cottage.' She eyed the tired décor in the kitchen and couldn't help grinning. 'Everyone in the village knows that I keep all my valuables in a bank vault.'

Old clothes, mud-stained wellies, tool kit for the hundreds of things that kept going wrong in the house, enviable selection of winter-woolly hats…just the sort of stuff any robber worth his salt would want to steal.

'I just thought, Becks, that you might venture out here and have a little fun for a while before summer comes and all those ghastly crowds. I know you came over for Christmas, but it was all so busy out here, what with Mum and Dad inviting every single friend over for drinks every single evening. I…I feel like I haven't seen you for absolutely ages! I mean, just the two of us, the way it used to be when we were younger and…well… Freddy and I…'

'I'm incredibly busy just at the moment, Ali. You know how it is around this time of year with the lambing season nearly on us, pregnant sheep in distress everywhere you look… But I'll come out as soon as I can. I promise.'

She didn't want to talk about Freddy, the guy she had

met at university, the guy she had fallen head over heels in love with, had he only known, the guy who had turned her into a good friend, who had met Alice, been smitten in the space of seconds and proposed in record time.

The guy who had broken her heart.

'Darling, Freddy and I have something to tell you and we would much rather tell you face to face...'

'What? What is it?' Filled with sudden consternation, Becky sat up, mind crash-banging into worst case scenarios.

'We're going to have a baby! Isn't it exciting?'

Yes, it was. Exciting, thrilling and something her sister had been talking about from the moment she had said *I do* and glided up the aisle with a band of gold on her finger.

Becky was thrilled for her. She really was. But, as she settled down for one of the rare Saturday nights when she wasn't going to be on call, she suddenly felt the weight of the choices she had made over the years bearing down on her.

Where were the clubs she should be enjoying? Where was the breathless falling in and out of love? The men in pursuit? The thrilling text messages? When Freddy had hitched his wagon to her sister, Becky had turned her back on love. Unlike Alice, she had spent her teens with her head in books. She'd always known what she'd wanted to be and her parents had encouraged her in her studies. Both were teachers, her father a lecturer, her mother a maths teacher at the local secondary school. She had always been the good girl who worked hard. Beautiful, leggy Alice had decided from an early age that academics were not for her and of course her parents—liberal, left wing and proud of their political correctness—had not batted an eyelid.

And so, while Becky had studied, Alice had partied.

'Everyone should be free to express themselves without being boxed into trying to live up or live down to other people's expectations!' had been her mother's motto.

At the age of eighteen, Becky had surfaced, startled and blinking, to university life with all its glorious freedom and had realised that a life of study had not prepared her for late-night drinking, skipping lectures and sleeping around.

She had not been conditioned to enjoy the freedom at her disposal, and had almost immediately developed a crush on Freddy, who had been in her year, studying veterinary science like her.

He, too, had spent his adolescence working hard. He, too, had had his head buried in text books between the ages of twelve and eighteen. He had been her soul mate and she had enjoyed his company, but had been far too shy to take it to another level, and had been prepared to bide her time until the inevitable happened.

Only ever having watched her sister from the sidelines, laughing and amused at the way Alice fell in and out of love, she had lacked the confidence to make the first move.

And in the end, thank goodness, because, had she done so, then she would have been roundly rejected. The boy she had considered her soul mate, the boy she had fancied herself spending her life with, had not been interested in her as anything but a pal. She had thought him perfect for her. Steady, hard-working, considerate, feet planted firmly on the ground…

He, on the other hand, had not been looking for a woman who shared those qualities.

He had wanted frothy and vivacious. He had wanted someone who shoved his books aside and sat on his lap.

He had wanted tall and blonde and beautiful, not small, dark-haired and plump. He hadn't wanted earnest.

As the dark night began to shed its first flurries of snow, Becky wondered whether retreating to the Cotswolds had been a good idea. She could see herself in the same place, doing the same thing, in ten years' time. Her kid sister felt sorry for her. Without even realising it, she was becoming a charity case, the sort of person the world *pitied.*

The house was falling down.

She was going to be jobless in a matter of months.

She would be forced to do something about her life, leave the security of the countryside, join the busy tide of bright young things in a city somewhere.

She would have to climb back on the horse and start dating again.

She felt giddy when she thought about it.

But think about it she did, and she only stopped when she heard the sharp buzz of the doorbell, and for once didn't mind having her precious downtime invaded by someone needing her help with a sick animal. In fact, she would have welcomed just about anything that promised to divert her thoughts from the grim road they were hell-bent on travelling.

She headed for the door, grabbing her vet's bag on the way, as well as her thick, warm, waterproof jacket, which was essential in this part of the world.

She pulled open the door with one foot in a boot, woolly hat yanked down over her ears and her car keys shoved in her coat pocket.

Eyes down as she reached for her bag, the first things she noticed were the shoes. They didn't belong to a farmer. They were made of soft, tan leather, which was already beginning to show the discolouration from the snow collecting outside.

Then she took in the trousers.

Expensive. Pale grey, wool. Utterly impractical. She was barely aware of her eyes travelling upwards, doing an unconscious inventory of her unexpected caller, registering the expensive black cashmere coat, the way it fell open, unbuttoned, revealing a fine woollen jumper that encased a body that was…so unashamedly *masculine* that for a few seconds her breath hitched in her throat.

'Plan on finishing the visual inspection any time soon? Because I'm getting soaked out here.'

Becky's eyes flicked up and all at once she was gripped by the most unusual sensation, a mixture of dry-mouthed speechlessness and heated embarrassment.

For a few seconds, she literally couldn't speak as she stared, wide-eyed, at the most staggeringly good-looking guy she had ever seen in her life.

Black hair, slightly long, had been blown back from a face that was pure, chiselled perfection. Silver-grey eyes, fringed with dramatically long, thick, dark lashes, were staring right back at her.

Mortified, Becky leapt into action. 'Give me two seconds,' she said breathlessly. She crammed her foot into wellie number two and wondered whether she would need her handbag. Probably not. She didn't recognise the man and, from the way he was dressed, he wasn't into livestock so there would be no sheep having trouble giving birth.

Which probably meant that he was one of those rich townies who had second homes somewhere in one of the picturesque villages. He'd probably descended for a weekend with a party of similarly poorly equipped friends, domestic pets in tow, and one of the pets had got itself into a spot of bother.

It happened. These people never seemed to realise that dogs and cats, accustomed to feather beds and grooming parlours, went crazy the second they were introduced to the big, bad world of the real countryside.

Then when their precious little pets returned to base camp, limping and bleeding, their owners didn't have a clue what to do. Becky couldn't count the number of times she had been called out to deal with weeping and wailing owners of some poor cat or dog that had suffered nothing more tragic than a cut on its paw.

In fairness, *this* man didn't strike Becky as the sort to indulge in dramatics, not judging from the cool, impatient look in those silver-grey eyes that had swept dismissively over her, but who knew?

'Right!' She stepped back, putting some distance between herself and the disconcerting presence by the door. The flurries of snow were turning into a blizzard. 'If we don't leave in five seconds, then it's going to be all hell getting back here! Where's your car? I'll follow you.'

'Follow me? Why would you want to follow me?'

His voice, Becky thought distractedly, matched his face. Deep, seductive, disturbing and very, very bad for one's peace of mind.

'Who *are* you?' She looked at him narrowly and her heart picked up pace. He absolutely towered over her.

'Ah. Introductions. Now we're getting somewhere. You only have to invite me in and normality can be resumed without further delay.'

Because this sure as hell wasn't normal.

Theo Rushing had just spent the past four-and-a-half hours in second gear, manoeuvring ridiculously narrow streets in increasingly inhospitable weather conditions, and cursing himself for actually thinking that it would be a good idea to get in his car and deal with this mission himself, instead of doing the sensible thing and handing it over to one of his employees to sort out.

But this trip had been a personal matter and he hadn't wanted to delegate.

In fact, what he wanted was very simple. The cottage into which he had yet to be invited.

He anticipated getting it without too much effort. After all, he had money and, from what his sources had told him, the cottage—deep in the heart of the Cotswolds and far from anything anyone could loosely describe as civilisation—was still owned by the couple who had originally bought it, which, as far as Theo was concerned, was a miracle in itself. How long could one family live somewhere where the only view was of uninterrupted countryside and the only possible downtime activity would be tramping over open fields? It worked for him, though, because said couple would surely be contemplating retirement to somewhere less remote…

The only matter for debate would be the price.

But he wanted the cottage, and he was going to get it, because it was the only thing he could think of that would put some of the vitality back into his mother's life.

Of course, on the list of priorities, the cottage was way down below her overriding ambition to see him married off, an ambition that had reached an all-time high ever since her stroke several months ago.

But that was never going to happen. He had seen first-hand the way love could destroy. He had watched his mother retreat from life when her husband, his father, had been killed suddenly and without warning when they should have been enjoying the bliss of looking towards their future, the young, energetic couple with their only child. Theo had only been seven at the time but he'd been sharp enough to work out that, had his mother not invested her entire life, the whole essence of her being, in that fragile thing called love, then she wouldn't have spent the following decades living half a life.

So the magic and power of love was something he could quite happily do without, thanks very much. It was a slice of realism his mother stoutly refused to contemplate and Theo had given up trying to persuade her into seeing his point of view. If she wanted to cling to unrealistic fantasies about him bumping into the perfect woman, then so be it. His only concession was that he would no longer introduce her to any of his imperfect women who, he knew from experience, never managed to pull away from the starting block as far as his mother was concerned.

Which just left the cottage.

Lavender Cottage…his parents' first home…the place where he had been conceived…and the house his mother had fled when his father had had his fatal accident. Fog…a lorry going over the speed limit… His father on his bicycle hadn't stood a chance…

Marita Rushing had been turned into a youthful widow and she had never recovered. No one had ever stood a chance against the perfect ghost of his father. She was still a beautiful woman but when you looked at her you didn't see the huge dark eyes or the dramatic black hair… When you looked at her all you saw was the sadness of a life dedicated to memories.

And recently she had wanted to return to the place where those memories resided.

Nostalgia, in the wake of her premature stroke, had become her faithful companion and she wanted finally to come to terms with the past and embrace it. Returning to the cottage, he had gathered, was an essential part of that therapy.

Right now, she was in Italy, and had been for the past six weeks, visiting her sister. Reminiscing about the cottage, about her desire to return there to live out her final days, had been replaced by disturbing insinuations that she might just return to Italy and call it quits with England.

'You're barely ever in the country,' she had grumbled a couple of weeks earlier, which was something Theo had not been able to refute. 'And when you are, well, what am I but the ageing mother you are duty-bound to visit? It's not as though there will ever be a daughter-in-law for me, or grandchildren, or any of those things a woman of my age should be looking forward to. What is the point of my being in London, Theo? I would see the same amount of you if I lived in Timbuktu.'

Theo loved his mother, but he could not promise a wife he had no intention of acquiring or grandchildren that didn't feature in his future.

If he honestly thought that she would be happy in Italy, then he would have encouraged her to stay on at the villa he had bought for her six years previously, but she had lived far too long away from the small village in which she had grown up and where her sister now lived. After two weeks, she would always return to London, relieved to be back and full of tales of Flora's exasperating bossiness.

Right now, she was recuperating, so Flora was full of tender, loving care. However, should his mother decide to turn her stay there into a permanent situation, then Flora would soon become the chivvying older sister who drove his mother crazy.

'Why are you getting dressed?' Theo asked the cottage's present resident in bemusement. She was small and round but he still found himself being distracted by the pure clarity of her turquoise eyes and her flawless complexion. Healthy living, he thought absently, staring down at her. 'And you still haven't told me who you are.'

'I don't think this is the time to start making chit chat.' Becky blinked and made a concerted effort to gather her wits because he was just another hapless tourist in need of her services. It was getting colder and colder in the little hallway and the snow was becoming thicker and thicker. 'I'll come with you but you'll have to drive me back.' She swerved past him, out into the little gravelled circular courtyard, and gaped at the racing-red Ferrari parked at a jaunty angle, as though he had swung recklessly into her drive and screeched to a racing driver's halt. 'Don't tell me that you came here in *that*!'

Theo swung round. She had zipped past him like a pocket rocket and now she was glaring, hands on her hips, woolly hat almost covering her eyes.

And he had no idea what the hell was going on. He felt like he needed to rewind the conversation and start again in a more normal fashion, because he'd obviously missed a few crucial links in the chain.

'Come again?' was all he could find to say, the man who was never lost for words, the man who could speak volumes with a single glance, a man who could close impossible deals with the right vocabulary.

'Are you *completely mad*?' Becky breathed an inward sigh of relief because she felt safer being the angry, disapproving vet, concerned for her safety in nasty weather conditions, and impatient with some expensive, arrogant guy who was clueless about the Cotswolds. 'There's no way I'm getting into that thing with you! And I can't believe you actually thought that driving all the way out here to get me was a good idea! Don't you people know anything *at all*? Not that you have to be a genius to work out that these un-gritted roads are *lethal* for silly little cars like that!'

'Silly little car?'

'*I'd* find the roads difficult and *I* drive a *sensible* car!'

'That *silly little car* happens to be a top-end Ferrari that cost more than you probably earn in a year!' Theo raked fingers frustratedly through his hair. 'And I have no bloody idea why we're standing out here in a blizzard having a chat about cars!'

'Well, how the heck are we supposed to get to your animal if we don't drive there? Unless you've got a helicopter stashed away somewhere? Have you?'

'Animal? What animal?'

'Your *cat*!'

'I don't have a cat! Why would I have a cat? Why would I have any sort of animal, and what would lead you to think that I had?'

'You mean you haven't come to get me out to tend to an animal?'

'You're a vet.' The weathered bag, the layers of warm, outdoor clothing, the wellies for tramping through mud. All made sense now.

Theo had come to the cottage to have a look, to stake his claim and to ascertain how much he would pay for the place. As little as possible, had been his way of thinking. It had been bought at a bargain-basement price from his mother, who had been so desperate to flee that she had taken the first offer on the place. He had intended to do the same, to assess the state of disrepair and put in the lowest possible offer, at least to start with.

'That's right—and if you don't have an animal, and don't need my services, then why the heck are you here?'

'This is ridiculous. It's freezing out here. I refuse to have a conversation in sub-zero temperatures.'

'I'm afraid I don't feel comfortable letting you into my house.' Becky squinted up at him. She was a mere five-foot-four and he absolutely towered over her. He was a tall, powerfully built stranger who had arrived in a frivolous boy-racer car out of the blue and she was on her own out here. No one would hear her scream for help. Should she *need* help.

Theo was outraged. No one, but no one, had ever had the temerity to say anything like that to him in his life before, least of all a woman. 'Exactly *what* are you suggesting?' he asked with withering cool, and Becky reddened but stoutly stood her ground.

'I don't know you.' She tilted her chin at a mutinous angle, challenging him to disagree with her. Every pore and fibre of her being was alert to him. It was as though, for the first time in her life, she was *aware* of her body, *aware* of her femininity, aware of her breasts—heavy and pushing against her bra—aware of her stiff and sensitive nipples, aware of her nakedness beneath her thick layer of clothes. Her discomfort was intense and bewildering.

'You could be *anyone*. I thought you were here because you needed my help with an animal, but you don't, so who the heck are you and why do you think I would let you into *my* house?'

'*Your* house?' Cool grey eyes skirted the rambling building and its surrounding fields. 'You're a little young to be the proud owner of a house this size, aren't you?'

'I'm older than you think.' Becky rushed into self-defence mode. 'And, not that it's any of your business, but yes, this house is mine. Or at least, I'm in charge while my parents are abroad and, that being the case, I won't be letting you inside. I don't even know your name.'

'Theo Rushing.' Some of the jigsaw immediately fell into place. He had expected to descend on the owners of the property. He hadn't known what, precisely, he would find but he had not been predisposed to be charitable to anyone who could have taken advantage of a distraught young woman, as his mother had been at the time.

At any rate, he had come with his cheque book, but without the actual owners at hand his cheque book was as useful as a three-pound note, because the belligerent little ball in front of him would not be able to make any decisions about anything.

Furthermore, she struck him as just the sort who *would* bite off the hand clutching the bank notes, or at least try and persuade her parents to…

He was accustomed to women wanting to please him. Faced with narrowed, suspicious eyes and the body language of a guard dog about to attack, he was forced to concede that announcing the purpose for his visit might not be such a good idea.

'I'm here to buy this cottage so you'll find yourself without a roof over your head in roughly a month and a half' wasn't going to win him brownie points.

He wanted the cottage and he was going to get it but he would have to be a little creative in how he handled the situation now.

He felt an unusual rush of adrenaline.

Theo had attained such meteoric heights over the years that the thrill of the challenge had been lost. When you could have anything you wanted, you increasingly lost interest in the things that should excite. Nothing was exciting if you didn't have to work to get it and that, he thought suddenly, included women.

Getting this cottage would be a challenge and he liked the thought of that.

'And I'm here…' He looked around him at the thick black sky. He had planned to arrive early afternoon but the extraordinary delays had dumped him here as darkness was beginning to fall. It had fallen completely now and there were no street lights to alleviate the unlit sky or to illuminate the fast falling snow.

His eyes returned to the woman in front of him. She was so heavily bundled up that he reckoned they could spend the next five hours out here and she would be immune to the freezing cold. He, on the other hand, having not expected to leave London and end up in a tundra, could not have been less well-prepared for the silent but deadly onslaught of the weather. Cashmere coats were all well and good in London but out here…

Waiting for an answer before she dispatched him without further ado, Becky could not help but stare. He was so beautiful that it almost hurt to tear her eyes away. In those crazy, faraway days, when she had been consumed by Freddy, she had enjoyed looking at him, had liked his regular, kind features, the gentleness of his expression and the warmth of his brown, puppy-dog eyes.

But she had never felt like this. There was something fascinating, *mesmerising*, about the play of shadow and darkness on his angular, powerful face. He was the last word in everything that *wasn't* gentle or kind and yet the pull she felt was overwhelming.

'Yes?' She clenched her gloved fists in the capacious pockets of her waterproof, knee-length, fleece-lined anorak. 'You're here because…?'

'Lost.' Theo spread his arm wide to encompass the lonely wilderness around him. 'Lost, and you're right—in a car that's not very clever when it comes to ice and snow. I'm not…accustomed to country roads and my satnav has had a field day trying to navigate its way to where I was planning on ending up.'

Lost. It made sense. Once you left the main roads behind—and that was remarkably easy to do—you could easily find yourself in a honeycomb of winding, unlit country lanes that would puzzle the best cartographer.

But that didn't change the fact that she was out here on her own in this house and he was still a stranger.

He read her mind. 'Look, I understand that you might feel vulnerable out here if you're on your own…' And she was, because there was no rush to jump in and warn him of an avenging boyfriend or husband wending his weary way back. 'But you will be perfectly safe if you let me in. The only reason I'm asking to be let in at all is because the weather's getting worse, and if I get into that car and try and make my way back to the bright lights I have no idea where I'll end up.'

Becky glanced at the racy, impractical sports car turning white as the snow gathered on it. *In a ditch*, was written all over its impractical bonnet.

Would her conscience allow her to send him off into the night, knowing that he would probably end up having an accident? What if the skittish car skidded off the road into one of the many trees and there was a fatality?

What if he ended up trapped in wreckage somewhere on an isolated country lane? If nothing else, he would perish from hypothermia, because his choice of clothing was as impractical for the weather as his choice of car.

'One night,' she said. 'And then I get someone to come and fetch you, first thing in the morning. I don't care if you have to leave the car here or not.'

'One night,' Theo murmured in agreement.

Becky felt the race of something dangerous slither through her.

She would give him shelter for one night and one night only…

What harm could come from that?

CHAPTER TWO

THE HOUSE SEEMED to shrink in size the minute he walked in. He'd fetched his computer from his car but that was all and Becky looked at him with a frown.

'Is that all you brought with you?'

'You still haven't told me your name.' The house was clearly on its last legs. Theo was no surveyor but that much was obvious. He now looked directly at her as he slowly removed his coat.

'Rebecca. Becky.' She watched as he carelessly slung his coat over one of the hooks by the front door. She could really appreciate his lean muscularity, now he was down to the jumper and trousers, and her mouth went dry.

This was as far out of her comfort zone as it was possible to get. Ever since Freddy, she had retreated into herself, content to go out as part of a group, to mingle with old friends—some of whom, like her, had returned to the beautiful Cotswolds, but to raise families. She hadn't actively chosen to discourage men but, as it happened, they had been few and far between. Twice she had been asked out on dates and twice she had decided that friendship was more valuable than the possibility of romance.

Truthfully, when she tried to think about relationships, she drew a blank. She wanted someone thoughtful and caring and those sorts of guys were already snapped up.

The guys who had asked her out had known her since for ever, and she knew for a fact that one of them was still recovering from a broken heart and had only asked her out on the rebound.

The other, the son of one of the farmers whom she had visited on call-out on several occasions, was nice enough, but nice enough just wasn't sufficient.

Or maybe she was being too fussy. That thought had occurred to her. When you were on your own for long enough, you grew careful, wary of letting anyone into your world, protective of your space. Was that what was happening to her?

At any rate, her comfort zone was on the verge of disappearing permanently unless she chose to stay where she was and travel long distances to another job.

She decided that inviting Theo in was good practice for what lay in store for her. She had opened her door to a complete stranger and she knew, with some weird gut instinct, that he was no physical threat to her.

In fact, seeing him in the unforgiving light in the hall did nothing to lessen the impact of his intense, sexual vitality. It was laughable to think that he would have any interest in her as anything other than someone offering refuge from the gathering snow storm.

'I can show you to one of the spare rooms.' Becky flushed because she could feel herself staring again. 'I don't keep them heated, but I'll turn the radiator on, and it shouldn't take too long to warm up. You might want to…freshen up.'

'I would love nothing more,' Theo drawled. 'Unfortunately, no change of clothing. Would you happen to have anything I could borrow? Husband's old gardening clothes? Boyfriend's…?' He wondered whether she intended to spend the rest of the evening in the shapeless anorak and mud-stained boots. She had to be the least fashion-conscious woman he had ever met in his entire life, yet for the life of him he was still captivated by something about her.

The eyes, the unruly hair still stuffed under the woolly hat, the lack of war paint…what was it?

He had no idea but he hadn't felt this alive in a woman's presence for a while.

Then again, it had been a while since he had been in the presence of any woman who wasn't desperate to attract his attention. There was a lot to be said for novelty.

'I can let you borrow something.' Becky shifted from foot to foot. She was boiling in the coat but somehow she didn't like the thought of stripping down to her jeans and top in front of him. Those sharp, lazy eyes of his made her feel all hot and bothered. 'My dad left some of his stuff in the wardrobe in the room you'll be in. You can have a look and see what might be able to work for you. And if you leave your stuff outside the bedroom door, then I guess I can stick it in the washing machine.'

'You needn't do that.'

'You're soaked,' Becky said flatly. 'Your clothes will smell if you leave them to dry without washing them first.'

'In that case, I won't refuse your charming offer,' Theo said drily and Becky flushed.

Very conscious of his eyes on her, she preceded him up the stairs, pointedly ignoring the bucket gathering water on the ground from the leaking roof, and flung open the door to one of the spare bedrooms. Had she actually thought things through when she had fled back to the family home, she would have realised that the 'cottage' was a cottage in name only. In reality, it was reasonably large, with five bedrooms and outbuildings in the acres outside. It was far too big for her and she wondered, suddenly, whether her parents had felt sorry for her and offered to allow her to stay there through pity. They hadn't known about Freddy and her broken heart but what must they have felt when she had dug her heels in and insisted on returning to the family home while Alice, already far flown from the nest, was busily making marriage plans so that the next phase of her life could begin?

Becky cringed.

Her parents would never, ever have denied her the cottage but they weren't rich. They had bought somewhere tiny in France when her grandmother had died, and they had both continued working part-time, teaching in the local school.

Becky had always thought it a brilliant way of integrating into life in the French town, but what if they'd only done that because they needed the money?

While she stayed here, paying a peppercorn rent and watching the place gradually fall apart at the seams…

She was struck by her own selfishness and it was something that had never occurred to her until now.

She would phone, she decided. Feel out the ground. After all, whether she liked it or not, her lifestyle was going to change dramatically once she was out of a job.

Theo looked at her and wondered what was going through her mind. He hadn't failed to notice the way she had neatly stepped past a bucket in the corridor which was quarter-full from the leaking roof.

It was startling enough that a woman of her age would choose to live out in the sticks, however rewarding her job might be, but it was even more startling that, having chosen to live out in the sticks, she continued to live in a house that was clearly on the verge of giving up the fight.

When he bought this cottage, he would be doing her a favour by forcing her out into the real world.

Where life happened.

Rather than her staying here...hiding away...which surely was what she was doing...?

Hiding from what? he wondered. He was a little amused at how involved he temporarily was in mentally providing an answer to that ridiculous question.

But if he had to get her onside, manoeuvre her into a position where she might see the sense of not standing in his way when it came to buying the cottage, then wouldn't it help to get to know her a little?

Of course, there was no absolute necessity to get anyone onside. He could simply bypass her and head directly to the parents. Make them an offer they couldn't refuse. But for once he wasn't quite ruthless enough to go down that road. There was something strangely alluring underneath the guard-dog belligerence. And he was not forgetting that there were times when money *didn't* open the door you wanted opening. If he bypassed her and leant on the parents, there was a real risk of them uniting with their daughter to shut him out permanently, whatever sums of money he chose to throw at them. Family loyalty could be a powerful wild card, and he should know... Wasn't family loyalty the very thing that had brought him to this semi-derelict cottage?

She was switching on the ancient heating, opening the wardrobe so that she could show him where the clothes were kept, fetching a towel from the corridor, dumping it on the bed and then informing him that the bathroom was just down the corridor, but that he would have to make sure that the toilet wasn't flushed before he turned on the shower or else he might end up with third-degree burns.

Theo walked slowly towards her and then stopped a few inches away.

When Becky breathed, she could breathe him in, masculinity mixed with the cold winter air, a heady, heady mix. Leaning against the doorframe, she blinked, suddenly unsteady on her feet.

He had amazing lashes, long, dark and thick. She wanted to ask him where he was from, because there was an exotic strain running through him that was quite… captivating.

He had shoved up the sleeves of his jumper and, even though she wasn't actually looking, she was very much aware of his forearms, the fine, dark hair on them, the flex of muscle and sinew…

Her breathing was so sluggish that it crossed her mind… *was it actually physically possible to forget how to breathe*?

'I don't get why you live here.' Theo was genuinely curious.

'Wh-what do you mean?' Becky stammered.

'The house needs a lot of work doing to it. I could understand if your parents wanted you in situ while work was being done but…can I call you Becky?…there's a bucket out in the corridor. And how long do you intend emptying it before you face the unpalatable fact that the roof probably needs replacing?'

Hard on the heels of the uncomfortable thoughts that had been preying on her mind, Theo's remarks struck home with deadly accuracy.

'I don't see that the state of this house is any of your business!' Bright patches of colour stained her cheeks. 'You're here for a night, *one night*, and only because I wouldn't have been able to live with myself if I had sent you on your way in this weather. But that doesn't give you the right to…to…'

'Talk?'

'You're not *talking*, you're—'

'I'm probably saying things that have previously occurred to you, things you may have chosen to ignore.' He shrugged, unwillingly intrigued by the way she was so patently uninterested in trying to impress him. 'If you'd rather I didn't, then that's fine. I have some work to do when I get downstairs and then we can pretend to have an invigorating conversation about the weather.'

'I'll be downstairs.' This for want of anything more coherent to say when she was so...*angry*...that he had had the nerve to shoot his mouth off! He was rude beyond words!

But he wasn't wrong.

And this impertinent stranger had provided the impetus she needed to make that call to her parents. As soon as she was in the kitchen, with the door firmly shut, because the man was as stealthy as a panther and obviously didn't wait for invitations to speak his mind. There was some beating around the bush but, yes, it *would* be rather lovely if the house *was* sold, not that they would ever dream of asking her to leave.

But...but...but...but.

Lots of *buts*, so that by the time Becky hung up fifteen minutes later she was in no doubt that not only was she heading for unemployment but the leaking roof over her head would not be hers for longer than it took for the local estate agent to come along and offer a valuation.

Mind still whirring busily away, she headed back up the stairs. She wished she could think more clearly and see a way forward but the path ahead was murky. What if she couldn't get a job? It should be easy but, then again, she was in a highly specialised field. What if she did manage to find a posting but it was in an even more remote spot than this? Did she really want the years ahead to be spent in a practice in the wilds of Scotland? But weren't the more desirable posts in London, Manchester or Birmingham going to be the first to be filled?

And underneath all those questions was the dissatisfaction that had swamped her after she had spoken to her sister.

Her life had been put into harsh perspective. The time she had spent here now seemed to have been wasted. Instead of moving forward, she had stayed in the same place, pedalling furiously and getting nowhere.

She surfaced from her disquieting thoughts to find that, annoyingly, the clothes she had asked to be placed outside the bedroom door were not there.

Did the man think that he was staying in a hotel?

Did he imagine that it was okay for her to hang around like a chambermaid until he decided that he could be bothered to hand over his dirty laundry for her to do? She didn't even have to wash his clothes! She could have sent him on his way in musty, semi-damp trousers and a jumper that smelled of pond water.

He obviously thought that he was so important that he could do as he pleased. Speak to her as he pleased. Accept her hospitality whilst antagonising her because he found it entertaining.

She had no idea how important or unimportant he was but, quite aside from the snazzy little racing-red number and the designer clothing, there was something about him that screamed *wealth.*

Or maybe it was *power.*

Well, none of that impressed *her.* She'd never had time for anyone who thought that money was the be all and end all. It just wasn't the way she had been brought up.

It was what was inside that counted. It was why, although Freddy had not been the one for her, there was a guy out there who was, a guy who had the sterling qualities of kindness, quiet intelligence and self-deprecating humour.

And, having ducked the dating scene for years, she would get back out there…because if she didn't then this was the person she would be in the years to come, entrenched in her singledom, godmother to all and sundry and maid of honour to her friends as they tied the knot and moved on with their fulfilling lives.

Swamped by sudden self-pity, she absently shoved open the door to the spare room, which was ajar, and… stopped. Her legs stopped moving, her hand froze on the door knob and her brain went into instant shutdown.

She didn't know where to look and somewhere inside she knew that it didn't matter because wherever she looked she would still end up seeing him. Tall, broad-shouldered, his body an amazing burnished bronze. She would still see the hardness of his six pack and the length of his muscular legs, the legs of an athlete.

Aside from a pair of low-slung boxers, he was completely naked.

Becky cleared her throat and opened her mouth and nothing emerged but an inarticulate noise.

'I was just about to stick the clothes outside…'

Without the woollen hat pulled down over her head, her hair was long, tumbling down her back in a cascade of unruly, dark curls, and without the layers upon layers of shriekingly unfashionable arctic gear…

She wasn't the round little beach ball he had imagined. Even with the loose-fitting striped rugby shirt, he could see that she had the perfect hourglass figure. News obviously hadn't reached this part of the world that the fashionable trend these days leaned towards long, thin and toned to athletic perfection, even if the exercise involved to get there never saw the outside of an expensive gym.

He could feel his whole body reacting to the sight of her lush curves and he hurriedly turned away, because a pair of boxers was no protection against an erection.

He was staring. Becky stood stock-still, conscious of herself and her body in ways she had never been before. Why was he staring at her like that? Was he even aware that he was doing it?

She couldn't believe that he was staring at her because she was the most glamorous woman he had ever set eyes on. She wasn't born yesterday and she knew that when it came to looks, well, a career could not be made out of hers. Alice had got the looks and she, Becky, had got the brains and it had always seemed like a fair enough deal to her.

He'd turned away now, thankfully putting on some ancient track pants her father had left behind and an even more ancient jumper, and by the time he turned back around to face her she wondered whether she had imagined those cool, grey eyes on her, skirting over her body.

Yes, she thought a little shakily. Of course she had. *She* had stared at *him* because he looked like a Greek god. *She* on the other hand was as average as they came.

Should she feel threatened? She was alone in this house…

She didn't feel threatened. She felt…excited. Something wicked and daring stirred inside her and she promptly knocked it back.

'The clothes.' She found her voice, one hand outstretched, watching as he gathered items of clothing and strolled towards her. 'I'll make sure they're washed and ready for you tomorrow morning.'

'First thing…before I'm sent on my way,' Theo murmured, still startled at the fierce grip of his libido that had struck from nowhere.

She couldn't wait to escape, he thought with a certain amount of disbelief.

Something had passed between them just then. Had she even been aware of it? A charge of electricity had shaken him and she hadn't been unaffected. He'd seen the reaction in the widening of her eyes as she had looked at him, and the stillness of her body language, as though one false move might have led her to do something…rash.

Did *rash* happen out here? he wondered. Or was she out here because she was escaping from something rash? Was the awkward, blushing, argumentative vet plagued by guilt over a misspent past? Had she thrown herself into a one-way relationship to nowhere with a con man? A married man? A rampant womaniser who had used her and tossed her aside? The possibilities were endless.

She certainly wasn't out here for the money. That bucket on the landing said it all. She might be living rent free at the place but she certainly wasn't earning enough to keep it maintained. Old houses consumed money with the greed of a gold-digger on the make.

'What if it's still snowing in the morning?'

She was clutching the bundle of clothes like a talisman and staring up at him with those amazing bright blue eyes. Her lips were parted. When she circled a nervous tongue over them, Theo had to fight down an urge to reach out and pull her against him.

'It won't be.'

'If you weren't prepared to risk my life by sending me on my way, then will you be prepared to risk someone else's life by asking them to come and collect me and take me away?'

'I could drive you myself. I have a four-wheel drive. It's okay in conditions like this.'

'When I knocked on your door…' Theo leant against the door frame '…I never expected someone like you to open it'

'What do you mean *someone like me*?' Becky stiffened, primed for some kind of thinly veiled insult.

Theo didn't say anything for a couple of seconds. Instead, he watched her, head tilted to one side, until she looked away, blushing. Very gently, he tilted her face back to his.

'You're on the defensive. Why?'

'Why do you think? I…I don't know you.' The feel of his cool finger resting lightly on her chin was as scorching-hot as the imprint from a branding iron.

'What do you think I'm going to do? When I said *someone like you*, I meant someone young. I expected someone much older to be living this far out in the countryside.'

'I told you, the house belongs to my parents. I'm just here… Look, I'm going to head downstairs, wash these things…' Her feet and brain were not communicating because, instead of spinning around and backing out of the room, she remained where she was, glued to the spot.

She wanted him to remove his hand…she wanted him to do more with it, wanted him to curve it over her face and then slide it across her shoulders, wanted him to find the bare flesh of her stomach and then the swell of her breasts… She didn't want to hear anything he had to say, yet he was making her think, and how could that be a bad thing?

She barely recognised her voice and she certainly didn't know what was going on with her body.

'Okay.' He stepped back, hand dropping to his side.

For a few seconds, Becky hovered, then she cleared her throat and stepped out of the room backwards.

By the time he joined her in the kitchen, the clothes were in the washing machine and she had regained her composure.

Theo looked at her for a few seconds from the doorway. She had her back to him and was busy chopping vegetables, while as background noise the television was giving an in-depth report of the various areas besieged by snow when spring should have sprung. He felt that her house would shortly be featured because there was no sign of the snow letting up.

Before he had come down, he had done his homework, nosed into a few of the rooms and seen for himself what he had suspected from the bucket on the landing catching water from the leaking roof.

The house was on its last legs. Did he think that he was doing anything underhand in checking out the property before he made an offer? No. He'd come here to conduct a business deal and, if things had been slightly thrown off course, nothing had fundamentally changed. The key thing remained the business deal.

And was the woman peeling the vegetables an unexpected part of acquiring what he wanted? Was she now part of the business deal that had to be secured?

In a way, yes.

And he was not in the slightest ashamed of taking this pragmatic view. Why should he be? This was the man he was and it was how he had succeeded beyond even his own wildest expectations.

If you allowed your emotions to guide you, you ended up a victim of whatever circumstances came along to blow you off course.

He had no intention of ever being one of life's victims.

His mother had so much to give, but she had allowed her damaged heart to take control of her entire future, so that, in the end, whatever she'd had to give to anyone else had dried up. Wasn't that one reason why she was so consumed with the thought of having grandchildren? Of seeing him married off?

Because her ability to give had to go somewhere and he was the only recipient.

That was what emotions did to a person. They stripped you of your ability to think. That was why he had never done commitment and never would. Commitment led to relationships and relationships were almost always train wrecks waiting to happen. Lawyers were kept permanently busy sorting out those train wrecks and making lots of money in the process.

He had his life utterly in control and that was the way he liked it.

He had no doubt that whatever had brought Becky to this place was a story that might tug on someone else's heartstrings. *His* heartstrings would be blessedly immune to any tugging. He would be able to find out about her and persuade her to accept that this was no place for her to be. When, inevitably, the house was sold from under her feet, she would not try and put up a fight, wouldn't try and coax her parents into letting her stay on.

He would have long disappeared from her life. He would have been nothing more than a stranger who had landed for a night and then moved on. But she would remember what he had said and she would end up thanking him.

Because, frankly, this was no place for her to be. It wasn't healthy. She was far too young.

He looked at the rounded swell of her derrière…

Far too young and far too sexy.

'What are you cooking?'

Becky swung round to see him lounging against the door frame. Her father was a little shorter and reedier than Theo. Theo looked as though he had been squashed into clothes a couple of sizes too small. And he was barefoot. Her eyes shot back to his face to find that he was staring right back at her with a little smile.

'Pasta. Nothing special. And you can help.' She turned her back on him and felt him close the distance between them until he was standing next to her, at which point she pointed to some onions and slid a small, sharp knife towards him. 'You've asked me a lot of questions,' she said, eyes sliding across to his hands and then hurriedly sliding back to focus on what she was doing. 'But I don't know anything about you.'

'Ask away.'

'Where do you live?'

'London.' Theo couldn't remember the last time he'd chopped an onion. Were they always this fiddly?

'And what were you doing in this part of the world? Aside from getting lost?'

Theo felt a passing twinge of guilt. 'Taking my car for some exercise,' he said smoothly. 'And visiting one or two…familiar spots en route.'

'Seems an odd thing to do at this time of year,' Becky mused. 'On your own.'

'Does it?' Theo dumped the half-peeled onion. 'Is there anything to drink in this house or do vets not indulge just in case they get a midnight call and need to be in their car within minutes, tackling the dangerous country lanes in search of a sick animal somewhere?'

Becky stopped what she was doing and looked at him, and at the poor job he had made of peeling an onion.

'I'm not really into domestic chores.' Theo shrugged.

'There's wine in the fridge. I'm not on call this evening and, as it happens, I don't get hundreds of emergency calls at night. I'm not a doctor. Most of my patients can wait a few hours and, if they can't, everyone around here knows where the nearest animal hospital is. And you haven't answered my question. Isn't it a bit strange for you to be here on your own…just driving around?'

Theo took his time pouring the wine, then he handed her a glass and settled into a chair at the kitchen table.

His own penthouse was vast and ultra-modern. He didn't care for cosy, although he had to admit that there was something to be said for it in the middle of a blizzard with the snow turning everything white outside. This was a cosy kitchen. Big cream Aga…worn pine table with mismatched chairs…flagstone floor that had obviously had underfloor heating installed at some point, possibly before the house had begun buckling under the effect of old age, because it wasn't bloody freezing underfoot…

'Just driving around,' he said slowly, truthfully, 'is a luxury I can rarely afford.' He thought about his life—high-voltage, adrenaline-charged, pressurised, the life of someone who made millions. There was no time for standing still. 'I seldom stop, and even when I do, I am permanently on call.' He smiled crookedly, at odds with himself for giving in to the unheard of temptation to confide.

'What on earth do you do?' Becky leant against the counter and stared at him with interest.

'I…buy things, do them up and sell them on. Some of them I keep for myself because I'm greedy.'

'What sorts of things?'

'Companies.'

Becky stared at him thoughtfully. The sauce was simmering nicely on the Aga. She went to sit opposite him, nursing her glass of wine.

Looking at her, Theo wondered if she had any idea of just how wealthy he was. She would now be getting the picture that he wasn't your average two-up, two-down, one holiday a year, nine-to-five kind of guy and he wondered whether, like every other single woman he had ever met, she was doing the maths and working out how profitable it might be to get to know him better.

'Poor you,' Becky said at last and he frowned.

'Come again?'

'It must be awful never having time to yourself. I don't have much but what I do have I really appreciate. I'd hate it if I had to get in my car and drive out into the middle of nowhere just to have some uninterrupted peace.'

She laughed, relaxed for the first time since he had landed on her doorstep. 'Our parents always made a big thing about money not being the most important thing in life.' Her bright turquoise eyes glinted with sudden humour. 'Alice and I used to roll our eyes but they were right. That's why…' she looked around her at the kitchen, where, as a family, they had spent countless hours together '…I can appreciate all this quiet, which I know you don't understand.'

The prospect of saying goodbye to the family house made her eyes mist over. 'There's something wonderfully peaceful about being here. I don't need the crowds of a city. I never have or I never would have returned here after… Well, this is where I belong.' And the thought of finding somewhere else to call home felt like such a huge mountain to climb that she blinked back a bout of severe self-pity. Her parents had moved on as had Alice. So could she.

Theo, watching her, felt a stab of alarm. A pep talk

wasn't going to get her packing her belongings and moving on and a wad of cash, by all accounts, wasn't going to cut it with her parents.

When was the last time he had met someone who wasn't impressed by money and what it could buy?

His mother, of course, who had never subscribed to his single-minded approach to making money, even though, as he had explained on countless occasions, making money per se was a technicality. The only point to having money was the security it afforded and that was worth its weight in gold. Surely, he had argued, she could see that—especially considering her life had been one of making ends meet whilst trying to bring up a child on her own?

He moved in circles where money talked, where people were impressed by it. The women he met enjoyed what he could give them. His was the sort of vast, bottomless wealth that opened doors, that conferred absolute freedom.

And what, he wondered, was wrong with that?

'Touching,' he said coolly. 'Clearly none of your family members are in agreement, considering they're nowhere to be seen. The opposite, in fact. They've done a runner and cleared off to a different country.'

'Do you know what?' Becky said with heartfelt sincerity. 'You may think you're qualified to look down your nose at other people who don't share your…your… materialism, but I feel sorry for anyone who thinks it's worth spending every minute of every day working! I feel sorry for someone who never has time off to just *do nothing.* Do you ever relax? Put your feet up? Listen to music? Or just watch television?' Becky's voice rang with self-righteous sincerity but she was guiltily aware that she was far from being the perfectly content person she was making herself out to be.

She hadn't rushed back to the cottage because she couldn't be without the vast, open peaceful spaces a second longer. She'd rushed back because her heart had been broken. And she hadn't stayed here because she'd been seduced by all the wonderful, tranquil downtime during which she listened to music or watched television with her feet up. She'd stayed because she'd fallen into a job and had then been too apathetic to do anything else about moving on with her life in a more dynamic way.

And it wasn't fun listening out for leaks. It wasn't fun waiting for the heating to pack up. And it certainly wasn't fun to know that, in another country, the rest of her family was busy feeling sorry for her and waiting for her to up sticks so that the house could be sold and valuable capital released.

'I relax,' Theo said softly.

'Huh?' She focused on a sharply indrawn breath, blinking like a rabbit caught in the headlights at the lazy, sexy smile curving his mouth.

'In between the work, I actually do manage to take time off to relax. It's just that my form of relaxation doesn't happen to include watching television or listening to music… But I can assure you that it's every bit as satisfying, if somewhat more energetic…'

CHAPTER THREE

'WHAT DO *YOU* do here?'

'What do you mean?' Becky asked in sudden confusion.

'To relax.' Theo sprawled back, angling the chair so that he could loosely cross his legs, ankle resting on thigh, one arm slung over the back of the chair, the other toying with the wine glass, twirling it slowly between his long fingers as he continued to look at her.

'I mean,' he continued pensively, 'it's all well and good killing time in front of the television with your feet up, while you congratulate yourself on how peaceful it is, but what else do you get up to when you've had your fill of the great open spaces and the lack of noise?'

'I grew up here' was all Becky could find to say.

'University must have been a very different change of scenery for you,' Theo mused. 'Which university did you go to?'

He could see her reluctance to divulge any personal details. It made him want to pry harder, to extract as much information as he could from her. Her dewy skin was pink and flushed. In a minute, she would briskly stand up and dodge his personal attack on her by busying herself in front of the Aga.

'Cambridge.'

'Impressive. And then you decided, after going to one of the top universities on the planet, that you would return here so that you could get a job at a small practice in the middle of nowhere?'

'Like I said, you wouldn't understand.'

'You're right. I don't. And you still haven't told me what you do for relaxation around here.'

'I barely have time to relax.' Becky stood up abruptly, uncomfortable with his questioning. She rarely found her motives questioned.

'But I thought you said…' A smile quirked at the corner of Theo's mouth.

'Yes, well,' snapped Becky, turning her back to him, more than a little flustered.

'But when you do…?' Theo followed her to where she was standing, clearing an already tidy counter.

He gently relieved her of the cloth and looked down at her.

Becky had no idea what was happening. Was this flirting? She had successfully convinced herself that there was no way the man could have any interest in her, aside from polite interest towards someone who had agreed to let him stay for the night because of the poor weather conditions. But when he looked at her the way he was looking at her now…

Her mind broke its leash and raced off in all sorts of crazy directions.

He was obnoxious. Of course he was, with his generalisations, his patronising assertions and that typical rich man's belief that money was the only thing that mattered.

He was just the sort of guy she had no time for.

But he was so outrageously beautiful and that was what gripped her imagination and held it. That was what was making her body react with such treacherous heat to his smoky grey eyes.

He'd painted a picture for her when he'd told her how he relaxed. *He hadn't had to go into details because in a few sentences she had pictured him naked...aroused... focusing all that glorious, masculine attention on one woman...*

'You surely must get a little lonely out here?' Theo murmured softly. 'However much you love the peace and isolation.'

'I...'

Her eyelids fluttered and her lips parted on an automatic denial of any such thing.

Theo drew in a sharp breath, riveted by the sight of those full, plump lips. She had no idea how alluring that mixture of apprehension and innocence was. It made him want to touch, even though he knew that it would be a mistake. This wasn't one of those women who'd stopped being green round the ears when they were sixteen. Whatever experiences this woman had had, whatever had driven her back to this house—and he was certain that something had—she was innocent.

He stepped back and raked his fingers through his hair, breaking the electric connection between them.

Becky was trembling. She could feel the tremor running through her body, as though she had had a shock and was still feeling the aftermath of it, even though he had returned to the table to sit back down. She couldn't look at him as he picked up the conversation, making sure to steer clear of anything personal.

He asked her about the sort of situations she had to deal with out in the country... How many were in the practice? Had she always wanted to be a vet? Why had she chosen that over a conventional medicine course?

He didn't ask her again whether she was lonely.

He didn't ask her why she had chosen to retreat to the country to live when she could have had a job anywhere in the country.

When he looked at her, it was without that lazy, assessing speculation that made her blood thicken and made her break out in a cold sweat.

He complimented her on the meal and asked her about her diet, about how she managed to fit in her meals with the hours she worked.

He could not have been more meticulously polite if he had been obeying orders with a gun held to his head and she hated it.

His arrival at the house was the most exciting thing that had happened to her in a long time and it had occurred just when she had been questioning her whole life, putting it into perspective, trying to figure out a way forward. It had occurred hard on the heels of her sister's phone call, which had stirred up a grey, sludgy mix of emotion in her, some of which she didn't like.

It also felt as though fate had sent him along to challenge her.

And how was she going to respond to that challenge? By running away? By retreating? She was going to be challenged a lot more when her job came to an end and the roof over her head was sold, and what was she going to do then? Dive for cover, close her eyes and hope for the best?

Where was the harm in getting into some practice now when it came to dealing with the unexpected? It wasn't as though there would be any repercussions, was it? You could bare your soul to a stranger on a plane and then walk away when the plane landed, safe in the knowledge that you wouldn't clap eyes on that person again, so if they happened to be a receptacle for all your secrets, what difference would that make?

She felt as though she had been on standby for someone just like him to come along and shake her world up a little because things had settled in a way that frightened her.

'It does get lonely,' she said, putting down her fork and spoon and cupping her chin in the palm of her hand to look at him. She cleared her throat, realising that this was something she had never said aloud to anyone. 'I mean, I'm busy most of the time, and of course I have friends here. It's a small place. Everyone knows everyone else and, since I returned, I've caught up with friends who went to school with me. It's nice enough but…' She took a deep breath. 'You're right. Sometimes, it gets a little lonely…'

Theo sat back to look at her narrowly. He had angled to find out more about her. He had reasoned that knowledge was power. To find out about her would help him when it came to buying the house. But, more than that, he had been strangely curious, curious to find out what had brought her and kept her here.

Now she was telling him—was it a good idea to encourage her in her confidences?

She wasn't the confiding sort. He could see that in the soft, embarrassed flush in her cheeks, as though she was doing something against her better judgement.

'Why are you telling me this?' he asked softly and Becky looked at him from under her lashes.

'Why not?'

'Because you've been resisting my questions ever since I turned up here and started asking them.'

Becky's flush deepened.

'I don't know you,' she said honestly, shrugging. 'And

once you leave my house I'll never see you again. You're not my type—you're not the sort of person I would ever want to continue having any sort of friendship with, despite the weird way we've happened to meet.'

'Such irresistible charm…' he murmured, catching her eye and countering her sheepishness with raised eyebrows.

Becky laughed and then warmed when he smiled back, a watchful, assessing smile. 'A girl doesn't get much chance to be irresistibly charming out here in the sticks,' she said. 'The livestock don't appreciate it.'

'But there's more than livestock out here, isn't there?' Theo prodded.

'Not much,' Becky confessed. She grimaced and then looked away, down to the wine glass which appeared to be empty. He had brought the bottle to the table and now he reached across to top her up. 'I say that I'm not on call-out twenty-four seven,' she laughed. 'Let's hope I don't get an emergency call tonight because I might just end up with my car in a ditch.'

'Surely no one would expect you to go out in weather like this?' Theo looked at her, startled, and she laughed again.

She had a lovely laugh, soft, ever so slightly self-conscious, the sort of laugh that automatically made you want to smile.

'No. Although I *have* had emergencies in snow before where I've had no choice but to get into my car, head out and hope for the best. Sheep. They sometimes have poor timing when it comes to lambing. They don't usually care whether it's snowing or whether it's three in the morning.'

'So just the demanding sheep to get your attention…' He considered that, in the absence of a significant other, she would be as free as a bird should she find herself having to leave the house at short notice.

To somewhere—he mentally justified the inevitable—where there might be more for a girl of her age than sheep and livestock.

'I don't suppose someone like you ever feels…like you're not too sure where you're going or what the next step might be.'

The question caught him by surprise because it wasn't often anyone ignored his 'no trespass' signs to ask anything as outrageously personal, and for a few seconds he contemplated not answering. But, then again, why not? Like she had so aptly said, they were ships passing in the night.

And besides, he liked that shy, tentative look on her face. It was so different from the feisty little minx who had first greeted him at the front door. He liked the fact that she was opening up to him. Normally uninterested in most women's predictable back stories—which were always spun as a prelude to someone trying to get to him—he had to admit that he was keen to hear hers.

She wanted nothing from him and that was liberating. He thought that it allowed him actually to *be himself*.

Of course, within certain limits, considering he had chosen to keep her in the dark about his real reasons for descending on her like a bolt from the blue, but there was no such thing as absolute truth between people, was there?

'No,' he drawled. 'I make it my business to always know where I'm going and I certainly have never been wrong-footed when it comes to the future.'

'Never?' Becky laughed uncertainly. He was so overwhelming, so blindingly self-assured. Those were character traits that should have left her cold but in him they were sexy, seductive, almost endearing. 'Nothing has ever happened in your life that you haven't been able to control?'

Theo frowned. Outside, through the kitchen window, he could see the driving fall of white, as fine and fierce as a dust storm, lit up and dazzling in the little patch outside the window where a light had been switched on.

Inside was warm and mellow. He hadn't felt so unstressed in a while and he recalled why he had been stressed for the past several months. Nothing to do with work. The stress of work was something he enjoyed, something he needed to survive, the way a plant needs rain or sun. He had been stressed out by his mother. This was the first time he could think about her without his gut tightening up.

'My mother has been ill,' he heard himself say abruptly. 'A stroke. Out of the blue. No one saw it coming, least of all me. So, yes, that could be categorised as something that has happened that has been out of my control.'

Becky wanted to reach across and squeeze his hand because he looked awkward with the confession. She wasn't accustomed to pouring her heart out to anyone and, clearly, neither was he. Not that she wouldn't have been able to see that for herself after five minutes in his company.

'I'm sorry. How is she now? How is your father dealing with it? And the rest of your family? Sometimes, it's almost harder for the family members.'

Theo wondered how he had managed to end up here, with a virtual stranger leaning towards him, face wreathed with sympathy.

'There's just me,' he said shortly. 'My father died…a long time ago and I'm an only child.'

'That's tough.' Becky thought of her own family arrangements.

'Do you feel sorry for me?' he prompted with silky smoothness. He smiled slowly, very slowly, and watched as the blood crept up to her hairline. She wanted to look away, but she couldn't, and that gave him a heady kick because the oldest game in the book was being played now and he liked that.

He liked it a lot more than spilling his guts like one of those emotional, touchy-feely types he had never had time for.

This was safe ground and known territory. When it came to sex, Theo was at home, and this was about sex. Why bother to beat about the bush? She wanted him and the feeling was mutual. He didn't understand why he found her so appealing, because she was not his type, but he did, and he wondered whether that had to do with the fact that for once there was no pressure. He wasn't even certain that she would take his hand if he offered it and allow herself to be led up to that bedroom of hers.

The uncertainty just lent another layer to the thrill of a chase he hadn't yet decided to embark upon.

Though she was so unknowingly sexy…

He wondered what she would look like without clothes on. He had to guess at a figure she was hell-bent on concealing and he was desperate to see what was there. He flexed his fingers and shifted.

'Of course I feel sorry for you,' Becky was saying with heartfelt sincerity. 'I'd be devastated if anything happened to one of my family.' She watched as he slowly eased his big body out of the chair. Her heart began to beat fast and it was beating even faster when he leaned over her to support himself on either side of her chair, caging her in.

She wanted to touch him. She wanted him to touch her. In no way did she feel in the slightest threatened by this tall, lean, powerful man physically dominating her with his presence.

She felt…feminine.

It was an unfamiliar feeling because femininity was something she had always presumed herself lacking. It went with good looks and both of those were the domain of her sister.

'How sorry?' Theo murmured huskily. Her excitement was contagious. He could feel it roaring through his veins, making him act in this unexpected way, because the caveman approach was just not his thing. He didn't sling women over his shoulder or rip their clothes off. That would have been on a par with beating his chest and swinging from tree to tree on a vine. But he wanted to sling this one over his shoulder, especially when she sat there, staring at him with those incredible eyes, chewing on her lower lip, refusing flippantly to give in to the massive charge of attraction between them.

'I…' Becky offered weakly. 'What's going on here?'

'Sorry?' Theo wondered whether he had misheard.

'I'm not sure I understand what's going on…'

'What do you think is going on? We're two adults and we're attracted to one another and what's going on is me making a pass at you…'

'Why?'

Theo straightened. He shot her a crooked smile and then perched on the edge of the table. 'This is a first for me.'

'What is?' Startled, Becky stared at him. She was so turned on that she could barely speak and she couldn't quite believe that this was happening. Not to her. Stuff like this never happened to her. She had always been the bookworm who attracted fellow bookworms. Face it, even Freddy had been a bookworm just like her. Guys like Theo didn't go for girls like her. They went for hot blondes in tight dresses who batted their eyelashes and knew what to do when it came to sex.

What did she know about sex? Nerves gripped her but the promise of that ride, with its speed, its thrills and its unbearable excitement, was much, much greater than any attack of nerves.

She wanted this.

'Never mind,' she said softly, eyes dipped. Her innate seriousness wanted to be reassured, wanted to be told that this was more than just sex, but of course it wasn't. It was purely about sex and that was part of its dragging appeal. This went against everything inside her and yet she couldn't resist its ferocious tug on all her senses.

'Look at me, Becky.'

She obeyed and waited with halted breath for him to say what he had to say.

'If you have any doubts at all, then say so right now and we both walk away from this.'

She shook her head and smiled, and Theo nodded. 'And Becky…' He leaned over her once again, his dark, lean face utterly serious. 'There's something I should tell you from the outset, just so that there are no misunderstandings. Don't invest in me and don't think that this is going to be the start of something big. It won't. I don't do relationships and, even if I did, we're from different worlds.'

He didn't do relationships and, even if he did, they were from different worlds…

He was giving her an out and he wasn't beating about the bush. This would be a one-night stand. She was going to hand her virginity over to someone who had made it clear that there was nothing between them bar physical attraction The one thing on which she had never placed any emphasis. Yet this was more than longing on her part. Her virginity felt like an albatross around her neck and she wanted to set herself free from it more than anything in the world.

'Message received and understood,' Becky murmured and blushed as he delivered her a slashing smile. 'You're not from my world either and, although I *do* do relationships, it would never, ever be with someone like you. So we're on the same page.' The dynamics of what happened next was making her perspire. Should she tell him that she was a virgin? No. Chances were he would never guess anyway…and she didn't want him to take fright and pull back.

'I've wanted you the minute I saw you,' Theo confessed unsteadily, fingers hooking under the waistband of the jogging bottoms he had borrowed.

'Even though I'm from a different world?' She tilted her chin up and stared at him.

'You've admitted the same about me' was his gruff response.

'I don't know why I find you attractive at all,' she muttered to herself and Theo laughed.

'Don't spare my ego, whatever you do.'

Their eyes tangled and she felt an affinity with him, this inappropriate stranger, that was so powerful it took her breath away. It was as if they were on exactly the same page, united, thinking as one, mixed up with one another as though they belonged.

Shaken, she stared at him.

Turned on beyond belief, Theo stayed her as she made to stand. 'Not yet,' he murmured. He stood in front of her and then he knelt and parted her legs, big hands on her inner thighs. Becky held her breath and then released it in a series of little gasps and sighs. She wanted to squirm. She wasn't naked but the way he was holding her, his position between her legs, made her feel exposed and daringly, recklessly wanton.

She flung back her head and half-closed her eyes. She felt his fingers dip under the waistband of her jeans and then the soft pop of the button being released, followed by the sound of the zipper being pulled down.

Everything was heightened.

She could hear the hammering of her heart against her rib cage, the raspy sound of her jerky breathing, the soft fluttering of her eyelids. She wriggled as he began to pull down her jeans.

This was surreal. The girl who had always thought that sex would be with someone she had given her heart to was desperate for a man who was just passing through. The girl who had quietly assumed that she'd *know* when love struck was being floored by something she had never anticipated—unbridled, hot, heady, sweat-inducing lust.

Cool air hit her legs. She half-opened her eyes and groaned softly, reaching out to curl her fingers in Theo's hair. He looked up and their eyes met.

'Enjoying yourself?' he asked in a wickedly soft voice and Becky nodded.

'Then why don't you get vocal and tell me?'

'I can't!'

'Of course you can. And you can tell me what you want me to do as well…' Her panties were still on. He could breathe in her musky scent through them and see the dampness of her desire, a patch of moisture against the pale pink cotton. He didn't pull them down. Instead, he gently peeled them to one side, exposing her, and blew softly against the mound.

'What should I do next?' he enquired.

'Theo...' Becky gasped in a strangled voice. She'd slipped a little down the chair.

'Tell me,' he ordered softly. 'Want me to lick you down there? Want to feel my tongue sliding in and teasing you?'

'Yes,' Becky whispered.

'Then give me some orders...' He was so hot for her, turned on by her shyness, which was so different from what he was accustomed to.

He had to shed his clothes. Urgently. The top, then the jogging bottoms, taking his boxer shorts with them. She was looking at him, eyes wide.

'Lick me...' Just saying that made her whole body burn. 'I'm so wet for you...' He was so beautiful that he took her breath away. Her mind had always drawn a convenient line at the bedroom door. In her head, the act of making love stopped with kissing, fumbling and whispering of sweet nothings.

She had never pictured the reality of the naked male, not really. This surpassed all her fantasies and she knew, somewhere deep down inside, that the benchmark he had set would never be reached by any other man. He was so gloriously masculine, his body so lean and exquisitely perfect, the burnished gold of his colouring so impossibly sexy.

Theo pulled off the panties, wanting to take his time, and knowing that it would require super-human control to do that, because he was so hard he was hurting. She was wonderfully wet and she shuddered as he slid his questing tongue against her, seeking out the little throbbing bud and then teasing it, feeling it swell and tighten.

Becky was on fire, burning up. Two of his fingers joined his tongue in its devastating assault on her senses.

She pushed his head harder against her. She felt so ready to take him into her. 'Come in me,' she begged.

'All in good time.' Theo barely recognised his voice. Having boasted about his formidable talent for exercising control all the time in all areas of his life, he was finding out what it felt like to lose it. He was free-falling, his body doing its own thing, refusing to listen to his head…

Head buried between her legs, he sucked hard and felt her come against his mouth, her body arching up, stiffening, her breath sucked in as her orgasm ripped through her, long and shuddering.

He rose up, watching her brightly flushed face and her feverish twisting as her orgasm subsided.

His good intentions to hang onto his self-control had disappeared faster than water being sucked down a plug hole.

'Hold me,' he commanded, legs straddled over her.

Dazed, Becky took him in her hand. Nothing had ever felt so good. Every inhibition she had ever had when she had thought about making love to a man for the first time disappeared the minute he touched her.

It felt *so right.*

He made her feel special, made it feel natural for her to open herself up to him in the most intimate way imaginable.

Touching him now, she was no longer apprehensive, even though her mind skittered away from the physical dynamics of having someone as big as he was inside her. She was so wet and so giddy for him that it wasn't going to be a problem…

She delicately traced her tongue along his rigid shaft then took him into her mouth and felt a surge of heady power as he groaned and arched back.

Instinct came naturally. She even knew when he was

nearing his orgasm…and she sensed that this was not how he had planned things to go.

Looking down at her, Theo could scarcely believe that his control had slipped so completely that he couldn't contain the orgasm he knew was a whisper away. Her mouth circling him was mind-blowingly erotic, as was the focused expression on her face and the slight trembling of her fingers cupping him.

Intent on not coming like *this*, he pulled away, and for a second he thought that he had succeeded, thought that he could hold himself in check for the length of time it would take them both to get upstairs. He was mistaken. He could no more control the inexorable orgasm that had been building from the moment she had looked at him with those turquoise eyes…the moment he had known that they would end up in bed together, whether it made sense or not, whether it was a good idea or not…than he could have controlled a fast approaching tsunami.

For Becky, still transported to another planet, this was inexplicably satisfying because it was proof positive that he was as out of control as she was.

Watching him come over her had rendered her almost faint with excitement. Her heated gaze met his and his mouth quirked crookedly.

'Would you believe me if I told you that this has never happened in my life before?' Theo was still breathing thickly and still shocked at his body's unexpected rebellion. 'I'm taking you upstairs before it happens again.' He lifted her up in one easy movement and took the stairs quickly. She could have been as light as a feather. Her hair was all over the place, her cheeks were bright with hectic colour and her eyes drowsy with desire.

The curtains hadn't been drawn and weak moonlight seeped into her bedroom. It was still snowing, a steady, silent fall of white that somehow enhanced the peculiar dream-like feel to what was going on.

Theo took a few seconds to look at her on the bed. Her dark hair was spread across the pillows and her pale, rounded body was a work of art. Her breasts were big, bigger than a generous handful, her nipples cherry-pink discs.

He was going to take his time.

He'd acted the horny teenager once and it wasn't going to happen again. He still couldn't compute how it had happened in the first place.

He joined her on the bed, pinned her hands to her side and straddled her.

'This time,' he said roughly, 'I'm going to take my time enjoying you...' He started with her breasts, working his way to them via her soft shoulders, down to the generous dip of her cleavage, nuzzling the heavy crease beneath her breasts until he settled on a nipple, and there he stayed, lathing it with his mouth, suckling, teasing and tasting, drawing the throbbing, stiffened bud into his mouth, greedy for her.

Becky writhed and groaned. She spread her legs and wrapped them around him, desperate to press herself against the hardness of his thigh so that she could relieve some of the sensitivity between them. But he wasn't having that and he manoeuvred her so that she was lying flat, enduring the sweet torment of his mouth all over her breasts.

He reached back to rub between her legs with the flat of his hand but not too much, not too hard and not for long.

He needed more than this erotic foreplay. He needed to be inside her, to feel that wetness all around him.

'My wallet's in my bedroom,' he whispered hoarsely. 'I need it to get protection. Don't go anywhere...'

Where was she going to go? Her body physically missed his for the half a minute it took for him to return and, during that time, she thought again about whether she should tell him the truth, tell him that she was a virgin…and, just as before, she quailed at the thought.

But as he applied the condom, looking directly at her as his fingers slid expertly along his huge shaft, she felt a twinge of nerves.

Theo settled between her legs and nudged her, pushing against her wetness gently. He wasn't going to go hard and fast. He was going to take his time and enjoy every second of her. He felt her momentarily tense but thought nothing of it. He was so fired up he could barely think at all and he certainly couldn't read anything from her response until he pushed into her, sinking deep and moving faster than he wanted but knowing that he just had to.

He heard her soft grunt of discomfort and stilled. 'I'm a big boy…tell me if I'm hurting you because you're really tight. Deliciously tight…' He sank deep into her and then it clicked.

Her blushing shyness, the way he had felt, as though everything he was doing was being done for the first time, that momentary wince…

'Bloody hell, Becky—tell me you're not a virgin…?'

'Take me, Theo. Please don't stop…'

He should have withdrawn but he couldn't. *A virgin.* His body was aflame at the thought. He'd never wanted any woman the way he wanted this one. Every sensation running through his body felt primitive. He was the caveman he never thought he could be, and the fact of her virginity made him feel even more primal, even more like a caveman.

Their bodies were slick with perspiration. With a groan, he thrust hard, deep into her tightness, and the feeling was indescribable as she rocked with him, wrapping her legs around his waist and coming seconds before he did, crying out as she raked her fingers along his back, the rhythm of her body matching his.

'You should have said.' He fell onto his back, disposing of the condom and thinking that he should be feeling a lot more alarmed that he had slept with someone as innocent as she was. So much for her escape to the country in the wake of some dastardly affair with a married man, or whoever it had been.

He was her first.

He'd never been more turned on.

'It doesn't make any difference.' She rolled so that she was half-balancing on his chest and staring down at him. 'Like I said, Theo, this isn't the beginning of anything for me. One night and then we exit one another's lives for ever…' She traced her finger around his flat, brown nipple. Why did it hurt when she said that?

'In that case…' Theo wasn't going to play mind games with himself as to whether he had done the right thing or not. 'Let's make the most of the night…'

CHAPTER FOUR

THEO STROLLED THROUGH into the kitchen of his sprawling four-bedroom penthouse and ignored the food that had been lavishly prepared by his personal chef, who kept him fed when he was in the country and actually in his apartment. The dish, with its silver dome, was on the counter, alongside a selection of condiments and some basic instructions on heating.

Instead, he headed straight for the cupboard, took down a squat whisky glass and proceeded to pour himself a stiff drink.

He needed it.

His mother, still in Italy, was back in hospital.

'A fall,' her sister Flora had told him when she had called less than an hour ago. 'She was on her way to get something to drink.' She had sounded vague and unsettled. 'And she tripped. You know those tiles, Theo, they can be very smooth and slippery. And I have told your mother a thousand times never to wear those stupid bedroom slippers when she is in the house! Those slippers with the fur and the suede are for your little box houses in England with lots of carpet! Not for nice tiles!'

'On her way to get something to drink?' Theo had picked up on the uneasy tone of his aunt's voice, and he had been right to, even though it had taken some prodding and nudging in the right direction to get answers out of her.

Now he sank into the long cream leather sofa and stared, frowning, past the stunning art originals on either side of the marble fireplace at nothing in particular. His mind was consumed by the very fundamental question…

What was he going to do?

His mother had not been on the way to fetch herself a glass of orange juice at a little after three-thirty in the afternoon. Nor had she tripped in her haste to make herself a fortifying cup of tea.

'She has been a little depressed,' Flora had admitted reluctantly. 'You know how it is, Theo. She likes it out here but she sees me…my grandchildren…I cannot hide any of this from Marita! I cannot put my children and my grandchildren in a cupboard and lock them away because my sister might find it upsetting!'

Theo had gritted his teeth and moved the grudging conversation along, to discover that depression was linked with drinking. His mother had gradually, over the weeks, become fond of a tipple or two before dinner and it seemed that the tipple or two had crept earlier and earlier up the day until she was having a drink with lunch and after lunch.

'Why haven't you told me this before?' he had asked coldly, but that had produced a flurry of indignant protests and Theo had been forced to concede that Flora had had a point. She didn't share the villa with his mother. She would not really have seen the steady progression of the problem until something happened to bring it to her notice.

Such as the fall.

'She's due out of hospital in a week's time,' Flora had said. 'But she doesn't want to return to London. She says that she has nothing there. She enjoys my grandchildren, Theo, even though it pains her to know that…'

There had been no need for his aunt to complete the sentence with all its barely concealed criticism.

Getting married and having hordes of children was the Italian way.

Going out with legions of unsuitable women, remaining stubbornly single and promising no grandchildren whatsoever was not.

And it wasn't as though he had siblings who could provide for his mother what he was unwilling to.

But he had to do *something...*

He glanced at his computer, lodged on the gleaming glass table on which he had stuck his feet. For a few seconds, he stopped thinking about the predicament with his mother and returned to what he had spent the last fortnight thinking about.

Becky.

The woman had occupied his mind so much that he hadn't been able to focus at work. The one night, as it happened, had turned into three because the snow had continued to fall, a wall of white locking them into a little bubble where, for a window in time, he had been someone else.

He had stopped being the powerhouse in charge of his own personal empire. He had stopped being responsible for all those people who depended on him for a livelihood. There'd been no fawning women trying to get his attention wherever he went or heads of companies trying to woo him into a deal of some sort or another. He was untroubled by the constant ringing of his mobile phone because service had been so limited that, after informing his PA that he couldn't get adequate reception, he had done the unthinkable and switched the phone off.

He had shed the billionaire persona just as he had shed the expensive clothes he had travelled in.

He had chopped wood, did his best to clear snow and fixed things around the house that had needed fixing.

And of course he had noted all the flaws with the cottage, which were not limited to the leaking roof. Everywhere he'd looked, things needed doing, and those things would only get worse as time went on.

He knew that if he played his cards right he would be able to get the place at a knockdown price. He could bypass her altogether. He had found out where her parents lived, even knew what they did for a living. He could simply have returned to London, picked up the phone and made them an offer they couldn't refuse. Judging from the state of the cottage, it wouldn't have had to be a high offer.

But that thought had not even occurred to him. He had played fast and loose with the truth when Becky had first asked him what had brought him to the Cotswolds and, like all good lies, it had been impossible to disconnect from it.

Maybe he had kidded himself that once he returned to London his usual ruthlessness would supplant his momentary lapse in character when he had been living with her. It hadn't worked that way and he had spent the past fortnight wondering what his next step was to be.

And, worse, wondering why he couldn't stop thinking about her. Thinking about her body, warm, soft and welcoming. Thinking about the way she laughed, the way she slid her eyes over to him, still shy even though they had touched each other everywhere. She haunted his dreams and wreaked havoc with his levels of concentration but he knew that there was no point picking up the phone and calling her because what they had enjoyed had not been destined to last.

They had both recognised that.

She had laughed when he had stood by her front door, back in his expensive cashmere, which was a little worse for wear thanks to the weather.

'Who *are* you?' she had teased, with a catch in her voice. 'I don't recognise the person standing in front of me!'

'It's been fun,' he had returned with a crooked smile but that about summed it up.

Back in the clothes she usually didn't step out of, she was the country vet, already thickly bundled up to go to the practice where she worked. He could no more have transported her to his world than he could have continued in her father's old clothes clearing snow and chopping wood for the fire.

But he'd felt something, something brief and piercing tugging deep inside him, a sharp ache that had taken him by surprise.

He focused now and looked around him at the fabulous penthouse, the very best that money could buy. He'd bought it three years previously and since then it had more than quadrupled in price. It sat at the top of an impressive converted glass and red brick government building which was formidably austere on the outside but outstandingly modern and well-appointed on the inside. Theo liked that. It gave him the pleasant illusion of living in a building of historic interest without having to endure any of the physical inconveniences that came with buildings of historic interest.

He wondered how Becky would fit in here. Not well. He wondered how she would fit into his lifestyle. Likewise, not well. He moved in circles where the women were either clothes horses, draped on the arms of very, very rich men, or else older, at ease with their wealth, often condescending to those without but in a terribly well-mannered and polite way.

And the women all dripped gold and diamonds, and were either chauffeured to and from their luxury destinations or else drove natty little sports cars.

But his mother…would like her. She was just the sort of natural girl his mother approved of. There was even something vaguely Italian about the way she looked, with her long, dark hair and her rounded, hourglass figure.

His mother would approve and so…

For the first time since he had returned to London after his sojourn in the back of beyond, Theo felt a weight lift from his shoulders.

Trying to deal with the annoying business of Becky playing on his mind when she should have been relegated to the past had interrupted the smooth running of his life and he could see now that he had been looking at things from the wrong angle.

He should have realised that there was only one reason why he hadn't been able to get her out of his mind. She was unfinished business. The time to cut short their sexual liaison had not yet come to its natural conclusion, hence he was still wrapped up with her and with thoughts of making love to her again.

He would make contact with her and see her again and he would take her to see his mother in Italy. She would be a tonic for his mother, who would be able at least to contemplate her son going out with a woman who wasn't completely and utterly inappropriate.

She would find her mojo once again and, when she was back to full strength, he would break the news that he and Becky were finished, but by then Marita

Rushing would be back on her feet and able to see a way forward.

And, he thought with even greater satisfaction, she would have the cottage to look forward to, the cottage she had wanted. Would Becky agree to speak to her parents about selling it to him? Yes. She would because it made financial sense and he had no doubt that he would be able to persuade her to see that. The house was falling down and would be beyond the point of reasonable sale in under a year, at which point the family home would either collapse into the ground or else be picked apart and sold to some developer with his eye on a housing estate.

Would she agree to this little game of pretend for the sake of his mother's health? Yes, she would, because that was the sort of girl she was. Caring, empathetic. When she had spoken about some of the animals she had treated in the course of her career, her eyes had welled up.

The various loose strands of this scheme began to weave and mesh in his mind.

And he felt good about all of it. He was solution-oriented and he felt good at seeing a way forward to solving the situation with his mother, or at least dealing with it in a way that could conceivably have a positive outcome.

And he felt great about seeing Becky again. In fact, he felt on top of the world.

He nudged his mobile phone into life and dialled…

Becky heard the buzz of her phone as she was about to climb into bed, and she literally couldn't believe her bad luck, because she had had two call-outs the past two nights and she really, *really* needed to get some sleep.

But then she drowsily glanced at the screen, saw who was calling and her heart instantly accelerated into fifth gear.

He had her number. He had taken it when he had been leaving on that last day because the roads had still been treacherous, even though the snow had lightened considerably, and she had been worried about him driving to London in his *silly little boy-racer car.*

'I'll call you if I end up in a ditch somewhere,' he had drawled, and then he had taken her number.

Noticeably, he hadn't given her his, and that had stung, even though she had made it perfectly clear that what they'd had was a done deal—there for the duration of the snow, and going just as the snow would go, disappearing into nothing until you couldn't even remember what it had been like to have it there.

Of course he hadn't called but for her the memory of him hadn't disappeared like the snow. Where white fields had faded from her mind, the memory of him was still as powerful after two weeks as it had been after two hours.

It didn't help either that, with the practice winding down, work was thinning out as the farmers, dog-owners, cat-owners and even one parrot-owner began transferring business to the nearest practice fifteen miles away. She had the feeling of being the last person at the party, hanging around after the crowd had dispersed when the lights were being switched on and the workers were beginning to clear the tables. The same sad, redundant feeling of someone who has outstayed their welcome.

And the house…

Becky had decided that she wouldn't think about the house until she had found herself a new job because there were only so many things one person could worry about.

But neither of those massive anxieties could eclipse the thoughts of Theo, which had lodged in her head and continued to occupy far too much space. She found herself regularly drifting off into dreamland. She wondered what he was doing. She longed to hear his voice. She checked her phone obsessively and then gave herself little lectures about being stupid because they had both agreed that theirs would only be a passing fling. She rehearsed fictional conversations with him, should they ever accidentally bump into one another, which was so unlikely it was frankly laughable.

She wondered why he had managed to get to her the way he had. Was it because he had come along at a point in time when she had been feeling especially vulnerable? With her job about to disappear and her sister finally achieving the picture-postcard life with her much-wanted baby on the way? Or was it because she had been starved of male attention for way too long? Or maybe it had been neither of those things.

Maybe she had never stood a chance because he was just so unbelievably good-looking and unbelievably sexy and she had just not had the arsenal to deal with his impact.

When she caught herself thinking that, she always and inevitably started thinking about the women he might now be seeing. She hadn't even asked him whether he had a girlfriend! He had seemed, for all his good looks, as the honourable sort of guy who would never have cheated on any woman he might have been seeing, but of course she could have been wrong.

He could have returned to London in his fancy car and immediately picked back up where he had left off with some gorgeous model type.

Realistically she had never expected him to get in touch so she stared open-mouthed at the buzzing mobile phone in her hand, too dumbstruck to do anything.

'Hello?'

Theo heard the hesitancy in her voice and immediately

knew that he had done the right thing in contacting her, had made the right decision. When he had driven away from her house two weeks ago, he had told himself that he had had a good time, but at the end of the day she had been a virgin and he'd been driving away from a potential problem. She had laughed off the fact that he had been the first man she had slept with, had told him that she was attracted to him, and why not?

'You're not the right guy for me,' she had said seriously. 'But, if I carry on waiting for Mr Right to come along, I might be waiting for a very long time.'

'In other words, you're using me!' he had laughed, amused, and she had laughed back.

'Are you hurt?' she had teased.

'I'll survive...'

And she hadn't been lying. There had been no clinging when the time had come for him to go. She hadn't tried to entice him into carrying on what they'd had. There had been no awkward questions asked about whether he would miss her. Her eyes hadn't misted over, her lips hadn't trembled and she hadn't clung to the lapels of his coat or given him one final, lingering kiss. She had smiled, waved goodbye and shut the door before he had had time to fire up the engine.

He might have been her first but he certainly wasn't going to be her last. Maybe that was another reason why he hadn't been able to get her out of his head. He'd effectively been dumped, and he'd never been dumped in his life before, simple as that.

'Becky...'

Becky heard that wonderful lazy drawl and the hairs on the back of her neck stood on end. She steeled herself to feel nothing, but curiosity was eating her up. Had he missed her? Had he been thinking about her every second of every minute, which was what it had felt like for her? Thinking about him all the time…

'How are you?'

'Been better.' They could spend time going around in polite circles before she asked him the obvious question—*why have you called?*—and Theo decided that he would skip the foreplay and get down to the main event. 'Becky, I could beat around the bush here, but the fact is I've called to ask you for…a favour. This would be a favour better asked face to face but…time is of the essence, I'm afraid. I just haven't got enough of it to woo you into helping me out.'

'A favour?' Of course he hadn't called because he'd missed her. Disappointment coursed through her, as bitter as bile.

'Do you remember I spoke to you about my mother? It would appear that…' He sighed heavily. 'Perhaps it would have been better to be having this conversation face to face after all. I know that this is asking a lot, Becky, but there have been some…unfortunate problems with my mother—problems that do not appear to have a straightforward solution.' The direct approach was failing. He stood up, paced and sat back down. 'I need you, Becky,' he said heavily.

'Need me to do what?' Her voice had cooled.

'Need you to come to London so that I can talk to you in person. I can send my driver for you.'

'Are you crazy, Theo? I don't know what's going on with your mother. I'm sorry if she's having problems but you can't just call me up out of the blue and expect me to jump to your summons.'

'I understand that what we had was… Look, I get it that, when you closed your front door, you didn't anticipate me getting in touch with you again.' Theo seriously found it hard to believe that this could actually be the case because the shoe was always on the other foot. Women were the ones desperate for him to make contact and he had always been the one keen to avoid doing any such thing.

He instinctively paused, waiting to hear whether she would refute that statement. She didn't.

Becky thought that he was certainly right on that count—she hadn't anticipated it—but she had hoped. It hadn't crossed her mind that she would indeed hear from him and he would be asking a favour of her!

That certainly put paid to any girlish illusions she might have had that their very brief fling had meant anything at all for him. She was thankful that she had waved him a cheery goodbye and not made any mention of hoping that they might meet again.

'You're right—I didn't—and I don't see how I could possibly do you any favours in connection with your mother. I don't even know her.'

'She fell,' Theo said bluntly. 'I've just come off the telephone with her sister. She apparently...' He paused, dealing with the unpalatable realisation that he was actually going to have to open up about a situation which felt intensely personal and which he instinctively thought should be kept to himself.

'Apparently what...?' Becky could feel vulnerability in his hesitation. He was so strong, so proud, so much the archetypal alpha male that any sort of personal confession would seem like an act of weakness to him.

Despite herself, she felt her heart go out to him, and then banked down that unwelcome tide of empathy.

'She's been depressed. The recovery we had all hoped for has been a physical success but...'

Again, that telling pause. She had a vivid picture of

him trying to find difficult words. She felt she knew him, and then she wondered how that was possible, considering they had spent a scant three days in one another's company. *Knowing* someone took a long time. It had taken her nearly two years before she had felt that she *knew* Freddy, and then it had turned out that she hadn't known him at all, so how likely was it that this sensation of being able to *sense* what Theo was feeling from down the end of a telephone was anything other than wishful thinking?

She wasn't going to give in to any misplaced feelings of sympathy. By nature, she was soft. It was why she had chosen to study veterinary science. Caring for sick and wounded animals was straight up her alley. But Theo was neither sick nor a wounded animal. He was a guy she had slept with who hadn't bothered to get in touch with her until now, when he obviously wanted something from her.

'She fell because she was drinking,' he said abruptly.

'Drinking?'

'No one knows how long it's been going on but it's reached a stage where she's drinking during the day and…a danger to herself. God knows what might have happened if she had been behind the wheel of a car…'

'I'm so sorry to hear that,' Becky said sincerely. 'You must be worried sick…'

'Which is why I called you. If my mother's problems are alcohol related, then it's obvious that she's slipping into a depressed frame of mind. There were signs of that happening before she left for Italy…' He sighed heavily. 'Perhaps I should have insisted that she go for therapy, for counselling of some sort, but of course I thought it was a straightforward case of being down because she had had a stroke, because she had had a brush with her own mortality.'

'That's understandable, Theo.' Becky automatically consoled him. 'I wouldn't beat myself up over it if I were you. Besides, there's nothing you can do about that now. Weren't you the person who made a big deal about telling me how important it was to live in the present because you can't worry over things that happened in the past which you can't change?'

'I told you that?'

'Over that tuna casserole you told me you hated.'

'Oh, yes. I remember…'

Becky's skin warmed. His voice had dropped to a husky drawl with just the ghost of a satisfied smile in it and she knew exactly what was going through his head.

He had pushed the dish of tuna bake to one side, pulled her towards him and they had made love in the kitchen. He had laid her on the table, her legs dangling, the dishes balanced in a heap that could have crashed to the floor at any given moment. He had parted her legs and had licked, sucked and nuzzled between them until she had been crying and whimpering for him to stop, for him to come inside her—and come inside her he had,with urgent, hungry, greedy force that had sent her soaring to an orgasm that had gone on and on and had left her shattered afterwards.

'So,' she said hurriedly, 'you couldn't have foreseen. Anyway, I'm sure everything will be fine when you bring her back to London, where you can keep an eye on her. You could even employ someone…'

She wondered whether that was the little favour he had phoned about. Perhaps he had returned to his busy tycoon lifestyle and was too preoccupied with making money to make time, so he'd decided that she might be able to see her way to helping him out. She'd been shortsighted enough to mention to him that the practice was going to close. Maybe he thought she'd have lots of free time on her hands.

'She's refusing to return to London.'

'Yes, well…'

'Nothing to come back here for, were, apparently—her words.'

'I still don't see why you've called me, Theo. I don't see how I could possibly help. Maybe you should…'

'Needs something to live for.'

'Yes, but…'

'She's old-fashioned, my mother. She wants what her sister has. She wants…a daughter-in-law.'

Becky thought she had misheard and then she figured that, even if she hadn't, she *still* had no idea what that had to do with her.

'Then you should get married,' she said crisply. 'I'm sure there would be hundreds of women falling over their feet to drag you up the altar.'

'But only one that fits the bill. You.'

Becky burst out laughing, manic, disbelieving laughter. 'You've telephoned out of the blue so that you can ask me to marry you because your mother's depressed?'

Theo's mouth compressed. He hadn't *asked her to marry him*. He loved his mother but even he could see a limit to the lengths he would go to in order to appease her. But, if he had, hysterical laughter would not have been the expected response.

'I'm asking you to go along with a fake engagement,' he gritted. 'A harmless pretence that would do wonders for my mother. We go to Italy…an all-expenses-paid holiday for you…and you smile a lot and then we leave. My mother will be delighted. She will have something to live for. Her depression will lift.'

'Until she discovers that it's all been a complete lie and there won't be any fairy-tale white wedding.'

'By which time two things will have been achieved. She will no longer be so depressed that she's dependent on a bottle to help her through, and she will realise that I'm capable of having a relationship with someone who isn't a bimbo.'

'So let me get this straight,' Becky said coldly. 'I'm the one for this *harmless pretence* because I have a brain and because—I'm reading between the lines here—I'm not tall, blonde and beautiful. I'm just an ordinary girl with an ordinary job so your mother will like me. Is that it?'

'You're not exactly what I would call *ordinary*,' Theo mused.

'No.' She was shaking with outrage and, underneath the outrage, hurt.

'Why not?'

'Why do you think, Theo? Because I'm not into deceiving people. Because I have some morals—'

'You're also heading for the unemployment line,' he said, cutting her off before she could carry on with her list of high-minded virtues. He was still scowling at her roar of laughter when she had thought he might have called to ask her to marry him. 'Not to mention living in a house that's falling apart at the seams.'

'Where are you going with this?'

'I could get you up and running with a practice of your own. You name the place and I'll provide the financial backing and cover all the advertising. In fact, I can do better than that—I'll set my team on it. And I'll get all those nasty little things that are wrong with your house repaired…'

'Are you trying to *buy* me so I do what you want?' And the weird thing was…she had thought about him so much, wanted him so much, would have picked up where they had left off if he had made the first move and called her. But this…

Theo wondered how his brilliant idea had managed to get derailed so easily. 'Not buying you, no,' he said heavily, shaking off the nasty feeling that yet again with this woman his self-control was not quite what it should be. 'Business transaction. You give me what I want and I give you…a great deal in return. Becky, that aside…' his voice dropped a notch or two '… I'm asking you from the bottom of my heart to do this for me. Please. You told me that you loved your parents. Put yourself in my shoes—I only want my mother to regain her strength.'

'It's not right, Theo.'

He heard the hesitation in her voice and breathed a heartfelt sigh of relief.

'I am begging you,' he told her seriously. 'And be assured that begging is something I never do.'

Becky closed her eyes tightly and took a deep breath. 'Okay. I'll do it, but on one condition…'

'Name it.'

'No sex. You want a business transaction, then a business transaction is what you'll get.'

CHAPTER FIVE

BECKY HAD WONDERED whether she would be given the fortnight off. She was owed it, had worked unpaid overtime for the past few months, but leaving someone in the lurch was not something she liked to do.

She had half-wished that she would be firmly told that she couldn't be spared, because as soon as she had agreed to Theo's crazy plan she had begun to see all the holes in it. On the contrary, her request was met with just the sort of kind-hearted sympathy that had made her realise how much she would miss working for the small practice.

'You come and go as you please until the place closes,' Norman had said warmly. 'Can't be nice for you, working here, knowing that it's winding down and that you won't be seeing our regulars again. Besides, you need to start thinking about your next job—and don't you worry about anything, Rebecca, you'll get a glowing reference from me.'

'The faster you can make it to London, the better, Becky,' Theo had said as soon as those fateful words—*okay, I agree*—had left her mouth, and he hadn't allowed her to sit on her decision and have any sort of rethink.

She'd needed a bit of time to get things sorted with her job and her house before she just breezed off abroad for two weeks.

'What things?' he had demanded.

She could practically hear him vibrating with impatience down the end of the line. He'd called her several times over the two-day period she'd taken to pack some stuff, check the house for incipient problems that might erupt the minute her back was turned and anxiously leave copious notes on some of the animals that had been booked in to have routine procedures done over the two-week period.

Already regretting her hasty decision, she'd plied him with questions about his mother.

She'd repeatedly told him that it was a crazy idea. He'd listened in polite silence and carried on as though she hadn't spoken, but he *had* talked about Marita Rushing and about the health problems that had afflicted her. He'd only closed up when she'd tried to unearth information prior to the stroke, to life before she had started worrying that her son might never marry and might never make her the grandmother she longed to be.

'Not relevant.' He swept aside her curiosity with the sort of arrogant dismissiveness that she recognised as part and parcel of his vibrant, restless personality.

'She won't believe that we have any kind of relationship,' Becky told him the night before she was due to leave for London. Ever since she had laid down the 'no sex' ground rules, he had been silent on the subject. He hadn't objected and she'd thought that he was probably glad that she had spared him the necessity of trying to resurrect an attraction that hadn't lasted beyond her front door.

That hurt but she told herself that it simplified things. He had suggested that she treat his proposition as a business transaction, and there was no reputable business transaction on the planet that included sex on tap. They'd had their fling and now this was something else. This was his way of doing the best he could to try and get his mother back on her feet and her way of trying to sort out her future.

In a way, accepting his generosity almost turned it into a job—an extremely well-paid job, but a job nevertheless—which meant she could distance herself from that flux of muddled emotions she still seemed to have for him.

It helped her to pretend to herself that there wasn't a big part of her that was excited at the prospect of seeing him again.

'People always believe what they want to believe, but we'll talk about that when you come,' he eventually said.

Becky had accepted that. She'd had too much on her mind to pay attention to whatever story line he might think up. He insisted on sending a driver for her, even though she had told him that the train was perfectly okay.

Now, sitting in the back seat of his chauffeur-driven black Range Rover, she felt the doubts and hesitations begin to pile up.

Along with a suffocating sense of heightened tension, which she valiantly tried to ignore. She told herself that he was not going to be as she remembered. She was looking back at that small window in time through rose-tinted specs. He wouldn't be as striking or as addictive as she had found him when he had stayed with her. Locked away in the cottage with the snow falling outside, she had built their brief fling into an impossibly romantic tryst.

The fact that they were so unsuitable for one another had only intensified the thrill. It was like putting the prissy, well-behaved head girl in the company of the bad boy who had roared into town on his motorbike. No matter how much the sparks might fly, it would all come crashing down because it wasn't reality.

When she went to London, reality would assert itself and she would see him as he really was. Not some tall, dark, dangerously sexy stranger who had burst into her humdrum life like an unexploded bomb, but a nice-looking businessman who wore suits and ties and carried a briefcase.

He would be hassled-looking, with worry lines on his face that she hadn't noticed because she had been swept away on a tide of novelty and adventure.

He hadn't been lying about his wealth. He'd never boasted, but he hadn't tried to hide it. She'd briefly wondered whether he had been enticing her by exaggerating just how much punch he packed, but any such vague doubts were put to rest as the silent, über-luxurious car pushed through the London traffic to glide into a part of the city that was so quiet it *breathed* wealth.

The tree-lined street announced its pedigree with the cars neatly parked outside fabulous, very pristine mansions. Some had driveways, most didn't. At the end of the street, a severe, imposing building dominated the cul-de-sac. It was gated, with a guard in a booth acting as sentry just within the ornate black wrought-iron gates. The very fact that the place was secured against anyone uninvited was an indication of the sort of people who lived there and her mouth fell open as the car drove through, directly to an underground car park.

Becky tugged her coat around her and thought about the two worn, battered cases she had brought with her. She hoped no one would see her on her way to his apartment because she would probably be evicted on the spot.

He had come into her world and he had slotted in, had replaced his city garb with her dad's country clothes and had mucked in as though he had spent his entire life in a shambolic cottage in the middle of nowhere.

But that was not his world. This was. And there was no way that she was going to fit in with the sort of seamless ease with which he had fitted into her world.

'I'll show you to the underground lift.' The chauffeur turned to glance at her. It was the first thing he had said since a polite 'Good morning' earlier when he had greeted her at the front door and taken her cases from her to stick them in the car trunk.

Becky nodded and they walked, in silence, through some glass doors into a reception area which housed a bank of four gleaming lifts, comfortable furniture for several people to relax and two very big, very well-cared-for plants that formed a feature on either side of the row of lifts. Yet another guard in uniform was sitting behind a circular desk and he nodded and exchanged a few pleasantries with Theo's driver, who had brought her bags out with him from the car.

This had all been a very bad idea. She should never have come. She didn't belong here. Their worlds had collided and then flown off in different directions. She should have left it there, just an exciting memory to draw upon now and again, something to put a smile on her face as her life, temporarily upset, carried on along its prescribed route.

Instead, she was here, listening to the porter tell her where to locate Theo, who would be waiting for her. Her battered bags were by her feet. She felt cumbersome and ungainly in her big coat, with all its useful pockets, and underneath the big coat there was nothing more glamorous. Her usual jeans, layers and baggy jumper. She wondered what the chauffeur had thought of her, and now she wondered what the porter was making of her, but she refused to give in to all the insecurities nudging at the door.

This was a business deal. She was doing him a favour and he was doing her one. There was no necessity for her to fit in or not fit in.

But her stomach was knotted with nerves as she was whooshed up in the mirrored lift to the fourteenth floor.

The lift opened out onto a plush carpeted landing. She stared straight ahead into an oversized mirror, on either side of which were two grand abstract paintings.

'Turn right,' the porter told her with a kindly smile, 'and you can't miss Mr Rushing's apartment.'

She turned right and saw the porter had not been kidding. The entire floor was clearly occupied by just one apartment. The corridor was more of an outside landing, with a glass and metal sideboard against the wall over which was another abstract work of art. It was very light and airy. She looked around her and just then, just as she was torn between moving forward and fleeing back to the sanctuary of the lift, a door opened and there he was.

Her heart fluttered erratically and her mouth went dry. He hadn't changed and it had been absurd wishful thinking to have hoped that he might. If anything, he was taller, more aggressively masculine and more sinfully sexy than she remembered. Wearing loafers, a pair of black jeans and a black, fitted short-sleeved polo, he was lounging against the doorframe, watching her as she tried to get herself together and present a composed image.

Theo looked at her. His mind, coolly analytical, recognised what he had known would present itself to him and that was a woman who, quite simply, didn't fit into the world of sophistication and glamour he occupied. He had known that she wouldn't have dressed for the occasion, and anyway, he doubted she had the sort of clothes that would allow her to blend in. She looked ill at ease, with her ancient suitcases on either side of her, and in the exceptionally practical sort of outfit that worked when she was tearing off to see to a sick animal but offered nothing more than functionality.

But then there was that other part of him…the part that remained uncontrolled by his coolly analytical mind… the part that had made him lose concentration at work because he hadn't been able to get her out of his mind…

The part that looked at her standing metres away from him and felt a surge in his libido that took his breath away. It didn't matter what she wore, how unfashionable her clothes were or how awkward she looked as she hovered suspiciously by her cases… She still turned him on.

But no sex.

Those had been her ground rules, and of course they made sense. It didn't matter whether he still wanted her or not. It had been short-sighted to imagine furthering what they had had by a fortnight so that he could somehow get her out of his system.

Perhaps if she had jumped at the opportunity to get back into bed with him again…

If she had greeted his phone call with the sort of breathless pleasure with which any other woman would have responded…

Well, under those circumstances, he would have had no problem in stepping up to the plate and taking what was on offer. But, if she had been the sort of woman to agree to two weeks of abandoned sex, then she wouldn't have been the woman he had gone to bed with.

She might have fancied him, she might have lost her virginity to him because she had been unable to fight the attraction and at that point in her life had chosen to allow the physical side of her to overrule the intellectual side of her, but essentially he wasn't the type of man she was interested in—hence the 'no sex' stipulation.

Common sense had reasserted itself. Of course, she was right. She was far too serious to indulge in a no-strings-attached liaison, especially when she would be going against the grain and faking a relationship with him for the sake of his mother.

The most important thing was his mother's health and he didn't want Becky to start questioning what she was doing because they were sleeping together, because she was having an affair with the wrong guy.

Besides, he had never chased any woman, and he wasn't about to start now.

Annoyed with himself because his libido wasn't playing ball, he pushed off from the doorframe and walked towards her. She looked as though, given half a chance, she would turn tail and scarper.

But of course she wouldn't do that, would she? She was being paid for the favour she was doing him. It didn't matter how morally high-minded you were, money always ruled the day.

She'd only been persuaded into this escapade because of the money. He had thought her different from all the other women he had ever dated in the past, women who had been impressed by his bank balance and the things he was capable of buying for them, but was she really?

His mouth thinned. At least the cards were on the table with no grey areas for misunderstandings. This was a business transaction and focusing on that would get his wayward libido back on the straight and narrow…

'You're here.' He picked up her bags and stood back, silver-grey eyes skirting over her. 'I wondered if you'd get cold feet at the last minute.'

Becky heard the cool in his voice and interpreted it as

what it was—the voice of a man who no longer had any physical interest in her. He needed her help and he was willing to pay a high price for it. This wasn't about any lingering attraction or affection on his part. This was about business and she shouldn't be surprised because, when it came to business, he was clearly at the top of the field and you didn't get there without ruthlessly being able to take advantage of opportunities.

He wanted to do what he felt was the best thing for his mother and she was an opportunity he had taken advantage of.

'I was tempted.' Becky fell into step alongside him and decided right there and then that she would have to be as cool and as detached as he was. 'But then I thought about what was on the table and I realised that I would be a fool to turn down your offer.'

'You mean the money.' His voice hardened as he stood back, allowing her to brush past him into the apartment.

Becky slipped past and was frozen to the spot. This wasn't an *apartment*...this was a *penthouse complex*. It was very open plan. Staring ahead, she looked at the wall of raw brick interrupted by a series of modern paintings that she knew, without being clued up on art, were priceless originals. Curving to the left was a short, twisting spiral staircase that led to an arrangement of rooms which she assumed to be bedrooms, although she could be wrong. But there were living spaces in front and on either side, from the glorious, huge sitting area with its white arrangement of leather sofas to a spacious kitchen in shades of grey and a dining area that was cool and contemporary. There were almost no walls, so the spaces all ebbed and flowed into one another in a beguiling mix of brick, wood and marble.

And it was vast. High ceilings, limitless space and

cool, subdued colours that always seemed to characterise immensely expensive houses. This was the sort of place where too much colour would be a rude intrusion and clutter was to be discouraged at all costs.

'Impressed?' Against his will, Theo felt a kick of pride at her awed expression. Other women had been awed. Frankly, all of them. This one was different.

'It's beautiful.' Becky turned to him, her glorious eyes sincere. 'You must feel very privileged living here…'

Theo shrugged. 'I've stopped noticing my surroundings,' he said, sweeping up the cases and striding off towards the staircase. 'Just as you, doubtless, have stopped noticing the leaking roof in your cottage.' Part of the deal had been to do repair work on the cottage, and Theo intended to do a damn good job so that the basics could be covered before he bought the place, because he had no doubt that it would be his in due course, especially now that setting her up in a practice of her own was part of the deal.

He wondered what it would be like to set her up with a practice in London…

Then he shook free the ridiculous notion.

'I'm not allowed to forget the leaking roof,' Becky said coldly, 'considering I have to avoid stepping in a bucket of water every other day.'

'Had it fixed yet?' He paused outside a bedroom door to look down at her.

Becky stared back up at him, angry with herself for the way he could still make her feel like this—hot, bothered and unsteady—when obviously everything had changed between them. She had to get a grip. She couldn't spend the next two weeks in a state of heightened awareness.

'One of my friends has offered to oversee the repair

work. I didn't think I could leave it leaking and unsupervised for two weeks.'

'I'll cover the costs.'

'There's no need.'

Theo pushed open the bedroom door but then stood in front of her, barring her path. 'Let's not skirt away from the base line here, Becky. There's a deal on the table and I intend to stick to it. You're doing me a great favour, and in return you get repair work done to your house and I set you up in a practice of your own so that you don't have to worry about whether you'll be able to get another job easily or not.'

Becky reddened. Put like that, without all the frilly business of helping him out to soften the *base line*, she couldn't quite believe what she was doing here. The practical side of this had not been the real reason she had ended up here, had it? It appalled and frightened her, if she was being brutally honest with herself, but she knew that the bigger part of her reason for standing right here, in front of a bedroom in this marvellous penthouse suite of rooms, was because she had nurtured the tiniest slither of hope that he might still find her as attractive now as he had a fortnight ago. She had broken all her rules when she had slept with him. It hadn't mattered how inappropriate he was for any kind of relationship, she had wanted to keep on breaking those rules for a little bit longer.

Now that she was here, it seemed like a ridiculous thing ever to have thought. She stuck out like a sore thumb and she wouldn't be surprised if he made sure to hide her away until they disappeared off to Italy, just in case he was spotted by anyone he knew.

Of course he wouldn't fancy her. Of course she had been a blip for him, just as he had been a blip for her. He would never have got in touch had the unfortunate situation with his mother not arisen. Thank goodness she had not shown her hand but instead had gone on the defensive the minute she had realised that he wanted her to do him a favour, and had laid down her 'no sex' ground rules. She knew that if he had chosen to break them, declared that he had missed her after all, then she would have cracked. She knew that if he had looked at her when she had stood there in that plush landing and then swept her up into his arms, her 'no sex' stipulation would have crumbled.

It hadn't happened and she had been an idiot to think that it might have.

'Fine.' She smiled brightly and peered around him to the bedroom which, like the rest of the place, was the last word in fabulous. 'Would you mind very much if I… er…had a shower? It's been a long drive down here…'

She risked a quick glance. She wanted to ask him why he was in a mood with her when he had been the one to ask her down here in the first place, but she didn't, because she needed to be as cool as he was. She wasn't going to start pleading with him to be *friendly.* Maybe he resented having her here in the first place. Maybe he felt as though he had been cornered into doing the only thing he could think of for his mother but, really, he didn't want to. He just didn't have a choice. Perhaps he had wanted to get back to his normal life of playing with beautiful, glamorous models but suddenly he had had to rummage up a feasible girlfriend to produce to his mother and she had been the only woman he knew plain enough to pass muster.

'And then,' she carried on, 'we could hammer out the details? If I'm supposed to be involved with you, we should at least get our stories straight.'

Theo marvelled at the speed with which she had abandoned her scruples about deceiving his mother and fallen in line now that there was a financial incentive dangling on the horizon.

'Quite,' he drawled. Her bags looked lost and out of place where he had placed them and he clenched his jaw, toughening up against any weakness inside him to imagine that those bags were a reflection of their owner, who must also be feeling lost and out of place.

'I...' She turned to him, burying her hands in her pockets so that she didn't impulsively and foolishly reach out to touch him. 'I've never done anything like this before...' She shuffled and then made herself stop, reminded herself that she was a qualified vet who dealt with far more important situations than this and handled herself competently and efficiently.

'Which is why we have to discuss what's going to happen. It's not going to be believable if you're a bag of nerves whenever you're around me. My mother will want to believe that I'm actually capable of being attracted to a woman with a brain, but even she is going to start having doubts if you act as though you're terrified of slipping up. Anyway, take your time, I'll be downstairs in the kitchen. We can...discuss how we proceed when you join me.'

He felt he needed a stiff drink.

By the time she emerged forty-five minutes later, he was wondering what exactly the details of his little ill-conceived adventure might be. His mother knew that he was bringing a girl to meet her and had already perked up because this was the first time in nearly two years he had done that.

There was no going back now.

His cool eyes swept over her as she slowly walked into the kitchen. She had changed into jeans and yet another baggy jumper and was wearing a pair of bedroom slippers.

Becky didn't miss the way he had given her the once-over and yet again she was burningly conscious of just not fitting in to the surroundings, a bit like a cheap souvenir from a package holiday amidst a collection of priceless pieces of china.

You didn't seem to mind this look when you were in my cottage, she thought with sudden resentment.

'You're doing it again,' Theo drawled, strolling to get a glass from the cupboard and pouring her some wine.

'Doing what?'

'Looking as though you'd rather be anywhere else but where you actually happen to be.'

'This is just such a stupid idea.'

'I suggest you move on from that. It's too late to get cold feet now and, besides, you have nothing to worry about.' He drained his glass and poured another. It was a little after seven and food had been prepared by his chef. From nowhere came the memory of her little kitchen and the way he would sit at her kitchen table, watching her as she cooked, anticipating touching her.

'What do you mean *I have nothing to worry about*?' She gulped down some wine and looked at him cautiously. He was just so beautiful. Why couldn't her imagination have been playing tricks on her?

'It's going to be two weeks,' Theo said drily. 'Two weeks for which you will be richly rewarded. In return, all you have to do is smile prettily and chat now and again. I will be with you at all times. I'm not asking you to turn into my mother's best friend. Your main purpose will be to…' he sighed heavily '…give her a purpose, make her see the future as something to look forward to.

It's a short-term plan,' he continued with a hint of dissatisfaction, 'but it's the only plan I have.'

'Why don't you just take someone you actually want to have a proper relationship with?' Becky suggested, frowning. 'Instead of this great big charade?'

Theo burst out laughing. 'If I had one of those stashed up my sleeve,' he mused, 'then don't you think I would have pulled her out by now? No, if I were to present my mother with any of the women from my little black book, she would run screaming in horror. She's had her fill of my women over the years. I honestly don't think her heart could take any more.'

'Why do you go out with them if they're so unsuitable?'

'Whoever said that they were unsuitable *for me*?' Theo answered smoothly. 'At any rate, it's irrelevant. Even if there was someone whose services I could avail myself of, it would be an unworkable arrangement.'

'Why?' Becky wondered whether he was actually aware of how insulting his remarks were.

'Because it would lead to all sorts of complications.' He thought of some of his girlfriends who had started daydreaming about rings and white dresses even though he had always made it clear from the outset that neither would be on the agenda. 'They might start blurring the line between fact and fiction.'

'How do you know that *I* won't do that?' Becky surprised herself by asking the question but this was a level playing field. He could say what he wanted, without any regard for her feelings, so why should she tiptoe round what she had to say to *him*?

'Because,' he countered silkily, 'you made it clear from the start that I wasn't your type and I don't see you getting any unfortunate ideas into your head.' She'd never told him what had driven her into the Cotswolds, what heartbreak had made her want to bury herself in the middle of nowhere. He wondered what the guy had been like. Nice, he concluded. So *nice* that he hadn't had the balls to entice her between the sheets. He couldn't stop a swell of pure, masculine satisfaction that *not nice* had done the trick.

'You're here because I offered you a deal you couldn't refuse and that suits me fine. No misunderstandings, no demands springing from nowhere, no unrealistic ambitions.'

And no sex… That could only be a good thing when it came to those nasty misunderstandings… Besides, if he had been having uninvited fantasies about her, then surely seeing her out of context, awkward and ill at ease in his territory as she was now, would slowly prove to him that her novelty value had been her only powerful draw…?

At the moment, he was still finding it difficult to look at her without mentally stripping her of her clothes, which was infuriating.

'But cutting to the chase…' He looked at the food which had been prepared earlier and was neatly in copper pans on the hob. He switched on the hob and had a quick think to ascertain the location of the plates. 'We met…?'

Becky shrugged. 'Why lie? Tell your mother where I live and that we met at my cottage. Tell her that you got lost because of the snow and ended up staying over for a few days.'

'That won't work,' Theo said sharply. He flushed and cursed the lie that could not now be retracted. 'Love at first sight might be a bit improbable.'

'Why?'

'Because it's not in my psyche, and anyone who knows me at all would know that.'

'So what *is* in your psyche?' Somehow, she had been so engrossed talking to him, that food had found its way to a plate and was now in front of her. Delicious, simple food, a fish casserole and some broad beans. With her nerves all over the place, her appetite should have deserted her, but it hadn't. The food was divine and she dug in with gusto.

Theo watched her, absently enjoying her lack of restraint. 'We met one another. After a diet of tall, thin models, beautiful but intellectually unchallenging, I fell, without even realising it, in love with someone who had a brain and made me jump through hoops to get her.'

Becky felt slow, hot colour invade her cheeks because, in that low, sexy, husky voice, it could have truly been a declaration of love. 'You mean you went for someone short and fat.' She covered over her embarrassment with a high-pitched, self-deprecating laugh and Theo frowned.

'Don't run yourself down,' he said gruffly. For a moment, he was weirdly disconcerted, but he recovered quickly and continued with cool speculation, 'There's no way I would ever have gone for someone who didn't like herself…'

'I like myself,' Becky muttered, glaring.

Theo grinned. 'Good. You should. Tall, thin and glamorous is definitely not all it's cracked up to be.'

Becky blushed, confused, because there was a flirtatious undercurrent to his voice, which she must have misheard because there had certainly been nothing flirtatious in his manner since she had arrived.

'And there's something else my mother would never buy,' he said slowly, pushing his plate to one side and relaxing back in the chair, his hands clasped behind his head so that he was looking down at her.

'What?'

'Your wardrobe.'

'I beg your pardon?'

'You can't show up in clothes you would wear on a house visit to see to a sick dog. You're going to have to lose the jeans and practical footwear. We're going to be staying on the coast, anyway. Much warmer than it is over here. You'll have to bid farewell to the jumpers, Becky, and the layers.'

'This is *me*,' she protested furiously. 'Aren't you supposed to have fallen for completely the opposite of the models you've always gone out with?'

'I'm not asking you to buy clothes that could be folded to the size of handkerchiefs but, if we're going to do this, then we're going to do it right. You'll have an unlimited budget to buy whatever you want…but it's time to kiss sweet goodbye to what you've brought with you…'

CHAPTER SIX

THEO GLANCED AT his watch and eyed the suite of rooms which Becky had been inhabiting with a hint of impatience.

His driver was waiting to take them to his private jet and he'd now been waiting for twenty minutes. Theo was all in favour of a woman's right to be late, except Becky wasn't that type, so what the hell was keeping her?

The vague dissatisfaction that had been plaguing him for the past forty-eight hours kicked in with a vengeance and he scowled, debating whether he should go and bang on her door to hurry her along.

The fact was that he had seen precious little of her since she had arrived at his apartment. They had discussed the nuts and bolts of what they would be doing but she had firmly rejected his offer to accompany her to the shops to buy a replacement wardrobe. She didn't want to do it in the first place, she had mutinously maintained, and she certainly wasn't going to have him traipsing around in her wake telling her what she could or couldn't wear. It was bad enough that he wanted her to try and project a persona she didn't have.

She'd made it quite clear that her decision to go along with the charade was one she had almost immediately regretted, and he'd been left in no doubt that only the prospect of having an uncertain future sorted out was the impetus behind her act of generosity. In other words, she'd been drawn by the offer of financial assistance. He was, above all else, practical. He could appreciate her sensible approach. He was grateful for the fact that there were absolutely no misplaced feelings of wanting more than the lucrative deal he had offered her. So, sex was off the agenda? He certainly wouldn't be chasing her although it was highly ironic that they were no longer physically intimate when they were going to have to convince his mother that they were.

He caught himself thinking that it would have been a damned sight more convenient if they had just fallen into bed with one another, for they were supposed to be a loved-up item, and then was furious with himself because he knew that he was simply trying to justify his own weakness.

If he'd thought that seeing her out of her comfort zone, an awkward visitor to *his* world, would cure him of his galloping, unrestrained libido, then he had been mistaken.

He still felt that he had unfinished business with her and for once his cool, detached, analytical brain refused to master the more primitive side of him that *wanted her.*

Had she brought a uniform of shapeless jumpers and faded jeans in a targeted attempt to ensure that he didn't try and make a pass?

Had she honestly thought that he would have forgotten what that body had felt like under his fingers?

He had become a victim of intense sexual frustration and he loathed it.

He wondered what she had bought to take to Italy and had already resigned himself to the possibility that she had just added to her supply of woefully unfashionable clothes as a protest against being told by him what to do.

Yet he had meant what he had told her...his mother knew him well enough to know that he liked well-dressed women. Or at least, she knew that the well-dressed woman was the sort of woman he was accustomed to dating. She'd certainly met enough of them over the years to have had that opinion well and truly cemented in her head. He might be able to sell her an intelligent woman as the woman who had finally won through but, intelligent or not, she'd never be convinced by a woman who couldn't give a damn about her appearance.

So how would she react if Becky decided to turn up in jeans and a baggy tee shirt? Trainers? Or, worse, sturdy, flat, laced-up shoes suitable for tramping through fields?

And yet, as he had told her, no other woman could possibly do for the role. And he couldn't think of a single one who would have held his interest long enough for his mother or anyone with two eyes in their head to believe that he was actually *serious.*

He smiled wryly because his mother would have been very amused if she could only see him here now, hovering by the door, glancing at his watch, prisoner of an unpredictable woman who wasn't interested in impressing him.

He was scrolling through messages on his phone when he became aware that she had emerged into the open-plan living area where he had now been tapping his feet for the past forty minutes.

He didn't have to look up.

He was as aware of her stealthy approach just as a tiger was aware of the soft tread of a gazelle.

He glanced up.

The battered bags, which he had insisted she replaced, were, of course, still there.

But everything else…

His eyes travelled the length of her, did a double take and then travelled the length of her all over again. He had been slouching against the wall. He now straightened. He knew that his mouth was hanging open but he had to make a big effort to close it because his entire nervous system seemed to have been rewired and had stopped obeying the commands from his brain.

Becky had had doubts about her drastic change of wardrobe. It had taken her far longer than necessary to get ready because she had wavered between wearing what she had bought and wearing what she was accustomed to wearing.

But he had got to her with those jibes about her clothes.

They had spent their glorious snatched time in the cottage snowed in, hanging around in old, comfy clothes. Because that was what the situation had demanded. But just how drab did he think she was? She had actually packed all of her summer wardrobe to take to Italy with her. She wasn't an idiot. She had known that thick layers would be inappropriate. How could he imagine that she would have presented herself as his so-called girlfriend dressed like a tramp?

She had never been more grateful for her decision to make sure he knew that the status of their relationship was purely business. If she had thought him not her type, then his stupid remarks about her having to change her appearance had consolidated that realisation.

How superficial was it to measure a woman's attractiveness by the type of clothes she wore?

But some devil inside her had decided to take him at his word. He wanted her to dress up like a doll? Then she would do it! She'd never been the sort to enjoying shopping. Buying clothes had always been a necessity rather than a source of pleasure. And in her line of work there was certainly no need to invest in anything other than purely functional wear. Durability over frivolity. She was all too aware that even the summer items she had packed were of a sensible nature. Flat sandals for proper walking in the countryside, sneakers, lightweight jeans and tee shirts in block colours, grey and navy, because bright colours had never been her thing. Her sister had always pulled off reds and yellows far more successfully.

But that was what Theo would be expecting. Perhaps even *dreading*. The fake girlfriend letting her side down by appearing like a pigeon to all the peacocks he had dated in the past. Maybe he had envisioned having to sit his mother down and persuade her to believe that he could actually fall for someone who didn't own a single mini-skirt and wouldn't have been caught dead wearing anything with sequins or glitter. Or lace, for that matter. And that included her underwear.

She had been timid in shop number one. Indeed, she had wondered what the point of being daring and rebellious was for a so-called liaison that wasn't destined to last longer than a fortnight.

But she had made herself go in and, by the time she had hit Harrods, she had found herself thoroughly enjoying the experience. How was it, she thought, that she had never sampled the carefree joy of trying on clothes, seeing herself as another person in a different light? How had she never realised that shedding her vet uniform could be downright liberating? She had retreated from trying to compete with her sister on the looks front and had pigeon-holed herself into the brainy bookworm with no time for playing silly dressing-up games. She had failed to see that there was a very healthy and very enjoyable middle ground.

In a vague way, as she had stood in one of the changing rooms, marvelling at the swirl of colour she had actually dared to try on, she had acknowledged that Theo was somehow responsible for this shift in her thinking. Just as he had been responsible, in a way, for hauling her out of her comfort zone, for taking her virginity, for being the one to make her enjoy the physical side of her.

Then she'd wondered what he would make of her change of wardrobe and that had spurred her on to be more daring than she might otherwise have been in colours, in styles, in shapes…

She'd even overhauled her lingerie, not that there had been any need, but why not?

And right now, in this breathless silence as he stood watching her with those amazing, brooding eyes, she thought that it had been worth every second of laborious trying on.

'I see you've gone for *barely there*…' Theo managed to get his legs working and his runaway brain back into gear.

The skirt was apricot and the top was dove-grey, and both fitted her like a glove, accentuating an hourglass figure that was the last word in sexy. The body that had driven him wild was on full display. Her tiny waist was clinched in, her full breasts were stunningly and lovingly outlined in the tight, stretchy top and even the grey trench-coat, which was as conventional as could be, seemed vaguely sensual because of the body it was incapable of covering up.

He'd told her that his mother would never have bought a girlfriend who dressed like a country vet, but he hadn't expected to be taken at his word.

And he didn't like it.

He scowled as he headed for her bags. 'I see you stuck to the ancient suitcases.'

'I thought it might be taking things a bit too far if I showed up with Louis Vuitton luggage considering I'm a working vet,' she snapped, stung by his lack of response to her outfit.

Would it be asking too much for him at least to acknowledge that she had done as asked and bought herself some peacock clothes?

Theo stood back and looked at her. 'No one would guess your profession from what you've got on.'

'Is that why you were staring at me?' she asked daringly. 'Because you think I should have bought stuff more in keeping with what a working vet on holiday would wear?'

They were outside and a driver was springing to open the passenger door for her.

Theo shot him a look of grim warning because he hadn't missed the man's eyes sliding surreptitiously over her, taking in her body in a quick sweep.

Harry had worked for him for two years and, as far as Theo could recall, had never so much as glanced at any of the women he had ferried from his apartment.

Theo flushed darkly. He turned to her as the car began purring away from the flash apartment block, through the impressive gates and in the direction of the airfield which, she had been told the day before, was an hour's drive away.

'When I suggested a change of wardrobe might be a good idea, I didn't think you'd go from one extreme to the other.'

'You said your mother would never find it credible that you would go out with someone who dressed the way I did. In other words, someone who looked like a bag lady.'

'That's quite the exaggeration.' But he had the grace to flush because she wasn't that far from the truth.

'You wanted me to be more like the kind of women you'd go out with so…' She shrugged.

Theo looked at her averted profile, the defensive tilt of her head, the way the skirt was riding provocatively up one thigh… He wondered whether she was wearing stockings or tights and his body responded enthusiastically to the direction of his thoughts.

'The women I'm accustomed to dating are…built a little differently to you,' he muttered truthfully. He had to shift to ease the pain of his sudden erection.

Becky's defences were instantly on red-hot alert but, before she could launch a counter attack, he continued, clearing his throat.

'They wouldn't be able to pull off an outfit like that quite like you're doing right now…'

'What do you mean?' Becky heard the husky breathlessness in her voice with dismay. This was a guy who had only got in touch because he had wanted something from her. A guy who had been happy to press on with his life after a couple of days. Even though she'd made a big deal of assuring him that there was no way he could ever have stayed the course with her, no way that she would want any more than the couple of days on offer, she'd be an idiot if she were to kid herself that she hadn't hoped for some sort of follow-up. Even a text to tell her that he missed her just a bit.

Because *she'd* missed *him* and thought about him a lot more after he'd gone than she should have.

She might not have played on his mind, but *he'd* played on *her* mind.

That had been part of the reason why she'd put down the 'no sex' rule when she'd agreed to his outrageous proposition.

If he thought that he could come to her for a favour,

tell her that she was the only one who fitted the bill because she was credibly average enough to convince his mother that he was serious about her, and then expect sex as some kind of bonus just because they'd been there before, then he was in for a shock!

But then, beneath that very sensible way of thinking was something she hardly dared admit even to herself. That *thing* she had felt for him and still felt for him after he'd disappeared back down to London frightened her. The power of his attraction had been so overwhelming that it had blitzed all her dearly held principles. In the face of it, she had had no choice but to throw herself into bed with him.

She was terrified that if she allowed herself to be weak, if she allowed herself to be overwhelmed by him again, then she would end up hurt and broken. She wasn't sure how she knew that but she just did.

So the last thing she should be doing right now was straying from the 'business arrangement' agenda and letting herself get side-tracked by personal asides.

'I mean…' he leaned towards her, his voice low '…my driver has never looked twice at any of the models who have stalked into this car over the years but he couldn't take his eyes off you.'

Becky went bright red. She wanted to put her hands to her cheeks to cool them. She glanced towards his driver, but the partition between the seats had been closed. Even so…

'If you think the stuff I bought is inappropriate, then I can easily, er, replace them…'

'Depends.'

'On what?'

'What else is in those suitcases of yours? Maybe I should have had a look before we left,' he continued in a low, thoughtful voice. 'Made sure you hadn't bought anything that would make my mother's hair curl…'

'You're being ridiculous,' Becky told him briskly. 'I doubt I've bought anything that any girl of my age wouldn't feel comfortable wearing, and your mother certainly wouldn't blink an eye at this outfit or any of the others if she's met any of your past girlfriends. I know, if they were all models, then what I'm wearing now would have been their idea of over-dressing.' Her skin was tingling all over and, although she wasn't looking at him, she was very much aware of his eyes on her, lazy and speculative.

Gazing at her pointedly averted profile, Theo had never felt such a surge of rampant desire. If this was what unfinished business felt like, then he wondered how he was going to cope for the next fortnight when he would be condemned to look without touching.

'At any rate, you've bought what you've bought,' Theo said roughly, dragging his mind off the prospect of trying to entice her into bed, because that would be a show of weakness he would never allow.

With the conversation abruptly closed down, Becky lapsed into nervous silence, while next to her Theo worked on his phone. When she glanced across, she could see him sending emails and scrolling through what appeared to be a mammoth report. He was completely oblivious to her. One minute it had felt so weird, so intimate…the next, she could have been invisible.

When she thought about the next fortnight, her stomach twisted into anxious knots, so instead she projected beyond that to where her life would be after they returned from Italy. He had told her that he would set her up in business, she only had to pick the spot, and she busied herself thinking about a possible location.

She wondered when the cottage would be sold. Her parents were unaware of the state of gradual disrepair into which it had fallen and that was something she had decided she would keep to herself. When it eventually sold—and there was no guarantee that would be soon, because the property market was hardly booming at the moment—it would get a far bigger price now that work was being done to fix the broken-down bits and she was pleased that her parents would reap the rewards from that. They had let her stay there for practically nothing.

Looking back at it, Becky could scarcely remember why she had felt so driven to run away when her sister and Freddy had tied the knot. She could scarcely remember what it had felt like to have a crush on Freddy or when, exactly, he had turned into just a pleasant guy who was perfect for her sister. She couldn't believe that some silly infatuation gone wrong had dictated her behaviour for years. If she hadn't allowed herself to lazily take the route of least resistance, she would not be here now, because she wouldn't have been at the cottage, pottering through life doing something she loved but without the necessary interaction with guys her own age.

She would never have met Theo. He had blasted into her life and galvanised her into really looking at the direction she had been taking. It just went to show how a series of coincidences could result in major life changes.

'Penny for them.'

Becky blinked and focused on him. He was leaning back against the door, his big body relaxed, legs spread slightly apart. Even like this, in repose, relaxed, he was the very image of the powerful alpha male and her heart gave a treacherous little leap.

'I was thinking about coincidences,' she said truthfully and Theo inclined his head.

'Explain.'

Becky hesitated. She knew that she needed to go on the defensive. She also knew that, if they were supposed to be *an item*, then for the duration of a fortnight she would have to stop treating him like the enemy.

He wasn't the enemy, she thought. Although he was... *dangerous.* Horribly, wonderfully, thrillingly, excitingly *dangerous.* And *that* was something she would never let on, because if there was one guy on the planet who would be tickled pink at being considered *dangerous* it was Theo Rushing. The more she agonised over the impact he still had on her, the more power she gave him over her state of mind.

He'd made those lazy little remarks to her about the way she looked and she'd practically gone into meltdown.

Well, it was going to be a nightmare if she went into a meltdown every time he turned his attention to her, especially considering they would have to pretend to be in love in front of his mother.

'I was thinking,' she ploughed on, determined to level the playing field between them so that she could be as cool as he was, 'that if you hadn't shown up out of the blue at the cottage, if it hadn't been snowing and you hadn't have ended up being stuck with me...'

'"Stuck" takes all the fun out of the memory.' Keen grey eyes noted the delicate colour that stained her cheeks and the way her eyelids fluttered as she breathed in sharply. Little giveaway signals that her 'no sex' rule had more holes in it than she probably would want to admit.

She'd made a big deal about how unsuited they were to one another and she was right. He could no more fall for someone as intensely romantic as she was than he could have climbed a mountain on roller skates. And, yet, the physical attraction was so strong that you could almost reach out and touch the electric charge between them.

She'd slept with him because she hadn't been able to fight that physical attraction. He hadn't been able to fight it either and he itched to touch her again.

Even though he knew that it probably wasn't a very good idea. He certainly wouldn't dream of going down the road of actively chasing her when a rebuff was waiting directly round the corner but…

He looked at her, eyes brooding and hooded.

There was no law against flirting, or pushing the barrier she had hastily erected, just to check and see how flimsy it was…was there…? Some might maintain that that would be a perfectly understandable response given that he was a red-blooded male with a more than healthy libido that just so happened to be fully operational when it came to her.

It would be a delicate compromise between maintaining his pride, holding on to his self-control and tipping his hat at common sense whilst testing the waters…and then playing a 'wait and see' game.

It would certainly enliven the next two weeks.

'I was drifting.' She ignored his little jibe. 'And you were a wake-up call.'

'Am I supposed to see a compliment in that?' he drawled. 'I don't think I've ever been described as any woman's *wake-up call*.'

'When this is over and done with, I feel that life can really start again for me.'

'I suggest we just get through the next couple of weeks before you start planning the rest of your life.'

'What if your mother doesn't like me?' Becky suddenly asked. 'I mean, you've taken it for granted that, because she hasn't approved of the women you've dated in the past, somehow she'll approve of me because I'm different from them—but she may not like me and, if she doesn't, then this whole charade will be a waste of time.'

Businesslike though this arrangement was, Theo was still irked to think that uppermost in her mind were worries about the financial side of things. 'Are you afraid,' he enquired coolly, 'That you might not get your money if things don't go according to plan?'

That had not occurred to Becky but she didn't refute it. She was going to be as cool about this as he was. She wasn't going to get bogged down in her own emotional issues. This was an exchange of favours and, the more she recognised that important aspect of their so-called relationship, the happier and more relaxed she would be. Their eyes met and she kept her stare as steady and as level as his.

'Well, nothing's been signed,' she pointed out with what she thought was an admirable amount of reasonable calm.

Theo gritted his teeth. One thing his mother was guaranteed to like about her was her honesty, he thought grimly. Marita Rushing had complained often and loudly that the bimbos she had met would have done whatever he asked because of his money.

'It must get boring for you,' she had declared a couple of years previously, after she had met one of the last of his leggy blondes before he had decided that introductions, always at his mother's insistence, were no longer a very good idea, however much she insisted.

His mother had never bought into the argument that having a woman do whatever he wanted was just what the doctor ordered for someone who had far too much stress on the work front to tolerate it on the home front. What he saw as soothing, she saw as unchallenging.

Becky took *challenging* to another level. If she didn't like anything else about his brand-new love interest, then that was something she would love. She would have first-hand insight into how frustrating the honest and challenging woman was capable of being.

By the end of the fortnight, he surmised that there was a good chance that his mother would be only too keen to concur when he'd say that there was a lot to be said for the eager-to-please lingerie model.

Instead of the woman who hadn't shied away from telling him that he wasn't her type, who had been frank about using him to please her, to teach her about making love, presumably so that she could implement the lessons learnt with a man more suitable… A woman who had agreed to help him out because of what she could get out of it in return and who, now, was worried that she might not reach the promised land if things did not go according to plan with his mother.

His lips thinned. 'Are you implying that I'm not a man of my word? That because I didn't get a lawyer to draw up an agreement for both parties to sign, that I would renege on what I promised to deliver?'

Becky sighed and lay back, eyes half-closed. 'You're the one who raised the subject.'

'Whatever the outcome of the next two weeks, you will get exactly what I have promised. In fact, name the place and I will get my people to start checking out suitable sites for a practice. Presumably you would want to go in with someone?'

She angled her head so that she was looking at him, and as always she had to fight not to respond outwardly to his masculine beauty.

'Maybe I'll go to France,' she thought aloud. 'Join the family. I'm going to be an aunt in a few months' time.'

And she wouldn't have a problem with Freddy. She could now, for the first time, fully admit what she had suspected for years. That, whilst she had been upset when he had chosen Alice over her, she hadn't been devastated. Whilst she had told herself that she needed to return to the family home, to be surrounded by what was familiar so that she could put heartbreak behind her, she had just given in to the indulgence of licking her wounds and then had stayed put because it had been easy. In truth, on the occasions when she had seen Freddy, she had secretly found him a little bland and boring—although to have admitted that, even to herself, would have opened up a Pandora's box of questions about the sort of man she was looking for.

She had always assumed that her soul mate would come in a package very much like Freddy's.

But Freddy was dull and so, she thought slowly, would be all those thoughtful, caring types she had held up as the perfect match for her.

She had allowed herself to assume, from a young age, that because Alice was the beautiful one in the family she would automatically be suited to guys as beautiful as she was. And for her, Becky, would come the steadier, more grounded, less beautiful types. But life had proved her very wrong, for her sister had fallen madly in love with the ordinary guy while she…

Her heart began to race. She felt nauseous, and suddenly she just couldn't look at the man next to her, even though she knew that she would still be able to see him with her eyes shut because he was so vividly remembered in her head. Like a diligent, top-of-the class student, the sort of student she had always been, she had filed away every single thing about him into her memory banks and all that information would now stay there a lifetime. She knew every small detail of his face, from the tiny lines that formed at the corners of his eyes when he smiled, to the slight dimple on just one side of his cheek when he laughed…from the way those silver-grey eyes could darken when he was roused, to the feel of his muscular shoulders under her fingertips.

She'd thought she was immune to him touching her heart because he hadn't ticked the right 'suitable for relationship' boxes in her head. She'd assumed that she hadn't been able to get him out of her mind after he had left for London because he had shaken her out of her comfort zone, so it was only natural that he had left behind a certain ache. What she hadn't done was ask herself the more fundamental question: why had she allowed him to break into her comfort zone in the first place?

Physical attraction was one thing but, of course, there had been much more to what she had felt for him, even after a day, two days…three days…

He had touched something deep inside her, stirred something into life. Why had no one warned her that love at first sight actually existed? Rather, why on earth hadn't she learnt from Alice and Freddy, both of whom had fallen head over heels in love from the very second their eyes had met?

And now here she was.

Panic and confusion tore through her. She felt she might faint. He was saying something about France, in that lazy, sexy voice of his but she barely heard him over the thundering of her heart. She wasn't aware of the car moving or didn't even know whether they were close to where his private jet would be waiting for them.

After a while, she heard herself responding to whatever he was saying. For the life of her, she had no idea what.

The only thing running through her head was the next two weeks and how she would survive them.

She could never let him suspect how she felt. She had her pride. If she had to live with memories, then she didn't want to add to the tally of difficult ones—the memory of him laughing incredulously at her or, maybe worse, backing away as if she were carrying a deadly infection.

The next two weeks weren't going to be a business arrangement to be endured as best as possible.

The next two weeks were going to be an assault course.

CHAPTER SEVEN

Becky had grudgingly accepted Theo's advice that she change her wardrobe or risk not being a credible girlfriend. He was rich and he was accustomed to dating women for whom shopping for clothes was a career choice. Even if he liked women who didn't care, his definition of 'not caring' would be designer jeans and designer silk blouses and designer high heels, accompanied by lots of gold and diamond jewellery. Dressing down in a no-expense-spared kind of way.

There was no way cheap, durable, all-weather clothing would have passed muster.

One glance at his fabulous apartment had told her that. Her old, tired suitcases had stuck out in the midst of all the luxurious splendour of his penthouse apartment like an elephant in a china shop.

But his private jet—which, he explained with an indifferent wave of his hand, was useful to his CEOs for whom time was usually a great deal of money—was a sharp reminder not only why he had pushed her to buy a new wardrobe but of the huge chasm between them.

Even in her fancy, expensive clothes, she was horribly conscious of *not quite fitting in.* She knew that she was gaping. Gaping at the pale, soft, butter-cream leather seats and the gleaming chestnut interior. It was a small plane, fast and light, and capable of seating only a dozen people, but it was truly exquisite inside, with a long sideboard, on which was a basket heaped with fresh fruit, and a marble bathroom that included a shower and thick, fluffy towels.

Looking at her, Theo knew that he should have been put off by her obvious open-mouthed awe. She didn't pretend to be blasé about flying in a private jet. She was impressed and it was written all over her face. There was no need for her to say *wow* for him to notice that.

He wasn't put off. He was as pleased as the cat that had just got the cream. He dumped all intentions of working on the short flight and instead gave her an amused, verbal, in-depth description of the plane, what it was capable of doing and where he'd flown on business.

'You must have really felt as though you were slumming it when you got stuck in my cottage,' Becky said ruefully and Theo looked away.

The thought of admitting at this late stage that he had hardly found himself *stuck* in her cottage by pure chance was unthinkable. It hardly made a difference, because what did it matter whether she eventually found out or not that he had appeared there by design? But something inside him twisted, an uneasy tug on his conscience, which was usually unassailable.

'But you just fitted in,' she pondered absently.

'I didn't always have money at my disposal,' he said abruptly and she looked at him, surprised, because this was the first time he had ever come right out and said anything at all about his past. During all that concentrated time when they had been trapped in the cottage, held prisoner by the weather, he had talked about what he did, various situations he had encountered…he had amused her and held her spellbound with stories of the places he had been to…

But he had not once reminisced about his past.

'You act as though you were born with a silver spoon in your mouth,' Becky said encouragingly.

This was just *small talk*, she told herself. But deep down she already knew she had fallen in love with the man. She had recognised that awful, awful truth just as she had recognised that falling in love with him had not been part of the deal. But the deal was for her to keep up the act of being the woman he had recruited to play this role, the woman who wouldn't be stupid enough to try and blur fact with fiction, so shouldn't she be as natural and as chatty as she possibly could be?

And, if she learnt a little more about him, then where was the harm in that? She preferred not to think of it as furtively feeding her greedy desire to know as much about him as she could, to take as much as she was capable of taking with her, so that in the long weeks and months ahead she could pull all those little details out of their hiding places and dwell on them at her leisure.

'Do I?' Theo didn't know whether to be taken aback or amused at her blunt honesty.

'You don't pay any attention at all to your surroundings,' Becky explained. 'You barely notice all those wonderful paintings in your apartment and you hardly looked around you when you stepped aboard this jet.'

'It's easy to become accustomed to what you know. The novelty wears off after a while.'

'When did that happen?' Becky asked with lively interest. 'I'm only asking,' she hurried on, 'because, if we're supposed to be an item, it's only natural that I would know a little bit about you…'

'You know a great deal about me,' Theo drawled.

'But I don't know anything about your…past.'

'The past is irrelevant.'

'No, it's not,' Becky disagreed stoutly. 'The past makes us the people we are. What if your mother says something about you, expecting me to know what she's talking about, and I look at her blankly and have to admit that I haven't got a clue what she's talking about?'

'I doubt she'd die of shock,' Theo responded drily. 'I'm a private person and my mother is all too aware of that.'

'You wouldn't be private with someone you're supposedly serious about.'

'I think you're confusing me with someone else,' Theo responded wryly. 'You're mixing me up with one of those touchy-feely types who think that relationships are all about outpourings of emotion and the high drama sharing of confidences.'

'You're so sarcastic, Theo,' Becky muttered.

'Realistic,' Theo contradicted calmly. 'I don't do emotional drama and I wouldn't expect any woman I was serious about to do it either.'

Becky stared at him. 'You mean you'd want someone to be as cold and detached as you?'

'I wouldn't say that I'm *cold and detached*, and if you think hard about it, Becky, I'm pretty sure you'd agree.' He shot her a wolfish smile, enjoying the hectic colour that flooded her cheeks as she clocked what he was saying and bristled.

'That remark is inappropriate,' Becky spat, all hot and bothered. She had laid down her ground rules, and it was even more important now that he obey them, because how was she going to keep a clear head if he did again what he had just done? Got under her skin like that, with a few words and a sexy little smile?

'Why? Because you've told me that you're not interested in going to bed with me?'

Becky went from pink to scarlet. 'This—this isn't what this is about,' she stuttered, her voice letting her down because it was high-pitched and cracked, not at all the voice of someone cool, confident and in control.

'You shouldn't dress like that if you want me to stay focused,' Theo told her bluntly.

Becky hated the stab of pleasure that raced through her. She'd made the fatal error of thinking that sex was just an act that could be performed without the emotions coming into play. She wasn't built like that.

But Theo was.

He'd said so himself. He took women to bed and then dispatched them when they began to outstay their welcome. He never involved his emotions because he had no emotions to involve.

Emotional drama. That was what most normal people would call *falling in love* and it was what she had stupidly gone and done with the last man on the planet who deserved it. At least Freddy had been a worthwhile candidate when it came to feelings, even if she hadn't been the one for him nor, as it turned out, he for her. At least he was capable of *feeling.*

'If you recall,' Becky told him coldly, 'I was told that none of my clothes were going to cut the mustard…'

Theo grunted. He thought that it was a good thing that they would be staying at his villa. Fewer men crashing into lamp posts as they turned around to stare. His blood boiled when he thought of young Italian boys looking at her with that open, avid interest that they never bothered to hide. Salivating.

'Anyway.' She was keen to get away from the topic of her clothes, keen to get away from anything that could make her skin prickle and tease her body into remembering what it had felt like to be touched by him. 'You were filling me in on your background.' She smiled and cleared her throat. 'You were going to try and convince me that you remember what it's like to have no money when you act as though you were born to the high life. I can't believe you've ever been anything but rich…'

It occurred to Theo that it had been a long, long time since he had let his guard down with any woman. She was looking at him, her bright blue eyes soft and questioning, her full lips parted on a smile, her body language so damned appealing that he couldn't tear his eyes away from her.

'You're not trying to turn me into a touchy-feely guy, are you?' he murmured, but returned her smile.

'I wouldn't dream of trying,' Becky said honestly.

'Are you going to feel sorry for me if I tell you my sob story?'

'I don't believe you have a sob story.' Her heart was beating so fast and so hard, she could actually feel it knocking against her rib cage. This definitely wasn't flirting, they were having a proper conversation, but it still felt like flirting. There was still something charged in the atmosphere that made her tingle.

'My mother…had her heart broken when she was a young woman.' Theo was startled that he was telling her this because it was an intensely private part of his past that he had never revealed to anyone. 'I was very young at the time.'

'What happened?' Becky asked breathlessly.

'My father was killed. Quite suddenly. One of those freak accidents you read about sometimes. Wrong place, wrong time. My mother was inconsolable. She…' This was skating on thin ice, and he paused, but then decided to push on. Again, that tug on his conscience. Again, he swept it uncomfortably aside. 'Packed her bags overnight, from what I understand, sold for a song the house they had shared and went as far away as she could. Of course, there was no money. Or very little. She worked in all manner of jobs so that she could give me whatever she felt I wanted…or needed. She instilled in me the importance of education and made sure I got the best on offer. She worked her fingers to the bone because, in the midst of her own personal heartbreak, I was the only person in the world who mattered to her.'

And she'd never moved on. Until she'd started talking about the cottage, talking wistfully about her desire to return there after her hasty departure over two decades ago. Coming to terms with the tragedy that had broken her had, to Theo, been a signal of her moving on at long last because, if she could reconcile herself to the past, then she would be free of the vice-like grip it had had over her.

He'd preferred that *moving on* solution to the other, which was moving on to become a mother-in-law and eventually a grandmother, moving on to a different and more rewarding phase in her life.

'I can see why this is so important to you,' Becky said simply and it took Theo a couple of minutes to drag his mind away from the surprise of his confession so that he could properly focus on her.

'Have you been moved by my heart-breaking tale?'

'Don't be so cynical.' Did he feel that his duty from a young age had been to fulfil the role of man of the family? Had their lack of money made him thirsty for financial security? Her liberal-minded parents had prided themselves on their lack of absorption when it came to money. Was that why they had never told her that they might have liked the cottage to be sold so that they could have more of a financial comfort blanket? Having boxed themselves into the position of people who didn't place any value on money, had they then been too embarrassed to tell her to move out? Had that sentiment been there alongside the sympathy they had felt for her as the daughter with the non-existent love life?

She felt as though Theo had burst into her life and opened a Pandora's box of feelings and realisations she had never been aware of before.

'My mother will probably be a little subdued when we get to Italy,' Theo said, changing the conversation with a slight frown. 'My aunt will not have told her that she's made me aware of the reason for her hospital visit, which is good, but my mother is a proud woman, and I think she'll be nursing a certain amount of…shame that she has become reliant on alcohol to help her get through the day.'

'I get that,' Becky murmured.

There was nothing cloying about her sympathy and Theo slanted an appreciative glance across at her. She was matter-of-fact about the circumstances for this charade—a result of working in a profession where she was alert to all sorts of vulnerability in people, he guessed, who harboured deep feelings about the pets she was called upon to treat. A tough man might shed tears if his dog had to be put down but Theo guessed that those tears would only be shed in the presence of the vet who administered the final injection.

Becky decided that it was better not to dwell on Theo's surprising show of confidence-sharing. This wasn't some side of him he was unexpectedly revealing to her. This was necessary information he felt he had to impart and he had done so dispassionately.

Some gut instinct also made her realise that, if she

tried to reach out to him and prolong the moment, he would retreat faster than a speeding bullet and resent her for being the one with whom this very private information had had to be imparted.

She had never met a man more proud or more guarded. She could understand why the thought of having any one else do what she was doing had been out of the question as far as he was concerned. Any woman who was in the slightest bit interested in the sort of relationship he clearly had no interest in would have seized the opportunity to take advantage of his need to confide, would have seen it as an opportunity to go beyond the skin-deep experience he was willing to have.

Becky shuddered when she thought of the irony of sitting here, in love with him, if only he knew it.

Deliberately, she changed the subject, and it wasn't very long before the jet was dipping down to the landing strip and then gliding to a smooth stop.

They had left behind a cold and grey London—not freezing, as it had been in the Cotswolds, but nevertheless miserable and dank.

They landed here to blue skies and a crispness in the air that felt like the touch of perfect spring.

A car was waiting for them.

Theo might have had hard times growing up but he had certainly not been tainted by the memory. He had made his fortune and had no qualms in spending his money with lavish extravagance. No expense was spared when it came to creature comforts.

He led her to the waiting car and ushered her into the back seat, moving round to the opposite side so that he could slide in next to her.

'My mother grew up in Tuscany,' Theo told her as she stared out at the mouth-watering scenery flashing past them. Lush green mountains were the backdrop to picturesque, colourful houses nestled into the greenery like a child's painting of match boxes in different, flamboyant colours.

'But,' he continued, 'she moved to England when she met and married my father. When her own mother died six years ago, I decided to invest in a villa near Portofino, because that's where her sister lives. Of course, that was before the place became flooded with A-listers. I, personally, think they should have both moved back to Tuscany when Flora's husband died three years ago, but they like the weather on the peninsula.'

'Shh!'

'Come again?'

'Don't talk,' Becky breathed. 'It's interrupting my looking.'

Theo laughed and then gazed at her rapt expression as she took in the outstandingly postcard-pretty harbour dotted with fishing boats and luxury yachts and lined with tall, graceful, colour-washed houses.

A tantalising view before the car swept up into the hills, curving and turning so that flashes of the harbour appeared and disappeared, getting smaller and smaller with each brief glimpse.

Becky had forgotten all her doubts, her apprehension, even the stark, dangerous reality of her feelings for the man sitting next to her. All had been swept aside by the sumptuous glamour of her surroundings. She realised that she hadn't actually had a proper holiday in ages and certainly nothing along these lines. This was a one-off. She was dipping her toes into another world and it wouldn't happen again.

She caught her breath as the car glided smoothly through some impressive gates, up a tree-lined drive and then into a little courtyard, in front of which was a lovely two-storeyed house, gaily painted a bright shade of salmon, with deep-green shutters which had been flung back.

There were tall trees everywhere, casting patterns of shade across the walls of the house, and on the leafy grass and clusters of flowers, and bushes were pressed against the walls, seemingly trying to clamber upwards to the roof.

The porch on the ground floor was broad enough to house a cluster of chairs and its replica was a balcony on the first floor, the white railings of which were laced with foliage that spilled over the sides, bursting with colourful flowers that stretched down to reach the bushes and flowers that were clambering up.

It was enchanting and Becky stood still for a minute as the chauffeur and Theo, with the cases, walked towards the front door.

'Is this another *shh* moment?' Theo asked, strolling back for her and leading her gently to the door.

'I think I'm in love.' She looked up at him, face flushed, poised wickedly on a perilous ledge where she was telling him nothing but the complete truth, just for this heartbeat moment. 'With this beautiful house...' she completed with the thrill of someone who had just managed a narrow escape from the jaws of untold danger.

She was unaware of being observed until she heard some delighted clapping and, when she blinked and turned round, it was to see a small, very pretty middle-aged woman standing in the doorway of the house with a broad smile on her face. She was propped up and leaning heavily on a cane.

And in that split instant Becky saw with her own eyes the depth of love that had driven Theo to take the drastic measure of setting up this charade for the benefit of his mother.

For he had walked quickly to the door to sweep his mother into a hug that was uncharacteristically gentle and very, very loving.

'Enough of you!' Marita Rushing was tenderly pushing her way out of his bear hug to beam around him at Becky, who had remained in the background, dithering, acutely self-conscious and not quite knowing what to do.

'At last, he brings a *real* woman for me to meet! Come here and let me see you, child!'

'I haven't seen her this happy in a long time' was the first thing Theo said to her hours later, after Marita Rushing had retired for the evening to her quarters, which were on the ground floor—a very happy situation, considering her mobility was not yet back up to speed after the accident. It also meant that there was no concerned surprise that a bedroom wasn't being shared by the love birds. Marita Rushing might have been traditional but Becky didn't think that she was so traditional that she wouldn't have been suspicious to discover that her vastly experienced son was sleeping in a different bedroom from the love of his life.

Becky turned to him, half-wanting to continue the conversation, half-wanting him to leave, because he was in the room she had been allocated and she had yet to recover from all the touching that had gone on throughout the course of the evening.

'Don't forget,' he had whispered at one point, his breath warm against her ear, sending all sorts of forbidden tingles up and down her spine, 'that you're the light of my life, that I can't keep my hands off you...'

At that point, he had been sitting next to her on the

sofa whilst opposite them his mother had been chattering away, excitement stamped into every fluttering gesture and every thrilled smile. His hand had been on her thigh, casually resting there with the heavy weight of ownership. She had tried to snap her legs together but the insistent slide of his thumb at the very acceptable point just above her knee had prohibited any such display of prudishness.

They were an item and he had had no qualms about running away with the concept.

At every turn, she had felt those lazy grey eyes on her. When he had touched her, he had managed to touch her in places that provoked the greatest physical arousal, even though you'd never have guessed if you'd been looking from the outside, because every touch was as light as a feather and as soft as a whisper, lingering just a little too long and in places that were just a little too intimate.

'I'm surprised your mother wasn't a bit more curious as to the circumstances of our meeting.' She walked towards the window and looked outside to a moonlit night and the soft glow the moon cast on the silent, gently swaying trees and bushes. The window was open and she could breathe in the cool, salty tang of sea breeze. Beyond the lawns, trees and shrubbery, she could see the black, unmoving stillness of the sea, a different shade of darkness from the darkness of the sky. She could have gazed out at the scenery for ever, were it not for the presence of Theo, lounging by the door, sending ripples of awareness zinging through her body as lightning-fast as quicksilver.

She turned back around, perching against the window ledge, hands gripping the sill on either side of her. 'I mean…you happened upon an injured dog at the side of the road, whilst out driving in the country? And, concerned citizen that you are, you took it to the nearest vet who just happened to be me?'

Theo flushed darkly and frowned. Deceiving his mother did not come naturally to him. In fact, he had never deceived her about anything, not even about the unsuitable women who had liberally littered his life in the past. But the physical change he had seen in her was worth it. He hadn't been lying when he had said that it was the happiest he had ever seen her.

He wasn't about to let anyone climb on the moral high ground and start lecturing him about the rights and wrongs of the decision he had made when all that mattered, as far as he was concerned, was the end result. Least of all when that *someone* was a woman who was only in it for the money.

He quietly shut the door and walked towards her. She had changed from one sexy-as-hell outfit into another sexy-as-hell outfit. What surprised him wasn't his mother's lack of suspicion at the story he had told her, but her lack of suspicion at just how damned sexy a country vet could look.

But it wasn't just the way the soft, straight elbow-length dress in pale coral outlined the curves of her body. In itself, the dress hardly shrieked *sexy*...on anyone else it would just have looked like a pleasant, relatively expensive silk dress. But on *her*... Something about the shape of her body, the slightness of her waist, the soft flare of her hips, the shapeliness of her legs, combined with an air of startled innocence...

Just looking at her now was doing all sorts of things to his body. She was wearing a strapless bra. She was too generously endowed to go braless but, bra or no bra, it didn't take much for him to recall the sight of those cherry-tipped breasts and the way those cherry tips had tasted.

He raked his fingers through his hair and stopped abruptly in front of her, glaring into narrowed, bright blue eyes.

'Why would my mother question how we met?' he asked roughly, looking away, but then looking at her again and trying hard to resist the temptation to stare down at the contour of her body under the wispy dress.

'It just seemed a very unlikely story,' Becky muttered, folding her arms and sliding her eyes away from him.

'No more unlikely than some of my other introductions to women,' Theo muttered.

'Like what?'

'Three years ago I did a charity parachute jump from my jet and landed in a field where there was a shoot going on. Some butter advert. She was tall, blonde, Swedish and almost ended up flattened by me when I landed. We went out for nearly three months. Ingrid was her name.'

'And now here you are. With a country vet.'

'Like I said, I've never seen my mother happier.'

'Because she thinks that we're going to give her a happy-ever-after story,' Becky murmured, eyes cast down. She shuffled and then glanced up at him.

'I know what's going through your head, Becky. You think I'm being cruel because sooner or later she will discover that there will be no happy-ever-after...'

'Aren't you?' Before she had met his mother, Marita Rushing had been a name. Now she was a delightful, living, breathing woman, shrouded in sadness, but still ready to smile at the prospect of her son settling down. Deceit had never felt so immediate and yet she could still recall the way they had hugged and that feeling she had had that he was simply doing something he hoped would be for the best in the long run. 'Forget I said that.' She sighed. 'Do you have any plans as to how we fill our time while we're here?'

Theo had planned to work, whilst ensuring he cast a constant supervisory eye on Becky to make sure she kept her distance. He wanted his mother to like her, wanted her truly to believe that he was capable of forming relationships with girls who weren't five-minute visitors to his life because they were so utterly unsuitable. He wanted Marita to regain her strength so that he could bring her back to London. But he didn't want Becky to bond too firmly with his mother. After all, she wasn't going to be a permanent fixture in his life.

He also planned to have a word with his aunt to establish just what his mother's frame of mind was whilst she was recuperating at the villa.

And, lastly, he wanted to probe her about any potential interests his mother might have mentioned which he could weave into her life once she was in London.

There was still the matter of the cottage which, once bought, would be a welcome distraction from any brooding thoughts.

He frowned, recognising that the whole cottage-purchase scenario was mired in all sorts of ethical tangleweed. Something else he would see to when the time came.

For now…

'One step at a time' seemed the best way forward. First thing in the morning, he would check the cupboards to see what alcohol there was lurking. His mother had been restrained that evening, with just the one glass of wine. He needed to make sure that any drinking had been a temporary blip and not something that might require an intervention.

Work would have to take a back seat.

Between all the things he knew he would have to do, all the necessary obligations he would have to see to, a sudden thought threaded its way through, curving, cornering and bypassing duty, obligation and necessity, like a tenacious weed pushing past the well-laid rose bushes in search of light and air…

Time out.

Two weeks.

'There's a lot to see here,' he told her huskily. 'It's to be expected that we do some exploring.'

Becky looked at him in some alarm. 'Exploring?'

'That's what couples sometimes get up to when they go on holiday together,' Theo inserted.

'But we're not a couple,' Becky pointed out uneasily.

'Go with the flow, Becky.'

'That's easy for you to say.'

'Meaning?'

'Nothing.' She sighed, very nearly trapped by her own treacherous thoughts. It was easy for him to treat this like just some situation that could be enjoyed while it lasted. His emotions weren't involved. Hers were. A spot of sightseeing would be, for him, just a *spot of sightseeing.* Whilst, for her, it would be more sinking into the quagmire that was already engulfing her, making it almost impossible for her to stand back and take an objective view of what they were doing.

'And you're going to have to stop all that touching stuff,' she heard herself say in a burst of defiance.

She'd been thinking of how vulnerable it made her feel just being in his company. She'd been imagining what it would be like for them to be out and about, like a normal couple, doing something normal like sightseeing. Then she'd thought about him holding her hand and how that would feel, the sparks that would run through her—the stolen sensation of it *actually* being true, that they *actually* weren't playing a part…

She'd never thought that it would be possible to project so many scenarios into such a small space of time. Ten seconds and she had seen her life flash past straight into a black void of a future where every minute snatching stolen moments in the present would be weeks spent trying to find a way back to the light in the future.

And then she'd thought of him touching her, those devastating little touches that had meant nothing to him…

Now she just couldn't meet his eyes, because he would be wondering where that cool, collected woman had gone, the one who had agreed to go through with this because of the tangible rewards at the end of it. The one who had chatted to his mother as though the charade were no more difficult than anything else she had ever been called upon to do.

'What *touching stuff*?' Theo murmured in a low, husky voice.

'You know what I mean…' She looked at him with sullen defiance and he smiled, a slow, utterly mesmerising smile that made the breath hitch in her throat and brought her out in a panicked cold sweat.

'I haven't been touching you,' he said softly. 'This…' He trailed one long finger along her collar bone and then allowed it to dip under the neckline of the dress, before pausing at the dip between her breasts, in that shadowy cleavage that was rising and falling as though she were recovering from running a marathon. '*This* is touching you. I haven't been doing that, have I?'

'Theo, please…'

'I like that. I like it when you beg for me…'

'This isn't what it's about. This is…is…' His finger

had slipped deeper, was now trailing over the top of her strapless bra, making gentle inroads underneath, and she could feel her nipples poking painfully against the bra, wanting the thing he was teasing her with. 'This is a business arrangement,' she finished in a breathless whisper, shifting her body, but not nearly firmly or fast enough to avoid his devastating caress.

'I know, but I can't seem to take my eyes off you, Becky. And where my eyes go, my hands itch to follow...'

'You promised.'

'I did no such thing.' He stepped back with an obvious show of reluctance. 'If you don't want *that* kind of touching, then I'll refrain, but Becky—if you look at me with those hot little stolen looks, and you lick your lips like you'd love nothing better than to taste me, you can't expect me to keep my hands to myself.'

'I don't mean to do that!'

Theo dropped his eyes, appreciating the subtle message that way of phrasing her words had given him. She 'didn't mean to do that' implied that she was fighting to uphold the 'no sex' stipulation she had put on this little game of theirs, if it could be called a game. Which meant that she still wanted him as much as he still wanted her, but she was a good girl whose innate moral code could not permit random sex with a man with whom there would and never could be any future. She had succumbed once, and had probably used every argument under the sun to justify that weakness, but she was determined not to succumb again.

And he itched to touch her. He'd wanted it the second he'd decided to get in touch with her again and he hadn't stopped, even though he had his own inner voices urging caution.

Or at least urging him to pay some attention to his

pride…irritating little voices reminding him that he had never chased a woman in his life before and that there was no reason to start now. But he'd spent the entire evening fighting a war with a libido that was out of control…

'But you do it anyway,' he drawled softly. He held his hands up in a gesture of phoney surrender before shoving them into the pockets of his trousers. 'And, while you do that, don't expect me to play ball…'

CHAPTER EIGHT

TEN DAYS AFTER they arrived, Becky woke to the crippling pain of a headache, aching bones and the first, nasty taste of fever in her mouth.

And, for the first time in living memory, she thought that she might actually be *pleased* that she was about to come down with a cold. Or flu. Or any other virus that would give her an excuse to stick to her bed for twenty-four hours because the past few days had been the sweetest of tortures.

Theo had laid his cards on the table. He wasn't going to play ball. She'd set her rules down and he'd coolly and calmly told her that he was going to ignore them.

So she had expected a full-on attack and had been bracing herself to deal with that. She had, as ammunition, plentiful supplies of simmering anger, self-righteous moral preaching and offended outrage that he should dare to ignore *her* wishes.

If he wanted to stage an assault, then she would be more than ready for the fight, and she knew she would fight like a cornered rat, because her defences were fragile and her determination was weak and full of holes.

She was utterly and completely vulnerable to him and that, in itself, gave her the strength to cast him in the role of veritable enemy, which she felt was something she could deal with.

But there was no assault.

If anything, some of that intimate touching stopped. She would feel his eyes on her, a lazy, brooding caress that did all sorts of things to her senses, but those intrusive fingers on her skin when there was nothing she could do about it were no more. Indeed, after dinner, when they had fallen into the habit of sitting in one of the downstairs sitting rooms—an airy space where, with the windows flung open, the sound of the distant sea was a steady background roll—he would often sit opposite her, legs loosely spread, arms resting on his thighs, leaning forward in a way that was relaxed whilst still being aggressively alert.

Peeling her eyes away from him was proving a problem.

And, without her armour to fall back on, she had been reduced to playing a waiting game of her own which meant that she was always on full alert.

Several times she had asked him whether he might not like to escape and do some work.

'I'm perfectly happy to find a quiet corner somewhere and read,' she had told him. There were lots of those in the villa, although her favourite space was outside, curled up in a swinging chair on the veranda, from where she could see the stretch of front lawn with its shady trees and foliage and beyond that the flat ocean, a distant band of varying shades of blue.

'Don't you go worrying about me,' he had delivered in a soothing tone, although his eyes had been amused. 'It's delightful that you're concerned but, in actual fact, I'm managing to keep on top of my work very well at night.'

Which meant that the long days were spent in one another's company. They had had two trips into Portofino, where he had shown her around the picturesque harbour with its rows upon rows of colourful houses nestled in the embrace of the lush hills rising behind them. They had lunched at an exquisite and very quaint restaurant and she had had far too much ice-cold Chablis for her own good.

But his self-restraint had turned her into a bag of nerves and she had a sneaking suspicion that he knew that, which in turn made him all the more restrained.

For much of the time they were together, however, his mother was chaperone and companion.

For that, Becky was relieved because it afforded her a certain amount of distance from Marita Rushing. Becky knew, without a shadow of a doubt, that if she and the older woman were alone together for long enough they would become firm friends and the deceit in which she was engaged would feel even more uncomfortable than it already did.

She also suspected that Theo was deliberately making sure that he worked late at night, when everyone was asleep, so that he could keep a watchful eye on his mother, to ascertain her levels of alcohol intake.

'I honestly don't think she has a problem,' Becky had told him quietly the evening before, as they had been about to head off to their separate quarters.

'How would you know?' he had said roughly, but then had shaken his head, as though physically trying to clear it of negative thoughts. 'Are you a doctor?'

'Are you?' she had responded with alacrity. 'And, in actual fact, I have a great deal more training in medicine than you—and I'm telling you that there's no need to watch over your mother like a hawk. She hasn't said a word to you about the drinking situation because it was a blip on her horizon, and she's probably ashamed when she thinks about it now. If you keep following her around, she's going to begin to suspect that Flora has said something to you and she'll never live it down. She's a very proud woman.'

He had glowered but she had stood her ground and eventually he had laughed shortly and shrugged, which she had taken as a sign that he had at least listened to what she'd had to say.

But being with him all the time…was exhausting. She felt as though she couldn't drop her guard, even though she was beginning to wonder whether he hadn't lost complete interest in her after his cocky assertion that her defences were there to be knocked down should he so choose.

He might have wanted her to begin with but he wasn't a man who pursued and, in the end, old habits had died hard. She'd stuck her hands out to ward him away and he'd decided to back off because he couldn't be bothered to do otherwise.

And what really troubled her was the fact that *she cared.*

Instead of basking in the relief that she didn't have to keep swatting him away, she found herself missing that brief window when he had looked at her as though she still mattered to him, at least on a physical level.

She caught herself, on more than one occasion, leaning forward to get something, knowing that one glimpse and he would be able to see down her flimsy, lacy bra to her barely contained breasts.

So now she felt miserable with the start of a cold and she couldn't have been happier because she needed the time out to try and regroup.

An internal line had been installed in his mother's

room, connecting her to the kitchen and the sitting room, should she ever need to be connected, but in the absence of any such convenience Becky did the next best thing and dialled through to Theo's mobile.

She looked around her at the beautiful suite of rooms into which she had been put. Marita Rushing couldn't handle the stairs up, and there was no reason for her to venture up, but every day a housekeeper came and cleaned the house from top to bottom, as well as making sure that food was cooked, if that was necessary.

The housekeeper was a very quiet young girl who barely spoke a word of English and had been mortified, on day one, when Becky had helpfully tried to join her in tidying the bedroom.

At first Becky had wondered whether the girl would report back to Theo's mother that the loved-up couple slept in separate quarters, but then she very quickly realised that that would never happen.

Now, she wondered what it might have been like if that half-formulated, barely realised fear, which had been there when this whole charade had first been suggested, had actually come to pass. When Theo had first contacted her, she had quailed at the thought of having to share a bedroom with him, after the initial biting disappointment that the only reason he had picked the phone up had been to ask a favour of her.

For surely, in this day and age, that would be a given? If his mother was expected to fall for them being a couple, then she would likewise expect them to share a bed.

And what if they had?

Would her 'no sex' stipulation have been swept aside under the overwhelming surge of her physical attraction, combined with the power of knowing that she had fallen in love with him? Would common sense have been obliterated by the deadly combination of love and lust? Between those twin emotions, would there have been any room left for her head to prevail?

And would she have been worse off than she was now? Because she was a wreck. Which was probably why she had succumbed to a bug. Her body was telling her that she needed to rest.

Theo picked up on the third ring and, even though it wasn't yet six thirty in the morning, he sounded as bright-eyed and bushy-tailed as if he had been awake for hours.

'Why are you up so early?' were his opening words, and Becky nearly smiled, because for all the frustration he engendered in her she had become accustomed to certain traits of his. A complete lack of social niceties was one of those traits.

'Why are you?' she countered.

'Why do you think?' In the outer room, which had been converted into an office years previously—indeed as soon as the villa had been bought and the prospect of going there, even for a couple of days at a time, had become inevitable—Theo pushed himself away from the sleek, metal-and-wood desk and swivelled his chair so that he was staring out of the floor-to-ceiling window.

She hadn't come to him.

He'd really and honestly believed that she would have cracked. After all, he had seen the flare of mutual attraction in those luminous eyes, and he hadn't banked on her resistance, whatever she might have said to the contrary.

Why would he have? Since when had he ever been prepared to withstand any woman's resistance? He didn't know the rules of that particular game but he had felt his way and decided that he'd said what he had to say, but he wasn't going to push things with her. If she wanted to huff and puff and flounce around with maidenly virtue wrapped round her like a security blanket, then sooner or later she would drop the act.

He knew women, after all.

He also knew the power of good sex. It was more than a worthy adversary for any amount of doubts, hesitations or last minute qualms.

And they'd had good sex. The best.

Unfortunately he'd misread the situation and, having taken up a certain stance, he was condemned to dig his heels in or risk being a complete loser by being the first to crack.

It was beginning to do his head in. They were both bloody adults! They'd already slept together! It wasn't as though they were tiptoeing around one another in some kind of slow burn of a courtship game! Plus his mother was living the dream life, loving every second of seeing her son with a woman of whom she seriously approved.

Throw hot attraction into the mix and he just couldn't work out why it was that he was barely able to focus on his work and was having to take cold showers twice a day when it all should have been so simple.

And now, hearing her voice down the end of the line, he couldn't stop his imagination from doing all sorts of weird and wonderful things to his body as he pictured her, sleep-rumpled, in only her birthday suit.

Or else covered from top to toe in a Victorian maiden's nightie, to match her crazy 'no sex' rules…

Either image worked for him.

'I'm working.' He shifted, trying to release some of the sudden painful pressure.

'Do you *ever*,' she was distracted enough to ask, 'get any sleep at all, Theo?'

'I try and avoid sleep. It's a waste of valuable time.

Is that why you've called at…six forty in the morning? To check and see whether I'm getting my essential fix of beauty sleep?'

'I've called because…I'm afraid today is going to be a bit of a write-off for me.'

'Why? What are you talking about?'

'I've woken up with a crashing headache and all sorts of aches and pains. I think I may have a cold. It won't last but I'm going to stay in bed today.'

'My mother will be disappointed.' Theo stood up, brow furrowed. 'She had planned on introducing you to her favourite tea shop…'

'I'm sorry, Theo. I could venture downstairs but I feel absolutely rotten and I wouldn't want to…pass anything on to your mother. She's had a pretty poor year and a half and the last thing she needs is to catch germs from her house guest. In fact, if you don't mind, I'm going to grab some more sleep and hopefully I'll be fighting fit by tomorrow…'

'What have you taken?'

'Are you concerned?' Becky couldn't resist asking. 'Do you think that you won't be getting value for money if I take a day off?' As soon as the words had left her mouth, she wished that she could snatch them and stuff them back in.

'Are you offering to stay an extra day, Becky? I know you have a very strong work ethic.'

'I'm sorry. I shouldn't have… Well, I'm sorry…'

'Go back to sleep, Becky. I'll get Ana to bring you up some food when she gets here.'

He cut the connection, mouth thin as he contemplated the due reminder of why she was in this villa, mutual attraction or no mutual attraction. There was nothing like a sudden sucker-punch to remind a person of priorities.

* * *

Becky struggled up, reluctantly rising from a disturbed, fever-ridden sleep. She had taken a couple of tablets two hours previously and she could feel the effects of the tablets beginning to wear a little thin.

In fairness, she felt better than she had two hours before, but she still needed a day off, a day during which she could gather herself.

She didn't see Theo immediately. The curtains were drawn, thick, heavy-duty curtains designed to plunge the room into darkness so that if you wanted to lie in you weren't wakened by the stealthy creep of dawn's fingers infiltrating the room.

Sleepy eyes rested on the now familiar pieces of furniture, then shifted to the glass of water, now empty, on the side table, then…

'You're up.'

Becky's heart sped up and her mouth fell open, before a wash of misplaced propriety had her yank the sheet over her bare arms.

She had bought a complete new wardrobe and that complete new wardrobe included lingerie that she would never have dreamed of buying before. Little wisps of lace and not much else. Her nightwear was along those lines. It left next to nothing to the imagination. It couldn't have been more different from the homely, comfy, warm, practical nightwear she had made her own for the past twenty-seven years. She had thrown caution to the winds when she had gone on her shopping spree and had robustly decided, *in for a penny, in for a pound…*

'What are you doing here?' She was acutely conscious of her nipples scraping against the lacy top and the brevity of the matching knickers.

'Doctor's orders. Breakfast. I'm on a mission of mercy for the invalid. What would you like to eat?'

'Please don't put Ana to any trouble,' Becky begged. 'She has enough to do around here without bringing me up breakfast in bed as though I'm Lady Muck. I just need to spend the day in bed sleeping and I'll be back on my feet by tomorrow.'

'And, while you're in bed, the diet of choice for returning to full health is starvation? Because you don't want to put the housekeeper out?'

Becky flushed. Theo's attitude to the hired help was very different from hers. He was pleasant and polite but, as far as he was concerned, they were paid handsomely to do their jobs and were no different from any of the other employees in his service working at any of the companies he owned. A business transaction. Simple.

'Doesn't matter.' He waved one hand in nonchalant dismissal. 'Ana is off sick. Probably has the same bug that you have.'

'How awful!' Becky was stricken.

'And please,' Theo interjected with wry amusement, 'don't start beating yourself up about being the carrier of germs. I expect Ana brought it to the house with her. She has five siblings—a lot of scope for bugs to find places to set up camp.'

'And your mother? Don't tell me she has it as well…?'

'Fortunately not but I've shipped her off to Flora's for two days. Her health is fragile and the last thing she needs is a dose of the flu.'

'You're probably going to be next,' Becky said glumly.

'I'm never ill.'

'Have you told those germs that have set up camp with Ana's siblings? Because they might not know. They might have already decided that you'd make an excellent playground for them to have some fun on.'

'I'm as strong as an ox. Right. Food order.'

So it was just Theo in the house. There was no need for apprehension because, had he wanted to keep touching her and provoking her, he could have. All that had bitten the dust. His declaration of intent had been empty.

And now the poor guy felt obliged to put himself out for her when he would probably rather be working on a day off from supervising his mother and chaperoning his so-called girlfriend in the guise of enthusiastic lover.

'I guess…' she allowed her voice to linger thoughtfully before tailing off. 'I *guess* I should really have something to eat. I mean, I *have* had a pretty restless night, to be honest.'

Theo raised his eyebrows. The duvet had slipped a little and, if he wasn't mistaken, she didn't seem to be clad in the all-encompassing Victorian meringue he would have imagined. In fact, those thin spaghetti straps, as wispy as strands of pale cotton, pointed to a completely different get-up underneath the duvet.

'So what will it be?' he asked gruffly, clearing his throat and concentrating one hundred percent on her flushed face.

'Perhaps a poached egg,' Becky murmured. 'And some toast. Maybe a bit of fried ham as well, but not fried in oil, maybe fried in a little butter, just a dash. Protein. Important for my recovery, I imagine. And if there's juice… that would be nice. I noticed Ana squeezing oranges with an electric juicer… And perhaps some tea as well…'

'You've done a complete turnaround from not being hungry and not wanting to put anyone out,' Theo complained in a voice that told her that he knew very well what that turnaround was all about, and Becky smiled sweetly and apologetically at him.

'I'd understand if you didn't want to make me breakfast, Theo. I don't suppose it's the sort of thing you've ever done for any woman in your life before. In fact, I'm guessing that no woman would ever have been brave enough to have fallen ill when you were around to see it. They'd probably have known that they would get short shrift from you.'

'And that,' Theo countered smoothly, 'shows just how special you are, doesn't it? Because here I am, offering to be your slave while you're bedridden…'

Becky reddened. She knew why he was here. His mother would probably have told him to make sure he took care of her. Marita was like that. She had had a brief but idyllic married life with a man she had fallen desperately in love with at a very young age. Her concept of love was romantic and idealised because that was what she had had. She actually had no idea how jaded her son was when it came to the concept of love and romance. In her heart, she truly believed that he was capable of falling in love and finding the happiness she had found with her partner and soul mate.

Becky had come to understand exactly what Theo had meant when he had told her that, introduced to a girl deemed suitable, she would happily believe the fiction played out for her benefit.

She had also come to understand why he had done what he had because, however uncomfortable she was with the deceit, she could see improvements in his mother practically from one hour to the next. Flora, in a quiet aside two evenings previously, had confirmed how much Marita Rushing's frame of mind had improved since Theo had come to visit with Becky on his arm.

'She's a different woman,' Flora had confided. 'She is my sister again and not this poor, frail woman who felt she had nothing to live for… It was different when Theo was young and needed her, but since all those heart problems…and realising that he had no interest in settling down… Well, it is good that you are here.'

'I'm fine with just toast' was all she could find to say, mouth downturned at his coolness.

'I wouldn't dream of depriving you of essential sustenance to overcome your cold.' Theo grinned and gave her a mock salute. 'Anything else to add to the order? Or should I exit while the going's good?'

Becky allowed herself a smile once he'd left the room.

He got to her on so many fronts and one of those was his sense of humour. He could be as ironic as he could be cheeky and those two strands, woven together, was a killer package.

Reminding herself of the reality of their situation and the reality of what he felt for her was a daily challenge.

Lying back against the pillows, she wondered whether she should quickly change into something more suitable, but then realised that in her haste to replace her entire wardrobe for the two week period she had recklessly omitted anything that remotely resembled sensible clothing. Even the shorts she had packed had been knee-length linen. A small but exquisitely inappropriate wardrobe for someone who was now bedridden with a severe cold.

Theo returned less than twenty minutes later with a tray. He nudged the bedroom door open with his shoulder, half-expecting to find her sitting primly on the chair by the window, clad in anything but whatever sexy nightwear she had been wearing. However, she was still in bed, with the duvet sternly pressed flat under both arms, a step away from encasing her completely like a mummy.

'Your breakfast…' He dragged a chair over to the bed, deposited the tray on her lap and proceeded to sit down next to her.

'There's no need for you to stay.' Becky looked at the muddle of food on her plate and was puzzled as to how her poached egg and ham had been translated into something that was unidentifiable.

'The poached egg,' Theo pointed out with an elegant shrug, 'didn't quite go according to plan. I'm afraid I had to be creative…'

How could she keep the duvet in place while she ate? She tried, but gradually it slipped a little lower.

From his advantageous position next to the bed, Theo felt like a voyeur as he looked at the soft, silky smoothness of her shoulders and back. He talked to distract himself from falling into a trance because there was something hypnotic about the movement of her shoulder blades as she tucked into the breakfast.

Becky could feel those brooding, silver-grey eyes on her. Even though she wasn't looking at him, wasn't even sneaking sidelong glances in his direction…

Hot little looks, as he had called them…

The fever-induced weakness had been overtaken by a thrilling edge-of-precipice feeling as she finished the last morsel of food on the plate and dutifully put down her knife and fork.

When she glanced down, she could see how the duvet had slipped and how the lacy top was peeking open ever so slightly, allowing a fine view of her pale skin underneath.

This was playing with fire and she didn't know why she was doing that. She had spent so long being strong. She had accepted that he had lost interest in her. She had beaten herself up over her stupidity in falling in love with the man and had been extra careful to make sure that she wasn't exposed.

But now she could feel his eyes on her and that little voice that she had listened to right at the very beginning—that stupid little voice that had lured her to touch the flame, to climb into bed with him—was once again doing its thing and getting under her skin to wreak havoc with the defences she had meticulously been building up.

So, she'd fallen in love with him… So it had to be the most stupid thing she could ever have done…not that she had been able to stop herself… But here she was, fighting hard and being a martyr, making sure he didn't come near her. She'd given him her best 'hands off' stance, had told him that sex wouldn't be on the agenda, but, aside from feeling morally smug, what good had it done her? Was she happy and content with her decision? Had it made him any less tempting?

She was so desperate to read into the future and protect herself against further hurt—so keen to make sure he didn't add to the tally of pain she would suffer at a later date should she repeat her original mistake and get into bed again—that she was in danger of having a complete nervous meltdown.

'That was very nice. Thank you.' She heard the telltale throaty nervousness in her voice and glanced across at him as he removed the tray. When she leaned back against the pillows, she didn't rush to yank the duvet back up into position.

She feigned innocence, half-closing her eyes with a sigh of contentment at being well fed. She'd been hungrier than she'd thought and the eggy stuff he'd served up had been a lot tastier than she had expected.

She half-opened one eye to find him towering over her, arms folded, his dark features inscrutable.

He'd pulled back the curtains but not all the way and the sun penetrated the room in a band of light, leaving the remainder of the room in shadow. The light caught him at an angle, defining the sharp jut of his cheekbones and the curve of his sensuous mouth. He wasn't smiling. Nor was he scowling. He was…just looking, and adding things up in his head, and that sent a frisson of awareness racing up and down her spine, because she knew what things he was adding up and she liked that.

She'd missed him. He'd gone AWOL on her and she hadn't liked it. Her brain might have patted itself on the back and thought it'd won the battle but her body was staging a rebellion and common sense didn't stand a chance.

'You wouldn't happen to be playing any games with me, would you?' Theo asked softly.

'Don't know what you mean…'

'Oh, really, Becky,' Theo said drily. 'Would that be because you're just a poor invalid who's feeling too under the weather to be thinking straight?'

'I feel a bit better now that I've had something to eat.'

'And that would account for the suddenly relaxed body language?'

Becky didn't say anything but their eyes tangled and neither could look away—neither wanted to break the electric charge zapping between them. She could hear her breathing slowing up and could almost feel the rush of hot blood through her veins. Her skin prickled and her nipples were tightening, pinching, hard, throbbing buds poking against the flesh-coloured lace.

For Theo, things seemed to be happening in slow motion, from the darkening of her turquoise eyes to the raspy unsteadiness of his breathing.

His erection was a sheath of steel and would be outlined against his lightweight tan khakis. *Dip your eyes a bit lower, baby,* he thought, *and you'll have more than your fill of exactly how turned on I am right now.*

She did.

And that, too, seemed to happen in slow motion, as did the way the tip of her tongue erotically wetted her full lips. Her hair was everywhere, spread against the white pillows and over her shoulders, wild and tangled and utterly provocative.

'No sex,' he reminded her in a rough, shaky undertone and Becky looked at him, eyes lacking all guile as she considered what he had just pointed out.

'You stopped touching,' she heard herself say in a breathy voice—because suddenly it seemed very important for him to tell her that he still fancied her, even though she could read that he did in his eyes, and in the very still, controlled way he was standing. And in the erection he was not bothering to hide. She just needed him to say it…

'As per your instructions.'

'I know, but…'

'Are you fishing for me to tell you that I wanted to keep touching you? Because you won't have to throw your line very far to hear me say it. I wanted to keep touching you…' He raked his fingers through his hair. This was what he wanted and it was what he had wanted all along. When he thought about her body and what it could do to him, he had to suck his breath in sharply just to control his wayward libido from doing what it shouldn't. 'I wanted you after I left the Cotswolds and I haven't stopped. It's been hell looking and not being able to touch. Is that more or less what you wanted to hear…?'

Becky thought that she would like to hear much, much more. But *want* was all she was going to hear and she was sick of pretending to herself that she could keep pushing that aside because it didn't come with *love*.

She was too weak.

She had a few days left here and she was too weak to keep trying to be strong.

Whatever capacity Theo had to love, it was never going to be her. Privately, she didn't think he would ever love anyone.

'He never saw me in love,' his mother had whispered sadly to her only the evening before when he had been called away on one of the rare emergency conference calls he had allowed through. 'He just saw me when I was sad and alone. That's made him the man he is today. Afraid of love… Until now…until he found you…'

Becky had ignored the bit about Theo being afraid of love until he found her, which was a joke, and analysed and analysed and analysed the rest of what his mother had said. It might have been an over-simplification, but it was probably grounded in truth. His background had made him what he was when it came to love. He would never trust anything that had the power to destroy and, in his mind, his mother had been destroyed by love. He couldn't see beyond that and never would.

What he had to give and all he had to give was…his touch.

'More or less,' Becky agreed on a broken sigh. She pushed down the duvet, revealing the lacy nonsense she was wearing, which concealed nothing. Her pink nipples were visible through the lace, as was the shadowy dark down between her thighs.

She rested her hand on the mound between her legs, wanting badly to squeeze her legs together to relieve the fierce burning between them. His eyes were practically black with unconcealed lust and a heady sense of power raced through her veins, obliterating everything in its path.

'Becky.' Theo barely recognised his voice. 'There's something you should know…' All those half-truths were coming home to roost but she needed to know, needed to know that in life there was no such thing as coincidence, needed to know the truth about her cottage. What had seemed a good idea at the time, concealing the purpose of his arrival there so that he could feel out the terrain, was now an unthinkable error of judgement.

'Don't say a word,' Becky rushed in before he could say what she knew he was going to, another one of those warnings that what they were about to do was meaningless. She just didn't want to hear it. She didn't need to have that rammed home to her. Again.

'We have a few more days and after that we go our separate ways. We won't see one another again, so nothing has to be explained. We can…just enjoy this window…and then tomorrow is another day…'

CHAPTER NINE

HE WOULD TELL HER. Of course he would. Instead of being an anonymous buyer in three months' time, he would show his hand. He would also pay over the odds for the cottage he had originally intended to buy at a knock-down price, poetic justice for the people who had bought it at a knock-down price from his mother.

In three months' time, what they had now would all be water under the bridge. They'd probably chuckle as they exchanged contracts because, face it, she would have emerged a winner. She would be in a brand-new job in a brand-new location, renting a brand-new apartment. Work would have been done on the cottage so that the time left spent there would be comfortable. No buckets collecting water from a leaking roof!

She wasn't interested in hearing long stories now about his appearance at the cottage and the reasons behind it.

And he wasn't that interested in killing the moment by telling her either, although, in fairness, he would have done had she not waved aside his interruption.

She was fired up.

He was fired up.

Talk was just something taking up too much time when there was so much they both wanted to do.

Becky watched Theo's momentary flicker of hesitation and found that she was holding her breath. This was as proactive as she was capable of being. She knew that if he decided to back away now…if he thought that he wasn't prepared to step back into the water, even though she had assured him that these last few days would simply be about giving in to lust and closing that door between them once and for all…then she would retreat.

She would have lost her pride but, even so, she would retreat without regret because she was no longer prepared to turn her back on what could be hers for a few days more.

She was sick to the back teeth of being a noble martyr.

In the heat of the moment and with surrender in her mind, she couldn't, for the life of her, remember what had propelled her to fling down that 'no sex' addendum to the proposal he had put forward. She'd been so strident and sure of herself.

'You're not well,' Theo said gruffly.

'Why are you being so thoughtful?' Becky teased, not quite certain of the response she would get, but he grinned rakishly at her.

'Because I'm a gentleman.'

'Maybe I don't want you to be a gentleman right now,' Becky murmured, wriggling slightly to make room for him on the double bed. 'Are you sure you're not scared of getting into bed with me because you might catch my germs? I know you said that germs would never dare attack you but…'

'You're a witch.' Theo half-groaned. He walked towards the window and drew the curtains, plunging the room into instant darkness. He had to adjust his trousers, had to control his erection, which was throbbing under the zipper. He took a few seconds to stand by the window and look at her.

Very slowly he began undressing. This was more for his benefit than it was for hers. Move too fast and he would have to take her quick and hard, and he didn't want that. He wanted to enjoy every second of this—he wanted to savour her body and remember the feel of it under his exploring mouth and hands.

He wanted to take his time.

Becky fell back against the pillows as he began to stroll towards her. Shirt discarded, trousers unzipped. He was physical perfection. He was lean and muscular and looked *strong*. The sort of man who would always emerge the winner in any street brawl. She could have kept looking at him for ever.

She had no idea where her cold had gone. She had woken up feeling rotten, and thinking that she could do with a day off to recover from the impact daily contact with him was having on her state of mind, and now here she was, cold forgotten, as though it had never existed.

She was on fire but not with fever. She was burning up for the man now staring down at her, his hand resting lightly on his zipper. She could see the prominent bulge of his erection underneath the trousers. He was well endowed and he was massively turned on. It showed. It thrilled her.

She reached forward and lightly touched that bulge and the soft sound of his indrawn hiss was as powerful as any drug, sending her already drugged senses into frantic overdrive.

She sat up while he remained standing next to the bed.

The duvet had been shrugged off. Theo looked down at her soft shoulders, her riotous hair and all the luscious places exposed by the very revealing, and for her very risqué, nightwear. He greedily took in the heaviness of her breasts, lovingly outlined by the lace, two shades of flesh combined, her flesh and the flesh-coloured fabric. The deep crease of her cleavage made him grind his teeth together and he had to clench his fists to avoid pressing her back against the pillows so that he could ravish her.

And now she was gently but firmly pulling down the zipper and tugging the trousers down.

'Becky...' He groaned.

'I like it when you lose control...' she said in a ragged voice. He had stepped out of the trousers and she knew that he was having to restrain himself from pushing her back against the mattress so that he could do what came so naturally for him, so that he could take control of the situation.

No way.

She tugged down the boxers and circled her fingers firmly around his massive erection. She felt it pulse and then she delicately began to lick it from the head, along the thick shaft, trailing wetness up and down and around until he couldn't contain his groans. His hand was tangled in her hair. He wanted to keep her right there, doing what she was doing, even though, at the same time, he also wanted to tug her away so that she could stop taking him to that point of no return.

She took him into her mouth, sucking gently, then firmly, then back to gently, building a rhythm that was exciting her as much as it was exciting him. He was groaning, urging her on, telling her how he liked it. Before she'd met him, she would never have thought that she could be this intimate with a man, intimate enough to taste him like this. She'd never thought that she would be able to hear him say the sort of things Theo said to her in the height of their lovemaking...telling her where to go, what to do, urging her to do the same...describing all the things he wanted to do to her until she was burning up and frantic with desire.

'Stop,' he ordered gruffly, but it was too late, as she pushed him over the edge.

It was the last thing he'd wanted. He'd wanted slow and thorough. But it just went to show the effect she had on him. He hadn't been able to stop himself and he cursed fluently under his breath as he came down from a mind-blowing orgasm.

'Shame on you,' he chided, settling onto the bed with her, depressing the mattress with his weight so that she slid towards him, her body pressed up hard against his nakedness. 'I wanted to take things easy…' He pushed some of her hair behind an ear and then nibbled her lobe, which sent little arrows of beautiful sensation zipping through her.

She squirmed and wriggled against him, then slid one thigh sinuously up along his leg, relieving some of the aching between her legs.

'Naughty girl,' he admonished softly, grinning. 'You know you're going to have to pay dearly for making me lose control like that, don't you?'

He'd missed this—missed it much more than he'd ever imagined possible. Having her here in bed with him made him feel…weirdly comfortable, as though the inevitable was happening, as though he was meant to be here, doing this.

Finishing business, he thought, shrugging off a suddenly uneasy feeling he couldn't quite define.

He smoothed her thigh with his hand. She was warm and he paused to ask her whether she was up to it.

'You took something for your cold, I'm assuming?'

'Since when are you a fussing mother hen?' Becky laughed and leaned up to kiss him. His lips were firm and cool and so, so familiar. It amazed her how readily her body could recall his.

For a second, just a second, Theo stilled, then the moment was lost as he curved his fingers under the lace, finding her breasts, cupping them, moving to tease her nipple between his fingers. He gently pushed her flat against the bed and levered himself into the most advantageous position for exploring her body.

He started with her mouth. She'd taken him over the edge, but he was building fast to another erection, and this time he was going to take her all the way…feeling her wrap herself around him.

He kissed her slowly, tracing her lips with his tongue, then tasting her the way a connoisseur might taste vintage wine. He gently smoothed her hair away from her face, kissed her eyes, the sides of her mouth, then her neck.

She arched back slightly and shivered as those delicate kisses wound their way along her neck and then across her shoulders.

Her staccato breathing sounded as loud as thunder in the quiet of the bedroom. It was all she could hear. It was louder than the gentle background whirring of the ceiling fan, which she had become accustomed to keeping on all night, and punctuated with small whimpers and little, gasping moans.

She was desperate to rip the lace nightwear off but he wouldn't let her. Instead, he traced his tongue over the fabric, inexorably finding her nipple and then suckling hard on it through the lace, rasping it with his tongue until he found a gap in the lace through which it peeped, dusky pink, a hard button standing to attention.

'You're going to wreck this brand-new top,' she rebuked with a breathless giggle as she watched him toy with the intricate lace pattern until he had engineered two slightly bigger gaps, which he proceeded to position expertly over her nipples so that they were now both poking through.

'You shouldn't have bought it,' he countered, glancing at her and meeting her fevered eyes. 'You should have stuck to the baggy cotton tee shirts, then you wouldn't mind if I ripped it to shreds to get to your delectable body.'

'I was only obeying orders and replacing my wardrobe, as per your request…'

'Since when do you ever obey orders?' Theo asked huskily. 'You're the most disobedient mistress I've ever had.'

'I'm not your mistress!'

'You prefer "lover"?'

'I'd prefer you to stop talking.' *Wife*, she thought. She'd prefer *wife*. But *lover* would do, just as these snatched few days and nights would also have to do.

'Happy to oblige.' Theo took his time at her breasts. He sucked her nipples, giving them both the attention they deserved. He liked the way they stuck out at him through the lace, perfect, pouting and slickly wet from his tongue. He was almost reluctant to lift the top higher, to free them from their constraints, but he wanted to hold them in his hands. He had big hands and her breasts filled them, heavy and sexy. He massaged them and she writhed as he did so, tossing and turning, her eyes drowsy and unfocused with lust.

This was how he liked her. It startled him to realise that he had pictured this almost from the very moment he had left the cottage, having been marooned there by the snow. He hadn't just had her on his mind. He'd stored all sorts of images of her and projected them into a place and time where they would be doing just what they were doing now. Making love.

He nuzzled the undersides of her breasts, then trailed languid kisses along her stomach. Her skin was as soft and as smooth as satin. He paused at the indentation of her belly button, explored it with his tongue and heard her tell him that she needed him, that she was burning up for him. Her legs were already parted and he could smell the sweet, musky scent of her femininity.

She was breathing fast, panting, her stomach rising and falling as if she were running a marathon.

He cupped her between her legs and felt her wetness through the lace shorts, then he slipped his hand underneath and ran his finger along the tender, sensitive slit of her womanhood, finding and feeling her pulsing core.

The lace shorts restricted movement of his hand and he moved the barrier to one side. In a minute, he would take off the damned things completely, but right now he was enjoying watching her face as she responded to the gentle probing and teasing of his fingers.

Her eyelids fluttered, her nostrils were flared and her mouth was half-open. Her breathing was raspy and uneven, halfway between moaning and whimpering.

She was the very picture of a woman at the mercy of her body's physical responses and he felt a kick of satisfaction that he was the one who had brought her to that place. She might make a big song and dance about his unsuitability but she couldn't deny how much he turned her on.

Which was probably why his mother had not questioned their relationship. Normally so perceptive, Marita Rushing had not doubted for an instant that they were seriously involved. Yes, she might have wanted to believe it, and so had avoided gazing too closely for discrepancies in the perfect picture on display, but something about their interaction had convinced her that they were truly an item. Theo could only ascribe that to the physical pull between them which had transmitted itself to his mother by some sort of osmosis, making the pretence very, very real.

'You have no idea how much you turn me on,' he breathed in a rough undertone and Becky looked at him with darkened eyes.

'You could try telling me. I need convincing after you've spent so long ignoring me…'

'I like to think of it as a slow burn…' He eased the shorts off and she half-sat up, tugged the top over her head and flung it to the ground, then lay back, propping herself against the pillows.

Theo paused, taking time out to look at her, so supple and soft and so very, very feminine. The height of femininity, with her rounded curves, her long hair and open, honest face.

He straddled her and then knelt, his legs on either side of her, so that he could continue his lazy exploration of her glorious body. He had to keep telling himself not to rush because he wanted to, badly. He had to make himself slow down, although it was nigh on impossible when he moved down her body and began to lick her between her legs, tasting her, savouring her dewy wetness in his mouth. He nudged his erection into some good behaviour because there was no way he was going to allow himself to lose control again. Once had been bad enough.

Becky could barely breathe. It was exquisite having him down there, head between her legs, his hands under her bottom, driving her up to his mouth so that not even the slightest fraction of sensation was lost.

She hooked her legs around his back and flattened

her hands at her sides. She could feel the steady rhythm of an orgasm building and eased away from his mouth, panting, not wanting to come, wanting and needing him inside her.

Theo straightened, lying lightly over her so that he could deliver a few little kisses to her mouth. 'You have no idea how long I've wanted this,' he confessed unsteadily. He pushed himself up and Becky traced the corded muscles of his arms.

'How long?' Becky made her voice light, teasing and mildly amused. She hoped that only she could hear the desperate plea to have something, *anything* to grab on to, that would turn this into more than just sex for him. It would never be love or anything like that, but affection, maybe… Would that be asking too much? She was only human, after all.

'Pretty much as soon as I stepped out of your front door.' He dealt her a slashing, wicked grin that made her toes curl.

'You could have stayed a little longer.'

'Unfortunately…' Theo nuzzled the side of her neck so that some of what he was saying was lost in the caress '…there was a certain little something called *reality* to be dealt with. Playing truant can only last so long…'

'A bit like what we're doing here.' Becky laughed lightly, although her heart was constricted with pain.

'This is a bit more than truancy.' Theo looked down at her seriously. 'It's not just about having some fun and then pushing on. There's someone else in the equation.'

'But essentially it *is* just fun and pushing on. I mean, we're here and we're in bed together, and then we'll leave and that'll be that…'

Theo shrugged. He wasn't going to cross any bridges until he was staring them in the face. 'I plan on bringing my mother back as soon as possible,' he admitted. 'It's all very well and good, her being out here—and I'm sure she's enjoying the weather, my aunt's company and my aunt's kids and grandchildren—but that's a form of truancy in itself, wouldn't you agree?'

'Maybe…'

'And, as for us pushing on… I admit things are slightly more complex on that front than I'd originally imagined.'

'How so?' Becky felt her racing heart begin to stutter. Tense as a bow string, she waited for him to elucidate.

'All this talk is killing the mood.' Theo shifted to turn onto his side and pulled her into position so that they were facing one another, belly to belly. 'I thought my mother would have been delighted to discover that I was capable of more than having flimsy relationships with unsuitable women. I imagined that that would have given her a fillip, so to speak. Bucked up her spirits and stopped her from having worst-case scenarios in her head about me remaining a bachelor for the rest of my days, because somehow I was incapable of forming bonds with any woman that might be permanent. I intended to insinuate that you might not be the one for me, but certainly there was a woman out there who would be…a woman who wasn't a supermodel with nothing much between her ears…'

'Not all models are like that.' Becky thought of her clever, lovely sister.

'I know,' Theo admitted. 'But maybe I've just made it my mission to find the ones who are. At any rate, I was perhaps a bit short-sighted. I also thought that I'd be able to break things off between us gently. A process of gradually growing apart because of the distance or my work commitments or your work commitments. No need for you to put in an appearance—just a slow and gradual demise which could be explained away without any visits from you. I had no idea that my mother would jump on board this charade with such rich enthusiasm or that she would…' he sighed and searched for the right words, and then shot her a crooked, sideways smile '…fall in love with you the way she has. It poses a problem, although it's not something we can't work with.'

'What problem?'

'It'll wait. I can't talk any more, Becky…' He dipped his fingers into her and slid them up and down. 'And neither can you, from the feel of things.'

He didn't give her time to pick up the threads of the conversation or even to dwell further on it, because he lowered himself down the length of her agitated body, hands on her sides, mouth kissing, licking and nibbling.

She gave a husky groan as he buried his head between her legs again, teasing with the same lingering thoroughness as he had earlier teased her tight, sensitive nipples. She curled her fingers into his hair, arched back and bucked in gentle, rotating movements, urging on his inquisitive tongue to taste every bit of her.

Her body was on fire and she feverishly played with her nipples, driving yet more sensation through her body. She was so close to coming…

But, when she could stand it no more, he reared up and rustled about, finding protection, giving her body a little time to breathe and for those almost-there sensations to subside.

She couldn't wait to have him inside her. Like him, she hadn't stopped wanting this. Unlike him, so much more was attached to her wanting, but for the moment she couldn't even begin to go down that road, not when she was burning up.

He inserted himself gently into her. He was big and

every time they had made love he had been careful to build his rhythm slowly, had eased himself slowly into her, before thrusting deeper and firmer.

She loved the feel of him in her, loved it when he began to move with surety and precision, knowing just how to rouse her, just where to touch her and when for maximum effect. It was as though her body had been groomed to respond to him in ways that she knew, in her heart, it would never, ever respond to any other man.

And this time it was no different. He pushed deep and hard and she automatically bent her knees, taking all of him inside her and feeling the rush of her orgasm as it hurtled towards her, sending her to a place where nothing existed but the sound of their breathing and movement, and then a splintering that was so intense that the world seemed to freeze completely.

Distantly, she knew that he was coming as well, felt the tension in his big body as he reared up with a strangled groan of completion and satisfaction.

She wrapped her arms around him, her eyes still closed and her breathing still laboured, shuddering as she came down from the high to which she had been catapulted. He stayed still for a while, his arms encasing her. It was such an illusion of absolute closeness that she wanted to cry.

Instead, she whispered softly, stroking his face until he opened his eyes and looked at her. 'You were telling me that there's a problem, Theo…'

'Isn't it usually the unthinking man who breaks the post-coital mood by talking? Or falling asleep? Or getting up to work?' Theo half-joked, kissing the tip of her nose.

'I wonder which of those three would be your preferred choice of atmosphere-breaking?' Becky darted a kiss on his mouth, which deepened into something more intense.

'With you…' Theo murmured, cupping her breast and absently playing with her nipple, rolling the pad of his thumb over it, thinking that he could easily dip down to suckle on it and just stay there until they were both ready to make love all over again, which, judging from the way his penis was behaving, would be sooner rather than later. 'With you, I could happily go for the repeat performance option…'

'Not yet.'

Theo flopped onto his back and laughed ruefully. 'Okay. Here's the problem.' He sighed and took a few seconds to get his brain back into gear before shifting onto his side to look at her. 'I don't think it's going to be easy for you to simply vanish from my life overnight, whilst I paper over your disappearance with as many limp excuses as I can think of. My mother may have had her spirit sapped by her ill health and worries but she's still vigorous enough to do something like demand a meeting with you to find out why we aren't making wedding plans. I asked you for a fortnight. It might not be long enough.'

'It has to be, Theo. I have a life to be getting on with.' She pushed herself away from him and then kept her hand flat on his chest to stop him from coming any closer.

'I get that.' Did he? Honestly? He didn't think that a few more days of this was going to be nearly enough to get her out of his system.

'I'm not going to be at your beck and call just because you think you might need me to put in an occasional appearance.'

'What about being at my beck and call because I can't seem to keep my hands off you and I don't want you to disappear from my life?'

If he hadn't said that…

If he'd just let her keep thinking that all he wanted was a continuation of the business arrangement they had embarked upon…

He didn't want her to disappear from his life. She knew that it was silly to read anything behind that but her romantic heart couldn't help but be swept away by the notion of fate having brought them together, delivered them to this place, this here and now, where possibilities were endless, if only he could see it.

'I know you don't mean that,' she muttered, confused and hearing the uncertainty in her voice with some alarm.

'I've never meant anything more in my life before, Becky,' Theo told her with driven urgency. He could sense her capitulation but he didn't feel the expected triumph. Instead, he felt a rush of heartfelt honesty that took him by surprise. This wasn't just about his mother. Oh, no…this was about *him.* She was a fever inside him and he knew that just a little bit longer with her would douse it. Overpowering *need* had never cut so deep.

'It's not practical, Theo, and besides…'

'Besides what…?' She didn't answer and he looked at her with deadly seriousness. 'Tell me you don't feel this too, Becky. This has nothing to do with my mother. I would be asking this of you were my mother not a factor in the equation. I don't want to let you go…'

Just yet, Becky reminded herself, clutching at sanity the way a drowning man clutched at a life raft. *You don't want to let me go just yet…*

She couldn't afford to let herself be lured any further along the road than she already had been. She was in love with him. Each day spent with him was a day deeper in love for her. She had cracked this time, had argued herself into a position of being able to justify her surrender.

So was she going to do that again? Until she was finally dispatched at some point in the not-too-distant future?

Theo knew that this was not only a tall order but an extremely rash one. It would be difficult to write her out of his life abruptly, but it could be done. There were always ways and means when it came to solving thorny problems. But he still really wanted her, and wanted her so badly that the need took precedence over clear judgement.

He was involved with her because of the cottage. Break up with her when they returned to England, and he could still buy the place after the dust had settled. They would have had a few sex-filled days in the Cotswolds and a dalliance in the sun generated from the extraordinary circumstance that had brought them together.

Continue, for whatever reason, when they returned to London, and like it or not they would be indulging in a full-blown relationship. What else could he possibly call it? Whatever she said about him not being her type, how long before that would change? Would she inevitably be seduced by a lifestyle she had never envisaged for herself? Once upon a time, he had doubted that she would fit in to his world, not that he'd really given a damn. He'd been wrong. Looking at the ease with which she'd pulled off the expensive couture clothes she had bought, he realised she fitted in just fine.

Haute couture was something a woman could get accustomed to very easily. How long, then, before she became just another woman trying to talk about marriage and planning things that would never materialise?

But none of that seemed to matter because the sex was just so good.

And anyway, he argued with himself, he would have *some* contact with her afterwards because of the practice he had promised to buy for her. He would have to have her input in sourcing somewhere suitable. It wasn't as though they could just walk away from one another without a backward glance.

There and then, he made his decision. The purchase of the cottage would have to be jettisoned. That had been an error of judgement, given everything that had come afterwards, and she would never find out about any of it. At any rate, Becky would soon be busy changing jobs and facing the challenges of living somewhere else. They would see one another but not regularly. His mother might see her again a few times but that would be it. Harmless dinners out where he would be able to manage the conversation.

It would be a shame about the cottage, but you won a few, you lost a few.

He slipped his hand between her legs and kissed her, a long, lingering, persuasive kiss. This was what he knew, the power of sex, and he was going to force her to admit to it too. He wasn't going to let her walk away in a haze of high-principled apologies and rambling, earnest lectures about what made sense and what didn't. If she walked away, then she was going to face what she was walking away from. Explosive, mind-blowing sex.

It was hitting below the belt, but Theo was nothing if not a man who knew how to take advantage of the situations life threw at him.

Becky moaned, her whole body quivering as he began devastating inroads into her self-control. He moved his fingers and touched her until she wanted to scream and beg him to take her. Her mind slipped its leash and she imagined all sorts of things she wanted him to do to her. She imagined what it would be like to pin down those powerful arms of his, restrain them with a nice leather strap and then torment his body by making love to him oh, so slowly…

She imagined them naked in a field making love under a black, starry sky, and touching one another in the back row of a cinema like a couple of teenagers…

And then the slideshow ended because none of that would happen if she walked away now.

She didn't want any of that to happen. She knew the consequences of prolonging this disastrous union.

But she still reached down anyway, held his erection in her slight hand and began massaging it before climbing on top of him and letting herself surrender…

CHAPTER TEN

How could you...? How could you do this...?

Ten days ago, that was exactly what Becky had wanted to scream and shout at the man who once again had become her lover, against her better judgement.

She had thought at the time that being bedridden for a day with a cold virus would give her breathing space. In fact, as it had turned out, being bedridden had placed her in just the right place for him to stage his very successful assault on what precious little had been left of her common sense.

She'd folded faster than the speed of light and they had spent the remainder of their stay in Italy unable to keep their hands off one another. Much to his mother's obvious delight.

And, after they had returned to England, she had kept telling herself that it was just a matter of time before it all fizzled out. That work commitments and all the details that had to be sorted out with her job and the new practice would reduce their time together until they simply drifted apart though lack of proximity. He wasn't the sort of man who could ever do a long-distance relationship or indeed any relationship where the woman he wanted was inaccessible.

Certainly, she had had to return to the Cotswolds, had

had to begin the process of dismantling her life there and beginning the search for somewhere new where a practice could be profitable. Yet, somehow, she seemed to have seen him over the ensuing fortnight with more regularity than she might have imagined, and then his mother had returned from Italy, earlier than he had anticipated.

Becky stared numbly around her, back where she had started at the cottage, which had now been renovated to a standard that was eminently saleable.

In fact, she barely recognised the place.

She blinked rapidly, squashing foolish tears at her own naivety. There was no such thing as a free lunch and especially not in the rarefied world that Theo occupied.

At the time, she had thought, unwisely, that the cottage and the practice were part of the deal that he had hired her to undertake. Play the game and she would be rewarded—and she had played the game, not for the rewards, but for the pleasure of playing because she had missed him. He had phoned and she had got herself in a lather and called upon her pride but, in the end, she had thrilled at the thought of just seeing him again and being with him again.

But, of course, the picture was a lot more complex than the one that had been painted for her benefit.

She paused to gaze at herself in the mirror in the newly painted hall. She'd dumped all the finery, the expensive dresses, the designer shoes and underwear.

This is who you are, she told her reflection. *A pleasant enough looking vet who's lived her entire life in the country. Not some glamorous sex kitten powerful enough to turn the head of a man like Theo Rushing.*

What on earth had got into her?

She knew, of course. Love had got into her. It had roared into her life and she had been knocked off her feet without even realising it because it had come in a format she hadn't recognised.

She'd expected someone like Freddy. She'd expected cuddles, kisses and, face it, polite, enjoyable sex.

She hadn't expected sex of the bodice-ripping variety, so she had written it off as lust until, of course, it had all been far too late for her adequately to protect herself.

Love had turned her into a puppet that had walked back into his arms, even though she had known that it was never going to be reciprocated. Love had effectively switched off all the burglar alarms that should have been up and running, protecting her.

And, disastrously, love had made her begin to hope.

She'd begun to think that he might just feel more for her than he had anticipated. People said one thing, but life had a way of getting in the way of all their well-grounded intentions.

Look at her!

Had it been the same for him? It surely wasn't just about the sex…? There'd been many times when they hadn't been rolling around on a bed, when they'd talked, when he'd given her advice on setting up a practice—brilliant, sensible advice from a guy who had done his own thing and come out on top.

It hadn't been the same for him. He'd had an agenda from the word *go* and, oh, how she had wanted to scream and shout when she had found out. Instead, she had absented herself and taken off to France for a week to be with her family, who had been overjoyed to see her.

For a while, she had almost been distracted enough to see a way forward. She had revelled in her sister's pregnancy and obvious happiness. She had allowed herself to be congratulated on her ambitions to move on and set up a practice while she had skirted around the precise explanation as to how, exactly, she was managing to do that. She had waffled a lot about excellent references, possible bank loans and the possibility of someone willing to invest for a share of the partnership…

Now she was back, though…

She peered through the window in the hall by the front door.

For the first time in ten days, ever since she had found out from his mother details of his past which he had conveniently kept from her, she would be seeing him.

She had no idea what was going through his head but she hadn't wanted him to know what had been going through hers. At least not then, not when she had been so boiling mad, so humiliated and mortified, that her emotions would have done the shouting and that would have made her incoherent and vulnerable.

And, when she confronted him, she wanted to be cool and detached.

She also wasn't even certain that she would mention anything at all. Perhaps she would just tell him that she felt that what they had had run its course. Maybe he had got the hint, because she hadn't been returning his calls, and on the couple of occasions when he had managed to get through to her she had been vague and distant, practically ending the conversation before it had begun.

She ducked away from the window the second she heard the throaty purr of his car and the crunch of gravel as it swerved into the little courtyard in front of the house.

Nerves gripped her. The doorbell sounded and she wiped her perspiring palms on her jeans and took a deep breath.

Experience told her that, when she pulled open the door, his impact on her would be as strong as it always was. Absence and time apart were two things that never seemed to diminish it. Unless he had gained two stone in the space of ten days and lost all his hair and teeth, his devastating good looks would still make the breath hitch in her throat and the flood of emotion she felt for him would still make her feel weak and powerless.

Not wanting to appear over-keen, she allowed him to stand pressing the doorbell for a few seconds before she opened the door.

And there he was.

The weather had changed from those heady few days when he had last been in the Cotswolds. Spring had long since arrived, and with it pale blue skies and wispy clouds were scurrying across the washed blue backdrop as though hurrying on urgent errands. The trees were in full bloom and the flowers were poking out wherever they could, eager to feel the first rays of sun on them, blues and violets and reds and pinks clambering out of the bushes and hedgerows and tumbling across fences and yellow stone walls.

It was Saturday. No work, hence his arrival at four in the afternoon, just a few hours after she herself had arrived back from France. He was long and lean in faded black jeans and a black polo shirt, casual jacket hooked over one shoulder. He'd propped his shades up and he looked every inch a drop-dead-sexy movie star.

And she felt all those predictable responses she always did whenever she clapped eyes on him.

'Theo,' she managed, stepping aside and then slightly back as he brushed past her.

His clean, woody scent filled her nostrils and made her feel faint.

'So...' Theo turned to look at her. His face was impassive. His body language was cool and controlled. Neither bore any resemblance to what was going on inside him because she'd spent the past ten days playing an avoidance game that had got on his nerves. She'd vanished off to France on a whim. She'd contrived to view possible practices up for grabs without him, even though he was going to be funding whatever purchase transpired.

'What's going on, Becky?'

They hadn't made it out of the narrow hall and already it was clear there were going to be no pleasantries to paper over the awkwardness of what she was going to say. Ending something was always tough but she was going to be ending this with an edge of bitterness that would live with her for ever, and that made it all the tougher.

'I thought I would show you the practice I'm thinking would be suitable. The head vet who runs it is retiring and he's looking for someone to take over. It'll be a similar sort of size to the one here and, if anything, the work will be less demanding and probably a lot more profitable because it's in a town.' She began edging towards the sitting room.

Two weeks ago, she would have flown into his arms and they wouldn't have made it to the bedroom.

If he hadn't got the message already that things were over between them, then he'd have to be blind not to be receiving the message loud and clear now. And he wasn't blind. Far from it.

'I know buying the practice was all…er…part of the deal that we had…'

Theo stayed her with one hand and spun her round to face him. 'This is how you greet me after nearly two weeks of absence, Becky?' He stepped closer towards her, a forbidding, towering presence that filled her with apprehension, nerves and that tingling excitement that was now taboo. 'With polite conversation about business deals?'

She whipped her arm away and stepped back, anger rising like a tide of bile at the back of her throat.

'Okay,' she snapped, reaching boiling point at the speed of light. 'How else would you like me to greet you? You must have guessed that…that…' She faltered, and he stepped into the sudden leaden silence like a predator sensing weakness.

'That…? Why don't you spell it out for me, Becky?'

'It's over. I…I'm moving on now and it's time for this to end.' She looked away because she just couldn't look at him. She could feel his grey eyes boring into her, trying to pull thoughts out of her head.

He knew. How could he not? One minute she had been full on and the next minute she had left the building. He'd tried to get in touch with her, and, sure, she'd picked up a few times, but conversation between them had been brief and stilted. He would have called a lot more because her silence had driven him crazy but pride, again, had intervened.

He felt sick. What was it they said about pride being a person's downfall? Except it had always been so much part and parcel of his personality. He wanted nothing more now than to shrug his shoulders and walk away. Let his lawyers deal with whatever had to be done in connection with the practice, sort out whatever paperwork needed sorting out.

He couldn't and he was afflicted by something alien to him. A wave of desperation.

He needed to move so he headed for the kitchen, barely glancing at the renovations his money had paid for. She was saying something from behind him, something about paying back whatever money he lent her. He spun around and cut her short with a slice of his hand,

'Why?' he grated savagely. 'And you can drop the

"time to move on" act. The last time we saw one another you were wriggling like an eel under me and begging me to take you.'

Becky went bright red. Trust him to bring sex into it—trust him to use it as a lever in his line of reasoning—yet why should she be surprised when it was the only thing that motivated him? That and the cool detachment that could allow him to see manipulation as something acceptable.

She moved to stand by the sink, pressed up against it with her hands behind her back because she was too restless to sit at the kitchen table.

'Maybe,' she burst out on a wave of uncontrolled anger that was heavily laced with fury at herself for ever, ever having thought that he might actually have proper feelings for her, 'it's because I've finally decided that having a bastard in my life is something I can do without!'

Theo went completely still. For once, his clever mind that could be relied upon to deal with any situation had stalled and was no longer functioning.

Their eyes met and she was the first to look away. Even in the grip of anger, he still exerted the sort of power over her that made her fearful because she knew how out of character it could make her behave.

'Explain.' He felt cold inside because he knew what she was going to say and, in retrospect, marvelled that he had ever thought that she wouldn't find out, marvelled that he had ever felt he could carry on having this relationship and then walk away from it with her none the wiser.

'You didn't just *happen to come here* while you were out taking your car for a little spin in the middle of nowhere, did you, Theo?' She had regained some of her self-control and her voice was low, but steady.

'You weren't just the *poor marooned billionaire* unfortunate enough to wash up on the doorstep of a country bumpkin with a house falling down around her ears, were you? You came here because you wanted to buy the place. Your mother told me. She told me how much she'd been hankering to return to the house where she and your father had lived as a young couple. She told me how she'd left in a hurry after he'd been killed in a road accident. She said that she'd never wanted to return but that lately she'd been wanting to make peace with her past and especially now that you seemed to be so happy and settled.' She laughed scornfully but her cheeks were bright red and her hands were shaking. 'When did you decide that it made more sense to check out the place and see for yourself how much it was worth? When did you decide that you would sleep with me so that it would be easier to talk me into selling it for the lowest possible price? The power of pillow talk and all that? Did you decide to put your little plan on hold temporarily because using me as a fake girlfriend was more important than yanking the house out from under my feet?

'After all, you'd already slept with me—why not keep it up for a few more weeks until your mother was over her little turn? Then a clean break-up and a speedy purchase! You'd already done the groundwork to get the place up to your standards. Were you ever going to tell me that you were behind the purchase? Or were you going to string me along for a while longer, until you got me to the point where you could convince me to sell it for a song before regrettably letting me go, like all those women you dated before me?'

Theo raked his fingers through his hair.

Consequences he had put on hold were ramming into him with the force of a runaway steam engine and fact was so intricately weaved with conjecture that he was well and truly on the back foot.

But that didn't bother him. What bothered him was that he had blown it.

He'd blown the only good thing to have happened in his life with his arrogance, his misplaced pride and his driving need to exert control over everything.

'Let me explain,' he said roughly, which provoked another bitter laugh, and he couldn't blame her. He couldn't have sounded more guilty of the accusations hurled at him if he'd tried.

'I don't want you to explain!'

'Why did you let me drive here if you didn't want to hear what I had to say?' he countered in a driven voice. He badly wanted to get closer to her, to close the distance between them, but it would be a big mistake. For once, words were going to have to be his allies. For once, he was going to have to say how he felt, and that scared him. He'd never done it before and now…

She hated him. It was written all over her face. But she hadn't, not before. No, she might have protested that he wasn't her type, but they'd clicked in a way he'd never clicked with a woman before.

He should have told her the truth when he'd had the chance in Portofino. He'd started but had allowed himself to be side-tracked. Now, he was paying a price he didn't want to pay.

'You're right. I did come here with the sole intention of buying this place. My mother had been making noises about wanting to return here. I had the money and I saw no reason not to take back what, I felt, had been taken from her at a knockdown price.' He held up his hand because he could see her bursting to jump in and, if nothing else, he would have his say. He had to. He had no choice.

'You used me.'

'I exploited a situation and at the time it felt like the right thing to do.' He looked at her with searing honesty and she squashed all pangs of empathy. 'I don't like having this conversation with you standing there. Won't you come here?'

'I don't like thinking that you used me. So that makes both of us not liking things that aren't about to change.'

Come nearer? Did anyone ever take up an invitation to jump into a snake pit?

And still her body keened for him in a way that was positively terrifying.

'Sleeping with me was all just part of your plan, wasn't it?'

'I would never have slept with you if I didn't fancy you, Becky. And fancy you more than I've ever fancied any woman in my life before. Okay, so you might think that what I did was unethical, but—'

'But?' She tilted her head to one side in a polite enquiry. At least he'd fancied her. He wasn't lying. That, in itself, was a comfort. *Small comfort*, she quickly reminded herself.

'But it was the only way I knew how to be,' he said in such a low, husky voice that she had to strain to hear him.

Unsettled, she felt herself relax a little, although she remained where she was, pressed against the counter, careful not to get too close. And she wasn't going to ask him what he meant either!

But her keen eyes noted the way he angled his big body so that he was leaning towards her, head lowered, arms resting on his thighs and his hands clasped loosely together. That looked like defeat in his posture, although she was probably wildly off the mark with that one. She seemed to have turned being wildly off the mark into a habit as far as this man was concerned.

Theo dealt her a hesitant glance.

He had such beautiful eyes, she thought, shaken by that hesitancy, such wildly extravagant eyelashes, and when he looked like that, as though he was searching in fog to find a way forward, was it any wonder that something inside her wasn't quite as steely as it should be?

'I've always been tough,' he admitted in the same low, barely audible voice and she took a couple of tentative steps towards him, then sat at the table, but at the opposite end. Theo glanced across and wondered if he dared let his hopes rise, considering she was no longer pressed against the counter like a cornered rat preparing to attack. 'I've had to be. Life wasn't easy when I was growing up, but I think I told you that.'

'Whilst omitting to tell me other things,' Becky pointed out with asperity, although her voice wasn't as belligerent as it had previously been.

'Granted.' He hung his head for a few seconds, then held her eyes once again. 'My mother was always unhappy. Not that she wasn't a good mother—she was a great mother—but she'd never recovered from my father's death. Love cut short in its prime will always occupy top position on the pedestal.' He shot her a crooked smile. 'She got very little for the cottage in the end. She sold low and, by the time the mortgage was paid off, she barely had enough to buy something else. She had to work her fingers to the bone to make sure we had food in the larder and heating during winter. That was what I saw and that was what, I guess, made me realise that love and emotion were weaknesses to be avoided at all costs. What mattered was security and only money could give you that. I locked my heart away and threw away the key. I was invincible. It never occurred to me that I wouldn't have to find the key to open it because someone else would do that for me.'

Becky felt prickles of something speckle her skin. She took a deep breath and held it.

'It made financial sense to buy the cottage cheap. My plan was to go there, fling money on the table and take what should have been my mother's as far as I was concerned. But then you opened the door and things changed—and then we slept together and after that everything kept changing. I kept telling myself that nothing had, that I was still going to buy the cottage, but I was in freefall without even realising it. Becky, I wanted to tell you why I'd shown up on your doorstep, but I'd boxed myself in and I couldn't get a grip to manoeuvre myself out.'

He shook his head ruefully. She was so still and for once he couldn't read what she was thinking. It didn't matter. He had to plough on anyway.

'In the end, I wasn't going to buy it,' he confessed heavily. 'I'd made that decision before we returned to this country. The only problem was that I never followed through with the reasoning because, if I had, I would have realised that the reason I dumped the plan to buy your house for my mother was because I'd fallen in love with you, and to do anything as underhand as try and buy you out, even if you agreed to sell, would have felt… somehow wrong.'

'You what? Say that again? I think…I think I must have missed something…'

'I've been an idiot.' Theo looked at her steadily. 'And I don't know how long I would have carried on being an idiot. I just know that the past ten days have been hell and, when you told me that you wanted me out of your life just now, my world felt like it was collapsing.

Becky…' He searched to find the words for a role he had never played before. 'I realise you don't consider me the ideal catch…'

'Stop.' Her head was buzzing from hearing stuff she'd never in a million years thought she'd ever hear. She was on cloud nine and now the distance between them seemed too great when all she wanted was to be able to reach out and touch him. She saw the shadow of defeat cross his face and her heart constricted.

'I *did* think that you weren't the sort of guy for me. I'd always made assumptions about the sort of guy who *would* be for me and you didn't fit the bill. There was so much about you that I'd never come across in my life before.' She smiled, eyes distant as she recalled those first impressions when he'd appeared on her doorstep in all his drop-dead, show-stopping glory. 'But you were irresistible,' she confessed. 'And it wasn't just about the way you looked, although it was easier for me to tell myself that. Everything about you was irresistible. I was hooked before I even went to bed with you, and then you disappeared without a backward glance.'

'Not so,' Theo murmured. 'If only you knew.' He patted his lap and she obediently and happily went to sit there. She sighed with pleasure because this was where she belonged. Close to him. If this turned out to be a dream, she was hoping not to wake any time soon.

'When you got in touch, I was so excited, then I realised that you'd only got in touch because you wanted something from me. That I was the only woman who could deliver that something, because I was plain and average and the sort of girl boys don't mind taking home to their mothers.'

'You're the sexiest woman I've ever known,' he assured her with a seriousness that made her smile again.

'The bonus is that you're also the type of woman I was proud to introduce to my mother.'

'I put down that "no sex" clause,' Becky said thoughtfully, 'but I was still excited to be seeing you again. Through it all, even when I was so angry—because some of the things you said, like me having to buy a whole new wardrobe to be a convincing girlfriend, were really offensive—I was still excited. It was like I could suddenly only come alive in your company.' She sighed. 'Which brings us right back to where we started. With the cottage and your reasons for showing up.'

'I think there's something my mother wants a lot more than a cottage.' He dropped a kiss on the side of her mouth and then, as she curved into him, looping her arms around his neck, the kiss deepened and deepened until he was in danger of forgetting what he wanted to say. Eventually he drew back and looked at her. 'She wants a daughter-in-law and I've realised that there's nothing more I want, my darling, than a wife. So…will you marry me?'

'You called me your darling…'

'And will you let me call you my *wife*?'

'My darling husband-to-be… Yes, I will.

* * * * *

COMING SOON!

We really hope you enjoyed reading this book. If you're looking for more romance, be sure to head to the shops when new books are available on

Thursday 27th December

To see which titles are coming soon, please visit **millsandboon.co.uk**

MILLS & BOON

LET'S TALK Romance

For exclusive extracts, competitions and special offers, find us online:

facebook.com/millsandboon

@MillsandBoon

@MillsandBoonUK

Get in touch on 01413 063232

For all the latest titles coming soon, visit millsandboon.co.uk/nextmonth

Want even more
ROMANCE?

Join our bookclub today!

'Mills & Boon books, the perfect way to escape for an hour or so.'

Miss W. Dyer

'Excellent service, promptly delivered and very good subscription choices.'

Miss A. Pearson

'You get fantastic special offers and the chance to get books before they hit the shops'

Mrs V. Hall

Visit millsandbook.co.uk/Bookclub and save on brand new books.

MILLS & BOON